**The New Copy Writer's Name Was Death—
His First Account Was Murder.**

Death Bredon had always been fascinated by the advertising business—almost as much as he was interested in the sport of his given name. He found both at Pym's Publicity, where murder became as commonplace as ad layouts.

"I think I never enjoyed a detective story so much—probably because it takes place in a large advertising agency and what goes on there in the everyday run of business is so steadily and even so uproariously funny that it would keep me reading even a mystery less double-end twisted than this."

Saturday Review

Other Avon books by
Dorothy L. Sayers

DOROTHY L. SAYERS

MURDER MUST ADVERTISE

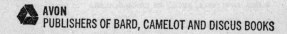
AVON
PUBLISHERS OF BARD, CAMELOT AND DISCUS BOOKS

AVON BOOKS
A division of
The Hearst Corporation
959 Eighth Avenue
New York, New York 10019

First Avon Printing, September, 1967
Eleventh Printing

AVON TRADEMARK REG. U.S. PAT. OFF. AND
FOREIGN COUNTRIES, REGISTERED TRADEMARK—
MARCA REGISTRADA, HECHO EN CHICAGO, U.S.A.

Printed in the U.S.A.

AUTHOR'S NOTE

I do not suppose that there is a more harmless and law-abiding set of people in the world than the Advertising Experts of Great Britain. The idea that any crime could possibly be perpetrated on advertising premises is one that could only occur to the ill-regulated fancy of a detective novelist, trained to fasten the guilt upon the Most Unlikely Person. If, in the course of this fantasy, I have unintentionally used a name or slogan suggestive of any existing person, firm or commodity, it is by sheer accident, and is not intended to cast the slightest reflection upon any actual commodity, firm or person.

CONTENTS

CHAPTER I

DEATH COMES TO PYM'S PUBLICITY

AND by the way," said Mr. Hankin, arresting Miss Rossiter as she rose to go, "there is a new copy-writer coming in today."

"Oh, yes, Mr. Hankin?"

"His name is Bredon. I can't tell you much about him; Mr. Pym engaged him himself; but you will see that he is looked after."

"Yes, Mr. Hankin."

"He will have Mr. Dean's room."

"Yes, Mr. Hankin."

"I should think Mr. Ingleby could take him in hand and show him what to do. You might send Mr. Ingleby along if he can spare me a moment."

"Yes, Mr. Hankin."

"That's all. And, oh, yes! Ask Mr. Smayle to let me have the Dairyfields guard-book."

"Yes, Mr. Hankin."

Miss Rossiter tucked her note-book under her arm, closed the glass-panelled door noiselessly after her and tripped smartly down the corridor. Peeping through another glass-panelled door, she observed Mr. Ingleby seated on a revolving chair with his feet on the cold radiator, and talking with great animation to a young woman in green, perched on the corner of the writing-table.

"Excuse me," said Miss Rossiter, with perfunctory civility, "but Mr. Hankin says can you spare him a moment, Mr. Ingleby?"

"If it's Tom-Boy Toffee," replied Mr. Ingleby defensively, "it's being typed. Here! you'd better take these two bits along and make it so. That will lend an air of verisimilitude to an otherwise—"

"It isn't Tom-Boy. It's a new copy-writer."

"What, already?" exclaimed the young woman. "Before those shoes were old! Why, they only buried little Dean on Friday."

"Part of the modern system of push and go," said Mr. Ingleby. "All very distressing in an old-fashioned, gentlemanly firm. Suppose I've got to put this blighter through his paces. Why am I always left with the baby?"

"Oh, rot!" said the young woman, "you've only got to warn him not to use the directors' lav., and not to tumble down the iron staircase."

"You are the most callous woman, Miss Meteyard. Well, as long as they don't put the fellow in with me—"

"It's all right, Mr. Ingleby. He's having Mr. Dean's room."

"Oh! What's he like?"

"Mr. Hankin said he didn't know, Mr. Pym took him on."

"Oh, gosh! friend of the management." Mr. Ingleby groaned.

"Then I think I've seen him," said Miss Meteyard. "Tow-coloured, supercilious-looking blighter. I ran into him coming out of Pymmie's room yesterday. Horn-rims. Cross between Ralph Lynn and Bertie Wooster."

"Death, where is thy sting? Well, I suppose I'd better push off and see about it."

Mr. Ingleby lowered his feet from the radiator, prised up his slow length from the revolving chair, and prowled unhappily away.

"Oh, well, it makes a little excitement," said Miss Meteyard.

"Oh, don't you think we've had rather too much of that lately? By the way, could I have your subscription for the wreath? You told me to remind you."

"Yes, rather. What is it? A bob? Here's half-a-crown, and you'd better take the sweep-money out of it as well."

"Thanks awfully, Miss Meteyard. I do hope you get a horse this time."

"High time I did. I've been five years in this beastly office and never even been placed. I believe you wangle the draw."

"Indeed we don't, Miss Meteyard, or we shouldn't let all the horses go to those people in the Printing. Wouldn't you like to come and draw for us this time? Miss Parton's just typing out the names."

"All right." Miss Meteyard scrambled down leggily and followed Miss Rossiter to the typists' room.

This was a small, inconvenient cubicle, crowded at the moment to bursting-point. A plump girl in glasses, with head tilted back and brows twisted to keep the smoke of a cigarette out of her eyes, was rattling off the names of Derby runners on her type-writer, assisted by a bosom-friend who dictated the list from the columns of the *Morning Star*.

A languid youth in shirt-sleeves was cutting the names of sweep-subscribers from a typed sheet, and twisting the papers into secretive little screws. A thin, eager young man, squatting on an upturned waste-paper basket, was turning over the flimsies in Miss Rossiter's tray and making sarcastic comments upon the copy to a bulky, dark youth in spectacles, immersed in a novel by P. G. Wodehouse and filching biscuits from a large tin. Draped against the door-posts and blocking the entrance to all comers, a girl and another young man, who seemed to be visitors from another department, were smoking gaspers and discussing lawn-tennis.

"Hullo, angels!" said Miss Rossiter, brightly. "Miss Meteyard's going to draw for us. And there's a new copy-writer coming."

The bulky young man glanced up to say "Poor devil!" and retreated again into his book.

"Bob for the wreath and sixpence for the sweep," went on Miss Rossiter, scrabbling in a tin cash-box. "Has anybody got two shillings for a florin? Where's your list, Parton? Scratch Miss Meteyard off, will you? Have I had your money, Mr. Garrett?"

"No money till Saturday," said the Wodehouse-reader.

"Hark at him!" cried Miss Parton, indignantly. "You'd think we were millionaries, the way we have to finance this department."

"Pick me a winner," replied Mr. Garrett, "and you can knock it off the prize-money. Hasn't that coffee come yet?"

"Have a look, Mr. Jones," suggested Miss Parton, addressing the gentleman on the door-post, "and see if you can see the boy. Just check these runners over with me, duckie. Meteor Bright, Tooralooral, Pheidippides II, Roundabout—"

"Roundabout's scratched," said Mr. Jones. "Here's the boy just coming."

"Scratched? No, when? What a shame! I put him down in the *Morning Star* competition. Who says so?"

"*Evening Banner* lunch special. Slip in the stable."

"Damn!" said Miss Rossiter, briefly. "There goes my thousand quid! Oh, well, that's life. Thank you, sonnie. Put it on the table. Did you remember the cucumber? Good boy. How much? One-and-five? Lend me a penny, Parton. There you are. Mind out a minute, Mr. Willis, do you mind? I want a pencil and rubber for the new bloke."

"What's his name?"

"Bredon."

"Where's he come from?"

"Hankie doesn't know. But Miss Meteyard's seen him. She says he's like Bertie Wooster in horn-rims."

11

"Older, though," said Miss Meteyard. "A well-preserved forty."

"Oh, gosh! When's he coming?"

"'Smorning. If I'd been him I'd have put it off till tomorrow and gone to the Derby. Oh, here's Mr. Ingleby. He'll know. Coffee, Mr. Ingleby? Have you heard anything?"

"Star of Asia, Twinkletoes, Sainte-Nitouche, Duke Humphrey . . ."

"Forty-two," said Mr. Ingleby. "No sugar, thanks. Never been in advertising before. *Balliol.*"

"Golly!" said Miss Meteyard.

"As you say. If there is one thing more repulsive than another it is Balliolity," agreed Mr. Ingleby, who was a Trinity man.

> *"Bredon went to Balliol*
> *And sat at the feet of Gamaliel,"*

chanted Mr. Garrett, closing his book.

> *"And just as he ought*
> *He cared for nought,"*

added Miss Meteyard. "I defy you to find another rhyme for Balliol."

"Flittermouse, Tom Pinch, Fly-by-Night . . ."

> *"And his language was sesquipedalial."*

"It isn't sesquipedalial, it's sesquipedalian."

"Brother!"

"Twist those papers up tight, duckie. Put them in the lid of the biscuit-tin. Damn! that's Mr. Armstrong's buzzer. Stick a saucer over my coffee. Where's my note-book?"

". . . two double-faults running, so I said . . ."

". . . I can't find the carbon of that Magnolia wholetreble . . ."

". . . started at fifty to one . . ."

"Who's bagged my scissors?"

"Excuse me, Mr. Armstrong wants his Nutrax carbons . . ."

". . . and shake 'em up well . . ."

". . . hail you all, impale you all, jail you all . . ."

"Mr. Ingleby, can you spare me a moment?"

At Mr. Hankin's mildly sarcastic accents, the scene dislimned as by magic. The door-post drapers and Miss Parton's bosom-friend melted out into the passage, Mr. Willis, rising

12

hurriedly with the tray of carbons in his hand, picked a paper out at random and frowned furiously at it, Miss Parton's cigarette dropped unostentatiously to the floor, Mr. Garrett, unable to get rid of his coffee-cup, smiled vaguely and tried to look as though he had picked it up by accident and didn't know it was there, Miss Meteyard, with great presence of mind, put the sweep counterfoils on a chair and sat on them, Miss Rossiter, clutching Mr. Armstrong's carbons in her hand, was able to look businesslike, and did so. Mr. Ingleby alone, disdaining pretence, set down his cup with a slightly impudent smile and advanced to obey his chief's command.

"This," said Mr. Hankin, tactfully blind to all evidences of disturbance, "is Mr. Bredon. You will—er—show him what he has to do. I have had the Dairyfields guard-books sent along to his room. You might start him on margarine. Er—I don't think Mr. Ingleby was up in your time, Mr. Bredon—he was at Trinity. Your Trinity, I mean, not ours." (Mr. Hankin was a Cambridge man.)

Mr. Bredon extended a well-kept hand.

"How do you do?"

"How do you do?" echoed Mr. Ingleby. They gazed at one another with the faint resentment of two cats at their first meeting. Mr. Hankin smiled kindly at them both.

"And when you've produced some ideas on margarine, Mr. Bredon, bring them along to my room and we'll go over them."

"Right-ho!" said Mr. Bredon, simply.

Mr. Hankin smiled again and padded gently away.

"Well, you'd better know everybody," said Mr. Ingleby, rapidly. "Miss Rossiter and Miss Parton are our guardian angels—type our copy, correct our grammar, provide us with pencils and paper and feed us on coffee and cake. Miss Parton is the blonde and Miss Rossiter the brunette. Gentlemen prefer blondes but personally I find them both equally seraphic."

Mr. Bredon bowed.

"Miss Meteyard—of Somerville. One of the brighter ornaments of our department. She makes the vulgarest limericks ever recited within these chaste walls."

"Then we shall be friends," said Mr. Bredon cordially.

"Mr. Willis on your right, Mr. Garrett on your left—both comrades in affliction. That is the whole department, except Mr. Hankin and Mr. Armstrong who are directors, and Mr. Copley, who is a man of weight and experience and does not come and frivol in the typists' room. He goes out for his elevenses, and assumes seniority though he hath it not."

13

Mr. Bredon grasped the hands extended to him and murmured politely.

"Would you like to be in on the Derby sweep?" inquired Miss Rossiter, with an eye to the cash-box. "You're just in time for the draw."

"Oh, rather," said Mr. Bredon. "How much?"

"Sixpence."

"Oh, yes, rather. I mean, it's jolly good of you. Of course, absolutely—must be in on the jolly old sweep, what?"

"That brings the first prize up to a pound precisely," said Miss Rossiter, with a grateful sigh. "I was afraid I should have to take two tickets myself. Type Mr. Bredon's for him, Parton. B,R,E,D,O,N—like summer-time on Bredon?"

"That's right."

Miss Parton obligingly typed the name and added another blank ticket to the collection in the biscuit-box.

"Well, I suppose I'd better take you along to your dog-kennel," said Mr. Ingleby, with gloom.

"Right-ho!" said Mr. Bredon. "Oh, rather. Yes."

"We're all along this corridor," added Mr. Ingleby, leading the way. "You'll find your way about in time. That's Garrett's room and that's Willis's, and this is yours, between Miss Meteyard and me. That iron staircase opposite me goes down to the floor below; mostly group managers and conference rooms. Don't fall down it, by the way. The man whose room you've got tumbled down it last week and killed himself."

"No, did he?" said Mr. Bredon, startled.

"Bust his neck and cracked his skull," said Mr. Ingleby. "On one of those knobs."

"Why do they put knobs on staircases?" expostulated Mr. Bredon. "Cracking fellows' skulls for them? It's not right."

"No, it isn't," said Miss Rossiter, arriving with her hands full of scribbling-blocks and blotting-paper. "They're supposed to prevent the boys from sliding down the hand-rail, but it's the stairs themselves that are so—oh, I say, push on. There's Mr. Armstrong coming up. They don't like too much being said about the iron staircase."

"Well, here you are," said Mr. Ingleby, adopting this advice. "Much the same as the rest, except that the radiator doesn't work very well. Still, that won't worry you just at present. This was Dean's room."

"Chap who fell downstairs?"

"Yes."

Mr. Bredon gazed round the small apartment, which contained a table, two chairs, a rickety desk and a bookshelf, and said:

"Oh!"

"It *was* awful," said Miss Rossiter.

"It must have been," agreed Mr. Bredon, fervently.

"Mr. Armstrong was just giving me dictation when we heard the most *frightful* crash. He said, 'Good God, what's that?' I thought it must be one of the boys, because one of them fell down last year carrying an Elliot-Fisher typewriter and it sounded exactly like it, only worse. And I said, 'I think one of the boys must have fallen downstairs, Mr. Armstrong,' and he said, 'Careless little devil,' and went on dictating and my hand was so shaky I could hardly make my outlines and then Mr. Ingleby ran past and Mr. Daniels' door opened and then we heard the most terrific shriek, and Mr. Armstrong said, 'Better go and see what's happened,' so I went out and looked down and I couldn't see anything because there was such a bunch of people standing round and then Mr. Ingleby came tearing up, with *such* a look on his face—you were as white as a sheet, Mr. Ingleby, you really were."

"Possibly," said Mr. Ingleby, a little put out. "Three years in this soul-searing profession have not yet robbed me of all human feeling. But that will come in time."

"Mr. Ingleby said, 'He's killed himself!' And I said, 'Who?' and he said, 'Mr. Dean,' and I said, 'You don't mean that,' and he said, 'I'm afraid so,' and I went back to Mr. Armstrong and said, 'Mr. Dean's killed himself,' and he said, 'What do you mean, killed himself?' and then Mr. Ingleby came in and Mr. Armstrong gave one look at him and went out and I went down by the other staircase and saw them carrying Mr. Dean along to the board-room and his head was all hanging sideways."

"Does this kind of thing happen often?" inquired Mr. Bredon.

"Not with such catastrophic results," replied Mr. Ingleby, "but that staircase is definitely a death-trap."

"I fell down it myself one day," said Miss Rossiter, "and tore the heels off both my shoes. It was awfully awkward, because I hadn't another pair in the place and—"

"I've drawn a horse, darlings!" announced Miss Meteyard, arriving without ceremony. "No luck for you, Mr. Bredon, I'm afraid."

"I always was unlucky."

"You'll feel unluckier still after a day with Dairyfields Margarine," said Mr. Ingleby, gloomily. "Nothing for me, I suppose?"

"Nothing, I'm afraid. Of course Miss Rawlings has drawn the favourite—she always does."

"I hope it breaks its beastly leg," said Mr. Ingleby. "Come

15

in, Tallboy, come in. Do you want me? Don't mind butting in on Mr. Bredon. He will soon become used to the idea that his room is a public place within the meaning of the act. This is Mr. Tallboy, group-manager for Nutrax and a few other wearisome commodities. Mr. Bredon, our new copy-writer."

"How do you do?" said Mr. Tallboy, briefly. "Look here, about this Nutrax 11-inch double. Can you possibly cut out about thirty words?"

"No, I can't," said Mr. Ingleby. "I've cut it to the bone already."

"Well, I'm afraid you'll have to. There isn't room for all this guff with a two-line sub-head."

"There's plenty of room for it."

"No, there isn't. We've got to get in the panel about the Fifty-six Free Chiming Clocks."

"Damn the clocks and the panel! How do they expect to display all that in a half-double?"

"Dunno, but they do. Look here, can't we take out this bit about 'When your nerves begin to play tricks on you,' and start off with 'Nerves need Nutrax'?"

"Armstrong liked that bit about playing tricks. Human appeal and all that. No, take out that rot about the patent spring-cap bottle."

"They won't stand for dropping that," said Miss Meteyard. "That's their pet invention."

"Do they think people buy nerve-food for the sake of the bottle? Oh, well! I can't do it straight away. Hand it over."

"The printer wants it by two o'clock," said Mr. Tallboy, dubiously.

Mr. Ingleby damned the printer, seized the proof and began cutting the copy, uttering offensive ejaculations between his teeth.

"Of all beastly days of the week," he observed, "Tuesday is the foulest. There's no peace till we get this damned 11-inch double off our chests. There! I've cut out twenty-two words, and you'll have to make it do. You can take that 'with' up into the line above and save a whole line, and that gives you the other eight words."

"All right, I'll try," agreed Mr. Tallboy. "Anything for a quiet life. It'll look a bit tight, though."

"Wish *I* was tight," said Mr. Ingleby. "Take it away, for God's sake, before I murder anybody."

"I'm going, I'm going," said Mr. Tallboy, and vanished hastily. Miss Rossiter had departed during the controversy, and Miss Meteyard now took herself out of the way, remarking, "If Pheidippides wins, you shall have a cake for tea."

"Now we'd better start *you* off," observed Mr. Ingleby.

"Here's the guard-book. You'd better have a look through it to see the kind of thing, and then think up some headlines. Your story is, of course, that Dairyfields' 'Green Pastures' Margarine is everything that the best butter ought to be and only costs ninepence a pound. And they like a cow in the picture."

"Why? Is it made of cow-fat?"

"Well, I daresay it is, but you mustn't say so. People wouldn't like the idea. The picture of the cow suggests the taste of butter, that's all. And the name—Green Pastures—suggests cows, you see."

"It suggests Negroes to me," said Mr. Bredon. "The play, you know."

"You mustn't put Negroes in the copy," retorted Mr. Ingleby. "Nor, of course, religion. Keep Psalm 23 out of it. Blasphemous."

"I see. Just something about 'Better than Butter and half the price.' Simple appeal to the pocket."

"Yes, but you mustn't knock butter. They sell butter as well."

"Oh!"

"You can say it's as good as butter."

"But in that case," objected Mr. Bredon, "what does one find to say in favour of butter? I mean, if the other stuff's as good and doesn't cost so much, what's the argument for buying butter?"

"You don't need an argument for buying butter. It's a natural, human instinct."

"Oh, I see."

"Anyway, don't bother about butter. Just concentrate on Green Pastures Margarine. When you've got a bit done, you take it along and get it typed, and then you buzz off to Mr. Hankin with the result. See? Are you all right now?"

"Yes, thanks," said Mr. Bredon, looking thoroughly bewildered.

"And I'll push along about 1 o'clock and show you the decentest place for lunch."

"Thanks frightfully."

"Well, cheerio!" Mr. Ingleby returned to his own room.

"*He* won't stay the course," he said to himself. "Goes to a damned good tailor, though. I wonder—"

He shrugged his shoulders and sat down to concoct a small, high-class folder about Slider's Steel Office Tables.

Mr. Bredon, left alone, did not immediately attack the subject of margarine. Like a cat, which, in his soft-footed inquisitiveness, he rather resembled, he proceeded to make himself acquainted with his new home. There was not very

17

much to see in it. He opened the drawer in his writing-table and found a notched and inky ruler, some bitten-looking pieces of india-rubber, a number of bright thoughts on tea and margarine scribbled on scraps of paper, and a broken fountain-pen. The book-case contained a dictionary, a repellent volume entitled *Directory of Directors*, a novel by Edgar Wallace, a pleasingly got-up booklet called *All about Cocoa*, *Alice in Wonderland*, Bartlett's *Familiar Quotations*, the *Globe* edition of the *Works of Wm. Shakespeare*, and five odd numbers of the *Children's Encyclopædia*. The interior of the sloping desk offered more scope for inquiry; it was filled with ancient and dusty papers, including a Government Report on the Preservatives in Food (Restrictions) Act of 1926, a quantity of rather (in every sense) rude sketches by an amateur hand, a bundle of pulls of advertisements for Dairyfields commodities, some private correspondence and some old bills. Mr. Bredon, dusting fastidious fingers, turned from this receptacle, inventoried a hook and a coat-hanger on the wall and a battered paperfile in a corner, and sat down in the revolving-chair before the table. Here, after a brief glance at a paste-pot, a pair of scissors, a new pencil and a blotting-pad, two scribbling-blocks and a grubby cardboard box-lid full of oddments, he propped up the Dairyfields guard-book before him, and fell to studying his predecessor's masterpieces on the subject of Green Pastures Margarine.

An hour later, Mr. Hankin pushed open the door and looked in upon him.

"How are you getting on?" he inquired kindly.

Mr. Bredon sprang to his feet.

"Not frightfully well, I'm afraid. I don't seem to get the atmosphere altogether, if you follow me."

"It will come," said Mr. Hankin. He was a helpfully-minded man, who believed that new copy-writers throve on encouragement. "Let me see what you are doing. You are starting with the headlines? Quite right. The headline is more than half the battle. IF YOU WERE A COW—no, no, I'm afraid we mustn't call the customer a cow. Besides, we had practically the same headline in—let me see—about 1923, I think. Mr. Wardle put it up, you'll find it in the last guard-book but three. It went 'IF YOU KEPT A COW IN THE KITCHEN you could get no better bread-spread than G. P. Margarine'—and so on. That was a good one. Caught the eye, made a good picture, and told the whole story in a sentence."

Mr. Bredon bowed his head, as one who hears the Law and the Prophets. The copy-chief ran a thoughtful pencil over the scribbled list of headlines, and ticked one of them.

"I like that.

That has the right feel about it. You might write copy for
that, and perhaps for this one,

YOU'D BE READY TO BET
IT WAS BUTTER—

though I'm not quite sure about it. These Dairyfields people
are rather strait-laced about betting."

"Oh, are they? What a pity! I'd done several about that,
'HAVE A BIT ON—' Don't you like that one?"

Mr. Hankin shook his head regretfully.

"I'm afraid that's too direct. Encouraging the working
classes to waste their money."

"But they all do it—why, all these women like a little
flutter."

"I know, I know. But I'm sure the client wouldn't stand
for it. You'll soon find that the biggest obstacle to good
advertising is the client. They all have their fads. That headline would do for Darling's, but it won't do for Dairyfields.
We did very well with a sporting headline in '26—'PUT YOUR
SHIRT ON Darling's Non-collapsible Towel-Horse'—sold 80,000
in Ascot week. Though that was partly accident, because we
mentioned a real horse in the copy and it came in at 50 to 1,
and all the women who'd won money on it rushed out and
bought Non-collapsible Towel-Horses out of sheer gratitude.
The public's very odd."

"Yes," said Mr. Bredon. "They must be. There seems to be
more in advertising than, so to speak, meets the eye."

"There is," said Mr. Hankin, a little grimly. "Well, get
some copy written and bring it along to me. You know
where to find my room?"

"Oh, yes—at the end of the corridor, near the iron staircase."

"No, no, that's Mr. Armstrong. At the other end of the
corridor, near the other staircase—not the iron staircase. By
the way—"

"Yes?"

"Oh, nothing," said Mr. Hankin, vaguely. "That is to
say—no, nothing."

Mr. Bredon gazed after his retreating figure, and shook his
fair head in a meditative manner. Then, applying himself to
his task, he wrote out, rather quickly, a couple of paragraphs
in praise of margarine and wandered out with them. Turning

to the right, he paused opposite the door of Ingleby's room and stared irresolutely at the iron staircase. As he stood there, the glass door of a room on the opposite side of the corridor opened and a middle-aged man shot out. Seeing Bredon, he paused in his rush for the stairhead and inquired:

"Do you want to know how to get anywhere or anything?"

"Oh! thanks awfully. No—I mean, yes. I'm the new copy-writer. I'm looking for the typists' room."

"Other end of the passage."

"Oh, I see, thanks frightfully. This place is rather confusing. Where does this staircase go to?"

"Down to a whole lot of departments—mostly group-managers' rooms and board-rooms and Mr. Pym's room and several of the Directors' rooms and the Printing."

"Oh, I see. Thanks ever so. Where does one wash?"

"That's downstairs too. I'll show you if you like."

"Oh, thanks—thanks most awfully."

The other man plunged down the steep and rattling spiral as though released by a spring. Bredon followed more gingerly.

"A bit precipitous, isn't it?"

"Yes, it is. You'd better be careful. One fellow out of your department smashed himself up here the other day."

"No, really?"

"Broke his neck. Dead when we picked him up."

"No, did he? was he? How on earth did he come to do that? Couldn't he see where he was going?"

"Slipped, I expect. Must have been going too fast. There's nothing really wrong with the staircase. I've never had an accident. It's very well-lit."

"Well-lit?" Mr. Bredon gaped vaguely at the skylight and up and down the passage, surrounded, like the one on the floor above, with glass partitions. "Oh, yes, to be sure. It's very well-lit. Of course he must have slipped. Dashed easy thing to slip on a staircase. Did he have nails in his shoes?"

"I don't know. I wasn't noticing his shoes. I was thinking about picking up the pieces."

"Did you pick him up?"

"Well, I heard the racket when he went down, and rushed out and got there one of the first. My name's Daniels, by the way."

"Oh, is it? Daniels, oh, yes. But didn't it come out at the inquest about his shoes?"

"I don't remember anything about it."

"Oh! then I suppose he didn't have nails. I mean, if he had, somebody would have mentioned it. I mean, it would be a sort of excuse, wouldn't it?"

"Excuse for whom?" demanded Daniels.

"For the firm; I mean, when people put up staircases and other people come tumbling down them, the insurance people generally want to know why. At least, I'm told so. I've never fallen down any staircases myself—touch wood."

"You'd better not try," retorted Daniels, evading the question of insurance. "You'll find the wash-place through that door and down the passage on the left."

"Oh, thanks frightfully."

"Not at all."

Mr. Daniels darted away into a room full of desks, leaving Mr. Bredon to entangle himself in a heavy swing door.

In the lavatory, Bredon encountered Ingleby.

"Oh!" said the latter. "You've found your way. I was told off to show you, but I forgot."

"Mr. Daniels showed me. Who's he?"

"Daniels? He's a group-manager. Looks after a bunch of clients—Sliders and Harrogate Bros. and a few more. Sees to the lay-outs and sends the stereos down to the papers and all that. Not a bad chap."

"He seems a bit touchy about the iron staircase. I mean, he was quite matey till I suggested that the insurance people would want to look into that fellow's accident—and then he kind of froze on me."

"He's been a long time in the firm and doesn't like any nasturtiums cast at it. Certainly not by a new bloke. As a matter of fact, it's better not to throw one's weight about here till one's been ten years or so in the place. It's not encouraged."

"Oh? Oh, thanks awfully for telling me."

"This place is run like a Government office," went on Ingleby. "Hustle's not wanted and initiative and curiosity are politely shown the door."

"That's right," put in a pugnacious-looking red-headed man, who was scrubbing his fingers with pumice-stone as though he meant to take the skin off. "I asked them for £50 for a new lens—and what was the answer? Economy, please, in all departments—the Whitehall touch, eh?—and yet they pay you fellows to write more-you-spend-more-you-save copy! However, I shan't be here long, that's one comfort."

"This is Mr. Prout, our photographer," said Ingleby. "He has been on the point of leaving us for the last five years, but when it comes to the point he realizes that we couldn't do without him and yields to our tears and entreaties."

21

"Tcha!" said Mr. Prout.

"The management think Mr. Prout so precious," went on Ingleby, "that they have set his feet in a large room—"

"That you couldn't swing a kitten in," said Mr. Prout, "and no ventilation. Murder, that's what they do here. Black holes of Calcutta and staircases that break people's heads open. What we want in this country is a Mussolini to organize trade conditions. But what's the good of talking? All the same, one of these days, you'll see."

"Mr. Prout is our tame firebrand," observed Ingleby, indulgently. "You coming up, Bredon?"

"Yes, I've got to take this stuff to be typed."

"Right-ho! Here you are. Round this way and up this staircase by the lift, through the Dispatching and here you are—right opposite the home of British Beauty. Children, here's Mr. Bredon with a nice bit of copy for you."

"Hand it here," said Miss Rossiter, "and oh! Mr. Bredon, do you mind putting down your full name and address on this card—they want it downstairs for the file."

Bredon took the card obediently.

"Block letters please," added Miss Rossiter, glancing with some dismay at the sheets of copy she had just received.

"Oh, do you think my handwriting's awful? I always think it's rather neat, myself. Neat, but not gaudy. However, if you say so—"

"Block letters," repeated Miss Rossiter, firmly. "Hullo! here's Mr. Tallboy. I expect he wants you, Mr. Ingleby."

"What, again?"

"Nutrax have cancelled that half-double," announced Mr. Tallboy with gloomy triumph. "They've just sent up from the conference to say that they want something special to put up against the new Slumbermalt campaign, and Mr. Hankin says will you get something out and let him have it in half an hour."

Ingleby uttered a loud yell, and Bredon, laying down the index-card, gazed at him open-mouthed.

"Damn and blast Nutrax," said Ingleby. "May all its directors get elephantiasis, locomotor ataxy and ingrowing toe-nails!"

"Oh, quite," said Tallboy. "You'll let us have something, won't you? If I can get it passed before 3 o'clock the printer— Hullo!"

Mr. Tallboy's eye, roving negligently round, had fallen on Bredon's index-card. Miss Rossiter's glance followed his. Neatly printed on the card stood the one word

"Look at that!" said Miss Rossiter.

"Oh!" said Ingleby, looking over her shoulder. "That's who you are, is it, Bredon? Well, all I can say is, your stuff ought to come home to everybody. Universal appeal, and so forth."

Mr. Bredon smiled apologetically.

"You startled me so," he said. "Pooping off that howl in my ear." He took up the card and finished his inscription:

DEATH BREDON,
12A, Great Ormond Street,
W.C.1

CHAPTER II

EMBARRASSING INDISCRETION
OF TWO TYPISTS

FOR the twentieth time, Mr. Death Bredon was studying the report of the coroner's inquest on Victor Dean.

There was the evidence of Mr. Prout, the photographer:

"It would be about tea-time. Tea is served at 3.30, more or less. I was coming out of my room on the top floor, carrying my camera and tripod. Mr. Dean passed me. He was coming quickly along the passage in the direction of the iron staircase. He was not running—he was walking at a good pace. He was carrying a large, heavy book under one arm. I know now that it was *The Times Atlas*. I turned to walk in the same direction that he was going. I saw him start down the iron staircase; it is rather a steep spiral. He had taken about half a dozen steps when he seemed to crumple together and disappear. There was a tremendous crash. You might call it a clatter—a prolonged crashing noise. I started to run, when Mr. Daniels' door opened and he came out and collided with the legs of my tripod. While we were mixed up together, Mr. Ingleby ran past us down the corridor. I heard a shrill scream from below. I put the camera down and Mr. Daniels and I went to the head of the staircase together. Some other people joined us—Miss Rossiter, I think, and some of the copy-writers and clerks. We could see Mr. Dean lying huddled together at the foot of the staircase. I could not say whether he had fallen down the stairs or through the banisters. He was lying all in a heap. The staircase is a right-handed spiral, and makes one complete turn. The treads are composed of pierced ironwork. The hand-rail has a number of iron knobs on it, about the size of small walnuts. The stairs are apt to be slippery. The stair is well lit. There is a sky-light above, and it receives light through the glass panels of Mr. Daniels' room and also from the glass-panelled corridor on the floor below. I have here a photograph taken by myself at 3.30 p.m. yesterday—that is the day after the accident. It shows the head of the spiral staircase. It was taken by ordinary daylight. I used an Actinax Special Rapid plate with the H & D number 450. The exposure was ⅕ second with the lens stopped down to ƒ.16. The light was then similar to what it was at the time of Mr. Dean's death. The sun was shining on both occasions. The corridor runs, roughly, north and south. As deceased went down the staircase, the light would be coming from above and behind him; it is not possible that he could have the sun in his eyes."

Then came Mr. Daniels' account:

"I was standing at my desk consulting with Mr. Freeman about an advertising lay-out. I heard the crash. I thought one of the boys must have fallen down again. A boy did fall down that staircase on a previous occasion. I do not consider it a dangerous structure. I consider that the boy was going too fast. I do not recollect hearing Mr. Dean go along the passage. I did not see him. My back was to the door. People pass along that passage continuously; I should not be paying attention. I went quickly out when I heard the noise of the fall. I encountered Mr. Prout and tripped over his tripod. I did not exactly fall down, but I stumbled and had to catch hold of him to steady myself. There was nobody in the corridor when I came out except Mr. Prout. I will swear to that. Mr. Ingleby came past us while we were recovering from the collision. He did not come from his own room, but from the south end of the passage. He went down the iron staircase and Mr. Prout and I followed as quickly as we could. I heard somebody shriek downstairs. I think it was just before, or just after I ran into Mr. Prout. I was rather confused at the time and cannot say for certain. We saw Mr. Dean lying at the bottom of the staircase. There were a number of people standing round. Then Mr. Ingleby came up the stairs very hastily and called out: 'He's dead!' or 'He's killed himself.' I cannot speak to the exact words. I did not believe him at first; I thought he was exaggerating. I went on down the staircase. Mr. Dean was lying bundled together, head downwards. His legs were partly up the staircase. I think somebody had already tried to lift him before I got there. I have had some experience of death and accidents. I was a stretcher-bearer in the War. I examined him and gave it as my opinion that he was dead. I believe Mr. Atkins had already expressed a similar opinion. I helped to lift the body and carry it into the Board-room. We laid him on the table and endeavoured to administer first-aid, but I never had any doubt that he was dead. It did not occur to us to leave him where he was till the police were summoned, because, of course, he might not have been dead, and we could not leave him head downwards on the staircase."

Then came Mr. Atkins, who explained that he was a

group-secretary, working in one of the downstairs rooms.

"I was just coming out of my room, the door of which commands a view of the iron staircase. It is not directly opposite the foot of the staircase, but it commands a view of the lower half of the staircase. Any one coming down the staircase would have his back turned to me as he stepped off. I heard a loud crash, and saw the deceased falling all of a heap down the stairs. He did not appear to make any attempt to save himself. He was clutching a large book in his arms. He did not loose his grip of the book as he fell. He seemed to cannon from one side of the staircase to the other and fall like a sack of potatoes, so to speak. He pitched on his head at the bottom. I was carrying a large tray full of glass jars. I set this down and ran towards him. I endeavoured to lift him up, but the moment I touched him I felt sure that he was dead. I formed the opinion that he had broken his neck. Mrs. Crump was in the passage at the time. Mrs. Crump is the head charwoman. I said to her: 'Good God! he's broken his neck,' and she screamed loudly. A number of other people arrived almost immediately upon the scene. Somebody said, 'Perhaps it's only dislocated.' Mr. Daniels said to me: 'We can't leave him here.' I think it was Mr. Armstrong who suggested that he should be taken into the Board-room. I assisted to carry him there. The book was held by the deceased in such a tight grip that we had difficulty in getting it away from him. He made no movement of any kind after he fell, and no attempt at speech. I never had the least doubt that he was dead from the moment that he fell."

Mrs. Crump confirmed this account to the best of her ability. She said: "I am head charwoman to the firm of Pym's Publicity, Ltd. It is my duty to take the tea-waggon round the office building at about 3.30 each afternoon. That is, I start my round at about 3.15 and finish at about 3.45. I had nearly finished doing the first floor, and was returning on my way to the lift to take tea up to the top floor. That would make the time about 3.30. I was coming along the corridor and was facing the foot of the iron staircase. I saw Mr. Dean fall. He fell all in a bunch-like. It was dreadful. He did not shout out or make any exclamation in falling. He fell like a dead thing. My heart seemed to stop. I was struck so I couldn't move for a minute or two. Then Mr. Atkins came running along to pick him up. He said: 'He's broke his neck,' and I let out a scream. I couldn't help myself, I was that upset. I think that staircase is a wicked dangerous place. I am always warning the other women against it. If you was to slip you couldn't hardly save yourself, not if you was carrying

26

anything. People run up and downstairs on it all day, and the edges of the steps gets that polished you wouldn't believe, and some of them is wore down at the edges."

The medical evidence was given by Dr. Emerson. "I reside in Queen's Square, Bloomsbury. It is about five minutes from my house to the offices of Pym's Publicity in Southampton Row. I received a telephone message at 3.40 p.m. and went round immediately. Deceased was dead when I arrived. I concluded that he had then been dead about 15 minutes. His neck was broken at the fourth cervical vertebra. He also had a contused wound on the right temple which had cracked the skull. Either of these injuries was sufficient to cause death. I should say he had died instantly upon falling. He had also the tibia of the left leg broken, probably through catching in the banister of the staircase. There were also, of course, a quantity of minor scratches and contusions. The wound on the head is such as might be caused through pitching upon one of the knobs on the handrail in falling. I could not say whether this or the broken vertebra was the actual cause of death, but in either case, death would be instantaneous. I agree that it is not a matter of great importance. I found no trace of any heart disease or any other disease which might suggest that deceased was subject to vertigo or fainting-fits. I observed no traces of alcoholic tendency or of addiction to drugs. I have seen the staircase, and consider that it would be very easy to slip upon it. So far as I can tell, deceased's eyesight would appear to have been normal."

Miss Pamela Dean, sister of deceased, gave evidence that her brother had been in good health at the time of the accident and that he had never been subject to fits or fainting. He was not short-sighted. He occasionally suffered from liverish attacks. He was a good dancer and usually very neat and nimble on his feet. He had once sprained his ankle as a boy, but so far as she knew, no permanent weakness of the joint had resulted.

Evidence was also called which showed that accidents had occurred on several previous occasions to persons descending the staircase; other witnesses expressed the opinion that the staircase was not dangerous to anybody exercising reasonable care. The jury returned a verdict of accidental death, with a rider to the effect that they thought the iron spiral should be replaced by a more solid structure.

Mr. Bredon shook his head. Then he drew a sheet of paper from the rack before him and wrote down:

1. He seemed to crumple together.
2. He did not make any attempt to save himself.

3. He did not loose his grip of the book.
4. He pitched on his head at the bottom.
5. Neck broken, skull cracked; either injury fatal.
6. Good health; good sight; good dancer.

He filled himself a pipe and sat for some time staring at this list. Then he searched in a drawer and produced a piece of notepaper, which seemed to be an unfinished letter, or the abandoned draft of one.

"DEAR MR. PYM,—I think it only right that you should know that there is something going on in the office which is very undesirable, and might lead to serious—"

After a little more thought, he laid this document aside and began to scribble on another sheet, erasing and rewriting busily. Presently a slow smile twitched his lips.

"I'll swear there's something in it," he muttered, "something pretty big. But the job is, to handle it. One's got to go for the money—but where's it coming from? Not from Pym, I fancy. It doesn't seem to be his personal show, and you can't blackmail a whole office. I wonder, though. After all, he'd probably pay a good bit to prevent—"

He relapsed into silence and meditation.

"And what," demanded Miss Parton, spearing another chocolate éclair, "do you think of our Mr. Bredon?"

"The Pimlico Pet?" said Miss Rossiter. "You'll put on pounds and pounds if you eat all that sweet stuff, duckie. Well, I think he's rather a lamb, and his shirts are simply too marvellous. He won't be able to keep that up on Pym's salary, bonus or no bonus. Or the silk socks either."

"He's been brought up silk-lined all right," agreed Miss Parton. "One of the new poor, I expect. Lost all his money in the slump or something."

"Either that, or his family have got tired of supporting him and pushed him out to scratch for himself," suggested Miss Rossiter. She slimmed more strenuously than her colleague, and was less inclined to sentiment. "I sort of asked him the other day what he did before he came here, and he said, all sorts of things, and mentioned that he'd had a good bit to do with motors. I expect he's been one of these gilded johnnies who used to sell cars on commission, and the bottom's dropped out of that and he's got to do a job of work—if you call copy-writing work."

"I think he's very clever," said Miss Parton. "Did you see that idiotic headline he put up for Margarine yesterday: 'IT'S

28

A FAR, FAR BUTTER THING'? Hankie nearly sniggered himself sick. I think the Pet was pulling his leg. But what I mean is, he wouldn't think of a silly thing like that if he hadn't got brains."

"He'll make a copy-writer," declared Miss Rossiter, firmly. She had seen so many new copy-writers come and pass like ships in the night, that she was as well able to size them up as the copy-chiefs themselves. "He's got the flair if you know what I mean. He'll stay all right."

"I hope he does," said Miss Parton. "He's got beautiful manners. Doesn't chuck the stuff at you as if you were dirt like young Willis. And he pays his tea-bill like a little gentleman."

"Early days," said Miss Rossiter. "He's paid *one* tea-bill. Gives me the pip, the way some of them make a fuss about it. There's Garrett. He was quite rude when I went to him on Saturday. Hinted that I made money out of the teas. I suppose he thinks it's funny. I don't."

"He means it for a joke."

"No, he doesn't. Not altogether. And he's always grumbling. Whether it's Chelsea buns or jam roll, there's always something wrong with it. I said to him, 'Mr. Garrett,' I said, 'if *you* like to give up *your* lunch-time every day to trying to find something that *everybody* will enjoy, you're welcome to do it.' 'Oh, no,' he said, 'I'm not the office-boy.' 'And who do you think I am,' I said, 'the errand-girl?' So he told me not to lose my temper. It's all very well, but you get very tired of it, especially this hot weather, fagging round."

Miss Parton nodded. The teas were a perennial grievance.

"Anyhow," she said, "friend Bredon is no trouble. A plain biscuit and a cup of tea every day. That's his order. And he said he was quite ready to pay the same subscription as everybody else, though really he ought to be let off with sixpence. I do like a man to be generous and speak to you nicely."

"Oh, the Pet's tongue runs on ball-bearings," said Miss Rossiter. "And talk of being a nosey-parker!"

"They all are," replied Miss Parton. "But I say, do you know what I did yesterday? It was dreadful. Bredon came in and asked for Mr. Hankin's carbons. I was in an awful rush with some of old Copley's muck—he always wants everything done in five minutes—and I said, 'Help yourself.' Well, what do you think? Ten minutes afterwards I went to look for something on the shelf and I found he'd gone off with Mr. Hankin's private letter-file. He must have been blind, because it's marked PRIVATE in red letters an inch high. Of course Hankie'd be in an awful bait if he knew. So I hared off to

Bredon and there he was, calmly reading Hankie's private letters, if you please! 'You've got the wrong file, Mr. Bredon,' I said. And he wasn't a bit ashamed. He just handed it back with a grin and said, 'I was beginning to think I might have. It's very interesting to see what salary everybody gets.' And, my dear, he was reading Hankie's departmental list. And I said, 'Oh, Mr. Bredon, you *oughtn't* to be reading that. It's frightfully confidential.' And he said, 'Is it?' He seemed quite surprised."

"Silly ass!" said Miss Rossiter. "I hope you told him to keep it to himself. They *are* all so sensitive about their salaries. I'm sure I don't know why. But they're all dying to find out what the others get and terrified to death anybody should find out what they get themselves. If Bredon goes round shooting his mouth off, he'll stir up some awful trouble."

"I warned him," said Miss Parton, "and he seemed to think it was awfully funny and asked how long it would take him to reach Dean's salary."

"Let's see, how much was Dean getting?"

"Six," replied Miss Parton, "and not worth much more in my opinion. The department will be better-tempered without him, I must say. He did rile 'em sometimes."

"If you ask me," said Miss Rossiter, "I don't think this business of mixing the University people with the other sort works very well. With the Oxford and Cambridge lot it's all give-and-take and bad language, but the others don't seem to fit in with it. They always think they're being sneered at."

"It's Ingleby upsets them. He never takes anything seriously."

"None of them do," said Miss Rossiter, putting an unerring and experienced finger on the point of friction. "It's all a game to them, and with Copley and Willis it's all deadly serious. When Willis starts on metaphysics, Ingleby recites limericks. Personally, I'm broad-minded. I rather like it. And I will say the 'varsity crowd don't quarrel like the rest of them. If Dean hadn't fallen downstairs, there'd have been a good old bust-up between him and Willis."

"I never could understand what that was all about," observed Miss Parton, thoughtfully stirring her coffee.

"*I* believe there was a girl in it," said Miss Rossiter. "Willis used to go about with Dean quite a lot at the week-end, and then it all stopped suddenly. They had an awful row one day last March. Miss Meteyard heard them going at it hammer and tongs in Dean's room."

"Did she hear what the fuss was?"

"No. Being Miss Meteyard, she first pounded on the partition and then went in and told them to shut up. She's no use for people's private feelings. Funny woman. Well, I suppose we'd better push off home, or we shan't be fit for anything in the morning. It was quite a good show, wasn't it? Where's the check? You had two cakes more than me. Yours is one-and-a-penny and mine's ninepence. If I give you a bob and you give me twopence and the waitress twopence and settle up at the desk, we shall be all square."

The two girls left the Corner House by the Coventry Street entrance, and turned to the right and crossed the Piccadilly merry-go-round to the Tube entrance. As they regained the pavement, Miss Rossiter clutched Miss Parton by the arm:

"Look! the Pet! got up regardless!"

"Go on!" retorted Miss Parton. "It isn't the Pet. Yes, it is! Look at the evening cloak and the gardenia, *and*, my dear, the monocle!"

Unaware of this commentary, the gentleman in question was strolling negligently towards them, smoking a cigarette. As he came abreast of them, Miss Rossiter broke into a cheerful grin and said, "Hullo!"

The man raised his hat mechanically and shook his head. His face was a well-bred blank. Miss Rossiter's cheeks became flooded with a fiery crimson.

"It isn't him. How *awful!*"

"He took you for a tart," said Miss Parton, with some confusion and perhaps a little satisfaction.

"It's an extraordinary thing," muttered Miss Rossiter, vexed. "I could have sworn—"

"He's not a bit like him, really, when you see him close to," said Miss Parton, wise after the event. "I told you it wasn't him."

"You said it was him." Miss Rossiter glanced back over her shoulder, and was in time to see a curious little incident.

A limousine car came rolling gently along from the direction of Leicester Square and drew up close to the kerb, opposite the entrance to the Criterion Bar. The man in dress-clothes stepped up to it and addressed a few words to the occupant, flinging his cigarette away as he did so, and laying one hand on the handle of the door, as though about to enter the car. Before he could do so, two men emerged suddenly and silently from a shop-entrance. One of them spoke to the chauffeur; the other put his hand on the gentleman's elegant arm. A brief sentence or two were exchanged; then the one man got up beside the chauffeur while the second man opened the door of the car. The man in dress-clothes got in, the other man followed, and the whole party drove off. The whole thing was so quickly done that almost before Miss Parton could turn round in answer to Miss Rossiter's exclamation, it was all over.

"An arrest!" breathed Miss Rossiter, her eyes shining. "Those two were detectives. I wonder what our friend in the monocle's been doing."

Miss Parton was thrilled.

"And we actually spoke to him and thought it was Bredon."

"*I* spoke to him," corrected Miss Rossiter. It was all very well for Miss Parton to claim the credit, but only a few minutes back she had rather pointedly dissociated herself from the indiscretion and she could not be allowed to have it both ways.

"You did, then," agreed Miss Parton. "I'm surprised at you, Rossie, trying to get off with a smart crook. Anyhow, if Bredon doesn't turn up tomorrow, we'll know it was him after all."

But it could hardly have been Mr. Bredon, for he was in his place the next morning just as usual. Miss Rossiter asked him if he had a double.

"Not that I know of," said Mr. Bredon. "One of my cousins is a bit like me."

Miss Rossiter related the incident, with slight modifications. On consideration, she thought it better not to mention that she had been mistaken for a lady of easy virtue.

"Oh, I don't think that would be my cousin," replied Mr. Bredon. "He's a frightfully proper person. Well known at Buckingham Palace, and all that."

"Go on," said Miss Rossiter.

"I'm the black sheep of the family," said Mr. Bredon. "He never even sees me in the street. It must have been some one quite different."

"Is your cousin called Bredon, too?"

"Oh, yes," said Mr. Bredon.

CHAPTER III

INQUISITIVE INTERVIEWS OF A
NEW COPY-WRITER

MR. BREDON had been a week with Pym's Publicity, and
had learnt a number of things. He learned the average number of words that can be crammed into four inches of copy;
that Mr. Armstrong's fancy could be caught by an elaborately-
drawn lay-out, whereas Mr. Hankin looked on art-work as
waste of a copy-writer's time; that the word "pure" was
dangerous, because, if lightly used, it laid the client open to
prosecution by the Government inspectors, whereas the
words "highest quality," "finest ingredients," "packed under
the best conditions" had no legal meaning, and were therefore safe; that the expression "giving work to umpteen thousand British employees in our model works at so-and-so" was
not by any means the same thing as "British made throughout"; that the north of England liked its butter and margarine salted, whereas the south preferred it fresh; that the
Morning Star would not accept any advertisements containing
the word "cure," though there was no objection to such
expressions as "relieve" or "ameliorate," and that, further,
any commodity that professed to "cure" anything might find
itself compelled to register as a patent medicine and use an
expensive stamp; that the most convincing copy was always
written with the tongue in the cheek, a genuine conviction of
the commodity's worth producing—for some reason—
poverty and flatness of style; that if, by the most far-fetched
stretch of ingenuity, an indecent meaning could be read into
a headline, that was the meaning that the great British Public
would infallibly read into it; that the great aim and object of
the studio artist was to crowd the copy out of the advertisement and that, conversely, the copy-writer was a designing
villain whose ambition was to cram the space with verbiage
and leave no room for the sketch; that the lay-out man, a
meek ass between two burdens, spent a miserable life trying
to reconcile these opposing parties; and further, that all
departments alike united in hatred of the client, who persisted in spoiling good lay-outs by cluttering them up with

coupons, free-gift offers, lists of local agents and realistic portraits of hideous and uninteresting cartons, to the detriment of his own interests and the annoyance of everybody concerned.

He also learned to find his way without assistance over the two floors occupied by the agency, and even up on to the roof, where the messenger boys did their daily physical jerks under the eye of the Sergeant, and whence a fine view of London might be obtained on a clear day. He became acquainted with a number of the group-managers, and was sometimes even able to remember off-hand which clients' accounts were in the control of which manager, while with most of the members of his own department he found himself established on a footing of friendly intimacy. There were the two copy-chiefs, Mr. Armstrong and Mr. Hankin, each brilliant in his own way and each with his own personal fads. Mr. Hankin, for example, would never accept a headline containing the word "magnificent"; Mr. Armstrong disliked any lay-out which involved the picture of a judge or a Jew, and was rendered so acutely wretched when the proprietors of "Whifflets" put out a new brand of smoke called "Good Judge" Mixture that he was obliged to hand the whole account over, lock, stock and barrel to Mr. Hankin. Mr. Copley, an elderly, serious-minded man, who had entered the advertising profession before the modern craze set in for public-school-and-University-trained copy-writers, was remarkable for a tendency to dyspepsia and a perfectly miraculous knack of writing appetizing copy for tinned and packeted foodstuffs. Anything that came out of a tin or a packet was poison to him, and his diet consisted of under-cooked beef-steak, fruit and whole-meal bread. The only copy he really enjoyed writing was that for Bunbury's Whole-Meal Flour, and he was perennially depressed when his careful eulogiums, packed with useful medical detail, were scrapped in favour of some light-headed foolishness of Ingleby's, on the story that Bunbury's Whole-Meal Flour took the Ache out of Baking. But on Sardines and Tinned Salmon he was unapproachable.

Ingleby specialized in snobbish copy about Twentyman's Teas ("preferred by Fashion's Favourites"), Whifflets ("in the Royal Enclosure at Ascot, in the Royal Yacht Club at Cowes, you find the discriminating men who smoke Whifflets") and Farley's Footwear ("Whether it's a big shoot or a Hunt Ball, Farley puts you on a sound footing"). He lived in Bloomsbury, was communistic in a literary way, and dressed almost exclusively in pull-overs and grey flannels. He was completely and precociously disillusioned and one of the most promising copy-writers Pym's had ever fathered. When released from Whiffles and fashionable footwear, he could be amusing on almost any subject, and had a turn for "clever" copy, wherever cleverness was not out of place.

Miss Meteyard, with a somewhat similar mental make-up, could write about practically anything except women's goods, which were more competently dealt with by Mr. Willis or Mr. Garrett, the former of whom in particular, could handle corsets and face-cream with a peculiar plaintive charm which made him more than worth his salary. The copy department on the whole worked happily together, writing each other's headlines in a helpful spirit and invading each other's rooms at all hours of the day. The only two men with whom Bredon was unable to establish genial relations were Mr. Copley, who held aloof from everybody, and Mr. Willis, who treated him with a reserve for which he was unable to account. Otherwise he found the department a curiously friendly place.

And it talked. Bredon had never in his life encountered a set of people with such active tongues and so much apparent leisure for gossip. It was a miracle that any work ever got done, though somehow it did. He was reminded of his Oxford days, when essays mysteriously wrote themselves in the intervals of club-meetings and outdoor sports, and when most of the people who took firsts boasted of never having worked more than three hours of any day. The atmosphere suited him well enough. He was a bonhomous soul, with the insatiable curiosity of a baby elephant, and nothing pleased him better than to be interrupted in his encomiums of Sopo ("makes Monday, Fun-day") or the Whoosh Vacuum-cleaner ("one Whoosh and it's clean") by a fellow-member of the department, fed-up with advertising and spoiling for a chat.

"Hullo!" said Miss Meteyard one morning. She had dropped in to consult Bredon about googlies—the proprietors of Tomboy Toffee having embarked upon a series of cricket advertisements which, starting respectively from "Lumme, what a Lob!" or "Yah! that's a Yorker!" led up by devious routes to the merits of Toffee—and had now reached the point when "Gosh! it's a Googly" had to be tackled. Bredon had demonstrated googlies with pencil and paper, and also in the corridor with a small round tin of Good Judge tobacco (whereby he had nearly caught Mr. Armstrong on the side of the head), and had further discussed the relative merits of "Gosh" and "Golly" in the headline; but Miss Meteyard showed no symptoms of departing. She had sat down at Bredon's table and was drawing caricatures, in which she

35

displayed some skill, and was rummaging in the pencil-tray for an india-rubber when she remarked, as above mentioned, "Hullo!"

"What?"

"That's little Dean's scarab. It ought to have been sent back to his sister."

"Oh, that! Yes, I knew that was there, but I didn't know whom it belonged to. It's not a bad thing. It's real onyx, though of course it's not Egyptian and it's not even very old."

"Probably not, but Dean adored it. He thought it was a sure-fire mascot. He always had it in his waistcoat pocket or sitting in front of him while he worked. If he'd had it on him that day, he wouldn't have tumbled downstairs—at least, that's what he'd have said himself."

Bredon poised the beetle on the palm of his hand. It was as big as a man's thumb-nail, heavy and shallowly carved, smooth except for a slight chip at one side.

"What sort of chap was Dean?"

"Well. *De mortuis*, and all that, but I wasn't exactly keen on him. I thought he was rather an unwholesome little beast."

"What way?"

"For one thing, I didn't like the people he went about with."

Bredon twitched an interrogative eyebrow.

"No," said Miss Meteyard, "I don't mean what you mean. At least, I mean, I can't tell you about that. But he used to tag round with that de Momerie crowd. Thought it was smart, I suppose. Luckily, he missed the famous night when that Punter-Smith girl did away with herself. Pym's would never have held its head up again if one of its staff had been involved in a notorious case. Pym's is particular."

"How old did you say this blighter was?"

"Oh, twenty-six or -seven, I should think."

"How did he come to be here?"

"Usual thing. Needed cash, I suppose. Had to have some sort of job. You can't lead a gay life on nothing, and he wasn't anybody, you know. His father was a bank-manager, or something, deceased, so I suppose young Victor had to push out and earn his keep. He knew how to look after himself all right."

"Then how did he get in with that lot?"

Miss Meteyard grinned at him.

"Somebody picked him up, I should think. He had a certain kind of good looks. There is a *nostalgie de la banlieue* as well as *de la boue*. And you're pulling my leg, Mr. Death Bredon, because you know that as well as I do."

"Is that a compliment to my sagacity or a reflection on my virtue?"

"How *you* came here is a good deal more interesting than how Victor Dean came here. They start new copy-writers without experience at four quid a week—about enough to pay for a pair of your shoes."

"Ah!" said Bredon, "how deceptive appearances can be! But it is evident, dear lady, that you do not do your shopping in the true West End. You belong to the section of society that pays for what it buys. I revere, but do not imitate you. Unhappily, there are certain commodities which cannot be obtained without cash. Railway fares, for example, or petrol. But I am glad you approve of my shoes. They are supplied by Rudge in the Arcade and, unlike Farley's Fashion Footwear, are actually of the kind that is to be seen in the Royal Enclosure at Ascot and wherever discriminating men congregate. They have a ladies' department, and if you will mention my name—"

"I begin to see why you chose advertising as a source of supply." The look of doubt left Miss Meteyard's angular face, and was replaced by a faintly derisive expression. "Well, I suppose I'd better get back to Tomboy Toffee. Thanks for your dope about googlies."

Bredon shook his head mournfully as the door closed after her. "Careless," he muttered. "Nearly gave the game away. Oh, well, I suppose I'd better do some work and look as genuine as possible."

He pulled towards him a guard-book pasted up with pulls of Nutrax advertising and studied its pages thoughtfully. He was not left long in peace, however, for after a couple of minutes Ingleby slouched in, a foul pipe at full blast and his hands thrust deep into his trousers-pockets.

"I say, is Brewer here?"

"Don't know him. But," added Bredon, waving his hand negligently, "you have my permission to search. The priest's hole and the concealed staircase are at your service."

Ingleby rooted in the bookcase in vain.

"Somebody's bagged him. Anyway, how do you spell Chrononhotonthologos?"

"Oh! I can do that. And Aldiborontophoscophornio, too. Crossword? Torquemada?"

"No, headline for Good Judges. Isn't it hot? And now I suppose we're going to have a week's dust and hammering."

"Why?"

"The fiat has gone forth. The iron staircase is condemned."

"Who by?"

"The Board."

"Oh, rot! they mustn't do that."

"What d'you mean?"

"Admission of liability, isn't it?"

"Time, too."

"Well, I suppose it is."

"You looked quite startled. I was beginning to think you
had some sort of personal feeling in the matter."

"Good lord, no, why should I? Just a matter of principle.
Except that the staircase does seem to have had its uses in
eliminating the unfit. I gather that the late Victor Dean was
not universally beloved."

"Oh, I don't know. I never saw much harm in him, except
that he wasn't exactly pukka and hadn't quite imbibed the
Pym spirit, as you may say. Of course the Meteyard woman
loathed him."

"Why?"

"Oh! she's a decent sort of female, but makes no al-
lowances. My motto is, live and let live, but protect your own
interests. How are you getting on with Nutrax?"

"Haven't touched it yet. I've been trying to get out a name
for Twentyman's shilling tea. As far as I can make Hankin
out, it has no qualities except cheapness to recommend it, and
is chiefly made of odds and ends of other teas. The name
must suggest solid worth and respectability."

"Why not call it 'Domestic Blend'? Nothing could sound
more reliable and obviously nothing could suggest so much
dreary economy."

"Good idea. I'll put it up to him." Bredon yawned. "I've
had too much lunch. I don't think anybody ought to have to
work at half-past two in the afternoon. It's unnatural."

"Everything's unnatural in this job. Oh, my God! Here's
somebody with something on a tray! Go away! go a-*way!*"

"I'm sorry," said Miss Parton, brightly, entering with six
saucers filled with a grey and steaming mess. "But Mr.
Hankin says, will you please taste these samples of porridge
and report upon them?"

"My dear girl, look at the time!"

"Yes, I know, it's awful, isn't it? They're numbered A, B
and C, and here's the questionnaire paper, and if you'll let
me have the spoons back I'll get them washed for Mr.
Copley."

"I shall be sick," moaned Ingleby. "Who's this? Peabody's?"

"Yes—they're putting out a tinned porridge, 'Piper Parritch.' No boiling, no stirring—only heat the tin. Look for the Piper on the label."

"Look here," said Ingleby, "run away and try it on Mr. McAllister."

"I did, but his report isn't printable. There's sugar and salt and a jug of milk."

"What we suffer in the service of the public!" Ingleby attacked the mess with a disgusted sniff and a languid spoon. Bredon solemnly rolled the portions upon his tongue, and detained Miss Parton.

"Here, take this down while it's fresh in my mind. Vintage A: Fine, full-bodied, sweet nutty flavour, fully matured; a grand masculine porridge. Vintage B: extra-sec, refined, delicate character, requiring only—"

Miss Parton emitted a delighted giggle, and Ingleby, who hated gigglers, fled.

"Tell me, timeless houri," demanded Mr. Bredon, "what was wrong with my lamented predecessor? Why did Miss Meteyard hate him and why does Ingleby praise him with faint damns?"

This was no problem to Miss Parton.

"Why, because he didn't play fair. He was always snooping round other people's rooms, picking up their ideas and showing them up as his own. And if anybody gave him a headline and Mr. Armstrong or Mr. Hankin liked it, he never said whose it was."

This explanation seemed to interest Bredon. He trotted down the passage and thrust his head round Garrett's door. Garrett was stolidly making out his porridge report, and looked up with a grunt.

"I hope I'm not interrupting you at one of those moments of ecstasy," bleated Bredon, "but I just wanted to ask you something. I mean to say, it's just a question of etiquette, don't you know, and what's done, so to speak. I mean, look here! You see, Hankie-pankie told me to get out a list of names for a shilling tea and I got out some awful rotten ones, and then Ingleby came in and I said, 'What would you call this tea?' just like that, and he said, 'Call it Domestic Blend,' and I said, 'What-ho! that absolutely whangs the nail over the crumpet.' Because it struck me, really, as being the caterpillar's boots."

"Well, what about it?"

"Well, just now I was chatting to Miss Parton about that fellow Dean, the one who fell downstairs you know, and why one or two people here didn't seem to be fearfully keen on him, and she said, it was because he got ideas out of other people and showed them up with his own stuff. And what I wanted to know was, isn't it done to ask people? Ingleby didn't say anything, but of course, if I've made a floater—"

"Well, it's like this," said Garrett. "There's a sort of un-written law—at our end of the corridor, anyway. You take any help you can get and show it up with your initials on it, but if Armstrong or whoever it is simply goes all out on it and starts throwing bouquets about, you're rather expected to murmur that it was the other bird's suggestion really, and you thought rather well of it yourself."

"Oh, I see. Oh, thanks frightfully. And if, on the other hand, he goes right up in the air and says it's the damn-silliest thing he's seen since 1919, you stand the racket, I suppose."

"Naturally. If it's as silly as that you ought to have known better than to put it up to him anyway."

"Oh, yes."

"The trouble with Dean was that he first of all snitched people's ideas without telling them, and then didn't give them the credit for it with Hankin. But, I say, I wouldn't go asking Copley or Willis for too much assistance if I were you. They weren't brought up to the idea of lending round their lecture notes. They've a sort of board-school idea that everybody ought to paddle his own canoe."

Bredon thanked Garrett again.

"And if I were you," continued Garrett, "I wouldn't men-tion Dean to Willis at all. There's some kind of feeling—I don't know quite what. Anyway, I just thought I'd warn you."

Bredon thanked him with almost passionate gratitude.

"It's so easy to put your foot in it in a new place, isn't it? I'm really most frightfully obliged to you."

Clearly Mr. Bredon was a man of no sensibility, for half an hour later he was in Willis's room, and had introduced the subject of the late Victor Dean. The result was an unequivo-cal request that Mr. Bredon would mind his own business. Mr. Willis did not wish to discuss Mr. Dean at all. In addition to this, Bredon became aware that Willis was suffer-ing from an acute and painful embarrassment, almost as though the conversation had taken some indecent turn. He was puzzled, but persisted. Willis, after sitting for some moments in gloomy silence, fidgeting with a pencil, at last looked up.

"If you're on Dean's game," he said, "you'd better clear out. I'm not interested."

He might not be, but Bredon was. His long nose twitched with curiosity.

"What game? I didn't know Dean. Never heard of him till I came here. What's the row?"

"If you didn't know Dean, why bring him up? He went about with a gang of people I didn't care about, that's all, and from the look of you, I should have said you belonged to the same bright crowd."

"The de Momerie crowd?"

"It's not much use your pretending you don't know all about it, is it?" said Willis, with a sneer.

"Ingleby told me Dean was a hanger-on of that particular bunch of Bright Young People," replied Bredon, mildly. "But I've never met any of them. They'd think me terribly ancient. They would, really. Besides, I don't think they're nice to know. Some of them are really naughty. Did Mr. Pym know that Dean was a Bright Young Thing?"

"I shouldn't think so, or he'd have buzzed him out double quick. What business is Dean of yours, anyway?"

"Absolutely none. I just wondered about him, that's all. He seems to have been a sort of misfit here. Not quite imbued with the Pym spirit, if you see what I mean."

"No, he wasn't. And if you take my advice, you'll leave Dean and his precious friends alone, or you won't make yourself too popular. The best thing Dean ever did in his life was to fall down that staircase."

"Nothing in life became him like the leaving it? But it seems a bit harsh, all the same. Somebody must have loved him. 'For he must be somebody's son,' as the dear old song says. Hadn't he any family? There is a sister, at least, isn't there?"

"Why the devil do you want to know about his sister?"

"I don't. I just asked, that's all. Well, I'd better tootle off, I suppose. I've enjoyed this little talk."

Willis scowled at his retreating form, and Mr. Bredon went away to get his information elsewhere. As usual, the typists' room was well informed.

"Only the sister," said Miss Parton. "She's something to do with Silkanette Hosiery. She and Victor ran a little flat together. Smart as paint, but rather silly, I thought, the only time I saw her. I've an idea our Mr. Willis was a bit smitten in that direction at one time, but it didn't seem to come to anything."

"Oh, I see," said Mr. Bredon, much enlightened.

He went back to his own room and the guard-books. But his attention wandered. He paced about, sat down, got up, stared out of the window, came back to the desk. Then, from a drawer, he pulled out a sheet of paper. It bore a list of

41

dates in the previous year, and to each date was appended a
letter of the alphabet, thus:

Jan.	7	G
"	14	O ?
"	21	A
"	28	P
Feb.	5	G

There were other papers in the desk in the same handwriting—presumably Victor Dean's—but this list seemed to interest Mr. Bredon unaccountably. He examined it with an
attention that one would have thought it scarcely deserved,
and finally folded it carefully away in his pocketbook.

"Who dragged whom, how many times, at the wheels of
what, round the walls of where?" demanded Mr. Bredon of
the world at large. Then he laughed. "Probably some sublime
scheme for selling Sopo to sapheads," he remarked, and this
time set himself soberly to work upon his guard-books.

Mr. Pym, the presiding genius of Pym's Publicity, Ltd.,
usually allowed a week or so to elapse before interviewing
new members of his staff. His theory was that it was useless
to lecture people about their work till they had acquired
some idea of what the work actually was. He was a conscientious man, and was particularly careful to keep before his
mind the necessity for establishing a friendly personal rela-
tion with every man, woman and child in his employment,
from the heads of departments down to the messenger-boys
and, not being gifted with any spontaneous ease and charm
of social intercourse, had worked out a rigid formula for
dealing with this necessity. At the end of a week or so, he
sent for any newly-joined recruits, interrogated them about
their work and interests, and delivered his famous sermon on
Service in Advertising. If they survived this frightful ordeal,
under which nervous young typists had been known to collapse and give notice, they were put on the list for the
monthly tea-party. This took place in the Little Conference
Room. Twenty persons, selected from all ranks and departments, congregated under Mr. Pym's official eye to consume
the usual office tea, supplemented by ham sandwiches from
the canteen, and cake supplied at cost by Dairyfields, Ltd.,
and entertained one another for an exact hour. This function
was supposed to promote inter-departmental cordiality, and
by its means the entire staff, including the Outside Publicity,
passed under scrutiny once in every six months. In addition

to these delights there were, for department and group managers, informal dinners at Mr. Pym's private residence, where six victims were turned off at a time, the proceedings being hilariously concluded by the formation of two bridge-tables, presided over by Mr. and Mrs. Pym respectively. For the group-secretaries, junior copywriters and junior artists, invitations were issued to an At Home twice a year, with a band and dancing till 10 o'clock; the seniors were expected to attend these and exercise the functions of stewards. For the clerks and typists, there was the Typists' Garden-Party, with tennis and badminton; and for the office-boys, there was the Office-Boys' Christmas Treat. In May of every year there was the Grand Annual Dinner and Dance for the whole staff, at which the amount of the staff bonus was announced for the year, and the health of Mr. Pym was drunk amid expressions of enthusiastic loyalty.

In accordance with the first item on this onerous programme, Mr. Bredon was summoned to the Presence within ten days of his first appearance at Pym's.

"Well, Mr. Bredon," said Mr. Pym, switching on an automatic smile and switching it off again with nervous abruptness, "and how are you getting on?"

"Oh, pretty well, thank you, sir."

"Find the work hard?"

"It is a little difficult," admitted Bredon, "till you get the hang of it, so to speak. A bit bewildering, if you know what I mean."

"Quite so, quite so," said Mr. Pym. "Do you get on all right with Mr. Armstrong and Mr. Hankin?"

Mr. Bredon said he found them very kind and helpful.

"They give me very good accounts of you," said Mr. Pym. "They seem to think you will make a good copy-writer." He smiled again and Bredon grinned back impudently.

"That's just as well, under the circumstances, isn't it?"

Mr. Pym rose suddenly to his feet and threw open the door which separated his room from his secretary's cubicle.

"Miss Hartley, do you mind going along to Mr. Vickers and asking him to look up the detailed appropriation for Darling's and let me have it? You might wait and bring it back with you."

Miss Hartley, realizing that she was to be deprived of hearing Mr. Pym's discourse on Service in Advertising, which —owing to the thinness of the wooden partition and the resonant quality of Mr. Pym's voice—was exceedingly familiar to her, rose and departed obediently. This meant that she would be able to have a nice chat with Miss Rossiter

43

and Miss Parton while Mr. Vickers was getting his papers together. And she would not hurry herself, either. Miss Rossiter had hinted that Mr. Willis had hinted all kinds of frightful possibilities about Mr. Bredon, and she wanted to know what was up.

"Now," said Mr. Pym, passing his tongue rapidly across his lips and seeming to pull himself together to face a disagreeable interview. "What have you got to tell me?"

Mr. Bredon, very much at his ease, leaned across with his elbows on the Managing Director's desk, and spoke for some considerable time in a low tone, while Mr. Pym's cheek grew paler and paler.

CHAPTER IV

REMARKABLE ACROBATICS
OF A HARLEQUIN

IT HAS already been hinted that Tuesday was a day of general mortification in Pym's copy-department. The trouble was caused by Messrs. Toule & Jollop, proprietors of Nutrax, Maltogene, and Jollop's Concentrated Lactobeef Tablets for Travellers. Unlike the majority of clients who, though all tiresome in their degree, exercised their tiresomeness by post from a reasonable distance and at reasonable intervals, Messrs. Toule & Jollop descended upon Pym's every Tuesday for a weekly conference. While there, they reviewed the advertising for the coming week, rescinding the decisions taken at the previous week's conference, springing new schemes unexpectedly upon Mr. Pym and Mr. Armstrong, keeping those two important men shut up in the Conference Room for hours on end, to the interruption of office-business, and generally making nuisances of themselves. One of the items discussed at this weekly séance was the Nutrax 11-inch double for Friday's *Morning Star*, which occupied an important position in that leading news-organ on the top right-hand corner of the Home page, next to the special Friday feature. It subsequently occupied other positions in other journals, of course, but Friday's *Morning Star* was the real matter of importance.

The usual procedure in respect of this exasperating advertisement was as follows. Every three months or so, Mr. Hankin sent out an S O S to the copy-department to the effect that more Nutrax copy was urgently required. By the united ingenuity of the department, about twenty pieces of copy were forthwith produced and submitted to Mr. Hankin. Under his severely critical blue-pencil, these were reduced to twelve or so, which went to the Studio to be laid out and furnished with illustrative sketches. They were then sent or handed to Messrs. Toule & Jollop, who fretfully rejected all but half-a-dozen, and weakened and ruined the remainder by foolish alterations and additions. The copy-department was then scourged into producing another twenty efforts, of which, after a similar process of elimination and amendment, a further half-dozen contrived to survive criticism, thus furnishing the necessary twelve half-doubles for the ensuing three months. The department breathed again, momentarily, and the dozen lay-outs were stamped in purple ink "Passed by Client," and a note was made of the proposed order of their appearance.

On Monday of each week, Mr. Tallboy, group-manager for Nutrax, squared his shoulders and settled down to the task of getting Friday's half-double safely into the *Morning Star*. He looked out the copy for the week and sent round to collect the finished sketch from the Studio. If the finished sketch was really finished (which seldom happened), he sent it down to the block-makers, together with the copy and a carefully drawn lay-out. The block-makers, grumbling that they never were allowed proper time for the job, made a line-block of the sketch. The thing then passed to the printers, who set up the headlines and copy in type, added a name-block of the wrong size, locked the result up in a forme, pulled a proof and returned the result to Mr. Tallboy, pointing out in a querulous note that it came out half an inch too long. Mr. Tallboy corrected the misprints, damned their eyes for using the wrong name-block, made it clear to them that they had set the headlines in the wrong fount, cut the proof to pieces, pasted it up again into the correct size and returned it. By this time it was usually 11 o'clock on Tuesday morning, and Mr. Toule or Mr. Jollop, or both of them, were closeted in the Conference Room with Mr. Pym and Mr. Armstrong, calling loudly and repeatedly for their 11-inch double. As soon as the new proof arrived from the printer's, Mr. Tallboy sent it down to the Conference Room by a boy, and escaped, if he could, for his elevenses. Mr. Toule or Mr. Jollop then pointed out to Mr. Pym and Mr. Armstrong a great number of weaknesses in both sketch and copy. Mr. Pym and Mr. Armstrong, sycophantically concurring in everything the client said, confessed themselves at a loss and invited suggestions from Mr. Toule (or Mr. Jollop). The latter, being, as most clients are, better at destructive than constructive criticism, cudgelled his brains into stupor, and thus reduced himself to a condition of utter blankness, upon which the persuasiveness of Mr. Pym and Mr. Armstrong could work with hypnotic effect. After half an hour of skilled treatment, Mr. Jollop (or Mr. Toule) found himself returning with a sense of relief and refreshment to the rejected lay-out. He then discovered that it was really almost exactly what he required. It only needed the alteration of a sentence and the introduction of a panel about gift-coupons. Mr. Armstrong then sent

46

the lay-out up again to Mr. Tallboy, with a request that he would effect these necessary alterations. Mr. Tallboy, realizing with delight that these involved nothing more drastic than the making of a new lay-out and the complete re-writing of the copy, sought out the copy-writer whose initials appeared on the original type-script, instructing him to cut out three lines and incorporate the client's improvements, while he himself laid the advertisement out afresh.

When all this had been done, the copy was returned to the printer to be re-set, the forme was sent to the block-makers, a complete block was made of the whole advertisement, and a fresh proof was returned. If, by any lucky chance, there turned out to be no defects in the block, the stereotypers got to work and made a sufficient number of stereos to be sent out to the other papers carrying the Nutrax advertising, with a proof to accompany each. On Thursday afternoon, the stereos were distributed by the despatching department to the London papers by hand, and to the provincial papers by post and train, and if nothing went wrong with these arrangements, the advertisement duly appeared in Friday's *Morning Star* and in other papers on the dates provided for. So long and arduous a history it is, that lies behind those exhortations to "Nourish your Nerves with Nutrax," which smite the reader in the eye as he opens his *Morning Star* in the train between Gidea Park and Liverpool Street.

On this particular Tuesday, exasperation was intensified. To begin with, the weather was exceptionally close, with a thunderstorm impending, and the top floor of Pym's Publicity was like a slow oven beneath the broad lead roof and the great glass skylights. Secondly, a visit was expected from two directors of Brotherhoods, Ltd., that extremely old-fashioned and religiously-minded firm who manufacture boiled sweets and non-alcoholic liquors. A warning had been sent round that all female members of the staff must refrain from smoking, and that any proofs of beer or whisky advertising must be carefully concealed from sight. The former restriction bore hardly upon Miss Meteyard and the copy-department typists, whose cigarettes were, if not encouraged, at least winked at in the ordinary way by the management. Miss Parton had been further upset by a mild suggestion from Mr. Hankin that she was showing rather more arm and neck than the directors of Brotherhoods, Ltd., would think seemly; out of sheer perversity, she had covered the offending flesh with a heavy sweater, and was ostentatiously stewing and grumbling and snapping the head off every one who approached her. Mr. Jollop, who was, if anything, slightly more captious than Mr. Toule, had arrived particularly early for the weekly Nutrax conference, and had distinguished himself by firmly killing no less than three advertisements which Mr. Toule had previously passed. This meant that Mr. Hankin had been obliged to send out his S O S nearly a month earlier than usual. Mr. Armstrong had toothache, and had been exceptionally short with Miss Rossiter, and something had gone wrong with Miss Rossiter's type-writer, so that its spacing was completely unreliable.

To Mr. Ingleby, perspiring over his guard-books, entered the detested form of Mr. Tallboy, a sheet of paper in his hand.

"Is this your copy?"

Mr. Ingleby stretched out a languid hand, took the paper, glanced at it and returned it.

"How often have I got to tell you blasted incompetents," he demanded amiably, "that those initials are on the copy for the purpose of identifying the writer? If you think my initials are DB you're either blind or potty."

"Who is DB anyway?"

"New fellow, Bredon."

"Where is he?"

Mr. Ingleby jerked his thumb in the direction of the next room.

"Empty," announced Mr. Tallboy, after a brief excursion,

"Well, have a look for him," suggested Ingleby.

"Yes, but look here," said Mr. Tallboy, persuasively, "I only want a suggestion. What the devil are the Studio to do with this? Do you mean to say Hankin passed that headline?"

"Presumably," said Ingleby.

"Well, how does he or Bredon or anybody suppose we're going to get it illustrated? Has the client seen it? They'll never stand for it. What's the point in laying it out? I can't think how Hankin came to pass it."

Ingleby stretched his hand out again.

"Brief, bright and brotherly," he observed. "What's the matter with it?"

The headline was:

———!

IF LIFE'S A BLANK
TAKE NUTRAX

"And in any case," grumbled Tallboy, "the *Morning Star* won't take it. They won't put in anything that looks like bad language."

48

"Your look-out," said Ingleby. "Why not ask 'em?"

Tallboy muttered something impolite.

"Anyway, if Hankin's passed it, it'll have to be laid out, I suppose," said Ingleby. "Surely the Studio—oh! hullo! here's your man. You'd better worry him. Bredon!"

"That's me!" said Mr. Bredon. "All present and correct!"

"Where've you been hiding from Tallboy? You knew he was on your tail."

"I've been on the roof," admitted Bredon, apologetically. "Cooler and all that. What's the matter. What have I done?"

"Well, this headline of yours, Mr. Bredon. How do you expect them to illustrate it?"

"I don't know. I left it to their ingenuity. I always believe in leaving scope to other people's imagination."

"How on earth are they to draw a blank?"

"Let 'em take a ticket in the Irish Sweep. That'll larn 'em," said Ingleby.

"I should think it would be rather like a muchness," suggested Bredon. "Lewis Carroll, you know. Did you ever see a drawing of a muchness?"

"Oh, don't fool," growled Tallboy. "We've got to do something with it. Do you really think it's a good headline, Mr. Bredon?"

"It's the best I've written yet," said Bredon enthusiastically, "except that beauty Hankie wouldn't pass. Can't they draw a man looking blank? Or just a man with a blank face, like those 'Are these missing features yours?' advertisements?"

"Oh, I suppose they *could*," admitted Tallboy, discontentedly. "I'll put it up to them anyhow. Thanks," he added, belatedly, and bounced out.

"Cross, isn't he?" said Ingleby. "It's this frightful heat. Whatever made you go up on the roof? It must be like a gridiron."

"So it is, but I thought I'd just try it. As a matter of fact, I was chucking pennies over the parapet to that brass band. I got the bombardon twice. The penny goes down with a tremendous whack, you know, and they look up all over the place to see where it comes from and you dodge down behind the parapet. It's a tremendous high parapet, isn't it? I suppose they wanted to make the building look even higher than it is. It's the highest in the street in any case. You do get a good view from up there. 'Earth hath not anything to show more fair.' It's going to rain like billy-ho in about two ticks. See how black it's come over."

"You seem to have come over pretty black, if it comes to that," remarked Ingleby. "Look at the seat of your trousers."

"You do want a lot," complained Bredon, twisting his spine alarmingly. "It is a bit sooty up there. I was sitting on the skylight."

"You look as if you'd been shinning up a pipe."

"Well, I did shin down a pipe. Only one pipe—rather a nice pipe. It took my fancy."

"You're loopy," said Ingleby, "doing acrobatics on dirty pipes in this heat. Whatever made you?"

"I dropped something," said Mr. Bredon, plaintively. "It went down on to the glass roof of the wash-place. I nearly put my foot through. Wouldn't old Smayle have been surprised if I'd tumbled into the wash-basin on top of him? And then I found I needn't have gone down the pipe after all; I came back by the staircase—the roof-door was open on both floors."

"They generally keep them open in hot weather," said Ingleby.

"I wish I'd known. I say, I could do with a drink."

"All right, have a glass of Sparkling Pompayne."

"What's that?"

"One of Brotherhood's non-alcoholic refreshers," grinned Ingleby. "Made from finest Devon apples, with the crisp, cool sparkle of champagne. Definitely anti-rheumatic and non-intoxicant. Doctors recommend it."

Bredon shuddered.

"I think this is an awfully immoral job of ours. I do, really. Think how we spoil the digestions of the public."

"Ah, yes—but think how earnestly we strive to put them right again. We undermine 'em with one hand and build 'em up with the other. The vitamins we destroy in the canning, we restore in Revito, the roughage we remove from Peabody's Piper Parritch we make up into a package and market as Bunbury's Breakfast Bran; the stomachs we ruin with Pompayne, we re-line with Peplets to aid digestion. And by forcing the damn-fool public to pay twice over—once to have its food emasculated and once to have the vitality put back again, we keep the wheels of commerce turning and give employment to thousands—including you and me."

"This wonderful world!" Bredon sighed ecstatically. "How many pores should you say there were in the human skin, Ingleby?"

"Damned if I know. Why?"

"Headline for Sanfect. Could I say, at a guess, ninety million? It sounds a good round number. 'Ninety Million

Open Doors by which Germs can Enter—Lock Those Doors with Sanfect.' Sounds convincing, don't you think? Here's another: 'Would you Leave your Child in a Den of Lions?' That ought to get the mothers."

"It'd make a good sketch— Hullo! here comes the storm and no mistake."

A flash of lightning and a tremendous crack of thunder broke without warning directly over their heads.

"I expected it," said Bredon. "That's why I did my roof-walk."

"How do you mean, that's why?"

"I was on the look-out for it," explained Bredon. "Well, it's here. Phew! that was a good one. I do adore thunderstorms. By the way, what has Willis got up against me?"

Ingleby frowned and hesitated.

"He seems to think I'm not nice to know," explained Bredon.

"Well—I warned you not to talk to him about Victor Dean. He seems to have got it into his head you were a friend of his, or something."

"But what *was* wrong with Victor Dean?"

"He kept bad company. Why are you so keen to know about Dean, anyway?"

"Well, I suppose I'm naturally inquisitive. I always like to know about people. About the office-boys, for instance. They do physical jerks on the roof, don't they? Is that the only time they're allowed on the roof?"

"They'd better not let the Sergeant catch 'em up there in office-hours. Why?"

"I just wondered. They're a mischievous lot, I expect; boys always are. I like 'em. What's the name of the redheaded one? He looks a snappy lad."

"That's Joe—they call him Ginger, of course. What's he been doing?"

"Oh, nothing. I suppose you get a lot of cats prowling about this place."

"Cats? I've never seen any cats. Except that I believe there's a cat that lives in the canteen, but she doesn't seem to come up here. What do you want a cat for?"

"I don't—anyway, there must be dozens of sparrows, mustn't there?"

Ingleby began to think that the heat had affected Bredon's brain. His reply was drowned in a tremendous crash of thunder. A silence followed, in which the street noises came thinly up from without; then heavy drops began to spit upon the panes. Ingleby got up and shut the window.

The rain came down like rods and roared upon the roof. In the lead gutters it danced and romped, rushing in small swift rivers into the hoppers. Mr. Prout, emerging from his room in a hurry, received a deluge of water down his neck from the roof and yelled for a boy to run along and shut the skylights. The oppression of heat and misery lifted from the office like a cast-off eiderdown. Standing at the window of his own room, Bredon watched the hurrying foot-passengers six stories below, open their umbrellas to the deluge, or, caught defenceless, scurry into shop doorways. Down below, in the Conference Room, Mr. Jollop suddenly smiled and passed six lay-outs and a three-colour folder, and consented to the omission of the Fifty-six Free Chiming Clocks from the current week's half-double. Harry, the lift-man, ushering a dripping young woman into the shelter of the cage, expressed sympathy with her plight, and offered her a wipedown with a duster. The young woman smiled at him, assured him that she was quite all right and asked if she could see Mr. Bredon. Harry handed her on to Tompkin, the reception clerk, who said he would send up, and what was her name, please?

"Miss Dean—Miss Pamela Dean—on private business."

The clerk became full of sympathetic interest.

"Our Mr. Dean's sister, miss?"

"Yes."

"Oh, yes, miss. A dreadful sad thing about Mr. Dean, miss. We were all very sorry to lose him like that. If you'll just take a seat, miss, I'll tell Mr. Bredon you're here."

Pamela Dean sat down and looked about her. The reception-hall was on the lower floor of the agency and contained nothing but the clerk's semi-circular desk, two hard chairs, a hard settle and a clock. It occupied the space which, on the upper floor, was taken up by the Dispatching, and just outside the door was the lift and the main staircase, which wound round the lift-shaft and went the whole way to the roof, though the lift itself went no further than the top floor. The clock pointed to 12.45, and already a stream of employees was passing through the hall, or clattering down from the floor above for a wash and brush-up before going out to lunch. A message from Mr. Bredon arrived to say that he would be down in a moment, and Pamela Dean entertained herself by watching the various members of the staff as they passed. A brisk, neat young man, with an immaculate head of wavy brown hair, a minute dark moustache and very white teeth (Mr. Smayle, had she known it, group-manager for Dairyfields, Ltd.); a large, bald man with a reddish, clean-shaven face and a masonic emblem (Mr. Harris of the

52

Outdoor Publicity); a man of thirty-five, with rather sulky good looks and restless light eyes (Mr. Tallboy, brooding on the iniquities of Messrs. Toule & Jollop); a thin, prim, elderly man (Mr. Daniels); a plump little man with a good-natured grin and fair hair, chatting to a square-jawed, snub-nosed red-head (Mr. Cole, group-manager for Herrogate Bros. of soap fame, and Mr. Prout, the photographer); a handsome, worried, grey-haired man in the forties, accompanying a prosperous baldpate in an overcoat (Mr. Armstrong escorting Mr. Jollop away to a mollifying and expensive lunch); an untidy, saturnine person with both hands in his trousers-pockets (Mr. Ingleby); a thin, predatory man with a stoop and jaundiced eyeballs (Mr. Copley, wondering whether his lunch was going to agree with him); then a lean, fair-haired, anxious-looking youth, who, at sight of her, stopped dead in his tracks, flushed, and then passed on. This was Mr. Willis; Miss Dean gave him a glance and a cool nod, which was as coolly returned. Tompkin, the reception clerk, who missed nothing, saw the start, the flush, the glance and the nods and mentally added another item to his fund of useful knowledge. Then came a slim man of forty or so, with a long nose and straw-coloured hair, wearing horn-rimmed glasses and a pair of well-cut grey trousers which seemed to have received recent ill-treatment; he came up to Pamela and said, more as a statement than as a question:

"Miss Dean."

"Mr. Bredon?"

"Yes."

"You ought not to have come here," said Mr. Bredon, shaking his head reproachfully, "it's a little indiscreet, you know. However—hullo, Willis, want me?"

It was evidently not Mr. Willis' lucky day. He had conquered his nervous agitation and turned back with the obvious intention of addressing Pamela, just in time to find Bredon in possession. He replied, "Oh, no, not at all"—with such patent sincerity that Tompkin made another ecstatic mental note, and was, indeed, forced to dive hurriedly behind his counter to conceal his radiant face. Bredon grinned amiably and Willis, after a moment's hesitation, fled through the doorway.

"I'm sorry," said Miss Dean. "I didn't know—"

"Never mind," said Bredon, and then, in a louder tone: "You've come for those things of your brother's, haven't you? I've got them here; I'm working in his room, don't you know. I say, er, how about, er, coming out and honouring me by taking in a spot of lunch with me, what?"

Miss Dean agreed; Bredon fetched his hat and they passed out.

"Ho!" said Tompkin in confidence to himself. "Ho! what's the game, I wonder? She's a smart jane all right, all right. Given the youngster a chuck and now she's out after the new bloke, I shouldn't be surprised. *And* I don't know as I blame her."

Mr. Bredon and Miss Dean went sedately down together in silence, affording no pasture for the intelligent ears of Harry the liftman, but as they emerged into Southampton Row, the girl turned to her companion:

"I was rather surprised when I got your letter . . ."

Mr. Willis, lurking in the doorway of a neighbouring tobacconist's shop, heard the words and scowled. Then, pulling his hat over his eyebrows and buttoning his mackintosh closely about him, he set out in pursuit. They walked through the lessening rain to the nearest cab-rank and engaged a taxi. Mr. Willis, cunningly waiting till they were well started, engaged the next.

"Follow that taxi," he said, exactly like somebody out of a book. And the driver, nonchalant as though he had stepped from the pages of Edgar Wallace, replied, "Right you are, sir," and slipped in his clutch.

The chase offered no excitement, ending up in the tamest possible manner at Simpson's in the Strand. Mr. Willis paid off his taxi, and climbed, in the wake of the couple, to that upper room where ladies are graciously permitted to be entertained. The quarry found a table near the window; Mr. Willis, ignoring the efforts of a waiter to pilot him to a quiet corner, squeezed in at the table next to them, where a man and woman, who obviously wanted to lunch alone, made way for him indignantly. Even so, he was not very well placed, for, though he could see Bredon and the girl, they had their backs to him, and their conversation was perfectly inaudible.

"Plenty of room at the next table, sir," suggested the waiter.

"I'm all right here," replied Willis, irritably. His neighbour glared, and the waiter, with a glance as much as to say, 'Loopy—but what can a man do?' presented the bill of fare. Willis vaguely ordered saddle of mutton and red-currant jelly with potatoes and gazed at Bredon's slim back.

". . . very nice today, sir."

"What?"

"The cauliflower, sir—very nice today."

"Anything you like."

The little black hat and the sleek yellow poll seemed very

54

close together. Bredon had taken some small object out of his pocket and was showing it to the girl. A ring? Willis strained his eyes—

"What will you drink, sir?"

"Lager," said Willis, at random.

"Pilsener, sir, or Barclay's London Lager?"

"Oh, Pilsener."

"Light or dark, sir?"

"Light—dark—no, I mean light."

"Large light Pilsener, sir?"

"Yes, yes."

"Tankard, sir?"

"Yes, no—damn it! Bring it in anything that's got a hole in the top." There seemed no end to the questions that could be asked about beer. The girl had taken the object, and was doing something with it. What? For heaven's sake, what?

"Roast or new potatoes, sir?"

"New." The man had gone, thank goodness. Bredon was holding Pamela Dean's hand—no, he was turning over the object that lay on her palm. The woman opposite Willis was stretching across for the sugar-basin—her head obstructed his view—deliberately, as it seemed to him. She moved back. Bredon was still examining the object—

A large dinner-wagon, laden with steaming joints under great silver covers was beside him. A lid was lifted—the odour of roast mutton smote him in the face.

"A little more fat, sir? You like it underdone?"

Great God! What monster helpings they gave one at this place! What sickening stuff mutton was! How vile were these round yellow balls of potato that the man kept heaping on his plate! What disgusting stuff cauliflower could be—a curdle of cabbage! Willis, picking with nauseated reluctance at the finest roast saddle in London, felt his stomach cold and heavy, his feet a-twitch.

The hateful meal dragged on. The indignant couple finished their gooseberry pie and went their affronted way without waiting for coffee. Now Willis could see better. The other two were laughing now and talking eagerly. In a sudden lull a few words of Pamela's floated clearly back to him: "It's to be fancy dress, so you'll slip in all right." Then she dropped her voice again.

"Will you take any more mutton, sir?"

Try as he would, Willis could catch nothing more. He sat on in Simpson's until Bredon, glancing at his watch, appeared to remind himself and his companion that advertising copy-writers must work sometimes. Willis was ready for them. His bill was paid. He had only to shelter behind the newspaper he had brought in with him until they had passed him and then—what? Follow them out? Pursue them again in a taxi, wondering all the time how closely they were clasped together, what they were saying to one another, what appointments they were making, what new devilment there was still in store for Pamela, now that Victor Dean was out of the way, and what he would or could do next to make the world safe for her to live in?

He was spared the decision. As the two came abreast of them, Bredon, suddenly popping his head over the Lunch Edition of the *Evening Banner,* observed cheerfully:

"Hullo, Willis! enjoyed your lunch? Excellent saddle, what? But you should have tried the peas. Can I give you a lift back to the tread-mill?"

"No, thanks," growled Willis; and then realized that if he had said, "Yes, please," he would at least have made an ardent tête-à-tête in the taxi impossible. But ride in the same taxi with Pamela Dean and Bredon he could not.

"Miss Dean, unhappily, has to leave us," went on Bredon. "You might come and console me by holding my hand."

Pamela was already half-way out of the room. Willis could not decide whether she knew to whom her escort was speaking and had studied to avoid him, or whether she supposed him to be some friend of Bredon's unknown to her. Quite suddenly he made up his mind.

"Well," he said, "it is getting a bit late. If you're having a taxi, I'll share it with you."

"That's the stuff," said Bredon. Willis rose and joined him and they moved on to where Pamela was waiting.

"I think you know our Mr. Willis?"

"Oh, yes," Pamela smiled a small, frozen smile. "Victor and he were great friends at one time."

The door. The stairs. The entrance. They were outside at last.

"I must be getting along now. Thank you so much for my lunch, Mr. Bredon. And you won't forget?"

"I certainly will not. 'Tisn't likely, is it?"

"Good afternoon, Mr. Willis."

"Good afternoon."

She was gone, walking briskly in her little, high-heeled shoes. The roaring Strand engulfed her. A taxi purred up to them.

Bredon gave the address and waved Willis in before him.

"Pretty kid, young Dean's sister," he remarked, cheerfully.

"See here, Bredon; I don't know quite what your game is,

56

but you'd better be careful. I told Dean and I tell you—if you get Miss Dean mixed up with that dirty business of yours—"

"What dirty business?"

"You know well enough what I mean."

"Perhaps I do. And what then? Do I get my neck broken, like Victor Dean?"

Bredon slewed round as he spoke and looked Willis hard in the eye.

"You'll get—" Willis checked himself. "Never mind," he said darkly, "you'll get what's coming to you. I'll see to that."

"I've no doubt you'll do it very competently, what?" replied Bredon. "But do you mind telling me exactly where you come into it? From what I can see, Miss Dean does not seem to welcome your championship with any great enthusiasm."

Willis flushed a dusky red.

"It's no business of mine, of course," went on Bredon, airily, while their taxi chugged impatiently in a traffic jam at Holborn Tube Station, "but then, on the other hand, it doesn't really seem to be any business of yours, does it?"

"It is my business," retorted Willis. "It's every decent man's business. I heard Miss Dean making an appointment with you," he went on, angrily.

"What a detective you would make," said Bredon, admiringly. "But you really ought to take care, when you are shadowing anybody, that they are not sitting opposite a mirror, or anything that will serve as a mirror. There is a picture in front of the table where we were sitting, that reflects half the room. Elementary, my dear Watson. No doubt you will do better with practice. However, there is no secret about the appointment. We are going to a fancy dress affair on Friday. I am meeting Miss Dean for dinner at Boulestin's at 8 o'clock and we are going on from there. Perhaps you would care to accompany us?"

The policeman dropped his arm, and the taxi lurched forward into Southampton Row.

"You'd better be careful," growled Willis, "I might take you at your word."

"I should be charmed, personally," replied Bredon. "You will decide for yourself whether Miss Dean would or would not be put in an embarrassing position if you joined the party. Well, well, here we are at our little home from home. We must put aside this light badinage and devote ourselves to Sopo and Pompayne and Peabody's Piper Parritch. A delightful occupation, though somewhat lacking in incident. But let us not complain. We can't expect battle, murder and sudden death more than once a week or so. By the way, where were you when Victor Dean fell downstairs?"

"In the lavatory," said Willis, shortly.

"Were you, indeed?" Bredon looked at him once more attentively. "In the lavatory? You interest me strangely."

The atmosphere of the copy-department was much less strained by tea-time. Messrs. Brotherhood had been and gone, having seen nothing to shock their sense of propriety; Mr. Jollop, mellowed by his lunch, had passed three large poster designs with almost reckless readiness and was now with Mr. Pym, being almost persuaded to increase his appropriation for the autumn campaign. The suffering Mr. Armstrong, released from attendance on Mr. Jollop, had taken himself away to visit his dentist. Mr. Tallboy, coming in to purchase a stamp from Miss Rossiter for his private correspondence, announced with delight that the Nutrax half-double had gone to the printer's.

"Is that 'KITTLE CATTLE'?" asked Ingleby. "You surprise me. I thought we should have trouble with it."

"I believe we did," said Tallboy. "Was it Scotch, and would people know what it meant? Would it suggest that we were calling women cows? And wasn't the sketch a little modernistic? But Armstrong got it shoved through somehow. May I drop this in your 'Out' basket, Miss Rossiter?"

"Serpently," replied the lady, with gracious humour, presenting the basket to receive the latter. "All billy-doos receive our prompt attention and are immediately forwarded to their destination by the quickest and surest route."

"Let's see," said Garrett. "I bet it's to a lady, and him a married man, too! No, you don't, Tallboy, you old devil—stand still, will you? Tell us who it is, Miss Rossiter."

"K. Smith, Esq.," said Miss Rossiter. "You lose your bet."

"What a swizz! But I expect it's all camouflage. I suspect Tallboy of keeping a harem somewhere. You can't trust these handsome blue-eyed men."

"Shut up, Garrett. I never," said Mr. Tallboy, extricating himself from Garrett's grasp and giving him a playful punch in the wind, "in my life, met with such a bunch of buttinskis as you are in this department. Nothing is sacred to you, not even a man's business correspondence."

"How should anything be sacred to an advertiser?" demanded Ingleby, helping himself to four lumps of sugar. "We spend our whole time asking intimate questions of perfect strangers and it naturally blunts our finer feelings. 'Mother! has your Child Learnt Regular Habits?' 'Are you Troubled with Fullness after Eating?' 'Are you satisfied about your Drains?' 'Are you *Sure* that your Toilet-Paper is Germ-free?' 'Your most Intimate Friends dare not Ask you this question.' 'Do you Suffer from Superfluous Hair?' 'Do you Like them to Look at your Hands?' 'Do you ever ask yourself about Body-Odour?' 'If anything Happened to you, would your Loved Ones be Safe?' 'Why Spend so much Time in the Kitchen?' 'You think that Carpet is Clean—but is it?' 'Are you a Martyr to Dandruff?' Upon my soul, I sometimes wonder why the long-suffering public doesn't rise up and slay us."

"They don't know of our existence," said Garrett. "They all think advertisements write themselves. When I tell people I'm in advertising, they always ask whether I design posters—they never think about the copy."

"They think the manufacturer does it himself," said Ingleby.

"They ought to see some of the suggestions the manufacturer does put up when he tries his hand at it."

"I wish they could." Ingleby grinned. "That reminds me. You know that idiotic thing Darling's put out the other day—the air-cushion for travellers with a doll that fits into the middle and sits up holding an 'ENGAGED' label?"

"What for?" asked Bredon.

"Well, the idea is, that you plank the cushion down in the railway carriage and the doll proclaims that the place is taken."

"But the cushion would do that without the doll."

"Of course it would, but you know how silly people are. They like superfluities. Well, anyway, they—Darling's, I mean—got out an ad. for the rubbish all by their little selves, and were fearfully pleased with it. Wanted us to put it through for them, till Armstrong burst into one of his juicy laughs and made them blush."

"What was it?"

"Picture of a nice girl bending down to put the cushion in the corner of a carriage. And the headline? 'DON'T LET THEM PINCH YOUR SEAT.'"

"Attaboy!" said Mr. Bredon.

The new copy-writer was surprisingly industrious that day. He was still in his room, toiling over Sanfect ("Wherever there's Dirt there's Danger!" "The Skeleton in the Water-closet," "Assassins Lurk in your Scullery!" "Deadlier than Shell-Fire—GERMS!!!") when Mrs. Crump led in her female army to attack the day's accumulated dirt—armed, one regrets to say, not with Sanfect, but with plain yellow soap and water.

"Come in, come in!" cried Mr. Bredon, genially, as the good lady paused reverently at his door. "Come and sweep me and my works away with the rest of the rubbish."

"Well, I'm sure, sir," said Mrs. Crump, "I've no need to be disturbing you."

"I've finished, really," said Bredon. "I suppose there's an awful lot of stuff to clear out here every day."

"That there is, sir—you'd hardly believe. Paper—well, I'm sure paper must be cheap, the amount they waste. Sackfuls and sackfuls every evening goes out. Of course, it's disposed of to the mills, but all the same it must be a dreadful expense. And there's boxes and boards and odds and ends—you'd be surprised, the things we picks up. I sometimes think the ladies and gentlemen brings up all their cast-offs on purpose to throw 'em away here."

"I shouldn't wonder."

"And mostly chucked on the floor," resumed Mrs. Crump, warming to her theme, "hardly ever in the paper-baskets, though goodness knows they makes 'em big enough."

"It must give you a lot of trouble."

"Lor', sir, we don't think nothing of it. We just sweeps the lot up and sends the sacks down by the lift. Though sometimes we has a good laugh over the queer things we finds. I usually just give the stuff a look through to make sure there's nothing valuable got dropped by mistake. Once I found two pound-notes on Mr. Ingleby's floor. He's a careless one and no mistake. And not so long ago—the very day poor Mr. Dean had his sad accident, I found a kind of carved stone lying round in the passage—looked as though it might be a charm or a trinket or something of that. But I think it must have tumbled out of the poor gentleman's pocket as he fell, because Mrs. Doolittle said she'd seen it in his room, so I brought it in here, sir, and put it in that there little box."

"Is this it?" Bredon fished in his waistcoat pocket and produced the onyx scarab, which he had unaccountably neglected to return to Pamela Dean.

"That's it, sir. A comical-looking thing, ain't it? Like it might be a beedle or such. It was lying in a dark corner under the iron staircase and at first I thought it was just a pebble like the other one."

"What other one?"

"Well, sir, I found a little round pebble in the very same place only a few days before. I said at the time, 'Well,' I said, 'that's a funny thing to find there.' But I reckon that one

60

must have come from Mr. Atkins's room, him having taken his seaside holiday early this year on account of having been ill, and you know how people do fill up their pockets with sea-shells and pebbles and such."

Bredon hunted in his pocket again.

"Something like that, was it?" He held out a smooth, water-rounded pebble, about the size of his thumbnail.

"Very like it, sir. Did that come out of the passage, sir, might I ask?"

"No—I found that up on the roof."

"Ah!" said Mrs. Crump. "It'll be them boys up to their games. When the Sergeant's eye is off them you never know what they're after."

"They do their drill up there, don't they? Great stuff. Hardens the muscles and develops the figure. When do they perform? In the lunch-hour?"

"Oh, no, sir. Mr. Pym won't have them running about after their dinners. He says it spoils their digestions and gives them the colic. Very particular, is Mr. Pym. Half-past eight regular they has to be on duty, sir, in their pants and singlets. Twenty minutes they has of it and then changed and ready for their dooties. After dinner they sets a bit in the boys' room and has a read or plays something quiet, as it might be, shove ha'penny or tiddley-winks or such. But in their room they must stay, sir; Mr. Pym won't have nobody about the office in the dinner-hour, sir, not without, of course, it's the boy that goes round with the disinfectant, sir."

"Ah, of course! Spray with Sanfect and you're safe."

"That's right, sir, except that they uses Jeyes' Fluid."

"Oh, indeed," said Mr. Bredon, struck afresh by the curious reluctance of advertising firms to use the commodities they extol for a living. "Well, we're very well looked after here, Mrs. Crump, what?"

"Oh, yes, sir. Mr. Pym pays great attention to 'ealth. A very kind gentleman, is Mr. Pym. Next week, sir, we has the Charwomen's Tea, down in the canteen, with an egg-and-spoon race and a bran-tub, and bring the kiddies. My daughter's little girls always look forward to the tea, sir."

"I'm sure they must," said Mr. Bredon, "and I expect they'd like some new hair-ribbons or something of that sort—"

"It's very kind of you, sir," said Mr. Crump, much gratified.

"Not at all." A couple of coins clinked. "Well, I'll push off now and leave you to it."

A very nice gentleman, in Mrs. Crump's opinion, and not at all proud.

61

It turned out precisely as Mr. Willis had expected. He had tracked his prey from Boulestin's, and this time he felt quite certain he had not been spotted. His costume—that of a member of the Vehmgericht, with its black cossack and black, eyeleted hood covering the whole head and shoulders—was easily slipped on over his every-day suit. Muffled in an old burberry, he had kept watch behind a convenient van in Covent Garden until Bredon and Pamela Dean came out; his taxi had been in waiting just round the corner. His task was made the easier by the fact that the others were driving, not in a taxi, but in an enormous limousine, and that Bredon had taken the wheel himself. The theatre rush was well over before the chase started, so that there was no need to keep suspiciously close to the saloon. The trail had led westward through Richmond and still west, until it had ended at a large house, standing in its own grounds on the bank of the river. Towards the end of the journey they were joined by other cars and taxis making in the same direction; and on arrival they found the drive a parking-place for innumerable vehicles. Bredon and Miss Dean had gone straight in, without a glance behind them.

Willis, who had put on his costume in the taxi, anticipated some difficulty about getting in, but there was none. A servant had met him at the door and asked if he was a member. Willis had replied boldly that he was and given the name of William Brown, which seemed to him an ingenious and plausible invention. Apparently the club was full of William Browns, for the servant raised no difficulty, and he was ushered straight in to a handsomely furnished hall. Immediately in front of him, on the skirts of a crowd of people drinking cocktails, was Bredon, in the harlequin black and white which had been conspicuous as he stepped into his car after dinner. Pamela Dean, in an exiguous swan's-down costume representing a powder-puff, stood beside him. From a room beyond resounded the strains of a saxophone.

"The place," said Mr. Willis to himself, "is a den of iniquity." And for once, Mr. Willis was not far wrong.

He was amazed by the slackness of the organization. Without question or hesitation, every door was opened to him. There was gambling. There was drink in oceans. There was dancing. There were what Mr. Willis had heard described as orgies. And at the back of it all, he sensed something else, something that he did not quite understand; something that he was not precisely kept out of, but to which he simply had not the key.

He was, of course, partnerless, but he soon found himself absorbed into a party of exceedingly bright young people, and watching the evolutions of a *danseuse* whose essential nakedness was enhanced and emphasized by the wearing of a top hat, a monocle and a pair of patent-leather boots. He was supplied with drinks—some of which he paid for, but the majority of which were thrust upon him, and he suddenly became aware that he would have made a better detective had he been more hardened to mixed liquors. His head began to throb, and he had lost sight of Bredon and Pamela. He became obsessed with the idea that they had departed into one of the sinister little cubicles he had seen—each heavily curtained and furnished with a couch and a mirror. He broke away from the group surrounding him and began a hurried search through the house. His costume was hot and heavy, and the sweat poured down his face beneath the stifling black folds of his hood. He found a conservatory full of amorous drunken couples, but the pair he was looking for was not among them. He pushed open a door and found himself in the garden. Cries and splashes attracted him. He plunged down a rose-scented alley beneath a pergola and came out upon an open space with a round fountain-pool in the centre.

A man with a girl in his arms came reeling past him, flushed and hiccuping with laughter, his leopard-skin tunic half torn from his shoulders and the vine-leaves scattering from his hair as he ran. The girl was shrieking like a steam-engine. He was a broad-shouldered man, and the muscles of his back gleamed in the moonlight as he swung his protesting burden from him and tossed her, costume and all, into the pool. Yells of laughter greeted this performance, renewed as the girl, draggled and dripping, crawled back over the edge of the basin and burst into a stream of abuse. Then Willis saw the black-and-white harlequin.

He was climbing the statue-group in the centre of the pool—an elaborate affair of twined mermaids and dolphins, supporting a basin in which crouched an amorino, blowing from a conch-shell a high spout of dancing water. Up and up went the slim chequered figure, dripping and glittering like a fantastic water-creature. He caught the edge of the upper basin with his hands, swung for a moment and lifted. Even in that moment, Willis felt a pang of reluctant admiration. It was the easy, unfretted motion of the athlete, a display of muscular strength without jerk or effort. Then his knee was on the basin. He was up and climbing upon the bronze cupid. Yet another moment and he was kneeling upon the figure's stooped shoulders—standing upright upon them, the spray of the fountain blowing about him.

"Good God!" thought Willis, "the fellow's a tight-rope

63

walker—or he's too drunk to fall." There were yells of applause, and a girl began to shriek hysterically. Then a very tall woman, in a moonlight frock of oyster satin, who had made herself the centre of the most boisterous of all the parties, pushed past Willis and stood out on the edge of the basin, her fair hair standing out like a pale aureole round her vivid face.

"Dive!" she called out, "dive in! I dare you to! Dive in!"

"Shut up, Dian!" One of the soberer of the men caught her round the shoulders and put his hand over her mouth. "It's too shallow—he'll break his neck."

She pushed him away.

"You be quiet. He shall dive. I want him to. Go to hell, Dickie. You wouldn't dare do it, but he will."

"I certainly wouldn't. Stow it."

"Come on, Harlequin, dive!"

The black and white figure raised its arms above its fantastic head and stood poised.

"Don't be a fool, man," bawled Dickie.

But the other women were fired with the idea and their screams drowned his voice.

"Dive, Harlequin, dive."

The slim body shot down through the spray, struck the surface with scarcely a splash and slid through the water like a fish. Willis caught his breath. It was perfectly done. It was magnificent. He forgot his furious hatred of the man and applauded with the rest. The girl Dian ran forward and caught hold of the swimmer as he emerged.

"Oh, you're marvellous, you're marvellous!" She clung to him, the water soaking into her draggled satin.

"Take me home, Harlequin—I adore you!"

The Harlequin bent his masked face and kissed her. The man called Dickie tried to pull him away, but was neatly tripped and fell with a jerk into the pool, amid a roar of laughter. The Harlequin tossed the tall girl across his shoulder.

"A prize!" he shouted. "A prize!"

Then he swung her lightly to her feet and took her hand. "Run," he called, "run! Let's run away, and let them catch us if they can."

There was a sudden stampede. Willis saw the angry face of Dickie as he lurched past him and heard him swearing. Somebody caught his hand. He ran up the rose-alley, panting. Something caught his foot, and he tripped and fell. His companion abandoned him, and ran on, hooting. He sat up, found his head enveloped in his hood and struggled to release himself.

A hand touched his shoulder.

"Come on, Mr. Willis," said a mocking voice in his ear, "Mr. Bredon says I am to escort you home."

He succeeded in dragging the black cloth from his head and scrambled to his feet.

Beside him stood Pamela Dean. She had taken off her mask, and her eyes were alight with mischief.

CHAPTER V

SURPRISING METAMORPHOSIS OF MR. BREDON

LORD PETER WIMSEY had paid a call upon Chief-Inspector Parker of Scotland Yard, who was his brother-in-law.

He occupied a large and comfortable arm-chair in the Chief-Inspector's Bloomsbury flat. Opposite him, curled upon the chesterfield, was his sister, Lady Mary Parker, industriously knitting an infant's vest. On the window-seat, hugging his knees and smoking a pipe, was Mr. Parker himself. On a convenient table stood a couple of decanters and a soda siphon. On the hearthrug was a large tabby cat. The scene was almost ostentatiously peaceful and domestic.

"So you have become one of the world's workers, Peter," said Lady Mary.

"Yes; I'm pulling down four solid quid a week. Amazin' sensation. First time I've ever earned a cent. Every week when I get my pay-envelope, I glow with honest pride."

Lady Mary smiled, and glanced at her husband, who grinned cheerfully back. The difficulties which are apt to arise when a poor man marries a rich wife had, in their case, been amicably settled by an ingenious arrangement, under which all Lady Mary's money had been handed over to her brothers in trust for little Parkers to come, the trustee having the further duty of doling out each quarter to the wife a sum precisely equal to the earnings of the husband during that period. Thus a seemly balance was maintained between the two principals; and the trifling anomaly that Chief-Inspector Parker was actually a mere pauper in comparison with small Charles Peter and still smaller Mary Lucasta, now peacefully asleep in their cots on the floor above, disturbed nobody one whit. It pleased Mary to have the management of their moderate combined income, and incidentally did her a great deal of good. She now patronized her wealthy brother with all the superiority which the worker feels over the man who merely possesses money.

66

"But what *is* the case all about, exactly?" demanded Parker.

"Blest if I know," admitted Wimsey, frankly. "I got hauled into it through Freddy Arbuthnot's wife—Rachel Levly that was, you know. She knows old Pym, and he met her at dinner somewhere and told her about this letter that was worrying him, and she said, Why not get somebody in to investigate it, and he said, Who? So she said she knew somebody—not mentioning my name, you see—and he said would she ask me to buzz along, so I buzzed and there I am."

"Your narrative style," said Parker, "though racy, is a little elliptical. Could you not begin at the beginning and go on until you come to the end, and then, if you are able to, stop?"

"I'll try," said his lordship, "but I always find the stopping part of the business so difficult. Well, look! On a Monday afternoon—the 25th of May, to be particular, a young man, Victor Dean by name, employed as a copy-writer in the firm of Pym's Publicity, Ltd., Advertising Agents, fell down an iron spiral staircase on their premises, situated in the upper part of Southampton Row, and died immediately of injuries received, to wit: one broken neck, one cracked skull, one broken leg and minor cuts and contusions, various. The time of this disaster was, as nearly as can be ascertained, 3.30 in the afternoon."

"Hum!" said Parker. "Pretty extensive injuries for a fall of that kind."

"So I thought, before I saw the staircase. To proceed. On the day after this occurence, the sister of deceased sends to Mr. Pym a fragment of a half-finished letter which she has found on her brother's desk. It warns him that there is something of a fishy nature going on in the office. The letter is dated about ten days previous to the death, and appears to have been laid aside as though the writer wanted to think over the wording a bit more carefully. Very good. Now, Mr. Pym is a man of rigid morality—except, of course, as regards his profession, whose essence is to tell plausible lies for money—"

"How about truth in advertising?"

"Of course, there is *some* truth in advertising. There's yeast in bread, but you can't make bread with yeast alone. Truth in advertising," announced Lord Peter sententiously, "is like leaven, which a woman hid in three measures of meal. It provides a suitable quantity of gas, with which to blow out a mass of crude misrepresentation into a form that the public can swallow. Which incidentally brings me to the delicate and important distinction between the words 'with' and 'from.' Suppose you are advertising lemonade, or, not to be invidious, we will say perry. If you say 'Our perry is made from fresh-plucked pears only,' then it's got to be made from pears only, or the statement is actionable; if you just say it is made 'from pears,' without the 'only,' the betting is that it is probably made chiefly of pears; but if you say, 'made *with* pears,' you generally mean that you use a peck of pears to a ton of turnips, and the law cannot touch you—such are the niceties of our English tongue."

"Make a note, Mary, next time you go shopping, and buy nothing that is not 'from, only.' Proceed, Peter—and let us have a little less of your English tongue."

"Yes. Well, here is a young man who starts to write a warning letter. Before he can complete it, he falls downstairs and is killed. Is that, or is it not, a darned suspicious circumstance?"

"So suspicious that it is probably the purest coincidence. But since you have a fancy for melodrama, we will allow it to be suspicious. Who saw him die?"

"I, said the fly. Meaning one Mr. Atkins and one Mrs. Crump, who saw the fall from below, and one Mr. Prout who saw it from above. All their evidence is interesting. Mr. Prout says that the staircase was well-lit, and that deceased was not going extra fast, while the other say that he fell all of a heap, forwards, clutching *The Times Atlas* in so fierce a grip that it could afterwards hardly be prised from his fingers. What does that suggest to you?"

"Only that the death was instantaneous, which it would be if one broke one's neck."

"I know. But look here! You are going downstairs and your foot slips. What happens? Do you crumple forwards and dive down head first? Or do you sit down suddenly on your tail and do the rest of the journey that way?"

"It depends. If it was actually a slip, I should probably come down on my tail. But if I tripped, I should very likely dive forwards. You can't tell, without knowing just how it happened."

"All right. You always have an answer. Well now—do you clutch what you're carrying with a deathly grip—or do you chuck it, and try to save yourself by grabbing hold 'of the banisters?"

Mr. Parker paused. "I should probably grab," he said, slowly, "unless I was carrying a tray full of crockery, or anything. And even then ... I don't know. Perhaps it's an instinct to hold on to what one's got. But equally it's an instinct to try and save one's self. I don't know. All this arguing about what you and I would do and what the reasonable man would do is very unsatisfactory."

Wimsey groaned. "Put it this way, doubting Thomas. If the death-grip was due to instantaneous rigor, he must have been dead so quickly that he couldn't think of saving himself. Now, there are two possible causes of death—the broken neck, which he must have got when he pitched on his head at the bottom, and the crack on the temple, which is attributed to his hitting his skull on one of the knobs on the banisters. Now, falling down a staircase isn't like falling off a roof— you do it in instalments, and have time to think about it. If he killed himself by hitting the banisters, he must have fallen first and hit himself afterwards. The same thing applies, with still more force, to his breaking his neck. Why, when he felt himself going, didn't he drop everything and break his fall?"

"I know what you want me to say," said Parker. "That he was sandbagged first and dead before he fell. But I don't see it. I say he would have caught his toe in something and tripped forwards and struck his head straight away and died of that. There's nothing impossible about it."

"Then I'll try again. How's this? That same evening, Mrs. Crump, the head charwoman, picked up this onyx scarab in the passage, just beneath the iron staircase. It is, as you see, rounded and smooth and heavy for its size, which is much about that of the iron knobs on the staircase. It has, as you also see, a slight chip on one side. It belonged to the dead man, who was accustomed to carry it in his waistcoat pocket or keep it sitting on the desk beside him while he worked. What about it?"

"I should say it fell from his pocket when he fell."

"And the chip?"

"If it wasn't there before—"

"It wasn't; his sister says she's sure it wasn't."

"Then it got chipped in falling."

"You think that?"

"I do."

"I think you were meant to think that. To continue: some few days earlier, Mrs. Crump found a smooth pebble of much the same size as the scarab lying in the same passage at the foot of the same iron staircase."

"Did she?" said Parker. He uncurled himself from the window-seat and made for the decanters. "What does she say about it?"

"Says that you'd scarcely believe the queer odds and ends she finds when she's cleaning out the office. Attributes the stone to Mr. Atkins, he having taken his seaside holiday early on account of ill-health."

"Well," said Parker, releasing the lever of the soda-siphon, "and why not?"

"Why not, indeed? This other pebble, which I here produce, was found by me on the roof of the lavatory. I had to shin down a pipe to get it, and ruined a pair of flannel bags."

"Oh, yeah?"

"Okay, captain. That's where I found it. I also found a place where the paint had been chipped off the skylight."

"What skylight?"

"The skylight that is directly over the iron staircase. It's one of those pointed things, like a young greenhouse, and it has windows that open all round—you know the kind I mean—which are kept open in hot weather. It was hot weather when young Dean departed this life."

"The idea being that somebody heaved a stone at him through the skylight?"

"You said it, chief. Or, to be exact, not *a* stone, but *the* stone. Meaning the scarab."

"And how about the other stones?"

"Practice shots. I've ascertained that the office is always practically empty during the lunch-hour. Nobody much ever goes on the roof, except the office-boys for their P.J.'s at 8.30 ack emma."

"People who live in glass skylights shouldn't throw stones. Do you mean to suggest that by chucking a small stone like this at a fellow, you're going to crack his skull open and break his neck for him?"

"Not if you just throw it, of course. But how about a sling or a catapult?"

"Oh, in that case, you've only got to ask the people in the neighbouring offices if they've seen anybody enjoying a spot of David and Goliath exercise on Pym's roof, and you've got him."

"It's not as simple as that. The roof's quite a good bit higher than the roofs of the surrounding buildings, and it has a solid stone parapet all round about three feet high—to give an air of still greater magnificence, I suppose. To sling a stone through on to the iron staircase you'd have to kneel down in a special position between that skylight and the next, and you can't be seen from anywhere—unless somebody happened to be *on* the staircase looking up—which nobody obviously was, except Victor Dean, poor lad. It's safe as houses."

"Very well, then. Find out if any member of the staff has frequently stayed in at lunch-time."

Wimsey shook his head.

"No bon. The staff clock in every morning, but there are no special tabs kept on them at 1 o'clock. The reception clerk goes out to his lunch, and one of the elder boys takes his place at the desk, just in case any message or parcel comes in, but he's not there necessarily every moment of the time. Then there's the lad who hops round with Jeyes' Fluid in a squirt, but he doesn't go on to the roof. There's nothing to prevent anybody from going up, say at halfpast twelve, and staying there till he's done his bit of work and then simply walking out down the staircase. The liftman, or his locum tenens, would be on duty, but you've only to keep on the blind side of the lift as you pass and he couldn't possibly see you. Besides, the lift might quite well have gone down to the basement. All the bloke would have to do would just be to bide his time and walk out. There's nothing in it. Similarly, on the day of the death. He goes through towards the lavatory, which is reached from the stairs. When the coast is clear, he ascends to the roof. He lurks there, till he sees his victim start down the iron staircase, which everybody does, fifty times a day. He whangs off his bolt and departs. Everybody is picking up the body and exclaiming over it, when in walks our friend, innocently, from the lav. It's as simple as pie."

"Wouldn't it be noticed, if he was out of his own room all that time?"

"My dear old man, if you knew Pym's! Everybody is always out of his room. If he isn't chatting with the copy-department, or fooling round the typists, he's in the studio, clamouring for a lay-out, or in the printing, complaining about a folder, or in the press-department, inquiring about an appropriation, or in the vouchers, demanding back numbers of something, or if he isn't in any of those places, he's somewhere else—slipping out for surreptitious coffee or hair-cuts. The word alibi has no meaning in a place like Pym's."

"Youre going to have a lovely time with it all, I can see that," said Parker. "But what sort of irregularity could possibly be going on in a place like that, which would lead to murder?"

"Now we're coming to it. Young Dean used to tag round with the de Momerie crowd—"

Parker whistled.

"Sinning above his station in life?"

"Very much so. But you know Dian de Momerie. She gets more kick out of corrupting the bourgeois—she enjoys the

71

wrestle with their little consciences. She's a bad lot, that girl. I took her home last night, so I ought to know."

"Peter!" said Lady Mary. "Quite apart from your morals, which alarm me, how did you get into that gang? I should have thought they'd as soon have taken up with Charles, here, or the Chief Commissioner."

"Oh, I went incog. A comedy of masks. And you needn't worry about my morals. The young woman became incapably drunk on the way home, so I pushed her inside her dinky little maisonette in Garlic Mews and tucked her up on a divan in the sitting-room to astonish her maid in the morning. Though she's probably past being astonished. But the point is that I found out a good bit about Victor Dean."

"Just a moment," interrupted Parker, "did he dope?"

"Apparently not, though I'll swear it wasn't Dian's fault if he didn't. According to his sister, he was too strong-minded. Possibly he tried it once and felt so rotten that he didn't try it again. . . . Yes—I know what you're thinking. If he was dopey, he might have fallen downstairs on his own account. But I don't think that'll work. These things have a way of coming out at post-mortems. The question was raised . . . no; it wasn't that."

"Did Dian have any opinion on the subject?"

"She said he wasn't a sport. All the same, she seems to have kept him in tow from about the end of November to the end of April—nearly six months, and that's a long time for Dian. I wonder what the attraction was. I suppose the whelp must have had something engaging about him."

"Is that the sister's story?"

"Yes; but she says that Victor 'had great ambitions.' I don't quite know what she thinks he meant by that."

"I suppose she realized that Dian was his mistress. Or wasn't she?"

"Must have been. But I rather gather his sister thought he was contemplating matrimony."

Parker laughed.

"After all," said Lady Mary, "he probably didn't tell his sister everything."

"Damned little, I should imagine. She was quite honestly upset by last night's show. Apparently the party Dean took her to wasn't quite so hot. Why did he take her? That's another problem. He said he wanted her to meet Dian, and no doubt the kid imagined she was being introduced to a future-in-law. But Dean—you'd think he'd want to keep his sister out of it. He couldn't, surely, really have wanted to corrupt her, as Willis said."

"Who is Willis?"

"Willis is a young man who foams at the mouth if you mention Victor Dean, who was once Victor Dean's dearest friend, who is in love with Victor Dean's sister, is furiously jealous of me, thinks I'm tarred with the same brush as Victor Dean, and dogs my footsteps with the incompetent zeal of fifty Watsons. He writes copy about face-cream and corsets, is the son of a provincial draper, was educated at a grammar school and wears, I deeply regret to say, a double-breasted waistcoat. That is the most sinister thing about him—except that he admits to having been in the lavatory when Victor Dean fell downstairs, and the lavatory, as I said before, is the next step to the roof."

"Who else was in the lavatory?"

"I haven't asked him yet. How can I? It's horribly hampering to one's detective work when one isn't supposed to be detecting, because one daren't ask any questions, much. But if whoever it was knew I was detecting, then whatsoever questions I asked, I shouldn't get any answers. It wouldn't matter if only I had the foggiest notion whom or what I was detecting, but looking among about a hundred people for the perpetrator of an unidentified crime is rather difficult."

"I thought you were looking for a murderer."

"So I am—but I don't think I shall ever get the murderer till I know why the murder was done. Besides, what Pym engaged me to do was to look for the irregularity in the office. Of course, murder is an irregularity, but it's not the one I'm commissioned to hunt for. And the only person I can fix a motive for the murder on to is Willis—and it's not the sort of motive I'm looking for."

"What was Willis's row with Dean?"

"Damn silliest thing in the world. Willis used to go home with Dean at week-ends. Dean lived in a flat with his sister, by the way—no parents or anything. Willis fell in love with sister. Sister wasn't sure about him. Dean took sister to one of Dian's hot parties. Willis found out. Willis, being a boob, talked to sister like a Dutch uncle. Sister called Willis a disgusting, stuck-up, idiotic, officious prig. Willis rebuked Dean. Dean told Willis to go to hell. Loud row. Sister joined in. Dean family united in telling Willis to go and bury himself. Willis told Dean that if he (Dean) persisted in corrupting his (Dean's) sister he (Willis) would shoot him like a dog. His very words, or so I am told."

"Willis," said Mary, "appears to think in clichés."

"Of course he does—that's why he writes such good corset-copy. Anyhow, there it was. Dean and Willis at daggers drawn for three months. Then Dean fell downstairs. Now Willis has started on me. I told off Pamela Dean to take him

73

home last night, but I don't know what came of it. I've explained to her that those hot-stuff parties are genuinely dangerous, and that Willis has some method in his madness, though a prize juggins as regards tact and knowledge of the sex. It was frightfully comic to see old Willis sneaking in after us in a sort of Ku Klux Klan outfit—incredibly stealthy, and wearing the same shoes he wears in the office and a seal-ring on his little finger that one could identify from here to the Monument."

"Poor lad! I suppose it wasn't Willis who tipped friend Dean down the staircase?"

"I don't think so, Polly—but you never know. He's such a melodramatic ass. He might consider it a splendid sin. But I don't think he'd have had the brains to work out the details. And if he had done it, I fancy he'd have gone straight round to the police-station, smitten the double-breasted waistcoat a resounding blow and proclaimed 'I did it, in the cause of purity.' But against that, there's the undoubted fact that Dean's connection with Dian and Co. definitely came to an end in April—so why should he wait till the end of May to strike the blow? The row with Dean took place in March."

"Possibly, Peter, the sister has been leading you up the garden. The connection may not have stopped when she said it did. She may have kept it up on her own. She may even be a drug-taker or something herself. You never know."

"No; but generally one can make a shrewd guess. No; I don't think there's anything like that wrong with Pamela Dean. I'll swear her disgust last night was genuine. It was pretty foul, I must say. By the way, Charles, where the devil do these people get their stuff from? There was enough dope floating about that house to poison a city."

"If I knew that," said Mr. Parker, sourly, "I should be on velvet. All I can tell you is, that it's coming in by the boat-load from somewhere or other, and is being distributed broadcast from somewhere or other. The question is, where? Of course, we could lay hands tomorrow on half a hundred of the small distributors, but where would be the good of that? They don't know themselves where it comes from, or who handles it. They all tell the same tale. It's handed to them in the street by men they've never seen before and couldn't identify again. Or it's put in their pockets in omnibuses. It isn't always that they won't tell; they honestly don't know. And if you did catch the man immediately above them in the scale, he would know nothing either. It's heart-breaking. Somebody must be making millions out of it."

"Yes. Well, to go back to Victor Dean. Here's another problem. He was pulling down six pounds a week at Pym's.

How does one manage to run with the de Momerie crowd on £300 a year? Even if he wasn't much of a sport, it couldn't possibly be done for nothing."

"Probably he lived on Dian."

"Possibly he did, the little tick. On the other hand, I've got an idea. Suppose he really did think he had a chance of marrying into the aristocracy—or what he imagines to be the aristocracy. After all, Dian is a de Momerie, though her people have shown her the door, and you can't blame them. Put it that he was spending far more than he could afford in trying to keep up the running. Put it that it took longer than he thought and that he had got heavily dipped. And then see what that half-finished letter to Pym looks like in the light of that theory."

"Well," began Parker.

"Oh, do step on the gas!" broke in Mary. "How you two darlings do love going round and round a subject, don't you? Blackmail, of course. It's perfectly obvious. I've seen it coming for the last hour. This Dean creature is looking round for a spot of extra income and he discovers somebody at Pym's doing something he shouldn't—the head-cashier cooking the accounts, or the office-boy pilfering from the petty cash, or something. So he says, 'If you don't square me, I'll tell Pym,' and starts to write a letter. Probably, you know, he never meant that letter to get to Mr. Pym, at all; it was just a threat. The other man stops him for the moment by paying up something on account. Then he thinks: 'This is hopeless, I'd better slug the little beast.' So he slugs him. And there you are."

"Just as simple as that," said Wimsey,

"Of course it's simple, only men love to make mysteries."

"And women love to jump to conclusions."

"Never mind the generalizations," said Parker, "they always lead to bad reasoning. Where do I come into all this?"

"You give me your advice, and stand by ready to rally round with your myrmidons in case there's any rough-housing. By the way, I can give you the address of that house we went to last night. Dope and gambling to be had for the asking, to say nothing of nameless orgies."

He mentioned the address and the Chief-Inspector made a note of it. "Though we can't do much," he admitted. "It's a private house, belonging to a Major Milligan. We've had our eye on it for some time. And even if we could get in on it, it probably wouldn't help us to what we want. I don't suppose there's a soul in that gang who knows where the dope comes from. Still, it's something to have definite evidence that that's where it goes. By the way, we got the goods on that couple you helped us to arrest the other night. They'll probably get seven years."

"Good. I was pretty nearly had that time, though. Two of Pym's typists were fooling round and recognized me. I gave them a fishy stare and explained next morning that I had a cousin who closely resembled me. That notorious fellow Wimsey, of course. It's a mistake to be too well known."

"If the de Momerie crowd get wise to you, you'll find yourself in Queer Street," said Parker. "How did you get so pally with Dian?"

"Dived off a fountain into a fish-pond. It pays to advertise. She thinks I'm the world's eighth wonder. Absolutely the lobster's dress-shirt."

"Well, don't kill yourself," said Mary, gently. "We rather like you, and small Peter couldn't spare his best uncle."

"It will do you no end of good," remarked his brother-in-law, callously, "to have a really difficult case for once. When you've struggled for a bit with a death that might have been caused by anybody for any imaginable motive, you may be less sniffy and superior about the stray murders all over the country that the police so notoriously fail to avenge. I hope it will be a lesson to you. Have another spot?"

"Thanks; I'll try to profit by it. In the meantime, I'll go on gulling the public and being Mr. Bredon, to be heard of at your address. And let me know of any developments with the Momerie-Milligan lot."

"I will. Should you care to make one in our next dope-raid?"

"Sure thing. When do you expect it?"

"We've had information about cocaine-smuggling on the Essex coast. Worst thing the Government ever did was to abolish the coast-guard service. It doubles our trouble, especially with all these privately-owned motor-boats about. If you're out for an evening's fun any time, you could come along—and you might bring that car of yours. It's faster than anything we've got."

"I see. Two for yourselves and one for me. Right you are. I'm on. Send me a line any time. I cease work at 5.30."

In the meantime, three hearts were being wrung on Mr. Death Bredon's account.

Miss Pamela Dean was washing a pair of silk stockings in her solitary flat.

"Last night was rather marvellous. . . . I suppose I oughtn't to have enjoyed it, with poor old Victor only just buried, the

76

darling ... but, of course, I really went for Victor's sake ...
I wonder if that detective man will find out anything about it
... he didn't say much, but I believe he thinks there was
something funny about Victor being killed like that ... anyhow, Victor suspected there was something wrong, and he'd
want me to do everything I could to ferret it out. ... I didn't
know private detectives were like that. . . . I thought they
were nasty, furtive little men ... vulgar ... I like his voice
... and his hands ... oh, dear! there's a hole ... I'll have to
catch it together before it runs up the instep ... and beautiful manners, only I'm afraid he was cross with me for
coming to Pym's ... he must be fearfully athletic to climb up
that fountain ... he swims like a fish ... my new bathing-
dress ... sun-bathing ... thank goodness I've got decent legs
... I'll really have to get some more stockings, these won't
go on much longer ... I wish I didn't look so washed-out in
black. . . . Poor Victor! . . . I wonder what I can possibly do
with Alec Willis ... if only he wasn't such a prig. . . . I don't
mind Mr. Bredon ... he's quite right about that crowd being
no good, but then he really knows what he's talking about,
and it isn't just prejudice. . . . Why will Alec be so jealous and
tiresome? . . . And looking so silly in that black thing ...
following people about. . . . Incompetent—I do like people to
be competent. . . . Mr. Bredon looks terribly competent ...
no, he doesn't exactly look it, but he is ... he looks as though
he never did anything but go to dinner-parties. . . . I suppose
high-class detectives have to look like that. . . . Alec would
make a rotten detective. . . . I don't like ill-tempered men ...
I wonder what happened when Mr. Bredon went off with
Dian de Momerie ... she is beautiful ... damn her, she's
lovely ... she does drink an awful lot ... they say it makes
you look old before your time ... you get coarse ... my
complexion's all right, but I'm not the fashionable type ...
Dian de Momerie is perfectly crazy about people who do
mad things ... I don't like aluminium blondes ... I wonder if
I could get an aluminium bleach. ..."

Alec Willis, hammering a rather hard pillow into a more
comfortable shape in his boarding-house bedroom, sought
slumber in vain:

"Gosh! what a head I had this morning ... that damned,
sleek brute! ... there's something up between Pamela and
him ... helping her with some business of Victor's my foot!
... He's out to make trouble ... and going off with that
white-headed bitch ... it's a damned insult ... of course
Pamela would lick his boots . . . women . . . put up with
anything ... wish I hadn't had all those drinks ... damn this
bed! damn this foul place ... I'll have to chuck Pym's ... it

isn't safe. . . . Murder? . . . anybody interfering with Pamela . . . Pamela. . . . She wouldn't let me kiss her . . . that swine Bredon . . . down the iron staircase . . . get my hands on his throat. . . . What a hope! damned posturing acrobat . . . Pamela . . . I'd like to show her . . . money, money, money . . . if I wasn't so damned hard up . . . Dean was a little squirt anyway . . . I only told her the truth . . . blast all women! . . . They like rotters . . . I haven't paid for that last suit . . . oh, hell! I wish I hadn't had those drinks . . . I forgot to get any bicarbonate . . . I haven't paid for those boots . . . all those naked women in the swimming-pool . . . black and silver . . . he spotted me, damn his eyes! . . . 'Hullo, Willis!' this morning, as cool as a fish . . . dives like a fish . . . fish don't dive . . . fish don't sleep . . . or do they? . . . I can't sleep . . . 'Macbeth hath murdered sleep.' . . . Murder . . . down the iron staircase . . . get my hands on his throat . . . oh, damn! damn! damn! . . ."

Dian de Momerie was dancing:
"My God! I'm bored. . . . Get off my feet, you clumsy cow. . . . Money, tons of money . . . but I'm bored. . . . Can't we do something else? . . . I'm sick of that tune . . . I'm sick of everything . . . he's working up to get all mushy . . . suppose I'd better go through with it . . . I was sozzled last night . . . wonder where the Harlequin man went to . . . wonder who he was . . . that little idiot Pamela Dean . . . these women . . . I'll have to make up to her, I suppose, if I'm ever to get his address . . . I got him away from her, any old how . . . wish I hadn't been so squiffy . . . I can't remember . . . climbing up the fountain . . . black and silver . . . he's got a lovely body . . . I think he could give me a thrill . . . my God! how bored I am . . . he's exciting . . . rather mysterious . . . I'll have to write to Pamela Dean . . . silly little fool . . . expect she hates me . . . rather a pity I chucked little Victor . . . fell downstairs and broke his silly neck . . . damn good riddance . . . ring her up . . . she's not on the 'phone . . . so suburban not to be on the 'phone . . . if this tune goes on, I shall scream . . . Milligan's drinks are rotten . . . why does one go there? . . . Must do something . . . Harlequin . . . don't even know his name. . . . Weedon . . . Leader . . . something or other . . . oh, hell! perhaps Milligan knows . . . I can't stand this any longer . . . black and silver . . . thank God! that's over!"

All over London the lights flickered in and out, calling on the public to save its body and purse: SOPO SAVES SCRUBBING—NUTRAX FOR NERVES—CRUNCHLETS ARE CRISPER—EAT

PIPER PARRITCH—DRINK POMPAYNE—ONE WHOOSH AND IT'S CLEAN—OH, BOY! IT'S TOMBOY TOFFEE—NOURISH NERVES WITH NUTRAX—FARLEY'S FOOTWEAR TAKES YOU FURTHER— IT ISN'T DEAR, IT'S DARLING—DARLING'S FOR HOUSEHOLD APPLIANCES—MAKE ALL SAFE WITH SANFECT—WHIFFLETS FASCINATE. The presses, thundering and growling, ground out the same appeals by the million: ASK YOUR GROCER—ASK YOUR DOCTOR—ASK THE MAN WHO'S TRIED IT—MOTHER'S! GIVE IT TO YOUR CHILDREN—HOUSEWIVES! SAVE MONEY—HUSBANDS! INSURE YOUR LIVES—WOMEN! DO YOU REALIZE?—DON'T SAY SOAP, SAY SOPO! Whatever you're doing, stop it and do something else! Whatever you're buying, pause and buy something different! Be hectored into health and prosperity! Never let up! Never go to sleep! Never be satisfied. If once you are satisfied, all our wheels will run down. Keep going—and if you can't, Try Nutrax for Nerves!

Lord Peter Wimsey went home and slept.

CHAPTER VI

SINGULAR SPOTLESSNESS OF A
LETHAL WEAPON

YOU know," said Miss Rossiter to Mr. Smayle, "our newest copy-writer is perfectly potty."

"Potty?" Mr. Smayle, showing all his teeth in an engaging smile, "you don't say so, Miss Rossiter? How, potty?"

"Well, loopy," explained Miss Rossiter. "Goofy. Blah. He's always up on the roof, playing with a catapult. I don't know *what* Mr. Hankin would say if he knew."

"With a catapult?" Mr. Smayle looked pained. "That doesn't seem quite the thing. But we in other spheres, Miss Rossiter, always envy, if I may say so, the happy youthful spirit of the copy-department. Due, no doubt," added Mr. Smayle, "to the charming influence of the ladies. Allow me to get you another cup of tea."

"Thanks awfully, I wish you would." The monthly tea was in full swing, and the Little Conference Room was exceedingly crowded and stuffy. Mr. Smayle edged away gallantly in pursuit of tea, and against the long table, presided over by Mrs. Johnson (the indefatigable lady who ruled the Dispatching, the office-boys and the first-aid cupboard) found himself jostled by Mr. Harris of the Outdoor Publicity.

"Pardon, old fellow," said Mr. Smayle.

"Granted," said Mr. Harris, "fascinating young fellows like you are privileged to carry all before them. Ha, ha, *ha!* I saw you doing the polite to Miss Rossiter—getting on like a house afire, eh?"

Mr. Smayle smirked deprecatingly.

"Wouldn't you like three guesses at our conversation?" he suggested. "One milk and no sugar and one milk and sugar, Mrs. J., please."

"Three's two too many," replied Mr. Harris. "I can tell you. You were talking about Miss Rossiter and Mr. Smayle, hey? Finest subjects of conversation in the world—to Mr. Smayle and Miss Rossiter, hey?"

"Well, you're wrong," said Mr. Smayle, triumphantly. "We were discussing another member of this community. The new copy-writer, in fact. Miss Rossiter was saying he was potty."

"They're all potty in that department, if you ask me," said Mr. Harris, waggling his chins. "Children. Arrested development."

"It looks like it," agreed Mr. Smayle. "Cross-words I am not surprised at, for everybody does them, nor drawing nursery pictures, but playing with catapults on the roof is really childish. Though what with Miss Meteyard bringing her Yo-Yo to the office with her—"

"I'll tell you what it is, Smayle," pronounced Mr. Harris, taking his colleague by the lapel and prodding him with his forefinger, "it's all this University education. What does it do? It takes a boy, or a young woman for that matter, and keeps him in leading-strings in the playground when he ought to be ploughing his own furrow in the face of reality—Hullo, Mr. Bredon! Was that your toe? Beg pardon, I'm sure. This room's too small for these social gatherings. I hear you are accustomed to seek the wide, open spaces on the roof."

"Oh, yes. Fresh air and all that, you know. Exercise. Do you know, I've been taking pot-shots at the sparrows with a catapult. Frightfully good training for the eye and that sort of thing. Come up one day and we'll have a competition."

"Not for me, thanks," replied Mr. Harris. "Getting too old for that kind of thing. Though when I was a boy I remember putting a pebble through my old aunt's cucumber-frame. Lord! how she did scold, to be sure!"

Mr. Harris suddenly looked rather wistful.

"I haven't had a catapult in my hand for thirty years, I don't suppose," he added.

"Then it's time you took it up again." Mr. Bredon half pulled a tangle of stick and rubber from his side-pocket and pushed it back again, with a wink and a grimace at the back of Mr. Pym, who now came into view, talking condescendingly to a lately-joined junior. "Between you and me, Harris, don't you find this place a bit wearisome at times?"

"Wearisome?" put in Mr. Tallboy, extricating himself from the crowd at the table, and nearly upsetting Mr. Smayle's two cups of tea, now at length achieved, "wearisome? You people don't know the meaning of the word. Nobody but a lay-out man knows what a lay-out man's feelings is."

"You should frivol with us," said Mr. Bredon. "If the lay-out lays you out, rejuvenate your soul in Roof Revels with Copy-writers. I bagged a starling this morning."

"What do you mean, bagged a starling?"

"Father, I cannot tell a lie. I did it with my little catapult.

81

But if it's found," added Mr. Bredon earnestly, "I expect they will lay the blame on the canteen cat."

"—apult," said Mr. Harris. He looked at Mr. Tallboy to see if this play upon words had been appreciated, and seeing that that gentleman looked more than ordinarily blank and unreceptive, he proceeded to rub it in.

"Like the old joke, eh? 'O take a pill! O take a pill! O take a pilgrim home!' "

"What do you say?" asked Mr. Tallboy, frowning in the effort to concentrate.

'O blame the cat, don't you see," persisted Mr. Harris, "O blame the cat! O blame the catapult! Got me?"

"Ha, ha! very good!" said Mr. Tallboy.

"There was another," Mr. Harris went on, "O for a man! O for a—"

"Are you a good hand with a catapult, Tallboy?" inquired Mr. Bredon, rather hastily, as though he feared something might explode unless he caused a diversion.

"I haven't the eye for it." Mr. Tallboy shook his head, regretfully.

"Eye for what?" demanded Miss Rossiter.

"For a catapult."

"Oh, go on, Mr. Tallboy! And you such a tennis champion!"

"It's not quite the same thing," explained Mr. Tallboy.

"A games' eye is a games' eye, surely!"

"An eye's an eye for a' that," said Mr. Harris, rather vaguely. "Ever done anything at darts, Mr. Bredon?"

"I won the pewter pot three years running at the Cow and Pump," replied that gentleman, proudly. "With right of free warren—I mean free beer every Friday night for a twelvemonth. It came rather expensive, though, because every time I had my free pot of beer I had to stand about fifteen to the pals who came to see me drink it. So I withdrew myself from the competition and confined myself to giving exhibition displays."

"What's that about darts?"

Mr. Daniels had roamed into view. "Have you ever seen young Binns throw darts? Really quite remarkable."

"I haven't yet the pleasure of Mr. Binns' acquaintance," acknowledged Mr. Bredon. "I am ashamed to say that there are still members of this great staff unknown to me except by sight. Which, of all the merry faces I see flitting about the passages, is the youthful Mr. Binns?"

"You wouldn't have seen him, I don't expect," said Miss Rossiter. "He helps Mr. Spender in the Vouchers. Go along there one day and ask for a back number of some obscure periodical, and Mr. Binns will be sent to fetch it. He's a terrific dab at any sort of game."

"Except bridge," said Mr. Daniels, with a groan. "I drew him one night at a tournament—you remember, Miss Rossiter, the last Christmas party but two, and he went three no trumps on the ace of spades singleton, five hearts to the king, queen and—"

"What a memory you have, Mr. Daniels! You'll never forget or forgive those three no trumps. Poor Mr. Binns! He must miss Mr. Dean—they often lunched together."

Mr. Bredon seemed to pay more attention to this remark than it deserved, for he looked at Miss Rossiter as though he were about to ask her a question, but the conclave was broken up by the arrival of Mrs. Johnson, who, having served out the tea and handed the teapot over to the canteen cook felt that the time had come for her to join in the social side of the event. She was a large, personable widow, with a surprising quantity of auburn hair and a high complexion, and being built on those majestic lines was, inevitably and unrelentingly, arch.

"Well, well," she said, brightly. "And how is Mr. Daniels day?"

Mr. Daniels, having suffered this method of address for nearly twelve years, bore up tolerably well under it, and merely replied that he was quite well.

"This is the first time you have been at one of our monthly gatherings, Mr. Bredon," pursued the widow. "You're *supposed* to make the acquaintance of the rest of the staff, you know, but I see you haven't strayed far from your own department. Ah, well, when we're fat and forty"—here Mrs. Johnson giggled—"we can't expect the same attention from the gentlemen that these young things get."

"I assure you," said Mr. Bredon, "that nothing but an extreme awe of your authority has hitherto prevented me from forcing my impertinent attentions upon you. To tell you the truth, I've been misbehaving myself, and I expect you would give me a rap over the knuckles if you knew what I'd been doing."

"Not unless you've been upsetting my boys," returned Mrs. Johnson, "the young scamps! Take your eye off them a minute and they're up to their games. Would you believe it, that little wretch they call Ginger brought a Yo-Yo to the office with him and broke the window in the boys' room practising 'Round the World' in his lunch-hour. That'll come out of young Ginger's wages."

"I'll pay up when I break a window," promised Mr. Bre-

83

don, handsomely. "I shall say: I did it with my little cata-pult—"

"Catapult!" cried Mrs. Johnson, "I've had quite enough of catapults. There was that Ginger, not a month ago— Let me catch you at it once again, I said."

Mr. Bredon, with raised and twisted eyebrows, exhibited his toy.

"You've been at my desk, Mr. Bredon!"

"Indeed I have not; I shouldn't dare," protested the accused. "I'm far too pure-minded to burgle a lady's desk."

"I should hope so," said Mr. Daniels. "Mrs. Johnson keeps all her letters from her admirers in that desk."

"That's quite enough of that, Mr. Daniels. But I really did think for a moment that was Ginger's catapult, but I see now it's a bit different."

"Have you still got that poor child's catapult? You are a hard-hearted woman."

"I have to be."

"That's bad luck on all of us," said Mr. Bredon. "Look here, let the kid have it back. I like that boy. He says 'Morning, sir,' in a tone that fills me with a pleasant conceit of myself. And I like red hair. To oblige *me,* Mrs. Johnson, let the child have his lethal weapon."

"Well," said Mrs. Johnson, yielding, "I'll hand it over to *you,* Mr. Bredon, and if any more windows are broken it's you will be responsible. Come along to me when the tea-party's over. Now I must go and talk to that other new member."

She bustled away, no doubt to tell Mr. Newbolt, Mr. Hamperley, Mr. Sidebotham, Miss Griggs and Mr. Woodhurst about the childish proclivities of copy-writers. The tea-party dwindled to its hour's end, when Mr. Pym, glancing at the Greenwich-controlled electric clock-face on the wall, bustled to the door, casting vague smiles at all and sundry as he went. The chosen twenty, released from durance, surged after him into the corridor. Mrs. Johnson found Mr. Bredon's slim form drooping deprecatingly beside her.

"Shall I come for the catapult before we both forget about it?"

"Certainly, if you like; you *are* in a hurry," said Mrs. Johnson.

"It promises me a few more minutes in your company," said Mr. Bredon.

"You *are* a flatterer," said Mrs. Johnson, not altogether ill-pleased. After all, she was not every much older than Mr. Bredon, and a plump widowhood has its appeal. She led the way upstairs to the Dispatching department, took a bunch of keys from her handbag and opened a drawer.

"You're careful with your keys, I see. Secrets in the drawer and all that, I suppose?"

"Stamp-money, that's all," said Mrs. Johnson, "and any odds and ends I have to confiscate. Not but what anybody *might* get at my keys if they wanted to, because I often leave my bag on the desk for a few moments. But we've got a very honest set of boys here."

She lifted out a sheet of blotting-paper and a cash-box and began to rummage at the back of the drawer. Mr. Bredon detained her by laying his left hand on hers.

"What a pretty ring you're wearing."

"Do you like it? It belonged to my mother. Garnets, you know. Old-fashioned, but quaint, don't you think?"

"A pretty ring, and it suits the hand," said Mr. Bredon, gallantly. He held the hand pensively in his. "Allow me." He slipped his right hand into the drawer and brought out the catapult. "This appears to be the engine of destruction—a good, strong one, from the look of it."

"Have you cut your finger, Mr. Bredon?"

"It's nothing; my penknife slipped and it's opened up again. But I think it has stopped bleeding."

Mr. Bredon unwound his handkerchief from his right hand, wrapped it carelessly round the catapult, and dropped both together into his pocket. Mrs. Johnson inspected the finger he held out to her.

"You'd better have a bit of sticking-plaster for that," she pronounced. "Wait a moment, and I'll get you some from the first-aid cupboard." She took up her keys and departed. Mr. Bredon, whistling thoughtfully to himself, looked round. On a bench at the end of the room sat four messenger-boys, waiting to be sent upon any errand that might present itself. Conspicuous among them was Ginger Joe, his red head bent over the pages of the latest *Sexton Blake*.

"Ginger!"

"Yessir."

The boy ran up and stood expectantly by the desk.

"When do you get off duty tonight?"

" 'Bout a quarter to six, sir, when I've taken the letters down and cleared up here."

"Come along then and find me in my room. I've got a small job for you. You need not say anything about it. Just a private matter."

"Yessir." Ginger grinned confidentially. A message to a young lady, his experience told him. Mr. Bredon waved him back to his bench as Mrs. Johnson's footsteps approached.

The sticking-plaster was fixed in its place.

"And now," said Mrs. Johnson, playfully, "you must run away, Mr. Bredon. I see Mr. Tallboy's got a little spot of trouble for me, and I've got fifty stereos to pack and dispatch."

"I want this got down to the printer urgently," said Mr. Tallboy, approaching with a large envelope.

"Cedric!" cried Mrs. Johnson.

A boy ran up. Another lad, arriving from the staircase, dumped a large tray full of stereo-blocks on the desk. The interlude was over. Mrs. Johnson addressed herself briskly to the important task of seeing that the right block went to the right newspaper, and that all were safely packed in corrugated cardboard and correctly stamped.

Punctually at a quarter to six, Ginger Joe presented himself at Mr. Bredon's door. The office was almost empty; the cleaners had begun their rounds, and the chink of pails, the slosh of soap and water and the whirr of the vacuum-cleaner resounded through the deserted corridors.

"Come in, Ginger; is this your catapult?"

"Yessir."

"It's a good one. Made it yourself?"

"Yessir."

"Good shot with it?"

"Pretty fair, sir."

"Like to have it back?"

"Yes, please, sir."

"Well, don't touch it for the moment. I want to see whether you're the sort of fellow to be trusted with a catapult."

Ginger grinned a little sheepishly.

"Why did Mrs. Johnson take it away from you?"

"We ain't supposed to carry them sort of things in our uniform pockets, sir. Mrs. Johnson caught me a-showin' it to the other fellows, sir, and constickated it."

"Confiscated."

"Confiscated it, sir."

"I see. Had you been shooting with it in the office, Ginger?"

"No, sir."

"H'm. You're the bright lad who's broken a window, aren't you?"

"Yessir. But that wasn't with a catapult. It was a Yo-Yo, sir."

"Quite so. You're sure you've never used a catapult in the office?"

"Oh, no, sir, never, sir."

"What made you bring this thing to the office at all?"

"Well, sir—" Ginger stood on one leg. "I'd been telling the other chaps about me shooting me Aunt Emily's tomcat, sir, and they wanted to see it, sir."

"You're a dangerous man, Ginger. Nothing is safe from you. Tom-cats and windows and maiden aunts—they're all your victims, aren't they?"

"Yessir." Understanding this to be in the nature of a jest, Joe sniggered happily.

"How long ago did this bereavement take place, Ginger?"

"Bereavement, sir? Did you mean Auntie's cat?"

"No, I meant, how long ago was your catapult confiscated?"

"Bit over a month ago, it would be, sir."

"About the middle of May?"

"That's right, sir."

"And you've never laid hands on it since?"

"No, sir."

"Have you any other catapult?"

"No, sir."

"Has any of the other boys got a catapult?"

"No, sir."

"Or a sling, or any other infernal machine for projecting stones?"

"No, sir; leastways, not here, sir. Tom Faggott has a pea-shooter at home, sir."

"I said stones, not peas. Did you ever shoot with this, or any other catapult, on the roof?"

"On the roof of the office, sir?"

"Yes."

"No, sir."

"Or anybody else that you know of?"

"No, sir."

"Are you absolutely sure?"

"Nobody that I know of, sir."

"Now, look here, son; I've got an idea that you're a straight sort of fellow, that mightn't like to split on a pal. You're quite sure there isn't anything at all about this catapult that you know and don't like to tell me? Because, if there is, I shall quite understand, and I'll explain to you exactly why it would be better that you should tell me."

Ginger's eyes opened very wide in bewilderment.

"Honest injun, sir," he said, with earnest sincerity, "I don't know nothing at all about no catapult, bar Mrs. Johnson taking that one and putting it away in her desk. Cross me heart and wish I may die, sir."

"All right. What was that book I saw you reading just now?"

Ginger, accustomed to the curious habit grown-up people have of interrogating their youngers and betters on any unrelated subjects that happen to strike a roving fancy, replied without hesitation or surprise:

"The Clue of the Crimson Star, sir. About Sexton Blake; he's a detective, you know, sir. It's a top-hole yarn."

"Like detective-stories, Ginger?"

"Oh, yes, sir. I reads a lot of them. I'm going to be a detective one day, sir. My eldest brother's in the police, sir."

"Is he? Splendid fellow. Well, the first thing a detective has to learn to do is to keep his mouth shut. You know that?"

"Yessir."

"If I show you something now, can you keep quiet about it?"

"Yessir."

"Very well. Here's a ten-bob note. Hop out to the nearest chemist and get me some grey powder and an insufflator."

"What sort of powder, sir?"

"Grey powder—mercury powder—the man will know. And an insufflator; it's a little rubber bulb with a nozzle to it."

"Yessir."

Ginger Joe hopped with speed.

"An ally," said Mr. Bredon to himself, "an ally—indispensable, I fear, and I fancy I've picked the right one."

Ginger came panting back in record time. He scented adventure. Mr. Bredon, in the meantime, had attached a discreet curtain of brown paper to the glass panel of his door. Mrs. Crump was not surprised. That proceeding was familiar to her. It usually meant that a gentleman was going out, and wished to change his trousers in a decent privacy.

"Now," said Mr. Bredon, shutting the door, "we will see whether your catapult can tell us anything about its adventures since it left your hands." He filled the insufflator with the grey powder and directed an experimental puff upon the edge of the desk. On blowing away the surplus powder, he thus disclosed a surprising collection of greasy finger-prints. Ginger was enthralled.

"Coo!" he said, reverently. "Are you going to test the catapult for prints, sir?"

"I am. It will be interesting if we find any, and still more interesting if we find none."

Ginger, goggle-eyed, watched the proceedings. The catapult appeared to have been well polished by use and presented an admirable surface for finger-prints, had there been any, but though they covered every half-inch of the thick Y-fork with powder, the result was a blank. Ginger looked disappointed.

"Ah!" said Bredon. "Now is it that it will not, or that it cannot speak? We will make that point clear. Catch hold of the thing, Ginger, as though you were whanging a shot off."

Ginger obeyed, clutching grimly with his greasy little paw.

"That ought to give 'em," said his new friend, "the whole of the palms of the fingers round the handle and the ball of the thumb in the fork. Now we'll try again."

The insufflator came once more into play, and this time a noble set of markings sprang into view.

"Ginger," said Mr. Bredon, "what do you, as a detective, deduce from this?"

"Mrs. Johnson must a-wiped it, sir."

"Do you think that's very likely, Ginger?"

"No, sir."

"Then go on deducing."

"Somebody else must a-wiped it, sir."

"And why should somebody else do that?"

Ginger knew where he was now.

"So that the police couldn't fix nothing on him, sir."

"The police, eh?"

"Well, sir, the police—or a detective—or somebody like as it might be yourself, sir."

"I can find no fault with that deduction, Ginger. Can you go further and say why this unknown catapult artist should have gone to all that trouble?"

"No, sir."

"Come, come."

"Well, sir, it ain't as though he stole it—and besides, it ain't worth nothing."

"No; but it looks as though somebody had borrowed it, if he didn't steal it. Who could do that?"

"I dunno, sir. Mrs. Johnson keeps that drawer locked."

"So she does. Do you think Mrs. Johnson has been having a little catapult practice on her own?"

"Oh, no, sir. Women ain't no good with catapults."

"How right you are. Well, now, suppose somebody had sneaked Mrs. Johnson's keys and taken the catapult and broken a window or something with it, and was afraid of being found out?"

"There ain't been nothing broke in this office, not between Mrs. Johnson pinching my catapult and me breaking the window with the Yo-Yo. And if one of the boys had took the catapult, I don't think they'd think about fingerprints, sir."

"You never know. He might have been playing burglars or something and just wiped his finger-prints away out of dramatic instinct, if you know what that is."

"Yessir," agreed Ginger, in a dissatisfied tone.

"Particularly if he'd done some really bad damage with it. Or of course, it might be more than dramatic instinct. Do you realize, Ginger, that a thing like this might easily kill anybody, if it happened to catch him in just the right spot?"

"Kill anybody? Would it, sir?"

"I wouldn't like to try the experiment. Was your aunt's tom-cat killed?"

"Yessir."

"That's nine lives at a blow, Ginger, and a man has only one. You're quite sure, sonnie, that nobody you know of was larking about with this catapult the day Mr. Dean fell downstairs?"

Ginger flushed and turned pale; but apparently only with excitement. His small voice was hoarse as he answered:

"No, sir. Wish I may die, sir, I never see nothing of that. You don't think somebody catapulted Mr. Dean, sir?"

"Detectives never 'think' anything," replied Mr. Bredon, reprovingly. "They collect facts and make deductions—God forgive me!" The last three words were a whispered lip-service to truth. "Can you remember who might have happened to be standing round or passing by when Mrs. Johnson took that catapult from you and put it in her desk?"

Ginger considered.

"I couldn't say right off, sir. I was just coming upstairs to the Dispatching when she spotted it. She was behind me, you see, sir, and it made me pocket stick out, like. A-jawing me, she was, all up the stairs, and took it off of me at the top and sent me down again with the basket to Mr. 'Ornby. I never see her put it away. But some of the other boys may have. 'Course, I knowed it was there, because all the things as is confisticated—"

"Confiscated."

"Yessir—confiscated, gets put in there. But I'll ask round, sir."

"Don't let them know why you're asking."

"No, sir. Would it do if I said I believed somebody had been borrowing of it and spiled the elastic for me?"

"That would do all right, provided—"

"Yessir. Provided I recollecks to spile the elastic."

Mr. Bredon, who had already jabbed a penknife into his

own finger that afternoon in the sacred cause of verisimilitude, smiled lovingly upon Ginger Joe.

"You are the kind of man I am proud to do business with," he said. "Here's another thing. You remember when Mr. Dean was killed. Where were you at the time?"

"Sittin' on the bench in the Dispatching, sir. I got an alibi." He grinned.

"Find out for me, if you can, how many other people had alibis."

"Yessir."

"It's rather a job, I'm afraid."

"I'll do me best, sir. I'll make up somefin', don't you worry. It's easier for me to do it than it is for you, I see that, sir. I say, sir!"

"Yes?"

"Are you a Scotland Yard 'tec?"

"No, I'm not from Scotland Yard."

"Oh! Begging your pardon for asking, sir. But I thought, if you was, you might be able, excuse me, sir, to put in a word for my brother."

"I might be able to do that, all the same, Ginger."

"Thank you, sir."

"Thank *you*," replied Mr. Bredon, with the courtesy which always distinguished him. "And mum's the word, remember."

"Wild 'orses," declared Ginger, finally and completely losing his grasp of the aitches with which a careful nation had endowed him at the expense of the tax-payer, "wild 'orses wouldn't get a word out o' me when I've give me word to 'old me tongue."

He ran off. Mrs. Crump, coming along the passage with a broom, was surprised to find him still hanging about the place. She challenged him, received an impudent answer, and went her way, shaking her head. A quarter of an hour later, Mr. Bredon emerged from his seclusion. As she had expected, he was in evening dress and looking, she thought, very much the gentleman. She obliged by working the lift for him. Mr. Bredon, the ever-polite, expanded and assumed his gibus during the descent, apparently for the express purpose of taking it off to her when he emerged.

In a taxi rolling south-west, Mr. Bredon removed his spectacles, combed out his side-parting, stuck a monocle in his eye, and by the time he reached Piccadilly Circus was again Lord Peter Wimsey. With a vacant wonder he gazed upon the twinkling sky-signs, as though, ignorant astronomer, he knew nothing of the creative hands that had set these lesser lights to rule the night.

CHAPTER VII

ALARMING EXPERIENCE OF A CHIEF-INSPECTOR

ON THAT same night, or rather in the early hours of the following morning, a very disagreeable adventure befell Chief-Inspector Parker. He was the more annoyed by it, in that he had done absolutely nothing to deserve it.

He had had a long day at the Yard—no thrills, no interesting disclosures, no exciting visitors, not so much as a disdiamonded rajah or a sinister Chinaman—only the reading and summarizing of twenty-one reports of interviews with police narks, five hundred and thirteen letters from the public in response to a broadcast S O S about a wanted man, and a score or so of anonymous letters, all probably written by lunatics. In addition, he had had to wait for a telephone call from an inspector who had gone down to Essex to investigate some curious movements of motor-boats in and about the estuary of the Blackwater. The message, if favourable, might call for immediate action, on which account Mr. Parker thought it better to wait for it in his office than go home to bed, with the prospect of being hawked out again at 1 o'clock in the morning. There, then, he sat, as good as gold, collating information and drawing up a schedule of procedure for the following day's activities, when the telephone duly rang. He glanced at the clock, and saw that it pointed to 1.10. The message was brief and unsatisfactory. There was nothing to report; the suspected boat had not arrived with that tide; no action was therefore called for; Chief-Inspector Parker could go home and get what sleep he could out of the small hours.

Mr. Parker accepted disappointment as philosophically as the gentleman in Browning's peom, who went to the trouble and expense of taking music lessons just in case his lady-love might demand a song with lute *obbligato*. Waste of time, as it turned out, but—suppose it hadn't been. It was all in the day's work. Putting his papers tidily away and locking his desk, the Chief-Inspector left the building, walked down to the Embankment, took a belated tram through the subway to

Theobald's Road and thence walked soberly to Great Ormond Street.

He opened the front door with his latch-key and stepped inside. It was the same house in which he had long occupied a modest bachelor flat, but on his marriage he had taken, in addition, the flat above his own, and thus possessed what was, in effect, a seven-roomed maisonette, although, on account of a fiddling L.C.C. regulation about access to the roof for the first-floor tenants in case of fire, he was not permitted to shut his two floors completely off by means of a door across the staircase.

The front hall, common to all the tenants, was in darkness when he got in. He switched on the light and hunted in the little glass-fronted box labelled "Flat 3—Parker" for letters. He found a bill and a circular and deduced, quite correctly, that his wife had been at home all evening and too tired or too slack to go down to fetch the 9.30 post. He was turning to go upstairs, when he remembered that there might be a letter for Wimsey, under the name of Bredon, in the box belonging to Flat 4. As a rule, of course, this box was not used, but when Wimsey had begun his impersonation at Pym's, his brother-in-law had provided him with a key to fit it and had embellished the box itself with a written label "Bredon," for the better information of the postman.

There was one letter in the "Bredon" box—the kind that novelists used to call a "dainty missive"; that is to say, the envelope was tinted mauve, had a gilt deckle-edge and was addressed in a flourishing feminine handwriting. Parker took it out, intending to enclose it with a note which he was sending to Wimsey in the morning, pushed it into his pocket and went on up to the first floor. Here he switched out the hall-light which, like the staircase lights, was fitted with two-way wiring, and proceeded to the second floor, containing Flat 3, which comprised his living-room, dining-room and kitchen. Here he hesitated, but, rather unfortunately for himself, decided that he did not really want soup or sandwiches. He switched off the lower light behind him and pressed down the switch that should have supplied light to the top flight. Nothing happened. Parker growled but was not surprised. The staircase lights were the affair of the landlord, who had a penurious habit of putting in cheap bulbs and leaving them there till the filament broke. By this means he alienated his tenants' affections, besides wasting more in electricity than he saved in bulbs, but then he was that kind of man. Parker knew the stairs as well as he knew the landlord's habits; he went on up in the dark, not troubling to light a match.

Whether the little incident had, however, put his profes-

sional subconsciousness on the alert, or whether some faint
stir of breath or movement gave him last-minute warning, he
never afterwards knew. He had his key in his hand, and was
about to insert it in the lock when he dodged suddenly and
instinctively to the right, and in that very instant the blow
fell, with murderous violence, on his left shoulder. He heard
his collar-bone crack as he flung himself round to grapple
with the villainous darkness, and even as he did so he found
himself thinking: "If I hadn't dodged, my bowler would have
broken the blow and saved my collar-bone." His right hand
found a throat, but it was protected by a thick muffler and a
turned-up collar. He struggled to get his fingers inside this
obstacle, at the same time that, with his semi-disabled left
arm, he warded off the second blow which he felt was about
to descend upon him. He heard the other man panting and
cursing. Then the resistance suddenly gave way, and, before
he could loose his grip he was lurching forward, while a
jerked knee smote him with brutal violence in the stomach,
knocking the wind out of him. He staggered, and his op-
ponent's fist crashed upon his jaw. In his last seconds of
consciousness before his head struck the ground, he thought
of the weapon in the other's hand and gave up hope.

Probably his being knocked out saved his life. The crash of
his fall woke Lady Mary. For a stunned moment she lay,
wondering. Then her mind rushed to the children, asleep in
the next room. She turned on the light, calling out as she did
so to ask whether they were all right. Receiving no answer,
she sprang up, threw on a dressing-gown and ran into the
nursery. All was peace. She stood puzzled, and asking herself
whether she had dreamed the crash. Then she heard feet
running down the staircase at headlong speed. She ran back
into the bedroom, pulled out the revolver which always lay
loaded in the dressing-table drawer and flung open the door
which gave upon the landing. The light streaming from
behind her showed her the crumpled body of her husband,
and as she stared aghast at this unnerving sight, she heard the
street-door slam heavily.

"What you ought to have done," said Mr. Parker, acidly,
"was not to have bothered about me, but dashed to the
window and tried to get a squint at the bloke as he went
down the street."

Lady Mary smiled indulgently at this absurd remark, and
turned to her brother.

"So that's all I can tell you about it, and he's uncommonly
lucky to be alive, and ought to be jolly well thankful instead
of grumbling."

"You'd grumble all right," said Parker, "with a bust collar-bone and a headache like nothing on earth and a feeling as though bulls of Bashan had been trampling on your tummy."

"It beats me," said Wimsey, "the way these policemen give way over a trifling accident. In the Sexton Blake book that my friend Ginger Joe has just lent me, the great detective, after being stunned with a piece of lead-piping and trussed up for six hours in ropes which cut his flesh nearly to the bone, is taken by boat on a stormy night to a remote house on the coast and flung down a flight of stone steps into a stone cellar. Here he contrives to release himself from his bonds after three hours' work on the edge of a broken wine-bottle, when the villain gets wise to his activities and floods the cellar with gas. He is most fortunately rescued at the fifty-ninth minute of the eleventh hour and, pausing only to swallow a few ham sandwiches and a cup of strong coffee, instantly joins in a prolonged pursuit of the murderers by aeroplane, during which he has to walk out along the wing and grapple with a fellow who has just landed on it from a rope and is proposing to chuck a hand-grenade into the cockpit. And here is my own brother-in-law—a man I have known for nearly twenty years—giving way to bad temper and bandages because some three-by-four crook has slugged him one on his own comfortable staircase."

Parker grinned ruefully.

"I'm trying to think who it could have been," he said. "It wasn't a burglar or anybody like that—it was a deliberate attempt at murder. The light-bulb had been put out of action beforehand and he had been hiding for hours behind the coal-bunker. You can see the marks of his feet. Now, who in the name of goodness have I got it in for to that extent? It can't be Gentleman Jim or Dogsbody Dan, because that's not their line of country at all. If it had happened last week, it might well have been Knockout Wally—he uses a cosh—but we jailed him good and hard for that business down in Limehouse on Saturday night. There are one or two bright lads who have it in for me one way or another, but I can't exactly fit it on to any of them. All I know is, that whoever it was, he must have got in here before 11 p.m., when the housekeeper shuts the street door and puts out the hall light. Unless, of course, he had a latch-key, but that's not so likely. He wasn't obliging enough to leave anything behind to identify him, except a Woolworth pencil."

"Oh, he left a pencil, did he?"

"Yes—one of those pocket propelling things—not a wooden one—you needn't hope for a handy mould of his front teeth on it, or anything like that."

"Show, show!" pleaded Wimsey.

"All right; you can see it if you like. I've tried it for finger-prints, but I can't get much—only vague smudges, very much superimposed. I've had our finger-print wallah round to look at 'em, but he doesn't seem to have made anything of 'em. See if you can find the pencil, Mary dear, for your little brother. Oh, and by the way, Peter, there's a letter for you. I've only just remembered. In my left coat-pocket, Mary. I'd just taken it out of the Flat 4 box when all this happened."

Mary sped away, and returned in a few minutes with the pencil and the coat.

"I can't find any letter."

Parker took the coat and, with his available hand, searched all the pockets carefully.

"That's funny," he said. "I know it was there. One of those fancy long-shaped mauve envelopes with gilt edges, and a lady's fist, rather sprawly."

"Oh!" said Wimsey, "the letter's gone, has it?" His eyes glinted with excitement. "That's very remarkable. And what's more, Charles, this isn't a Woolworth pencil—it's one of Darling's."

"I meant Darling's—same thing. Anybody might carry one of them."

"Ah!" said Wimsey, "but this is where my expert knowledge comes in. Darling's don't sell these pencils—they give them away. Anybody buying more than a pound's worth of goods gets a pencil as a good-conduct prize. You observe that it carries an advertising slogan: IT ISN'T DEAR, IT'S DARLING. (One of Pym's best efforts, by the way.) The idea is that, every time you make a note on your shopping list, you are reminded of the superior economy of purchasing your household goods from Darling's. And a very remarkable firm it is, too," added his lordship, warming to the subject. "They've carried the unit system to the pitch of a fine art. You can sit on a Darling chair, built up in shilling and sixpenny sections and pegged with patent pegs at sixpence a hundred. If Uncle George breaks the leg, you buy a new leg and peg it in. If you buy more clothes than will go into your Darling chest of drawers, you unpeg the top, purchase a new drawer for half a crown, peg it on and replace the top. Everything done by numbers, and kindness. And, as I say, if you buy enough, they give you a pencil. If you mount up to five pounds' worth, they give you a fountain pen."

"That's very helpful," said Parker, sarcastically. "It ought to be easy to identify a criminal who has bought a pound's worth of goods at Darling's within the last six months or so."

"Wait a bit; I said I had expert knowledge. This pencil—a natty scarlet, as you observe, with gold lettering—didn't come from any of Darling's branches. It's not on the market yet. There are only three places it could have come from: one, from the pencil manufacturer's; two, from Darling's head office; three, from our place."

"Do you mean Pym's?"

"I do. This is the new pencil design, with an improved propelling mechanism. The old ones only propelled; his repels also, with a handy twist of the what-d'ye-call. Darling's obligingly presented us with half a gross of them to try out."

Mr. Parker sat up so suddenly that he jarred his shoulder and his head, and groaned dismally.

"I think it highly improbable," went on Lord Peter, lusciously, "that you have a deadly enemy at the pencil manufacturer's or at Darling's head office. It seems to me much more likely that the gentleman with the cosh, or knuckle-duster, or sand-bag, or lead-piping, in short, the blunt instrument, came from Pym's, guided by the address which, with your usual amiability, you kindly allowed me to give as mine. Observing my name neatly inscribed on the letter-box of Flat 4, he mounted confidently, armed with his cosh, knuckle—"

"Well, I'm dashed!" exclaimed Lady Mary, "do you mean to say that it's really you, you devil, who ought to be lying there mangled and bruised in the place of my afflicted husband?"

"I think so," said Wimsey, with satisfaction, "I certainly do think so. Particularly as the assailant seems to have walked off with my private correspondence. I know who—or to be grammatical, whom—that letter was from, by the way."

"Who?" demanded Parker, disregarding the grammatical nicety.

"Why, from Pamela Dean, to be sure. I recognize your description of the envelope."

"Pamela Dean? The victim's sister?"

"As you say."

"Willis's young woman?"

"Precisely."

"But how should he know about the letter?"

"I don't suppose he did. I rather fancy this is the result of a little bit of self-advertisement I put in yesterday afternoon at the office tea-party. I made it clear to all and sundry that I had been experimenting on the roof with a catapult."

"Did you? Who, exactly, were the all and sundry?"

"The twenty people taking tea and all the other people they mentioned it to."

"Rather a wide limit."

"M'm, yes. I thought I might get some reaction. What a pity it reacted on you and not on me."

"A very great pity," agreed Mr. Parker, with feeling.

"Still, it might have been worse. We've got three lines to go upon. The people who heard about the catapult. The people who knew, or inquired for, my address. And, of course, the bloke who's lost his pencil. But, I say—" Wimsey broke off with a shout of laughter—"what a shock it must have been for whoever it was when I turned up this morning without so much as a black eye! Why in the name of creation didn't you let me have all the details first thing this morning, so that I could have kept a look-out?"

"We were otherwise employed," said Lady Mary.

"Besides, we didn't think it had anything to do with you."

"You should have guessed. Wherever trouble turns up, there am I at the bottom of it. But I'll overlook it this time. You have been sufficiently punished, and no one shall say that a Wimsey could not be magnanimous. But this blighter—you didn't manage to mark him, Charles, did you?"

"Afraid not. I got a clutch on his beastly throat, but he was all muffled up."

"You did that badly, Charles. You should have socked him one. But, as I said before, I forgive you. I wonder if our friend will have another shot at me."

"Not at this address, I hope," said Mary.

"*I* hope not. I'd like to have him under my own eye next time. He must have been pretty smart to get that letter. Why in the world—ah! now I understand."

"What?"

"Why nobody fainted at the sight of me this morning. He must have had a torch with him. He knocks you down and turns on the torch to see if you're properly dead. The first thing he spots is the letter. He grabs that—why? Because—we'll come back to that. He grabs it and then looks at your classic features. He realizes that he's slugged the wrong man, and at that very moment he hears Mary making a hulla-baloo. So he clears. That's perfectly plain now. But the letter? Would he have taken any letter that happened to be there, or did he know the writing? When was that letter delivered? Yes, of course, the 9.30 post. Suppose, when he came in to look for my flat, he saw the letter in the box and

98

recognized whom it was from. That opens up a wide field of speculation, and possibly even offers us another motive."

"Peter," said Lady Mary, "I don't think you ought to sit here exciting Charles with all this speculation. It'll send his temperature up."

"So it will, by Jove! Well, look here, old boy, I'm really fearfully sorry you copped that packet that was meant for me. It's perfectly damnable luck and I'm dashed thankful it was no worse. I'll buzz off now. I've got to, anyhow. I've got a date. So-long."

Wimsey's first action after leaving the flat was to ring up Pamela Dean, whom he fortunately found at home. He explained that her letter had been lost in transmission, and asked what was in it.

"Only a note from Dian de Momerie. She wants to know who you are. You seem to have made a remarkable hit."

"We aim to please," said Peter. "What have you done about it?"

"Nothing. I didn't know what you would like me to do."

"You didn't give her my address?"

"No. That was what she was asking for. I didn't want to make another mistake, so I passed it all on to you."

"Quite right."

"Well?"

"Tell her—does she know that I'm at Pym's?"

"No, I was very careful to say absolutely nothing about you. Except your name. I did tell her that, but she seems to have forgotten it."

"Good. Listen, now. Tell bright Dian that I'm a most mysterious person. You never know where to find me yourself. Hint that I'm probably miles away—in Paris or Vienna, or anything that sounds fruity. You can convey the right impression, I know. Phillips Oppenheim, with a touch of Ethel M. Dell and Elinor Glyn."

"Oh, yes, I can do that."

"And you might say that she will probably see me some time when she least expects it. Suggest, if you don't mind being so vulgar, that I am a sort of yellow-dog dingo, very truly run after and hard to catch. Be stimulating. Be intriguing."

"I will. Am I at all jealous, by the way?"

"Yes, if you like. Give the impression that you're sort of putting her off. It's a hard chase and you're not keen on competitors."

"All right. That won't be difficult."

"What did you say?"

"Nothing. I said I could manage that all right."

"I know you'll do it beautifully. I rely on you very much."

"Thank you. How is the enquiry getting on?"

"So-so."

"Tell me all about it some time, won't you?"

"Rather! As soon as there's anything to report."

"Will you come to tea one Saturday or Sunday?"

"I should love to."

"I'll keep you to that."

"Oh, yes, rather! Well, goodnight."

"Goodnight—Yellow-Dog Dingo."

"Bung-ho!"

Wimsey put down the receiver. "I hope," he thought, "she isn't going to make an awkwardness. You cannot trust these young women. No fixity of purpose. Except, of course, when you particularly want them to be yielding."

He grinned with a wry mouth, and went out to keep his date with the one young woman who showed no signs of yielding to him, and what he said or did on that occasion is in no way related to this story.

Ginger Joe hoisted himself cautiously up in bed and looked round the room.

His elder brother—not the policeman, but sixteen-year-old Bert, the nosey one—was reassuringly asleep, curled up dog-fashion, and dreaming, no doubt, of motor-cycles. The faint light from the street lamp outlined the passive hump he made in the bedclothes, and threw a wan gleam across Ginger's narrow bedstead.

From beneath his pillow, Ginger drew out a penny exercise book and a stubby pencil. There was very little privacy in Ginger's life, and opportunities had to be seized when they occurred. He licked the pencil, opened the book, and headed a page in a large, round hand: "Report."

There he paused. It was desirable to do this thing really creditably, and the exercises in English composition they had given him at school did not seem to help. "My Favourite Book," "What I Should Like to Do when I Grow Up," "What I Saw at the Zoo"—very good subjects but not of great assistance to a rising young detective. He had once been privileged to take a glimpse at Wally's note-book (Wally being the policeman), and remembered that the items had all begun somewhat in this fashion: "At 8.30 p.m., as I was proceeding along Wellington Street"—a good opening, but not applicable to the present case. The style of *Sexton Blake*, also, though vigorous, was more suited for the narration of

100

stirring adventures than for the compilation of a catalogue of names and facts. And on the top of all this, there was the awkward question of spelling—always a stumbling-block. Ginger felt vaguely that an ill-spelt report would have an untrustworthy appearance.

In this emergency, he consulted his native commonsense, and found it a good guide.

"I better just begin at the beginning," he said to himself, and, pressing heavily upon the paper and frowning desperately, began to write.

"REPORT
by Joseph L. Potts
(aged 14½)"

On consideration, he thought this needed a little more corroborative detail, and added his address and the date. The report then proceeded:

"I had a talk with the boys about the *catter* (erased) cattapult. Bill Jones says he reckollects of me standing in the Dispatch and Mrs. Johnson collering of the cattapult. Sam Tabbit and George Pyke was there too. What I says to them was as Mr. Bredon give me back the cattapult and it have the bit of leather tore and I wants to know who done it. They all says they never been to Mrs. Johnson's draw and I think they was tellin the truth sir because Bill and Sam is good sorts and you can always tell if George is fibbing because of the way he looks and he was looking alright. So then I says could it have been any of the others and they says they have not seen none of them with cattapults so I makes out to be very angry and says it's a pitty a boy can't have his cattapult *confist* confiskcated without somebody goes and tears of it. And then Clarence Metcalfe comes along which he is head boy sir and asks what's up so I tells him and he says if anybody's been at Mrs. Johnsons draw its very serious. So he gets arsking them all and they all says no but Jack Bolter remembers of Mrs. Johnson leaving her bag on the desk one day and Miss Parton picking it up and taking of it down to the canteen. I says when? And he says it was about two days after my cattapult was *confik* took away, and the time just after lunch sir. So you see sir it would have been laying there an hour sir when nobody was about.

Now sir about who else was there and might have seen it took. Now I comes to think I remember Mr. Prout was there at the head of the stairs because he passed a remark to Mrs. Johnson and pulled my ear and there was one of the young ladies I think it was Miss Hartley waiting to get a messenger.

101

And after I gone down to Mr. Hornby Sam says as Mr. Wedderburn came along and him and Mrs. Johnson had a bit of a joke about it. But sir I expecks lots of people knew about it because Mrs. Johnson would tell them in the canteen. She is always telling tales on we boys sir I suppose she thinks its funny.

This is all I has to report about the cattapult sir. I has not yet made any inquiry about the other matter thinking one was enough at a time or they might think I was askin a lot of questions but I have thought of a plan for that.

Yours respeckfully
J. POTTS.

"What the devil are you doing there, Joe?"

Ginger, too absorbed in his report to have kept a proper look-out upon Bert, started violently, and thrust the exercise book under his pillow.

"Never you mind," he said, nervously. "It's private."

"Oh, is it?"

Bert flung the bedclothes aside and advanced, a threatening figure.

"Writing poitry?" he demanded, with contempt.

"It's nothing to do with you," retorted Ginger. "You leave me be."

" 'And that there book over," said Bert.

"No, I won't."

"You won't, won't you?"

"No, I won't. Get out!"

Ginger clasped the document with agitated hands.

"I'm going to 'ave a look—leggo!"

Ginger was a wiry child for his years and spirited, but his hands were hampered by the book, and the advantages of height, weight and position were with Bert. The struggle was noisy.

"Let me go, you beastly great bully."

"I'll teach you to call names! Cheeky little beast."

"Ow!" wailed Ginger. "I won't, I won't, I tell you! it's private!"

Whack! wallop!

"Nah then!" said a stately voice, "wot's all this?"

"Wally, tell Bert to leave me be."

"He didn't oughter cheek me. I only wanted ter know wot he was doin', sittin' up writin' poitry w'en he oughter a-bin asleep."

"It's private," persisted Ginger. "Really and truly, it's frightfully private."

"Can't yer leave the kid alone?" said P. C. Potts, magisterially, "makin' all this noise. You'll wake Dad and then you'll both get a 'iding. Now both of you 'op back to bed or I'll 'ave ter take you up for disturbing the peace. And you did oughter be asleep, Joe, and not writing poitry."

"It ain't poitry. It's something I was doing for a gentleman at the office and he said I wasn't to tell nobody."

"Well, see here," said Wally Potts, extending a vast official fist. "You 'and over that there book to me, see? I'll put it away in my drawer and you can 'ave it again in the morning. And now go to sleep for goodness' sake, both on yer."

"You won't read it, will yer, Wally?"

"All right, I won't read it if you're so bloomin' perticler."

Ginger, reluctant but confident of Wally's honour, reluctantly released the exercise-book.

"That's right," said Wally. "and if I 'ear any more larkin' about you're for it, both of yer. See wot I mean?"

He stalked away, gigantic in his striped pyjamas.

Ginger Joe, rubbing the portions of himself which had suffered in the assault, rolled the bed-clothes about him and took comfort in telling himself a fresh instalment of that nightly narrative of which he was both author and hero.

"Bruised and battered, but unshaken in his courage, the famous detective sank back on his straw pallet in the rat-ridden dungeon. In spite of the pain of his wounds, he was happy, knowing that the precious documents were safe. He laughed to think of the baffled Crime King, gnashing his teeth in his gilded oriental saloon. 'Foiled yet again, Hawk-eye!' growled the villainous doctor, 'but it will be my turn next!' Meanwhile . . ."

The life of a detective is a hard one.

CHAPTER VIII

CONVULSIVE AGITATION OF AN
ADVERTISING AGENCY

IT WAS on the Friday of the week in which all these stirring incidents occurred that Pym's Publicity, Ltd. became convulsed by the Great Nutrax Row, which shook the whole office from the highest to the lowest, turned the peaceful premises into an armed camp and very nearly ruined the Staff Cricket Match against Brotherhood's, Ltd.

The hardworking and dyspeptic Mr. Copley was the prime mover of all the trouble. Like most fomenters of schism, he acted throughout with the best intentions—and indeed, when one looks back upon the disturbance in the serene perspective of distance and impartiality, it is difficult to see what he could have done, other than what he did. But as Mr. Ingleby observed at the time, "It isn't what Copley *does,* it's the way he does it"; and in the heat and fury of the battle, when the passions of strong men are aroused, judgment easily becomes warped.

The thing started in this way:

At a quarter past six on the Thursday evening, the office was deserted, except for the cleaners and Mr. Copley, who, by an altogether exceptional accident, was left working overtime upon a rush series of cut-price advertisements for Jamboree Jellies. He was getting along nicely, and hoped to be through by half-past six and home in good time for 7.30 supper, when the telephone in the Dispatching rang violently and insistently.

"Dash it!" said Mr. Copley, annoyed by the din, "they ought to know the office is closed. You'd think they expected us to work all night."

He went on working, trusting that the nuisance would cease of itself. Presently it did cease, and he heard the shrill voice of Mrs. Crump informing the caller that there was nobody in the office. He took a soda-mint tablet. His sentence was shaping itself beautifully. "The authentic flavour of the fresh home-grown orchard fruit—of apricots ripening in the sunny warmth of an old, walled garden . . ."

"Excuse me, sir."

Mrs. Crump, shuffling apologetically in her carpet slippers, poked a nervous head round the door.

"What is it now?" said Mr. Copley.

"Oh, if you please, sir, it's the *Morning Star* on the telephone very urgent, asking for Mr. Tallboy. I told them they was all gone 'ome, but they says it's very important, sir, so I thought I'd better ask you."

"What's it all about?"

"Somethink about the advertisement for tomorrow morning, sir—somethink's gone wrong and they say, did it ought to be left out altogether or can we send them somethink else, sir?"

"Oh, well!" said Mr. Copley, resigned, "I suppose I'd better come and speak to them."

"I dunno whether I done right, sir," continued Mrs. Crump, anxiously pattering after him, "but I thought, sir, if there *is* a gentleman in the office I ought to tell him about it, because I didn't know but what it mightn't be important—"

"Quite right, Mrs. Crump, quite right," said Mr. Copley. "I daresay I can settle it."

He strode competently to the telephone and grasped the receiver.

"Hullo!" he said, petulantly, "Pym's here. What's the matter?"

"Oh!" said a voice. "Is that Mr. Tallboy?"

"No. Mr. Tallboy's gone home. Everybody's gone home. You ought to know that by this time. What is it?"

"Well," said the voice, "it's about that Nutrax half-double for tomorrow's feature page."

"What about it? Haven't you had it?"

(Just like Tallboy, thought Mr. Copley. No organization. You never could trust these younger men.)

"Yes, we've got it," said the voice, doubtfully, "but Mr. Weekes says we can't put it in. You see—"

"Can't put it in?"

"No. You see, Mr.—"

"I'm Mr. Copley. It's not in my department. I really know nothing about it. What's the matter with it?"

"Well, if you had it there before you, you'd see what I mean. You know the headline—"

"No, I don't," snapped Mr. Copley, exasperated. "I tell you it's not my business and I've never seen the thing."

"Oh!" said the voice, with irritating cheerfulness. "Well, the headline is: ARE YOU TAKING TOO MUCH OUT OF YOUR-SELF? And, taken in conjunction with the sketch, Mr. Weekes thinks it might lay itself open to an unfortunate interpretation. If you had it there before you, I think you'd see what he means."

"I see," said Mr. Copley, thoughtfully. Fifteen years' experience told him that this was disaster. There was no arguing with it. If the *Morning Star* got it into their heads that an advertisement contained some lurking indelicacy, that advertisement would not be printed, though the skies fell. Indeed, it was better that it should not. Errors of this kind lowered the prestige of the product and of the agency responsible. Mr. Copley had no fancy for seeing copies of *Morning Star* sold at half-a-crown a time in the Stock Exchange to provide a pornographer's holiday.

In the midst of his annoyance, he felt the inward exultation of the Jeremiah whose prophecies have come true. He had always said that the younger generation of advertising writers were No Good. Too much of the new-fangled University element. Feather-headedness. No solid business sense. No thought. But he was well-trained. He carried the war instantly into the enemy's camp.

"You ought to let us know earlier," he said, severely. "It's ridiculous to ring up at a quarter past six, when the office is closed. What do you expect us to do about it?"

"Not our fault," said the voice, brightly. "It only came in ten minutes ago. We're always asking Mr. Tallboy to let us have the blocks in better time, just to prevent this kind of situation."

More and more confirmation of Mr. Copley's prophecies. General slackness—that was what it was. Mr. Tallboy had left promptly at 5.30. Mr. Copley had seen him go. Clock-watchers, the whole lot of them. Tallboy had no business to leave before he had got an assurance from the paper that the block was received and that all was in order. Moreover, if the messenger had not delivered the parcel to the *Morning Star* till 6.5, he had either started too late, or had dawdled on the way. More bad management. That Johnson woman—no control, no discipline. Before the War there would have been no women in advertising offices, and none of these silly mistakes.

Still, something must be done.

"Very unfortunate," said Mr. Copley. "Well, I'll see if I can get hold of somebody. What's your last moment for making an alteration?"

"Must have it down here by 7 o'clock," said the voice, ineluctably. "As a matter of fact, the foundry is waiting for that sheet now. We only want your block to lock the forme. But I've spoken to Wilkes, and he says he can give you till seven."

106

"I'll ring you," said Mr. Copley, and rang off.

Rapidly his mind raced over the list of people who were fitted to cope with the situation. Mr. Tallboy, the Group-manager; Mr. Wedderburn, his Group-secretary; Mr. Armstrong, the copy-chief responsible; the writer of the copy, whoever he was; in the last resort, Mr. Pym. It was a most unfortunate moment. Mr. Tallboy lived at Croydon, and was probably still swaying and sweltering in the train; Mr. Wedderburn—he really had no idea where he lived, except that it was probably in some still more remote suburb. Mr. Armstrong lived in Hampstead; he was not in the tele-phone-book, but his private number would doubtless be on the telephone-clerk's desk; there was some hope of catching him. Mr. Copley hurried downstairs, found the list and the number and rang up. After two wrong numbers, he got the house. Mr. Armstrong's housekeeper replied. Mr. Armstrong was out. She could not say where he had gone or when he would return. Could she take a message? Mr. Copley replied that it didn't matter and rang off again. Half-past six.

He consulted the telephonist's list again. Mr. Wedderburn did not appear upon it and presumably was not on the 'phone. Mr. Tallboy's name was there. Without much hope, Mr. Copley got on to the Croydon number, only to hear, as he expected, that Mr. Tallboy had not yet returned. His heart sinking, Mr. Copley rang up Mr. Pym's house. Mr. Pym had just that minute left. Where for? It was urgent. Mr. and Mrs. Pym were dining at Frascati's with Mr. Armstrong. This sounded a little more hopeful. Mr. Copley rang up Frascati's. Oh, yes. Mr. Pym had engaged a table for 7.30. He had not yet arrived. Could they give a message when he did arrive? Mr. Copley left a message to ask Mr. Pym or Mr. Armstrong to ring him up at the office before 7 o'clock if possible, but he felt convinced that nothing could possibly come of it. No doubt these gadding directors had gone to a cocktail party somewhere. He looked at the clock. It was 6.45. As he looked, the telephone rang again.

It was, as he had expected, the *Morning Star*, impatient for instructions.

"I can't get hold of anybody," explained Mr. Copley.

"What are we to do? Leave it out altogether?"

Now, when you see in a newspaper a blank white space, bearing the legend: "THIS SPACE RESERVED FOR SO-AND-SO LTD.," it may mean nothing very much to you, but to those who know anything of the working of advertising agencies, those words carry the ultimate, ignominious brand of incom-petency and failure. So-and-so's agents have fallen down on their job; nothing can be alleged in mitigation. It is the Thing That Must Not Happen.

Mr. Copley, therefore, while savagely reflecting that it would serve the whole bunch of slackers and half-wits right if the space *was* left blank, ejaculated hastily: "No, no! on no account. Hold the line one moment. I'll see what I can do." In so doing he acted very properly, for it is the first and almost the only rule of business morality that the Firm must come first.

Dashing hastily along the passage, he entered Mr. Tallboy's room, which was on the same floor as the Dispatching and Copy departments, on the far side of the iron staircase. One minute brought him there; another minute, spent rummaging in Mr. Tallboy's drawers, gave him what he wanted—an advance proof of the wretched Nutrax half-double. A glance showed him that Mr. Weekes's doubts were perfectly justified. Each harmless enough in itself, sketch and headline together were deadly. Without waiting to wonder how so obvious a gaffe had escaped the eagle eyes of the department chiefs, Mr. Copley sat down and pulled out his pocket pencil. Nothing now could be done about the sketch; it must stand; his job was to find a new headline which would suit the sketch and the opening line of the copy, and contain approximately the same number of letters as the original.

Hurriedly he jotted down ideas and crossed them out. "WORK AND WORRY SAP NERVE-STRENGTH"—that was on the right lines, but was a few letters short. It was rather flat, too; and besides, it wasn't quite true. Not work—over-work was what the copy was talking about. "WORRY AND OVERWORK"— no good, it lacked rhythm. "OVERWORK AND OVERWORRY"— far better, but too long. As it stood, the headline filled three lines (too much, thought Mr. Copley, for a half-double), being spaced thus:

Are You Taking
TOO MUCH OUT
OF YOURSELF?

He scribbled desperately, trying to save a letter here and there. "NERVOUS FORCE"? "NERVE-FORCE"? "NERVE-POWER"? The minutes were flying. Ah? how about this?

OVER-WORK &
OVER-WORRY—
waste Nerve-Power!

Not brilliant, but dead on the right note, unexceptionable and offering no difficulties about spacing. On the point of rushing back to the 'phone it occurred to him that the instrument on Mr. Tallboy's desk might have been left connected to the switchboard. He removed the receiver; a reassuring buzz assured him that it was so. He spoke urgently:

"Are you there?"

"Yes."

"Look here. Can you cut away the headline and re-set in Goudy Bold?"

"Ye-es—Yes, we can just do that if we get it at once."

"I'll dictate it."

"Right-ho! Fire away."

"Start exactly where you start now with 'ARE YOU TAKING.' First line in caps, same size as the caps you've got there for 'TOO MUCH OUT.' Right. This is the line: 'OVER-WORK &'—with hyphen in Over-work and an ampersand. Got that?"

"Yes."

"Next line. Same size. Start two ems further in. 'OVER-WORRY,' Hyphen. Dash. Got that?"

"Yes."

"Now, third line, Goudy 24-point upper and lower. Start under the W. 'Waste Nerve-Power!' Capital N, capital P, and screamer. Got that?"

"Yes; I'll repeat. First line Goudy caps., starting level with cap A of present headline. O,V,E,R, hyphen, W,O,R,K, ampersand; second line, same fount, 2 ems to the right, O,V,E,R, hyphen, W,O,R,R,Y, dash. Third line. Start under W, Goudy 24 point upper and lower: lower-case w,a,s,t,e, capital N,e,r,v,e hyphen, capital P,o,w,e,r, screamer. That O.K.?"

"That's right. Much obliged."

"Not at all. Much obliged to you. Sorry to bother you. Good-bye."

"Good-bye."

Mr. Copley sank back, mopping his brow. It was done. The firm was saved. Men had been decorated for less. When it came to an emergency, when all the jumped-up jacks-in-office had deserted their posts, it was on him, Mr. Copley, the old-fashioned men of experience, that Pym's Publicity had to depend. A man who could grapple with a situation. A man not afraid of responsibility. A man whose heart and soul were wrapped up in his job. Suppose he had rushed off home on the stroke of half-past five, like Tallboy, caring nothing whether his work was done or not—what would have happened? Pym's would have been in the cart. He would have something to say about it in the morning. He hoped it would be a jolly good lesson to them.

He pulled the roll-top of Mr. Tallboy's desk down again over the disgracefully untidy set of pigeon-holes and the cluttered mass of paper that it nightly concealed, and as he did so, received fresh proof of the disorderliness of Mr. Tallboy's habits. From some mysterious nook where it had become caught up, a registered envelope dislodged itself, and fell with a plump little flop to the floor.

Mr. Copley stooped at once and picked it up. It was addressed in block letters to J. Tallboy, Esq., at the Croydon address, and had already been opened. Peeping in at the slit end, Mr. Copley observed what could be nothing but a thickish wad of green currency notes. Yielding to a not unnatural impulse, Mr. Copley pulled them out, and counted, to his astonishment and indignation, no less than fifty of them.

If there was one action more than another which Mr. Copley condemned as Thoughtless and Unfair (long advertising practice had given him a trick of thinking in capital letters), it was Putting Temptation in People's Way. Here was the colossal sum of Fifty Pounds, so carelessly secured that the mere opening of the desk sent it skittering to the floor, for Mrs. Crump and her corps of charladies to find. No doubt they were all very honest women, but in these Hard Times, a working woman could hardly be blamed if she succumbed. Worse still, suppose the precious envelope had got swept up and destroyed. Suppose it had fallen into the wastepaper basket and thence made its way to the sack and the paper-makers, or, still worse, to the furnace. Some innocent person might have been Falsely Accused, and laboured for the rest of her life under a Stigma. It was intolerable of Mr. Tallboy. It was Really Wicked.

Of course, Mr. Copley realized exactly what had happened. Mr. Tallboy had received this Large Sum (from whom? there was no covering letter; but that was hardly Mr. Copley's business. Possibly these were winnings on dog-races, or something equally undesirable) and had brought it to the office, intending to bank it at the Metropolitan & Counties Bank at the corner of Southampton Row, where the majority of the staff kept their accounts. By some accident, he had been prevented from doing this before the Bank closed. Instead of bestowing the envelope safely in his pocket, he had thrust it into his desk, and at 5.30 had rushed off home in his usual helter-skelter way, and forgotten all about it. And if he had since given another thought to it, reflected Mr. Copley indignantly, it was probably only to assume that it would be "perfectly all right." The man really ought to be given a lesson.

Very well, he *should* be given a lesson. The notes should be placed in safe custody and he, Mr. Copley, would give Mr. Tallboy a good talking-to in the morning. He hesitated for a moment as to the best plan. If he took the notes away with him, there was the possibility that he might have his pocket picked on the way home, which would be very unfortunate and expensive. It would be better to take them to his own room and lock them securely in the bottom drawer of his own desk. Mr. Copley congratulated himself upon the conscientious foresight that had prompted him to ask for a drawer with a proper lock.

He accordingly carried the packet to his room, put it safely away underneath a quantity of confidential papers dealing with future campaigns for tinned food and jellies, tidied up his own desk and locked it, pocketed the keys, brushed his hat and coat and took his virtuous departure, not forgetting to replace the telephone receiver upon its hook as he passed through the Dispatching.

He emerged from the doorway into the street, and crossed the road before turning south to the Theobalds Road tram-terminus. On gaining the opposite pavement, he happened to glance back, and saw the figure of Mr. Tallboy coming up on the other side from the direction of Kingsway. Mr. Copley stood still and watched him. Mr. Tallboy turned into Pym's entrance and disappeared.

"Aha!" said Mr. Copley to himself, "he's remembered about the money after all."

It is at this point that Mr. Copley's conduct is perhaps open to censure. A charitable fellow-feeling would, one imagines, have prompted him to dodge back through the traffic, to return to Pym's, to take the lift to the top floor, to seek out the anxious Mr. Tallboy and to say to him: "Look here, old man, I found a registered packet of yours sculling about and put it away in safety and, by the bye, about that half-double for Nutrax—" But he did not.

Let us remember, in mitigation, that it was now half-past seven, that there was no chance of his getting back to his evening meal much before half-past eight, that he was of dyspeptic habit and dependent upon regular hours, and that he had had a long day, concluding with an entirely unnecessary piece of worry and hustle occasioned by Mr. Tallboy's tiresomeness.

"Let him suffer for it," said Mr. Copley, grimly. "It serves him right."

He caught his tram and departed on his tedious way to a remote northern suburb. As he jolted and ground along, he planned to himself how, next day, he would score over Mr.

111

Tallboy and earn commendations from the powers that were.

There was one factor with which Mr. Copley, in his anticipatory triumph, had failed to reckon; namely, that to obtain the full effect and splendour of his *coup de théâtre* it was necessary for him to get to the office before Mr. Tallboy. In his day-dream, he had taken this for granted—naturally so, since he was a punctual man at all times, and Mr. Tallboy was apt to be more punctual in departing than in arriving. Mr. Copley's idea was that, after making a stately report to Mr. Armstrong at 9 o'clock, in the course of which Mr. Tallboy would be called in and admonished, he should then take the repentant Group-manager privately to one side, read him a little lecture on orderliness and thought for others, and hand him over his fifty pounds with a paternal caution. Meanwhile, Mr. Armstrong would mention the Nutrax incident to the other directors, who would congratulate themselves on having so reliable, experienced, and devoted a servant. The words sang themselves into a little slogan in Mr. Copley's head: "You can Count on Copley in a Crisis."

But things did not turn out that way. To begin with, Mr. Copley's late arrival on the Thursday night plunged him into a domestic storm which lasted into the night and still muttered with thunderous reverberations on the following morning.

"I suppose," said Mrs. Copley, acidly, "that while you were telephoning to all these people, it was too much trouble to think of your *wife*. I don't count at all, naturally. It's nothing to *you* that I should be left imagining all kinds of things. Well, don't blame *me* if the chicken is roasted to a chip and the potatoes are sodden, and you get indigestion."

The chicken *was* roasted to a chip; the potatoes *were* sodden; and, in consequence, Mr. Copley did get a violent indigestion, to which his wife was obliged to minister with soda-mint and bismuth and hot-water bottles, voicing her opinion of him at every application. Not until six o'clock in the morning did he fall into a heavy and unrefreshing slumber, from which he was aroused at a quarter to eight by hearing Mrs. Copley say:

"If you are going to the office today, Frederick, you had better get up. If you are *not* going, you may as well say so, and I will send a message. I have called you three times, and your breakfast is getting cold."

Mr. Copley, with a bilious headache over his right eye and a nasty taste in his mouth, would gladly have authorized her to send the message—gladly have turned over upon his pillow and buried his woes in sleep, but the recollection of the

Nutrax half-double and the fifty pounds rushed over him in a flood and swept him groaning from between the sheets. Seen in the morning light, to the accompaniment of black spots dancing before his eyes, the prospect of his triumph had lost much of its glamour. Still, he could not let it go with a mere explanation by telephone. He must be on the spot. He shaved hastily, with a shaking hand and cut himself. The flow of blood would not be staunched. It invaded his shirt. He snatched the garment off, and called to his wife for a clean one. Mrs. Copley supplied it—not without reprimand. It seemed that the putting on of a clean shirt on a Friday morning upset the entire economy of the household. At ten minutes past eight, he came down to a breakfast he could not eat, his cheek ludicrously embellished with a tuft of cotton-wool and his ears ringing with migraine and conjugal rebuke.

It was impossible, now, to catch the 8.15. Sourly, he caught the 8.25.

At a quarter to nine, the 8.25 was hung up for twenty minutes outside King's Cross on account of an accident to a goods train.

At 9.30, Mr. Copley crawled drearily into Pym's, wishing he had never been born.

As he entered the office from the lift, the reception-clerk greeted him with a message that Mr. Armstrong would like to see him at once. Mr. Copley, savagely signing his name far away below the red line which divided the punctual from the dilatory, nodded, and then wished he had not, as a pang of agony shot through his aching head. He mounted the stair and encountered Miss Parton, who said brightly:

"Oh, *here* you are, Mr. Copley! We thought you were lost. Mr. Armstrong would like to see you."

"I'm just going," said Mr. Copley, savagely. He went to his room and took off his coat, wondering whether a phenacetin would cure his headache or merely make him sick. Ginger Joe knocked at the door.

"If you please, sir, Mr. Armstrong says, could you spare him a moment."

"All right, all right," said Mr. Copley. He tottered out into the passage, and nearly fell into the arms of Mr. Ingleby.

"Hullo!" said the latter, "you're wanted, Copley! We were just sending out the town-crier. You'd better nip along to Armstrong pronto. Tallboy's out for your blood."

"Ar'rh!" said Mr. Copley.

He shouldered Mr. Ingleby aside and went on his way, only to encounter Mr. Bredon, lurking at the door of his own room, armed with an imbecile grin and a jew's harp.

"See the conquering hero comes," cried Mr. Bredon, following up this remark with a blast upon his instrument.

"Jackanapes!" said Mr. Copley. Whereupon, to his horror, Mr. Bredon executed three handsome cart-wheels before him down the passage, finishing up accurately before Mr. Armstrong's door, and just out of Mr. Armstrong's line of sight.

Mr. Copley knocked upon the glass panel, through which he could see Mr. Armstrong, seated at his desk, Mr. Tallboy, upright and indignant, and Mr. Hankin standing, with his usual air of mild hesitation, on the far side of the room. Mr. Armstrong looked up and beckoned Mr. Copley in.

"Ah!" said Mr. Armstrong, "here's the man we want. Rather late this morning, aren't you, Mr. Copley?"

Mr. Copley explained that there had been an accident on the line.

"Something must be done about these accidents on the line," said Mr. Armstrong. "Whenever Pym's staff travels, the trains break down. I shall have to write to the Superintendent of the line. Ha, ha!"

Mr. Copley realized that Mr. Armstrong was in one of his frivolous and tiresome moods. He said nothing.

"Now, Mr. Copley," said Mr. Armstrong, "what's all this about the Nutrax half-double? We've just had an agitated telegram from Mr. Jollop. I can't get hold of the *Morning Star* man—what's his name?"

"Weekes," said Mr. Tallboy.

"Weekes—golly, what a name! But I understand—or Mr. Tallboy understands—from somebody or other, that you altered the Nutrax headline last night. I've no doubt you've got an excellent explanation, but I should like to know just what we've got to say to Mr. Jollop."

Mr. Copley pulled himself together and embarked on an account of the previous night's crisis. He felt that he was not doing himself justice. Out of the tail of his eye, he could see the dab of cotton-wool on his cheek waggling absurdly as he spoke. He pointed out with emphasis and acerbity the extremely unfortunate suggestion conveyed by the sketch and the original headline.

Mr. Armstrong burst into a hoot of laughter.

"My God!" he shouted. "They've got us there, Tallboy! Ho, ho, ho! Who wrote the headline? I must tell Mr. Pym about this. Why the devil didn't you catch it, Tallboy?"

"It never occurred to me," said Mr. Tallboy, unaccountably crimson in the face. Mr. Armstrong hooted again.

"I think Ingleby wrote it," added Mr. Tallboy.

"Ingleby, of all people!" Mr. Armstrong's mirth was not to

114

be restrained. He pushed the buzzer on his desk. "Miss Parton, ask Mr. Ingleby to step in here."

Mr. Ingleby arrived, cool and insolent as ever. Mr. Armstrong, half speechless with joy, thrust the original pull of the advertisement at him, with a comment so barbarically outspoken that Mr. Copley blushed.

Mr. Ingleby, unabashed, capped the comment with a remark still more immodest, and Miss Parton, lingering, notebook in hand, gave a refined snigger.

"Well, sir," said Ingleby, "it's not my fault. My original rough was illustrated with a very handsome sketch of a gentleman overwhelmed with business cares. If the innocents in the Studio choose to turn down my refined suggestion in favour of a (male epithet) and a (female epithet) who look as though they'd been making a night of it, I refuse to be responsible."

"Ha, ha!" said Mr. Armstrong. "That's Barrow all over. I don't suppose Barrow—"

The end of the sentence was more complimentary to the Studio-chief's virtue than to his virility. Mr. Hankin suddenly exploded into a loud snicker of laughter.

"Mr. Barrow is rather fond of cashiering any suggestion put forward by the Copy Department," said Mr. Copley. "I hardly like to suggest that there is any inter-departmental jealousy behind it, but the fact remains—"

But Mr. Armstrong was feeling hilarious, and paid no attention. He recited a limerick, amid applause.

"Well, it's all right, Mr. Copley," he said, when he had partially recovered himself. "You did quite right. I'll send an explanation to Mr. Jollop. He'll have a fit."

"He'll be surprised that *you* passed it," said Mr. Hankin.

"Well, he may be," agreed Mr. Armstrong, pleasantly. "It isn't often I overlook anything indecent. I must have been off-colour that day. So must you, Tallboy, Oh, dear! Mr. Pym will have something to say about it. I shall enjoy seeing his face. I only wish it had gone through. He'd have sacked the whole department."

"It would have been very serious," said Mr. Copley.

"Of course it would. I'm very glad the *Morning Star* spotted it. All right. Now that's settled. Mr. Hankin, about that whole page for Sopo—"

"I hope," said Mr. Copley, "you are satisifed with what I did. There wasn't much time—"

"Quite all right, quite all right," said Mr. Armstrong. "Very much obliged to you. But, by the way, you might have let somebody know. I was left rather up in the air this morning."

Mr. Copley explained that he had endeavoured to get into touch with Mr. Pym, Mr. Armstrong, Mr. Tallboy and Mr. Wedderburn, but without success.

"Yes, yes, I see," said Mr. Armstrong. "But why didn't you ring up Mr. Hankin?"

"I am always at home by six," added Mr. Hankin, "and it is very seldom that I go out. When I do, I always leave directions where I am to be found." (This was a dig at Mr. Armstrong.)

Dismay seized upon Mr. Copley. He had clean forgotten Mr. Hankin, and he knew well enough that Mr. Hankin, mild as were his manners, was quick to resent anything in the nature of a slight.

"Of course," he stammered. "Of course, yes, I might have done that. But Nutrax being your client, Mr. Armstrong—I thought—it never occurred to me that Mr. Hankin—"

This was a bad tactical error. It was, to begin with, contrary to the great Pym Principle that any member of the Copy Department was supposed to be ready to carry on with any part of the work at any time, if called upon. And it also suggested that Mr. Hankin was, in that respect, less versatile than Mr. Copley himself.

"Nutrax," said Mr. Hankin, in a thin manner, "is certainly not a favourite account of mine. But I have coped with it in my time." (This was another side-blow at Mr. Armstrong, who had temperamental periods when he was apt to hand all his clients over to Mr. Hankin, pleading nervous exhaustion.) "It is really no further outside my scope than that of the junior copy-writers."

"Well, well," said Mr. Armstrong, perceiving that Mr. Hankin was on the point of doing the undesirable thing, and ticking off a member of the department before a member of another department, "it's not of any great consequence, and you did your best in an awkward crisis. Nobody can think of everything. Now, Mr. Hankin"—he dismissed the small fry with a nod—"let's get this Sopo question settled once and for all. Don't go, Miss Parton, I want you to take a note. I'll see to Nutrax, Mr. Tallboy. Don't worry."

The door closed behind Mr. Copley, Mr. Ingleby and Mr. Tallboy.

"My God!" said Ingleby, "what a howl! Went with a bang from start to finish. It only wanted Barrow to make it complete. That reminds me, I'll have to go and pull his leg. This'll teach him to turn down my intelligent suggestions. Hullo! there's the Meteyard. I must tell her what Armstrong said about old Barrow."

He dived into Miss Meteyard's room, from which unladylike shouts of mirth were soon heard to proceed. Mr. Copley, feeling as though his head were filled with hard knobs of spinning granite that crashed with sickening thuds against his brain-pan, walked stiffly away to his own quarters. As he passed the Dispatching, he had a vision of Mrs. Crump, in tears, standing before Mrs. Johnson's desk, but he paid no attention. His one agonized yearning was to shake off Mr. Tallboy, who padded grimly at his heels.

"Oh, Mr. Tallboy!"

Mrs. Johnson's rather shrill voice came to Mr. Copley like an order of release. He shot home like a bolting rabbit. He must try phenacetin and chance the consequences. Hastily he swallowed three tablets without even troubling to fetch a glass of water, sat down in his revolving chair and closed his eyes.

Crash, crash, crash, went the lumps of granite in his brain. If only he could remain where he was, quite quietly, for half an hour—

The door was flung violently open.

"Look here, Copley," said Mr. Tallboy, in a voice like a pneumatic drill, "when you were hugger-muggering round with my desk last night did you have the unprintable bloody impertinence to interfere with my private belongings?"

"For heaven's sake," moaned Mr. Copley, "don't make such a row. I've got a splitting headache."

"I don't care a highly-coloured damn if you've got a headache or not," retorted Mr. Tallboy, flinging the door to behind him with a slam like the report of an 11-inch gun. "There was an envelope in my desk last night with fifty pounds in it, and it's gone, and that old (epithet) Mrs. Crump says she saw you (vulgar word)-ing about among my papers."

"I have your fifty pounds here," replied Mr. Copley, with as much dignity as he could muster. "I put it away safely for you, and I must say, Tallboy, that I consider it extremely thoughtless of you to leave your property about for the charwomen to find. It's not fair. You should have more consideration. And I did not rummage about in your desk as you suggest. I merely looked for the pull of the Nutrax half-double, and when I was closing the desk, this envelope fell out upon the floor."

He stooped to unlock the drawer, experiencing a ghastly qualm as he did so.

"You mean to tell me," said Mr. Tallboy, "that you had the all-fired cheek to take my money away to your own damned room—"

"In your own interests," said Mr. Copley.

117

"Interests be damned! Why the devil couldn't you leave it in a pigeon-hole and not be so blasted interfering?"

"You do not realize—"

"I realize this," said Mr. Tallboy, "that you're an expurgated superannuated interfering idiot. What you wanted to come poking your blasted nose in for—"

"Really, Mr. Tallboy—"

"What business was it of yours, anyway?"

"It was anybody's business," said Mr. Copley—so angry that he almost forgot his headache—"who had the welfare of the firm at heart. I am considerably older than you, Tallboy, and in my day, a Group-manager would have been ashamed to leave the building before ascertaining that all was well with his advertisement for the next day's paper. How you came to let such an advertisement pass in the first place is beyond my understanding. You were then late with the block. Perhaps you do not know that it was not received by the *Morning Star* till five minutes past six—*five minutes past six*. And instead of being at your post to consider any necessary corrections—"

"I don't want you to teach me my job," said Mr. Tallboy.

"Pardon me, I think you do."

"Anyhow, what's that got to do with it? The point is, you stick your nose into my private affairs—"

"I did not. The envelope fell out—"

"That's a bloody lie."

"Pardon me, it is the truth."

"Don't keep saying 'pardon me' like a bloody kitchen-maid."

"Leave my room!" shrieked Mr. Copley.

"I'm not going to leave your damned room till I get an apology."

"I think I ought to receive the apology."

"*You?*" Mr. Tallboy became almost inarticulate. "You—! Why the hell couldn't you have had the decency to ring me up and tell me, anyway?"

"You weren't at home."

"How do you know? Did you try?"

"No. I knew you were out, because I saw you in Southampton Row."

"You saw me in Southampton Row, and you hadn't the ordinary common decency to get hold of me and tell me what you'd been after? Upon my word, Copley, I believe you jolly well *meant* to get me into a row. And collar the cash for yourself, too, I shouldn't wonder."

"How dare you suggest any such thing?"

"And all your rot about consideration for the charwomen! It's sheer damned hypocrisy. Of course I thought one of them had had it. I told Mrs. Crump—"

"You accused Mrs. Crump?"

"I didn't accuse her. I told her I had missed fifty pounds."

"That just shows you," began Mr. Copley.

"And fortunately she'd seen you at my desk. Otherwise, I suppose I should never have heard anything more about my money."

"You've no right to say that."

"I've a damn sight more right to say it than you had to steal the money."

"Are you calling me a thief?"

"Yes, I am."

"And I call you a scoundrel," gasped Mr. Copley, beside himself, "an insolent scoundrel. And I say that if you came by the money honestly, which I doubt, sir, which I very much doubt—"

Mr. Bredon poked his long nose round the door.

"I say," he bleated anxiously, "sorry to butt in, and all that, but Hankie's compliments and he says, would you mind talking a little more quietly? He's got Mr. Simon Brotherhood next door."

A pause followed, in which both parties realized the thinness of the beaverboard partition between Mr. Hankin's room and Mr. Copley's. Then Mr. Tallboy thrust the recovered envelope into his pocket.

"All right, Copley," he said. "I shan't forget your kind interference." He bounced out.

"Oh, dear, oh, dear," moaned Mr. Copley, clasping his head in his hands.

"Is anything up?" queried Mr. Bredon.

"Please go away," pleaded Mr. Copley, "I'm feeling horribly ill."

Mr. Bredon withdrew on catlike feet. His inquisitive face beamed with mischief. He pursued Mr. Tallboy into the Dispatching, and found him earnestly talking to Mrs. Johnson.

"I say, Tallboy," said Mr. Bredon, "what's wrong with Copley? He looks jolly fed-up. Have you been twisting his tail?"

"It's no affair of yours, anyway," retorted Mr. Tallboy, sullenly. "All right, Mrs. J., I'll see Mrs. Crump and put it right with her."

"I hope you will, Mr. Tallboy. And another time, if you have any valuables, I should be obliged if you would bring

119

them to me and let me put them in the safe downstairs. These upsets are not pleasant, and Mr. Pym would be greatly annoyed if he knew about it."

Mr. Tallboy fled for the lift without vouchsafing any reply.

"Atmosphere seems a bit hectic this morning, Mrs. Johnson," observed Mr. Bredon, seating himself on the edge of the good lady's desk. "Even the presiding genius of the Dispatching looks a trifle ruffled. But a righteous indignation becomes you. Gives sparkle to the eyes and a clear rosiness to the complexion."

"Now that'll do, Mr. Bredon. What will my boys think if they hear you making fun of me? Really, though, some of these people are *too* trying. But I must stand up for my women, Mr. Bredon, and for my boys. There isn't one of them that I wouldn't trust, and it isn't right to bring accusations with nothing to support them."

"It's simply foul," agreed Mr. Bredon. "Who's been bringing accusations?"

"Well, I don't know if I ought to tell tales out of school," said Mrs. Johnson, "but it's really only justice to poor Mrs. Crump to say—"

Naturally, in five minutes' time, the insinuating Mr. Bredon was in possession of the whole story.

"But you needn't go and spread it all round the office," said Mrs. Johnson.

"Of course I needn't," said Mr. Bredon. "Hullo! is that the lad with our coffee?"

He sprang alertly from his perch and hastened into the typists' room, where Miss Parton was detailing to a prick-eared audience the more juicy details of the morning's scene with Mr. Armstrong.

"That's nothing," announced Mr. Bredon. "You haven't heard the latest development."

"Oh, *what* is it?" cried Miss Rossiter.

"I've promised not to tell," said Mr. Bredon.

"Shame, shame!"

"At least, I didn't exactly promise. I was asked not to."

"Is it about Mr. Tallboy's money?"

"You do know, then? What a disappointment!"

"I know that poor little Mrs. Crump was crying this morning because Mr. Tallboy had accused her of taking some money out of his desk."

"Well, if you know that," said Mr. Bredon artlessly, "in justice to Mrs. Crump—"

His tongue wagged busily.

"Well, I think it's too bad of Mr. Tallboy," said Miss

120

Rossiter. "He's always being rude to poor old Copley. It's a shame. And it's rotten to accuse the charwomen."

"Yes, it is," agreed Miss Parton, "but I've no patience with that Copley creature. He's a tiresome old sneak. He went and told Hankie once that he'd seen me at the dog-races with a gentleman friend. As if it was any business of his what a girl does out of business hours. He's too nosey by half. Just because anybody's a mere typist it doesn't mean one's a heathen slave. Oh! here's Mr. Ingleby. Coffee, Mr. Ingleby? I say, *have* you heard about old Copley pinching Mr. Tallboy's fifty quid?"

"You don't say so," exclaimed Mr. Ingleby, shooting a miscellaneous collection of oddments out of the waste-paper basket as a preliminary to up-turning it and sitting upon it. "Tell me quickly. Golly! what a day we're having!"

"Well," said Miss Rossiter, lusciously taking up the tale, "somebody sent Mr. Tallboy fifty pounds in a registered envelope—"

"What's all this?" interrupted Miss Meteyard, arriving with some sheets of copy in one hand and a bag of bulls' eyes in the other. "Here are some lollipops for my little ones. Now let's hear it all from the beginning. I only wish people would send *me* fifty poundses in registered envelopes. Who was the benefactor?"

"I don't know. Do you know, Mr. Bredon?"

"Haven't the foggiest. But it was all in currency notes, which is suspicious, for a start."

"And he brought them to the office, meaning to take them to the Bank."

"But he was busy," chimed in Miss Parton, "and forgot all about them."

"Catch me forgetting about fifty pounds," said Miss Parton's bosom-friend from the Printing.

"Oh, we're only poor hardworking typists. Fifty pounds or so is nothing to Mr. Tallboy, obviously. He put them in his desk—"

"Why not in his pocket?"

"Because he was working in his shirt-sleeves, and didn't like to leave all that wealth hanging on a coat-peg—"

"Yes; well, he forgot them at the lunch-hour. And in the afternoon, he found that the blockmaker had done something silly with the Nutrax block—"

"Was that what delayed it?" inquired Mr. Bredon.

"Yes, that was it. And, I say, I've found out something else. Mr. Drew—"

"Who's Mr. Drew?"

"That stout man from the Cormorant Press. He said to

Mr. Tallboy he thought the headline was a bit hot. And Mr. Tallboy said he had a nasty mind and anyhow, everybody had passed it and it was too late to alter it then—"

"Jiminy!" said Mr. Garrett, suddenly bursting into speech, "it's a good thing Copley didn't get hold of that. He'd have rubbed it in, all right. I must say, I think Tallboy ought to have done something about it."

"Who told you that?"

"Mr. Wedderburn. Drew asked him about it this morning. Said he noticed they'd thought better of it after all."

"Well, get on with the story."

"By the time Mr. Tallboy had had the block put right, the Bank was shut. So he forgot about it again, and went off, leaving the fifty quid in his desk."

"Does he often do that sort of thing?"

"Goodness knows. And old Copley was working late on his jellies—"

Clack, clack, clack. The story lost nothing in the telling.

"—poor old Mrs. Crump was weeping like a sponge—"

"—Mrs. Johnson was in *such* a bait—"

"—making a most *awful* row. Mr. Bredon heard them. What did he call him, Mr. Bredon?"

"—accused him of stealing the money—"

"—thief and scoundrel—"

"—what Mr. Brotherhood must have thought—"

"—give them the sack, I shouldn't wonder—"

"—my dear, the *thrills* we get in this place!"

"And, by the way," observed Mr. Ingleby, maliciously, "I pulled Barrow's leg all right about that sketch."

"You *didn't* tell him what Mr. Armstrong said?"

"No. At least, I didn't tell him Mr. Armstrong said it. But I gave him a hint to that effect off my own bat."

"You are awful!"

"He's out for the blood of this department—especially Copley's."

"Because Copley went to Hankie last week about a Jamboree display and complained that Barrow didn't follow his directions, and so now he thinks this business is a plot of Copley's to—"

"Shut up!"

Miss Rossiter leapt at her typewriter and began to pound the keys deafeningly.

Amid a pointed silence of tongues, Mr. Copley made his entrance.

"Is that Jelly copy of mine ready, Miss Rossiter? There doesn't seem to be much work being done here this morning."

"You've got to take your turn, Mr. Copley. I have a report of Mr. Armstrong's to finish."

"I shall speak to Mr. Armstrong about the way the work is done," said Mr. Copley. "This room is a bear-garden. It's disgraceful."

"Why not give Mr. Hankin a turn?" snapped Miss Parton, unpleasantly.

"No, but really, Copley, old sport," pleaded Mr. Bredon, earnestly. "You mustn't let these little things get your goat. It's not done, old thing. Positively not done. You watch me squeeze copy out of Miss Parton. She eats out of my hand. A little kindness and putting her hair in papers will work wonders with her. Ask her nicely and she'll do anything for you."

"A man of your age, Bredon, should know better," said Mr. Copley, "than to hang round here all day. Am I the only person in this office with work to do?"

"If you only knew it," replied Mr. Bredon, "I'm working away like anything. Look here," he added, as the unhappy Mr. Copley withdrew, "do the poor old blighter's muck for him. It's a damned sha.ne to tease him. He's looking horribly green about the gills."

"Right-ho!" said Miss Parton, amiably, "I don't mind if I do. May as well get it over."

The typewriters clacked again.

CHAPTER IX

UNSENTIMENTAL MASQUERADE
OF A HARLEQUIN

DIAN DE MOMERIE was holding her own. True, the big Chrysler and the Bentley ahead of her had more horsepower, but young Spenlow was too drunk to last out, and Harry Thorne was a notoriously rotten driver. She had only to tail them at a safe distance till they came to grief. She only wished "Spot" Lancaster would leave her alone. His clumsy grabs at her waist and shoulders interfered with her handling of the car. She eased the pressure of her slim sandal on the accelerator, and jabbed an angry elbow into his hot face.

"Shut up, you fool! you'll have us into the ditch, and then they'd beat us."

"I say!" protested Spot, "don't do that. It hurts."

She ignored him, keeping her eye on the road. Everything was perfect tonight. There had been a most stimulating and amusing row at Tod Milligan's, and Tod had been very definitely told where he got off. All the better. She was getting tired of Tod's hectoring. She was keyed up just enough and not too much. The hedges flashed and roared past them; the road, lit by the raking headlights, showed like a war-worn surface of holes and hillocks, which miraculously smoothed themselves out beneath the spinning wheels. The car rode the earth-waves like a ship. She wished it were an open car and not this vulgar, stuffy saloon of Spot's.

The Chrysler ahead was lurching perilously, thrashing her great tail like a fighting salmon. Harry Thorne had no business with a car like that; he couldn't hold it on the road. And there was a sharp S-bend coming. Dian knew that. Her senses seemed unnaturally sharpened—she could see the road unrolled before her like a map. Thorne was taking the first bend—far too wide—and young Spenlow was cutting in on the left. The race was hers now—nothing could prevent it. Spot was drinking again from a pocket-flask. Let him. It left her free. The Chrysler, wrenched brutally across the road, caught the Bentley on the inner edge of the bend, smashing it

124

against the bank and slewing it round till it stood across the road. Was there room to pass? She pulled out, her off wheels bumping over the grass verge. The Chrysler staggered on, swaying from the impact—it charged the bank and broke through the hedge. She heard Throne yell—saw the big car leap miraculously to earth without overturning, and gave an answering cry of triumph. And then the road was suddenly lit up as though by a searchlight, whose powerful beam swallowed her own headlights like a candle in sunlight.

She leant over to Spot.

"Who's that behind us?"

"Dunno," grunted Spot, twisting ineffectually to stare through the small pane at the rear of the car. "Some blighter or other."

Dian set her teeth. Who the hell, who the *hell* had a car like that? The driving mirror showed only the glare of the enormous twin lights. She drove the accelerator down to its limit, and the car leaped forward. But the pursuer followed easily. She swung out on the crown of the road. Let him crash if he wanted to. He held on remorselessly. A narrow, hump-backed bridge sprang out of the darkness. She topped it and seemed to leap the edge of the world. A village, with a wide open square. This would be the man's chance. He took it. A great dark shape loomed up beside her, long, low and open. Out of the tail of her eye she sought the driver. For five seconds he held beside her, neck and neck, and she saw the black mask and skull-cap and the flash of black and silver. Then, in the narrowing of the street, he swept ahead. She remembered what Pamela Dean had told her:

"You will see him when you least expect him."

Whatever happened, she must hold on to him. He was running ahead now, lightly as a panther, his red tail-lamp tantalizingly only a few yards away. She could have cried with exasperation. He was playing with her.

"Is this all your beastly Dutch-oven will do?"

Spot had fallen asleep. His head rolled against her arm and she shook it off violently. Two miles, and the road plunged beneath over-arching trees, with a stretch of woodland on either side. The leading car turned suddenly down a side-road and thence through an open gate beneath the trees; it wound its way into the heart of the wood, and then abruptly stopped; all its lights were shut off.

She jammed on her brakes and was out upon the grass. Overhead the treetops swung together in the wind. She ran to the other car; it was empty.

She stared round. Except for the shaft of light thrown by her own headlamps, the darkness was Eygptian. She stumbled over her long skirts among briars and tufts of bracken. She called:

"Where are you? Where are you hiding? Don't be so *silly!*"

There was no answer. But presently, far off and mockingly, there came the sound of a very high, thin fluting. No jazz tune, but one which she remembered from nursery days:

> *Tom, Tom the piper's son*
> *Learned to play when he was young,*
> *And the only tune that he could play*
> *Was: "Over the hills and far away—"*

"It's too *stupid*," said Dian.

> *Over the hills and a great way off*
> *The wind is blowing my top-knot off.*

The sound was so bodiless that it seemed to have no abiding-place. She ran forward, and it grew fainter; a thick bramble caught her, tearing her ankles and her sheer silk stockings. She wrenched herself pettishly away and started off in a new direction. The piping ceased. She suddenly became afraid of the trees and the darkness. The good, comforting drinks were taking back the support they gave and offering her instead a horrible apprehensiveness. She remembered Spot's pocket-flask and began scrambling back towards the car. Then the beaconing lights went out, leaving her alone with the trees and the wind.

The high spirits induced by gin and cheerful company do not easily survive siege by darkness and solitude. She was running now, desperately, and screaming as she ran. A root, like a hand about her ankles, tripped her, and she dropped, cowering.

The thin tune began again.

> *Tom, Tom the piper's son—*

She sat up.

"The terror induced by forests and darkness," said a mocking voice from somewhere over her head, "was called by the Ancients, Panic fear, or the fear of the great god Pan. It is interesting to observe that modern progress has not altogether succeeded in banishing it from ill-disciplined minds."

Dian gazed upwards. Her eyes were growing accustomed to the night, and in the branches of the tree above her she caught the pale gleam of silver.

"What do you want to behave like an idiot for?"

"Advertisement, chiefly. One must be different. I am always different. That is why, my dear young lady, I am the pursued and not the pursuer. You may say it is a cheap way of producing an effect, and so it is; but it is good enough for gin-soaked minds. On such as you, if you will pardon my saying so, subtlety would be wasted."

"I wish you would come down."

"Possibly. But I prefer to be looked up to."

"You can't stay there all night. Think how silly you would look in the morning."

"Ah! but by comparison with yourself I shall retain an almost bandbox perfection of appearance. My costume is better suited than yours to acrobatic exercise in a wood at midnight."

"Well, what are you doing it for, anyway?"

"To please myself—which is the only reason you would admit for doing anything."

"Then you can sit up there and do it all alone. I'm going home."

"Your shoes aren't very suitable for a long walk—but if it amuses you, go home by all means."

"Why should I have to walk?"

"Because I have the ignition keys of both cars in my pocket. A simple precaution, my dear Watson. Nor do I think it will be very much good to try to send a message by your companion. He is plunged in the arms of Morpheus—an ancient and powerful god, though not so ancient as Pan."

"I hate you," said Dian.

"Then you are on the high road to loving me—which is only natural. We needs must love the highest when we see it. Can you see me?"

"Not very well. I could see you better if you came down."

"And love me better, perhaps?"

"Perhaps."

"Then I am safer where I am. Your lovers have a knack of coming to bad ends. There was young Carmichael—"

"I couldn't help that. He drank too much. He was an idiot."

"And Arthur Barrington—"

"I told him it wasn't any good."

"Not a bit of good. But he tried, all the same, and blew his brains out. Not that they were very good brains, but they were all the brains he had. And Victor Dean—"

"The little rotter! That wasn't anything to do with me."

127

"Wasn't it?"

"Why, he fell down a staircase, didn't he?"

"So he did. But why?"

"I haven't the faintest idea."

"Haven't you? I thought you might have. Why did you send Victor Dean about his business?"

"Because he was a silly little bore and just like all the rest."

"You like them to be different?"

"I like everything to be different."

"And when you find them different, you try to make them all alike. Do you know anybody who is different?"

"Yes; you're different."

"Only so long as I stay on my branch, Circe. If I come down to your level, I should be just like all the rest."

"Come down and try."

"I know when I am well off. You had better come up to me."

"You know I can't."

"Of course you can't. You can only go down and down."

"Are you trying to insult me?"

"Yes, but it's very difficult."

"Come down, Harlequin—I want you here."

"That's a new experience for you, isn't it? To want what you can't get. You ought to be grateful to me."

"I always want what I can't get."

"What do you want?"

"Life—thrills—"

"Well, you're getting them now. Tell me all about Victor Dean."

"Why do you want to know about him?"

"That's a secret."

"If I tell you, will you come down?"

"Perhaps."

"What a funny thing to want to know about."

"I'm famous for being funny. How did you pick him up?"

"We all went out one night to some frightful sort of suburban dancing place. We thought it would be such a scream."

"And was it?"

"No, it was rather dull really. But he was there, and he fell for me and I thought he was rather a pet. That's all."

"A simple story in words of one syllable. How long was he your pet?"

"Oh, about six months. But he was terribly, terribly boring. And such a prig. Imagine it, Harlequin darling. He got all cross and wanted bread and cheese and kisses. Are you laughing?"

"Hilariously."

"He wasn't any fun. He was all wet."

"My child, you are telling this story very badly. You made him drink and it upset his little tummy. You made him play high, and he said he couldn't afford it. And you tried to make him take drugs and he didn't like it. Anything else?"

"He was a little beast, Harlequin, really he was. He was out for what he could get."

"Aren't you?"

"Me?" Dian was really surprised. "I'm terribly generous. I gave him everything he wanted. I'm like that when I'm fond of anybody."

"He took what he could get but didn't spend it like a gentleman?"

"That's it. Do you know, he actually called himself a gentleman. Wouldn't that make you laugh? Like the middle ages, isn't it? Ladies and Gentlemen. He said we needn't think he wasn't a gentleman because he worked in an office. Too mirth-making, Harlequin, darling, wasn't it?"

She rocked herself backwards and forwards in amusement.

"Harlequin! Listen! I'll tell you something funny. One night Tod Milligan came in and I told him: 'This is Victor Dean, and he's a gentleman, and he works for Pym's Publicity.' Tod said: 'Oh, you're the chap, are you?' and looked too utterly murderous. And afterwards he asked me, just like you, how I got hold of Victor. That's queer. Did Tod send you out here to ask me?"

"No. No one ever sends me. I go where I like."

"Well, then, why do you all want to know about Victor Dean?"

"Too mystery-making, isn't it? What did Milligan say to Dean?"

"Nothing much, but he told me to string him along. And afterwards, quite suddenly, he told me to give him the push."

"And you did as you were told, like a good girl?"

"I was fed up with Victor, anyhow. And it doesn't do to get wrong with Tod."

"No—he might cut off supplies, mightn't he? Where does he get it from?"

"Coke, do you mean? I don't know."

"No, I suppose you don't. And you can't get him to tell you, either. Not with all your charms, Circe."

"Oh, Tod! he doesn't give anything away. He's a dirty

129

swine. I loathe him. I'd do anything to get away from Tod.
But he knows too much. And besides, he's got the stuff. Lots
of people have tried to chuck Tod, but they always go back
again—on Fridays and Saturdays."

"That's when he hands it out, is it?"

"Mostly. But—" she began to laugh again—"you weren't
there tonight, were you? It was too amusing. He'd run short,
or something. There was a hellish row. And that septic
woman Babs Woodley was screaming all over the place. She
scratched him. I do hope he gets blood-poisoning. He promised it would be there tomorrow, but he looked the most
perfect idiot, with blood running down his chin. She said
she'd shoot him. It was too marvellous."

"Rabelaisian, no doubt."

"Fortunately I'd got enough, so I gave her enough to keep
her quiet, and then we thought we'd have a race. I won—at
least, I should have, if it hadn't been for you. How did you
happen along?"

"Oh, I just happened along. I always happen."

"You don't. You only seem to happen occasionally. You
aren't one of Tod's regular lot, are you?"

"Not at present."

"Do you want to be? Because, don't. I'll get the stuff for
you if you want it. But Tod's a beast. You'd better keep clear
of him."

"Are you warning me for my good?"

"Yes, I am."

"What devotion!"

"No, I mean it. Life's hell, anyway, but it's worse if you
get mixed up with Tod."

"Then why don't you cut loose from Tod?"

"I can't."

"Afraid of him?"

"Not so much of him. It's the people behind him. Tod's
afraid too. He'd never let me go. He'd kill me first."

"How fascinating! I think I must know Tod better."

"You'd end by being afraid, too."

"Should I? Well, there's a kick in being afraid."

"Come down here, Harlequin, and I'll show you how to
get a kick out of life."

"Could you?"

"Try and see."

There was a rustle among the leaves, and he slid down to
stand beside her.

"Well?"

"Lift me up. I'm all cramped."

He lifted her, and she felt his hands hard as iron under her

130

breast. She was tall, and as she turned to look at him she could see the glint of his eyeballs, level with her own.

"Well, will I do?"

"For what?"

"For you?"

"For me? What are you good for, to me?"

"I'm beautiful."

"Not so beautiful as you were. In five years' time you will be ugly."

"Five years? I wouldn't want you for five years."

"I wouldn't want you for five minutes."

The cold daybreak was beginning to filter through the leaves; it showed her only a long, implacable chin and the thin curl of a smiling mouth. She made a snatch at his mask, but he was too quick for her. Very deliberately he turned her towards him, putting both her arms behind her back and holding them there.

"What next?" she demanded, mockingly.

"Nothing. I shall take you home."

"You will? Ah, you will, then?"

"Yes, as I did once before."

"Exactly as you did before?"

"Not exactly, because you were drunk then. You are sober now. With that trifling difference, the programme will be carried out according to precedent."

"You might kiss me, Harlequin."

"Do you deserve kissing? Once, for your information. Twice, for your disinterested effort to save me from the egregious Mr. Milligan. And the third time, because the fancy takes me that way."

He bestowed the kisses like deliberate insults. Then he picked her up bodily, still holding her arms imprisoned, and dumped her into the back of the open car.

"Here's a rug for you. You'll need it."

She said nothing. He started up the engine, turned the car and drove it slowly along the path. As they came abreast of the saloon, he leaned out and tossed the ignition key on to the knees of Spot Lancaster, happily snoring in his seat. In a few minutes, they had turned out from the wood into the main road. The sky was faintly streaked with the ghostly glimmer of the false dawn.

Dian de Momerie slid from under the rug and leaned forward. He was driving easily, slumped down in his seat, his black poll leaning carelessly back, his hand slack on the wheel. With a twist, she could send him and herself into the ditch, and he would deserve it.

"Don't do it," he said, without turning his head.

131

"You devil!"

He stopped the car.

"If you don't behave, I shall leave you by the roadside, sitting on a milestone, like the bailiff's daughter of Islington. Or, if you prefer it, I can tie you up. Which is it to be?"

"Be kind to me."

"I am being kind. I have preserved you from boredom for two solid hours. I beg you not to plunge us both into the horrors of an anti-climax. What are you crying for?"

"I'm tired—and you won't love me."

"My poor child, pull yourself together. Who would believe that Dian de Momerie could fall for a fancy-dress and a penny whistle?"

"It isn't that. It's you. There's something queer about you. I'm afraid of you. You aren't thinking about me at all. You're thinking of something horrible. What is it? What is it? Wait!"

She put out a cold hand and clutched his arm.

"I'm seeing something that I can't make out. I've got it now. Straps. They are strapping his elbows and dropping a white bag over his head. The hanged man. There's a hanged man in your thoughts. Why are you thinking of hanging?"

She shrank away from him and huddled into the farthest corner of the car. Wimsey re-started the engine and let in the clutch.

"Upon my word," he thought, "that's the oddest after-effect of drink and drugs I've met yet. Very interesting. But not very safe. Quite a providential interposition in one way. We may get home without breaking our necks. I didn't know I carried such a graveyard aura about with me."

Dian was fast asleep when he lifted her out of the car. She half woke, and slipped her arms round his neck.

"Darling, it's been lovely." Then she came to with a little start. "Where have we got to? What's happened?"

"We're home. Where's your latch-key?"

"Here. Kiss me. Take that mask off."

"Run along in. There's a policeman thinking we look rather disreputable." He opened the door.

"Aren't you coming in?"

She seemed to have forgotten all about the hanged man.

He shook his head.

"Well, good-bye then."

"Good-bye."

He kissed her gently this time and pushed her into the house. The policeman, stumping inquisitively nearer, revealed a face that Wimsey knew. He smiled to himself as the official gaze swept over him.

132

"Good morning, officer."

"Morning, sir," said the policeman, stolidly.

"Moffatt, Moffatt," said his lordship, reprovingly, "you will never get promotion. If you don't know me, you should know the car."

"Good lord, your lordship, I beg your pardon. Didn't somehow expect to see you here."

"Not so much of the lordship. Somebody might be listening. You on your beat?"

"Just going home, my—sir."

"Jump in and I'll drive you there. Ever see a fellow called Milligan round this way?"

"Major Tod Milligan? Yes, now and then. He's a bad hat, he is, if ever there was one. Runs that place down by the river. Mixed up with that big drug-gang as Mr. Parker's after. We could pull him in any day, but he's not the real big noise."

"Isn't he, Moffatt?"

"No, my lord. This car's a treat, ain't she? Shouldn't think there's much catches *you* on the road. No. What Mr. Parker wants is to get him to lead us to the top man of all, but there don't seem to be much chance of it. They're as cunning as weasels, they are. Don't suppose he knows himself who the other fellow is."

"How's it worked, Moffatt?"

"Well, my lord, as far as we've been told, the stuff is brought in from the coast once or twice a week and run up to London. We've had a try at catching it on the way more than once, that is to say, Mr. Parker's special squad have, but they've always given us the slip. Then it'll be taken somewhere, but where we don't know, and distributed out again to the big distributors. From them it goes to all kinds of places. We could lay hands on it there—but lord! what's the use? It'd only be in another place next week."

"And whereabouts does Milligan come into it?"

"We think he's one of the high-up distributors, my lord. He hands it out at that house of his, and in other places."

"In the place where you found me, for instance?"

"That's one of them."

"But the point is, where does Milligan get his supplies?"

"That's it, my lord."

"Can't you follow him and find out?"

"Ah! but he don't fetch it for himself, my lord. There's others does that. And you see, if we was to open his parcels and search his tradesmen and so on, they'd just strike him off their list, and we'd be back where we was before."

"So you would. How often does he give parties in that house of his?"

"Most evenings, my lord. Seems to keep open house, like."

"Well, keep an eye open on Friday and Saturday nights, Moffatt."

"Fridays and Saturdays, my lord?"

"Those are the nights when things happen."

"Is that so, my lord? I'm much obliged to you. We didn't know that. That's a good tip, that is. If you'll drop me at the next corner, my lord, that'll do me champion. I'm afraid I've took your lordship out of your way."

"Not a bit, Moffatt, not a bit. Very glad to have seen you. And, by the way, you have not seen me. Not a question of my morals, you understand, but I've a fancy that Major Milligan might not approve of my visiting that particular house."

"That's all right, my lord. Not being on duty at the time, I ain't bound to put it in a report. Good morning, my lord, and thank you."

CHAPTER X

DISTRESSING DEVELOPMENTS
OF AN OFFICE ROW

ALL very well for you to talk, Bill Jones," said Ginger Joe, "but bet you sixpence if you was called as a witness in a case, you'd get into a 'owling mess. Why, they might ask you what you was doin' a month ago and what'd you know about that?"

"Bet you I'd know all right."

"Bet you you wouldn't."

"All right, bet you anything I would."

"Bet you if I was a 'tec—"

"Cor lumme, you'd be a good 'tec, you would."

"Bet you I would, anyhow."

" 'Oo ever 'eard of a carrotty-'eaded 'tec?"

This objection appeared to Ginger to be irrelevant. He replied, however, automatically:

"Bet you I'd be a better 'tec 'or you."

"Bet you you wouldn't."

"Bet you if I was a 'tec and arst you w'ere you was when Mr. Dean fell downstairs, you wouldn't 'ave no alleybi."

"That's silly, that is," said Bill Jones. "I wouldn't want no alleybi for Mr. Dean falling downstairs, 'cause it was accidental death."

"All right, Suet-face. I was only sayin', supposin' I *was* a 'tec an' I was investigatin' Mr. Dean's fallin' downstairs, and I arst you wot you was a-doin' of, you wouldn't be able to tell me."

"Bet you I would, then. I was on the lift, that's where I was, and 'Arry could prove it. So just you stick that in your silly face and shut up."

"Oh, you was on the lift, was you? 'Ow d'you know that was when it was?"

"When wot was?"

"When Mr. Dean fell downstairs?"

" 'Cos the first thing I 'ears when I comes off of the lift is Mr. Tompkin a-telling Sam there all about it. Didn't I, Sam?"

Sam Tabbitt glanced up from a copy of *Radio for Amateurs* and nodded briefly.

"That don't prove nothing," persisted Ginger. "Not without you know 'ow long it took Mr. Tompkin to shoot 'is mouth off."

"Not long it didn't," said Sam. "I'd just come out of the Big Conference room—takin' tea to Mr. Pym and two clients, I was—Muggleton's, if you want ter know—and I hears an awful screeching and I says to Mr. Tompkin, 'Coo, lumme!' I says, 'wot's up?' An' he says as Mr. Dean's fallen down and broke 'is neck an' they've jest rung up for a doctor."

"That's right," added Cyril, who was the boy in attendance on the Executive and the Switchboard. "Mr. Stanley comes running along full pelt into our place and says, 'Oh, Miss Fearney, Mr. Dean's fell downstairs and we're afraid he's killed himself and you're to telephone for a doctor.' So Miss Fearney tells Miss Beit to put the call through and I hops out quick through the other door so as Miss Fearney can't see me—that's the door behind Mr. Tompkin's desk—and I says, 'Mr. Dean's tumbled down and killed hisself,' and he says, 'Run and see what's happened, Cyril.' So I runs and I see Sam jest a-comin' out from the Big Conference room. Didn't I, Sam?"

Sam agreed.

"And that's when I heard the screeching," he added.

"Who was a-screeching?"

"Mrs. Crump was a-screeching in the Executive. Said she'd just seen Mr. Dean fall down and kill hisself and they was a-bringin' 'im along. So I looked into the passage and there they was, a-carryin' of him. He did look awful."

"And that was when I come up," said Bill, sticking to the point at issue. "I hears Mr. Tompkin telling Sam about it, and I runs after Sam and I calls to Mr. Tompkin as they're a-bringing him through, and he comes and looks on too. So they takes him into the Board-room, and Miss Fearney says, 'What about telling Mr. Pym?' and Mr. Tompkin says, 'He's still in the conference,' and she says, 'I know he is. We don't want the clients to hear about it.' So Mr. Tompkin says, 'Better telephone through to him.' So she does and then she gets hold of me and says, 'Bill, get a sheet of brown paper and run along to the Board-room and tell them to put it over the glass door,' and just as I was a-going, Mr. Atkins comes along and says, 'Is there any dust-sheets?' he says. 'He's gone,' he says, 'and we got to have somethink to put over him.' And Miss Fearney says, sharp-like, 'Dust-sheets is nothing to do with this department,' she says, 'what are you thinking about? Go up and ask Mrs. Johnson.' Coo! that was a set-out, that was." Bill grinned, as one who looks back to a grand gala-day, a brilliant green oasis in a desert of drudgery. Then he remembered once more what the dispute had been about.

"So where's your blinkin' alleybi?" he demanded, sternly.

"Where's yours, Ginger, if it comes to that?"

By such methods, serpentine but effective, Ginger Joe pursued his inquiries. The eyes of the office-boy are everywhere, and his memory is retentive. Five days of inquiry brought the whole inside staff of Pym's under review—all that was necessary, since the day of Dean's death had not been the day that brought the Outside Publicity men into the office.

Out of the ninety-odd inside members of the staff, only ten remained unaccounted or partially unaccounted for. These were: in the Copy Department:

Mr. Willis. He had arrived from the outside staircase about five minutes after the accident, had gone straight through the hall, up the stair to the Dispatching and so into his own room, speaking to nobody. About a quarter of an hour later, he had gone to Mr. Dean's room and, not finding him, had gone back to the typists' room. Here, on asking for Mr. Dean, he had been greeted with the news, which appeared to startle and horrify him. (Witness: the boy George Pyke, who had heard Miss Rossiter telling Mrs. Johnson all about it.)

Mr. Hankin. He had been absent from the office since half-past two, on private business, and did not return till half-past four. Harry had informed him of the catastrophe as soon as he came in, and, as soon as he stepped out of the lift, Mr. Tompkin had requested him to go and see Mr. Pym. (Witnesses: Harry and Cyril.)

Mr. Copley. Presumably in his room all the time, but this could not be substantiated, since he never took tea and was accustomed to work at his "slope," which was set against the inner wall and not visible to any one casually passing his door. He was an assiduous worker, and was not likely to emerge from his room, however much noise or running about there might be in the passages. At a quarter to five, he had walked in the most ordinary way into the typists' room to ask why his copy had not been typed. Miss Parton had told him, rather tartly, that she didn't see how he could expect anything to be ready under the circumstances. He had then asked what circumstances and, on being told about Mr. Dean's fatal accident, had expressed astonishment and regret, but added that he could see no reason why the work of the

137

department should not be carried on. (Witnesses: four boys who, on separate occasions, had heard this shocking exhibition of callousness discussed with and by Mrs. Johnson.)

In the Vouchers:

Mr. Binns. An elegant youth who had gone out at 3 o'clock to inquire for last September's number of the *Connoisseur* for Mr. Armstrong, and had unaccountably taken an hour and a half over the transaction. (Witness: Sam, whose elder sister was a typist in the Vouchers, and had given it as her opinion that young Binns had had a date for tea with his best girl.) (Note: Mr. Binns was already known to Mr. Bredon as the darts expert who had often lunched with Victor Dean.)

In the various Group-managers' offices:

Mr. Haagedorn (Sopo and allied products). Leave of absence all day to attend aunt's funeral. But said to have been seen during the afternoon attending a matinée at the Adelphi. (Witnesses: Jack Dennis, the boy who thought he had seen him, and Mr. Tompkin's attendance-register consulted by Cyril.)

Mr. Tallboy. Exact location at the moment of the action not quite certain. At 3.30 or thereabouts, Mr. Wedderburn had come down to the Vouchers to ask for certain back numbers of the *Fishmonger's Gazette,* saying that Mr. Tallboy wanted them in a hurry. On returning ten minutes later, after having the required numbers sorted out for him, Mr. Wedderburn had run into all the excitement about Mr. Dean and had forgotten the *Fishmonger's Gazette.* He had, in fact, been talking to Miss Fearney in the Executive, when Mr. Tallboy had come in and rather abruptly asked whether he was expected to wait all night for them. Mr. Wedderburn had explained that the alarm about Mr. Dean had put the matter out of his head, and Mr. Tallboy had replied that the work had got to be done, notwithstanding. (Witnesses: Horace, the messenger-boy in the Vouchers, and Cyril.)

Mr. McAllister. Group-secretary to Dairyfields, Ltd., under Mr. Smayle. Absent all afternoon on visit to dentist. (Witness: Mr. Tompkin's register.)

In the Studio:

Mr. Barrow. At British Museum, studying Greek vases with view to advertising display for Klassika Corsets. (Witness: Mr. Barrow's time-sheet.)

Mr. Vibart. Supposed to be at Westminster, making a sketch of the Terrace of the House of Commons for Farley's Footwear. ("The feet that tread this historic pavement are more often than not, clad in Farley Fashion Footwear.") Absent 2.30-4.30. (Witnesses: Mr. Vibart's time-sheet and the sketch itself.)

Wilfred Cotterill. At 3 o'clock complained of nose-bleeding and sent to lie down by himself in the Boys' Room, the other boys being told to leave him alone. Completely forgotten by everybody till 5 o'clock, when he was discovered, asleep, by the boys going in to change their tunics. Alleged that he had slept through the whole of the excitement. (Witnesses: All the other boys.) Wilfred Cotterill was a small, pale, excitable child of fourteen, but looking much younger. When told what he had missed he merely remarked "Oo-er!"

A very creditable piece of work on Ginger Joe's part, thought Mr. Bredon, if we may continue so to call him during office-hours, but leaving much room for further inquiry. His own investigations were not going too well. In his search for Darling Special Pencils he had been brought face to face with the practical communism of office life. The Copy Department preferred 5B or even 6B drawing-pencils for writing its roughs, and was not much interested in Darling's product, except, of course, Mr. Garrett, who had been drawing up a little panel for display in Darling's advertisements, calling attention to the generous offer of the pencil. He had two specimens, and four, in various stages of decay, were found in the typists' room. There was one on Mr. Armstrong's desk. Mr. Hankin had none. Mr. Ingleby admitted to having thrown his out of the window in a fit of temper, and Miss Meteyard said she thought she had one somewhere if Mr. Bredon really wanted it, but he had better ask Miss Parton. The other departments were even worse. The pencils had been taken home, lost, or thrown away. Mr. McAllister, mysteriously but characteristically, said he had no less than six. Mr. Wedderburn had lost his, but produced one which he had bagged from Mr. Tallboy. Mr. Prout said he couldn't be bothered; the pencil was a silly, gimcrack thing anyway; if Bredon really wanted a propelling pencil he ought to get an Eversharp. He (Mr. Prout) had never seen the thing since he'd had it to photograph; he added that for a first-class photographer to spend his life photographing tin pencils and jelly cartons was enough to drive any sensitive person to suicide. It was heart-breaking work.

In the matter of his own address, Bredon did get one piece of information. Mr. Willis had asked for it one day. Discreet questioning fixed the date to within a day or so, one way or another, of Chief-Inspector Parker's unfortunate encounter on the stairs. Nearer than this, Miss Beit (the telephonist, who also presided over the office address-book) could not go. It was all rather unnerving as well as exasperating. Mr.

Bredon hoped that the assailant would have been sufficiently alarmed by the failure of his first attempt to forswear blunt instruments and violence for the future; nevertheless, he developed a habit of keeping a careful lookout for following footsteps whenever he left the office. He went home by circuitous routes, and when engaged on his daily duties, found himself avoiding the iron staircase.

Meanwhile, the great Nutrax row raged on with undiminished vigour, developing as it went an extraordinary number of offshoots and ramifications, of which the most important and alarming was a violent breach between Mr. Smayle and Mr. Tallboy.

It began, rather absurdly, at the bottom of the lift, where Mr. Tallboy and Miss Meteyard were standing, waiting for Harry to return and waft them to their sphere of toil above. To them, enter Mr. Smayle, fresh and smiling, his teeth gleaming as though cleaned with Toothshine, a pink rosebud in his buttonhole, his umbrella neatly rolled.

"Morning, Miss Meteyard, morning, morning," said Mr. Smayle, raising his bowler, and replacing it at a jaunty angle. "Fine day again."

Miss Meteyard agreed that it was a fine day. "If only," she added, "they wouldn't spoil it with income-tax demands."

"Don't talk about income-tax," replied Mr. Smayle with a smile and a shudder. "I said to the wife this morning, 'My dear, we shall have to take our holiday in the back garden, I can see.' And I'm sure it's a fact. Where the money for our usual little trip to Eastbourne is to come from, I don't know."

"The whole thing's iniquitous," said Mr. Tallboy. "As for this last budget—"

"Ah! *you* must be paying super-tax, old man," said Mr. Smayle, giving Mr. Tallboy a prod in the ribs with his umbrella.

"Don't do that," said Mr. Tallboy.

"Tallboy needn't worry," said Mr. Smayle, with a rallying air. "He's got more money than he knows what to do with. We all know that, don't we, Miss Meteyard?"

"He's luckier than most, then," said Miss Meteyard.

"He can afford to chuck his quids over the office, fifty at a time," pursued Mr. Smayle. "Wish I knew where he gets it from. Daresay the income-tax authorities would like to know too. I'll tell you what, Miss Meteyard, this man's a dark horse. I believe he runs a dope-den or a bucket-shop on the sly, eh? You're a one, you are," said Mr. Smayle, extending a roguish forefinger and jabbing it into Mr. Tallboy's second waistcoat button. At this moment the lift descended and Miss

140

Meteyard stepped into it. Mr. Tallboy, rudely thrusting Mr. Smayle aside, stepped in after her.

"Here!" said Mr. Smayle, "manners, manners! The trouble with you, old man," he went on, "is that you can't take a joke. No offence meant, I'm sure—and none taken, I hope."

He clapped Mr. Tallboy on the shoulder.

"Do you mind keeping your hands off me, Smayle," said Mr. Tallboy.

"Oh, all right, all right, your Highness. Got out of bed the wrong side, hasn't he?" He appealed to Miss Meteyard, being troubled by an obscure feeling that men should not quarrel before ladies, and that it was somehow up to him to preserve the decencies by turning the whole thing into a joke.

"Money's a sore point with us all, I'm afraid, Mr. Smayle," replied Miss Meteyard. "Let's talk about something jollier. That's a nice rose you've got there."

"Out of my own garden," replied Mr. Smayle, with pride. "Mrs. Smayle's a wonder with the roses. I leave it all to her, bar the digging and mulching, of course." They emerged from the lift and signed their names at the desk. Miss Meteyard and Mr. Smayle passed on through the anteroom and turned by common consent to the left up the stair by the Dispatching. Mr. Tallboy shouldered past them and took a lone and frosty course down the main corridor to ascend by the iron staircase.

"I'm reelly very sorry," said Mr. Smayle, "that Tallboy and I should have indulged in anything approaching to words in your presence, Miss Meteyard."

"Oh, that's nothing. He seems a little irritable. I don't think he likes that little upset of his with Mr. Copley to be talked about."

"No, but reelly," said Mr. Smayle, lingering at the door of Miss Meteyard's room, "if a man can't take a harmless joke, it's a great pity, isn't it?"

"It is," said Miss Meteyard. "Hullo! What are all you people doing here?"

Mr. Ingleby and Mr. Bredon, seated on Miss Meteyard's radiator with a volume of the *New Century Dictionary* between them, looked up unabashed.

"We're finishing a Torquemada cross-word," said Ingelby, "and naturally the volume we wanted was in your room. Everything always is."

"I forgive you," said Miss Meteyard.

"But I do wish you wouldn't bring Smayle in here with you," said Mr. Bredon. "The mere sight of him makes me think of Green Pastures Margarine. You haven't come to dun me for that copy, have you? Because don't, there's a good fellow. I haven't done it and I can't do it. My brain has dried up. How you can live all day with Margarine and always look so fresh and cheerful passes my understanding."

"I assure you it's an effort," said Mr. Smayle, displaying his teeth. "But it reelly is a great refreshment to see you copywriters all so cheerful and pleasant together. Not like some people I could name."

"Mr. Tallboy has been unkind to Mr. Smayle," said Miss Meteyard.

"I like to be agreeable with everybody," said Mr. Smayle, "but reelly, when it comes to shoving your way past a person into the lift as if one wasn't there and then telling you to keep your hands off as if a person was dirt, a man may be excused for taking offence. I suppose Tallboy thinks I'm not worth speaking to, just because he's been to a public school and I haven't."

"Public school," said Mr. Bredon, "first I've heard of it. What public school?"

"He was at Dumbleton," said Mr. Smayle, "but what I say is, I went to a Council School and I'm not ashamed of it."

"Where's Dumbleton?" demanded Ingleby. "I shouldn't worry, Smayle. Dumbleton isn't a public school, within the meaning of the act."

"Isn't it?" said Mr. Smayle, hopefully. "Well, you and Mr. Bredon have had college educations, so you know all about it. What schools do *you* call public schools?"

"Eton," said Mr. Bredon, promptly, "—and Harrow," he added, magnanimously, for he was an Eton man.

"Rugby," suggested Mr. Ingleby.

"No, no," protested Bredon, "that's a railway junction."

Ingleby delivered a brisk left-hander to Bredon's jaw, which the latter parried neatly.

"And I've heard," Bredon went on, "that there's a decentish sort of place at Winchester, if you're not too particular."

"I once met a man who'd been to Marlborough," suggested Ingleby.

"I'm sorry to hear that," said Bredon. "They get a terrible set of hearty roughs down there. You can't be too careful of your associates, Ingleby."

"Well," said Mr. Smayle, "Tallboy always says that Dumbleton is a public school."

"I daresay it is—in the sense that it has a Board of Governors," said Ingleby, "but it's nothing to be snobbish about."

"What is, if you come to that?" said Bredon. "Look here,

Smayle, if only you people could get it out of your heads that these things matter a damn, you'd be a darn sight happier. You probably got a fifty times better education than I ever did."

Mr. Smayle shook his head. "Oh, no," he said, "I'm not deceiving myself about that, and I'd give anything to have had the same opportunities as you. There's a difference, and I know there's a difference, and I don't mind admitting it. But what I mean is, some people make you feel it and others don't. I don't feel it when I'm talking to either of you, or to Mr. Armstrong or Mr. Hankin, though you've been to Oxford and Cambridge and all that. Perhaps it's just because you've been to Oxford and Cambridge."

He struggled with the problem, embarrassing the other two men by his wistful eyes.

"Look here," said Miss Meteyard, "I know what you mean. But it's just that these two here never think twice about it. They don't have to. And you don't have to, either. But the minute anybody begins to worry about whether he's as good as the next man, then he starts a sort of uneasy snobbish feeling and makes himself offensive."

"I see," said Mr. Smayle. "Well, of course, Mr. Hankin doesn't have to try and prove that he's better than me, because he is and we both know it."

"Better isn't the right word, Smayle."

"Well, better educated. You know what I mean."

"Don't worry about it," said Ingleby. "If I were half as good at my job as you are at yours, I should feel superior to everybody in this tom-fool office."

Mr. Smayle shook his head, but appeared comforted.

"I do wish they wouldn't start that kind of thing," said Ingleby when he had gone, "I don't know what to say to them."

"I thought you were a Socialist, Ingleby," said Bredon, "it oughtn't to embarrass you."

"So I am a Socialist," said Ingleby, "but I can't stand this stuff about Old Dumbletonians. If everybody had the same State education, these things wouldn't happen."

"If everybody had the same face," said Bredon, "there'd be no pretty women."

Miss Meteyard made a grimace.

"If you go on like that, I shall be getting an inferiority complex too."

Bredon looked at her gravely.

"I don't think you'd care to be called pretty," he said, "but if I were a painter I should like to make a portrait of you. You have very interesting bones."

143

"Good God!" said Miss Meteyard. "I'm going. Let me know when you've finished with my room."

There was a mirror in the typists' room, and in this Miss Meteyard curiously studied her face.

"What's the matter, Miss Meteyard?" asked Miss Rossiter. "Got a spot coming?"

"Something of the sort," said Miss Meteyard, absently. "Interesting bones indeed!"

"Pardon?" said Miss Rossiter.

"Smayle is getting unbearable," grumbled Mr. Tallboy to Mr. Wedderburn. "Vulgar little tick. I hate a fellow who digs you in the ribs."

"He means no harm," rejoined Mr. Wedderburn. "He's quite a decent sort, really."

"Can't stand those teeth," grumbled Mr. Tallboy. "And why must he put that stinking stuff on his hair?"

"Oh, well," said Mr. Wedderburn.

"I'm not going to have him playing in the cricket match, anyhow," pursued Mr. Tallboy, viciously. "Last year he wore white suède shoes with crocodile vamps, and an incredible blazer with Old Borstalian colours."

Mr. Wedderburn looked up, rather startled.

"Oh, but you're not going to leave him out? He's quite a good bat and very nippy on the ball in the field."

"We can do without him," said Mr. Tallboy, firmly. Mr. Wedderburn said no more. There was no regular cricket eleven at Pym's, but every summer a scratch team was got together to play a couple of matches, the selection being entrusted to Mr. Tallboy, who was energetic and had once carried his bat out for 52 against Sopo. He was supposed to submit a list of cricketers for Mr. Hankin's final decision, but Mr. Hankin seldom questioned his selection, for the sufficient reason that there were seldom more than eleven candidates available to choose from. The important point was that Mr. Hankin should bat third, and field at mid-on. If these points were taken note of, he raised no further objections.

Mr. Tallboy pulled out a list.

"Ingleby," he said, "and Garrett. Barrow. Adcock. Pinchley. Hankin. Myself. Gregory can't play; he's going away for the week-end, so we'd better have McAllister. And we can't very well leave out Miller. I wish we could, but he's a Director. Yourself."

"Leave me out," said Mr. Wedderburn. "I haven't touched a bat since last year and I didn't put up much of a show then."

144

"We've nobody else who can bowl slow spinners," said Mr. Tallboy. "I'll put you down No. 11."

"All right," said Mr. Wedderburn, gratified by the recognition accorded to his bowling, but irrationally provoked by being put down No. 11. He had expected his companion to say, "Oh, but that was just a fluke," and send him in higher up the list. "How about a wicket-keeper? Grayson says he won't do it again, not after getting his front tooth knocked out last year. He seems to have got the wind up properly."

"We'll make Haagedorn do it. He's got hands like a pair of hams. Who else? Oh, that chap in the printing—Beesely—he's not much good with a bat, but we can rely on him for a few straight balls."

"What about that new fellow in the Copy Department? Bredon? He's a public school man. Is he any good?"

"Might be. He's a bit ancient, though. We've got two aged stiffs already in Hankin and Miller."

"Aged stiff be blowed. That chap can move, I've seen him do it. I wouldn't be surprised if he could show us a bit of style."

"Well, I'll find out. If he's any good, we'll stick him in instead of Pinchley."

"Pinchley can swipe 'em up," said Mr. Wedderburn.

"He never does anything but swipe. He's jam for the fielders. He gave them about ten chances last year and was caught both innings."

Mr. Wedderburn agreed that this was so.

"But he'll be awfully hurt if he's left out," he said.

"I'll ask about Bredon," said Mr. Tallboy.

He sought out that gentleman, who was, for once, in his own room, singing soup-slogans to himself.

> *A meal begun with Blagg's Tomato*
> *Softens every husband's heart-oh!*
>
> *Hubbies hold those wives most dear*
> *Who offer them Blagg's Turtle Clear.*
>
> *Fit for an Alderman—serve it up quick—*
> *Rum-ti-ty, tum-ti-ty, Blagg's Turtle Thick.*

"Rum-ti-ty, tum-ti-ty," said Mr. Bredon. "Hullo, Tallboy what's the matter? Don't say Nutrax has developed any more innuendos."

"Do you play cricket?"

"Well, I used to play for—" Mr. Bredon coughed; he had been about to say, "for Oxford," but remembered in time

145

that these statements could be checked. "I've played a good deal of country-house cricket in the old days. But I'm rapidly qualifying to be called a Veteran. Why?"

"I've got to scrape up an eleven for a match against Brotherhood's. We play one every year. They always beat us, of course, because they have their own playing-fields and play together regularly, but Pym likes it to be done. He thinks it fosters fellow-feeling between client and agent and all that sort of thing."

"Oh! when does it come off?"

"Saturday fortnight."

"I daresay I might keep my end up for a bit, if you can't get anybody better."

"You anything of a bowler?"

"Nothing."

"Better with the willow than the leather, eh?"

Mr. Bredon, wincing a little at this picturesqueness, admitted that, if he was anything, he was a batsman.

"Right. You wouldn't care to open the ball with Ingleby, I suppose?"

"I'd rather not. Put me down somewhere near the tail."

Tallboy nodded.

"Just as you like."

"Who captains this Eleven?"

"Well, I do, as a rule. At least, we always ask Hankin or Miller, just out of compliment, but they generally decline with thanks. Well, righty-ho; I'll just buzz round and see that the others are O.K."

The selected team went up on the office notice-board at lunch-time. At ten minutes past two, the trouble began with Mr. McAllister.

"I observe," said he, making a dour appearance in Mr. Tallboy's room, "that ye're no askin' Smayle to play for ye, and I'm thinkin' it'll be a wee bit awkward for me if I play and he does not. Workin' in his room all day and under his orders, it will make my poseetion not just so very comfortable."

"Position in the office has nothing to do with playing cricket," said Mr. Tallboy.

"Ay, imph'm, that's so. But I just do not care for it. So ye'll oblige me by leavin' my name oot."

"Just as you like," said Tallboy, annoyed. He struck Mr. McAllister's name off the list, and substituted that of Mr. Pinchley. The next defection was that of Mr. Adcock, a stolid youth from the Voucher Department. He inconsiderately fell off a step-ladder in his own home, while assisting his

146

mother to hang a picture, and broke the small bone of his leg.

In this extremity, Mr. Tallboy found himself compelled to go and eat humble pie to Mr. Smayle, and request him to play after all. But Mr. Smayle had been hurt in his feelings by being omitted from the first list, and showed no eagerness to oblige.

Mr. Tallboy, who was, indeed, a little ashamed of himself, endeavoured to gloss the matter over by making it appear that his real object in leaving out Mr. Smayle had been to make room for Mr. Bredon, who had been to Oxford and was sure to play well. But Mr. Smayle was not deceived by this specious reasoning.

"If you had come to me in the first instance," he complained, "and put the matter to me in a friendly way, I should say nothing about it. I like Mr. Bredon, and I appreciate that he has had advantages that I haven't had. He's a very gentlemanly fellow, and I should be happy to make way for him. But I do not care for having things done behind my back in a hole-and-corner fashion."

If Mr. Tallboy had said at this point, "Look here, Smayle, I'm sorry; I was rather out of temper at the time over that little dust-up we had, and I apologize"—then Mr. Smayle, who was really an amiable creature enough, would have given way and done anything that was required of him. But Mr. Tallboy chose to take a lofty tone. He said:

"Come, come, Smayle. You're not Jack Hobbs, you know."

Even this might have passed over with Mr. Smayle's ready admission that he was not England's premier batsman, had not Mr. Tallboy been unhappily inspired to say:

"Of course, I don't know about you, but *I* have always been accustomed to have these things settled by whoever was appointed to select the team, and to play or not, according as I was put down."

"Oh, yes," retorted Mr. Smayle, caught on his sensitive point, "you would say that. I am quite aware, Tallboy, that I never was at a public school, but that is no reason why I shouldn't be treated with ordinary, common courtesy. And from those who have been to real public schools, I get it, what's more. You may think a lot of Dumbleton, but it isn't what *I* call a public school."

"And what do *you* call a public school?" inquired Mr. Tallboy.

"Eton," retorted Mr. Smayle, repeating his lesson with fatal facility, "and Harrow, and—er—Rugby, and Winchester

147

and places like those. Places where they send gentlemen's sons to."

"Oh, do they?" said Mr. Tallboy. "I suppose you are sending *your* family to Eton, then."

At this, Mr. Smayle's narrow face became as white as a sheet of paper.

"You cad!" he said, choking. "You unspeakable swine. Get out of here or I'll kill you."

"What the devil's the matter with you, Smayle?" cried Mr. Tallboy, in considerable surprise.

"Get out!" said Mr. Smayle.

"Now, I'd just like a word wi' ye, Tallboy," interposed Mr. McAllister. He laid a large, hairy hand on Mr. Tallboy's arm and propelled him gently from the room.

"What on airth possessed ye to say such a thing to him?" he asked, when they were safely in the passage. "Did ye not know that Smayle has but the one boy and him feeble-minded, the poor child?"

Mr. Tallboy was really aghast. He was stricken with shame, and, like many shame-stricken people, took refuge in an outburst of rage against the nearest person handy.

"No, I didn't know. How should I be expected to know anything about Smayle's family? Good God! I'm damned sorry and all that, but why must the fellow be such an ass? He's got a mania about public schools. Eton, indeed! I don't wonder the boy's feeble-minded if he takes after his father."

Mr. McAllister was deeply shocked. His Scottish sense of decency was outraged.

"Ye ought to be damn well ashamed o' yersel'," he said, severely, and releasing Tallboy's arm, stepped back into the room he shared with Mr. Smayle and slammed the door.

Now, it is not very clear at the first glance what this disagreement between Mr. Tallboy and Mr. Smayle about a cricket match had to do with the original disagreement between the former and Mr. Copley. True, one may trace a remote connection at the beginning of things, since the Tallboy-Smayle row may be said to have started with Mr. Smayle's indiscreet jest about Mr. Tallboy's fifty pounds. But this fact has no very great importance. What is really important is that as soon as Mr. McAllister made known all the circumstances of the Tallboy-Smayle affair (which he did as soon as he could find a listener), public opinion, which, in the Tallboy-Copley dispute had been largely on Mr. Tallboy's side, veered round. It was felt that since Mr. Tallboy could behave

148

with so much unkindness to Mr. Smayle, he was probably not guiltless towards Mr. Copley. The office staff was divided like the Red Sea and rose up in walls on either hand. Only Mr. Armstrong, Mr. Ingleby, and Mr. Bredon, sardonic Gallios, held themselves apart, caring little, but fomenting the trouble for their own amusement. Even Miss Meteyard, who abominated Mr. Copley, experienced an unwonted uprush of feminine pity for him, and pronounced Mr. Tallboy's behaviour intolerable. Old Copley, she said, might be an interfering old nuisance, but he wasn't a cad. Mr. Ingleby said he really didn't think Tallboy could have meant what he said to Smayle. Miss Meteyard said: "Tell that to the marines," and, having said so, noted that the phrase would make a good headline for something-or-other. But Mr. Ingleby said, "No, that had been done."

Miss Parton, of course, was an anti-Copleyite whom nothing could move, and therefore smiled on Mr. Tallboy when he happened into the typists' room to borrow a stamp. But Miss Rossiter, though superficially more peppery, prided herself on possessing a well-balanced mind. After all, she insisted, Mr. Copley had probably meant well over the matter of the fifty pounds and, when you came to think of it, he had got Tallboy and all the rest of the Nutrax contingent out of a very tiresome sort of mess. She thought that Mr. Tallboy thought rather a lot of himself, and he had certainly had no business to speak as he had done to poor Mr. Smayle.

"And," said Miss Rossiter, "I don't like his lady friends."

"Lady friends?" said Miss Parton.

"Well, I'm not one to talk, as you know," replied Miss Rossiter, "but when you see a married man coming out of a restaurant at past midnight with somebody who is obviously not his wife—"

"No!" exclaimed Miss Parton.

"My dear! and got up regardless ... one of those little hats with an eye-veil ... three-inch diamanté heels ... such bad taste with a semi-toilette ... fish-net stockings and all. . . ."

"Perhaps it was his sister."

"My *dear!* ... And his wife's having a baby, too. . . . He didn't see me. . . . Of course, I wouldn't say a word, but I do think ..."

Thus the typewriters clacked.

Mr. Hankin, though officially impartial, was a Tallboyite. Himself a precise and efficient man, he was nevertheless perennially irritated by the precision and efficiency of Mr. Copley. He suspected, what was quite true, that Mr. Copley criticized the conduct of the department and would have liked to be given a measure of authority. Mr. Copley had a

149

way of coming to him with suggestions: "Would it not be better, Mr. Hankin, if ..." "If you will excuse my making a suggestion, Mr. Hankin, could not a stricter control be kept ... ?" "Of course, I know I am in an entirely subordinate position here, Mr. Hankin, but I have had over thirty years' experience of advertising, and in my humble opinion ..."— excellent suggestions, always, and having only the one drawback that they threatened either to annoy Mr. Armstrong, or to involve a quantity of tedious and time-wasting supervision, or to embroil the whole temperamental Copy Department and put it off its stroke. Mr. Hankin grew weary of saying: "Quite so, Mr. Copley, but Mr. Armstrong and I find it works better, on the whole, to have as few restrictions as possible." Mr. Copley had a way of saying that he quite understood, which always left Mr. Hankin with the impression that Mr. Copley thought him weak and ineffectual, and this impression had been confirmed by the Nutrax incident. When a point had arisen about which Mr. Hankin might, and ought to, have been consulted, Mr. Copley had passed him over—conclusive proof to Mr. Hankin that all Mr. Copley's valuable suggestions about departmental management were so much window-dressing, put forward to show how brilliant Mr. Copley was, and not in the least with the desire of aiding Mr. Hankin or the department. In this, Mr. Hankin's shrewdness saw much more clearly into Mr. Copley's motives than did Mr. Copley himself. He was quite right. Consequently, he was not inclined to bother himself about Mr. Copley, and was determined to give any necessary support to Mr. Tallboy. The Smayle incident was, naturally, not reported to him: he therefore made no comment upon the Cricket Eleven except to ask, mildly, why Mr. Smayle and Mr. McAllister were excluded. Mr. Tallboy replied briefly that they were unable to play, and that was the end of the matter.

Mr. Tallboy had a further ally in Mr. Barrow, who disliked the whole Copy Department on principle, because, as he complained, they were a conceited lot who were always trying to interfere with his artists and dictate to him about his displays. He admitted that, as a general proposition, the sketch was supposed to illustrate the copy, but he maintained (and with truth) that the displays suggested by the copywriters were often quite impracticable and that the copywriters took unnecessary offence over the very necessary modifications which he had to make in their "roughs." Further, he had been deeply insulted by Mr. Armstrong's remarks about himself, too faithfully reported by Mr. Ingleby, whom he detested. In fact, he was within an ace of refusing altogether to play in the same match as Mr. Ingleby.

"Oh, but, look here!" protested Mr. Tallboy, "you simply can't let me down like that! You're the best bat we've got."

"Can't you leave Ingleby out?"

This was more than awkward, for in fact Mr. Barrow, though a good and reliable bat, was by no means so good a bat as Mr. Ingleby. Mr. Tallboy hesitated:

"I don't quite see how I can do that. He made 63 last year. But I'll tell you what. I'll put him in fourth and leave you to open with somebody else—say Pinchley. Will you start with Pinchley?"

"You can't put Pinchley in first. He's nothing but a slogger."

"Who else is there?"

Mr. Barrow scanned the list mournfully.

"It's a weak bunch, Tallboy. Is that really the best you can do?"

"Afraid so."

"Pity you've managed to get across Smayle and McAllister."

"Yes—but that can't be helped now. You'll *have* to play, Mr. Barrow, or we'll have to scratch—one or the other!"

"I know what you'd better do. Put yourself in first with me."

"They won't like that. They'll think it's swank."

"Then put Garrett in."

"Very well. You'll play, then?"

"I suppose I must."

"That's very sporting of you, Mr. Barrow."

Mr. Tallboy ran down, sighing, to pin the revised list on the board:

MATCH AGAINST BROTHERHOOD'S

1. Mr. Barrow
2. Mr. Garrett
3. Mr. Hankin
4. Mr. Ingleby
5. Mr. Tallboy (Captain)
6. Mr. Pinchley
7. Mr. Miller
8. Mr. Beeseley
9. Mr. Bredon
10. Mr. Haagedorn
11. Mr. Wedderburn

He stood for a moment looking at it rather hopelessly. Then he went back to his room and took up a large sheet of foolscap, with the intention of marking off the figures for a client's appropriation over the next three months. But his mind was not on the figures. Presently he pushed the sheet aside, and sat staring blankly out of the window across the grey London roofs.

"What's up, Tallboy?" inquired Mr. Wedderburn.

"Life's the devil," said Mr. Tallboy. Then, in a sudden outburst:

"My God! how I hate this blasted place. It gets on my nerves."

"Time you had your holiday," said Mr. Wedderburn, placidly. "How's the wife?"

"All right," rejoined Mr. Tallboy, "but we shan't be able to get away till September."

"That's the worst of being a family man," replied Mr. Wedderburn. "And that reminds me. Have you done anything about that series for *The Nursing Times* about 'Nutrax for Nursing Mothers'?"

Mr. Tallboy thoughtlessly cursed the nursing mothers, dialled Mr. Hankin's room on the inter-office 'phone and in a mournful tone put in a requisition for six 4-inch doubles on that inspiring subject.

CHAPTER XI

INEXCUSABLE INVASION OF A
DUCAL ENTERTAINMENT

TO LORD PETER WIMSEY, the few weeks of his life spent in unravelling the Problem of the Iron Staircase possessed an odd dreamlike quality, noticeable at the time and still more insistent in retrospect. The very work that engaged him—or rather, the shadowy simulacrum of himself that signed itself on every morning in the name of Death Bredon—wafted him into a sphere of dim platonic archetypes, bearing a scarcely recognizable relationship to anything in the living world. Here those strange entities, the Thrifty Housewife, the Man of Discrimination, the Keen Buyer and the Good Judge, for ever young, for ever handsome, for ever virtuous, economical and inquisitive, moved to and fro upon their complicated orbits, comparing prices and values, making tests of purity, asking indiscreet questions about each other's ailments,. household expenses, bed-springs, shaving cream, diet, laundry work and boots, perpetually spending to save and saving to spend, cutting out coupons and collecting cartons, surprising husbands with margarine and wives with patent washers and vacuum cleaners, occupied from morning to night in washing, cooking, dusting, filing, saving their children from germs, their complexions from wind and weather, their teeth from decay and their stomachs from indigestion, and yet adding so many hours to the day by labour-saving appliances that they had always leisure for visiting the talkies, sprawling on the beach to picnic upon Potted Meats and Tinned Fruit, and (when adorned by So-and-so's Silks, Blank's Gloves, Dash's Footwear, Whatnot's Weatherproof Complexion Cream and Thingummy's Beautifying Shampoos), even attending Rane-lagh, Cowes, the Grand Stand at Ascot, Monte Carlo and the Queen's Drawing-Rooms. Where, Bredon asked himself, did the money come from that was to be spent so variously and so lavishly? If this hell's-dance of spending and saving were to stop for a moment, what would happen? If all the adver-tising in the world were to shut down tomorrow, would people still go on buying more soap, eating more apples.

153

giving their children more vitamins, roughage, milk, olive oil, scooters and laxatives, learning more languages by gramophone, hearing more virtuosos by radio, re-decorating their houses, refreshing themselves with more non-alcoholic thirst-quenchers, cooking more new, appetizing dishes, affording themselves that little extra touch which means so much? Or would the whole desperate whirligig slow down, and the exhausted public relapse upon plain grub and elbow-grease? He did not know. Like all rich men, he had never before paid any attention to advertisements. He had never realized the enormous commercial importance of the comparatively poor. Not on the wealthy, who buy only what they want when they want it, was the vast superstructure of industry founded and built up, but on those who, aching for a luxury beyond their reach and for a leisure for ever denied them, could be bullied or wheedled into spending their few hardly won shillings on whatever might give them, if only for a moment, a leisured and luxurious illusion. Phantasmagoria—a city of dreadful day, of crude shapes and colours piled Babel-like in a heaven of harsh cobalt and rocking over a void of bankruptcy—a Cloud Cuckoo-land, peopled by pitiful ghosts, from the Thrifty Housewife providing a Grand Family Meal for Four-pence with the aid of Dairyfields Butter Beans in Margarine, to the Typist capturing the affections of Prince Charming by a liberal use of Muggins's Magnolia Face Cream.

Among these phantasms, Death Bredon, driving his pen across reams of office foolscap, was a phantasm too, emerging from this nightmare toil to a still more fantastical existence amid people whose aspirations, rivalries and modes of thought were alien, and earnest beyond anything in his waking experience. Nor, when the Greenwich-driven clocks had jerked on to half-past five, had he any world of reality to which to return; for then the illusionary Mr. Bredon dislimned and became the still more illusionary Harlequin of a dope-addict's dream; an advertising figure more crude and fanciful than any that postured in the columns of the *Morning Star;* a thing bodiless and absurd, a mouthpiece of stale clichés shouting in dull ears without a brain. From this abominable impersonation he could not now free himself, since at the sound of his name or the sight of his unmasked face, all the doors in that other dream-city—the city of dreadful night—would be closed to him.

From one haunting disquietude, Dian de Momerie's moment of inexplicable insight had freed him. She no longer desired him. He thought she rather dreaded him; yet, at the note of the penny whistle she would come out and drive with him, hour after hour, in the great black Daimler, till night turned to daybreak. He sometimes wondered whether she believed in his existence at all; she treated him as though he were some hateful but fascinating figure in a hashish-vision. His fear now was that her unbalanced fancy might topple her over the edge of suicide. She asked him once what he was and what he wanted, and he told her stark truth, so far as it went.

"I am here because Victor Dean died. When the world knows how he died, I shall go back to the place from which I came."

"To the place from which you came. I've heard that said before, but I can't remember where."

"If you ever heard a man condemned to death, then you heard it said then."

"My God, yes! That was it. I went to a murder trial once. There was a horrible old man, the Judge—I forget his name. He was like a wicked old scarlet parrot, and he said it as though he liked it. 'And may the Lord have mercy upon your soul.' Do we have souls, Harlequin, or is that all nonsense? It is nonsense, isn't it?"

"So far as you are concerned, it probably is."

"But what have I got to do with Victor's death?"

"Nothing, I hope. But you ought to know."

"Of course I had nothing to do with it."

And indeed, she might not have. This was the most phantasmal part of the illusion—the border where daydream and night-dream marched together in an eternal twilight. The man had been murdered—of that he was now certain; but what hand had struck the blow and why was still beyond all guessing. Bredon's instinct told him to hold fast to Dian de Momerie. She was the guardian of the shadow-frontier; through her, Victor Dean, surely the most prosaic denizen of the garish city of daylight, had stepped into the place of bright flares and black abysses, whose ministers are drink and drugs and its monarch death. But question her as he might, he could get no help from her. She had told him one thing only, and over and over again he pondered it, wondering how it fitted into the plot. Milligan, the sinister Milligan, knew something about Pym's, or somebody who worked at Pym's. He had known of this before he met Dean, for he had said on meeting him: "So you're the chap, are you?" What connection was there? What had Dean, at Pym's, had to do with Milligan, before Milligan knew him? Was it merely that Dian had boasted, laughing, of having a lover from that respectable agency? Had Victor Dean died merely because of Dian's fancy for him?

Wimsey could not believe it; the fancy had died first, and

the death of Dean was, after that, surely superfluous. Besides, when they of the city of night slay for passion's sake, they lay no elaborate schemes, wipe off no finger-prints and hold no discreet tongues before or after. Brawls and revolver-shots, with loud sobs and maudlin remorse, are the signs and tokens of fatal passion among leaders of the bright life.

One other piece of information Dian had indeed given him, but at that moment he could not interpret it, and was not even aware that he held it. He could only wait, like a cat at a mouse-hole, till something popped out that he could run after. And so he passed his nights very wearily, driving the car and playing upon a penny whistle, and snatching his sleep in the small hours, before taking up the daily grind at Pym's.

Wimsey was quite right about Dian de Momerie's feeling for him. He excited her and frightened her, and, on the whole, she got a sensation of rather titillating horror at the sound of the penny whistle. But the real reason of her anxiety to propitiate him was founded on a coincidence that he could not have known and that she did not tell him.

On the day after their first encounter, Dian had backed an outsider called Acrobat, and it had come in at 50 to 1. Three days after the adventure in the woods, she had backed another outsider called Harlequin, each way, and it had come in second at 100 to 1. Thereafter, she had entertained no doubt whatever that he was a powerful and heaven-sent mascot. The day after a meeting with him was her lucky day, and it was a fact that on those days she usually succeeded in winning money in one way or another. Horses, after those first two brilliant coups, had been rather disappointing, but her fortune with cards had been good. How much of this good fortune had been due to sheer self-confidence and the will to win, only a psychologist could say; the winnings were there, and she had no doubt at all about the reason for them. She did not tell him that he was a mascot, from a superstitious feeling that to do so would be to break the luck, but she had been to a crystal-gazer, who, reading her mind like a book, had encouraged her in the belief that a mysterious stranger would bring her good fortune.

Major Milligan, sprawling upon the couch in Dian's flat with a whisky-and-soda, turned on her a pair of rather bilious eyes. He was a large, saturnine man, blank as to morals but comparatively sober in his habits, as people must be who make money out of other people's vices.

"Ever see anything of that Dean girl nowadays, Dian?"

"No, darling," said Dian, absently. She was getting rather tired of Milligan, and would have liked to break with him, if only he had not been so useful, and if she had not known too much to make a break-away healthy.

"Well, I wish you would."

"Oh, why? She's one of Nature's worst bores, darling."

"I want to know if she knows anything about that place where Dean used to work."

"The advertising place? But, Tod, how too yawn-making. Why do you want to know about advertising?"

"Oh, never mind why. I was on to something rather useful there, that's all."

"Oh!" Dian considered. This, she thought, was interesting. Something to be made out of this, perhaps. "I'll give her a ring if you like. But she's about as wet as a drowned eel. *What* do you want to know?"

"That's my business."

"Tod, I've often wanted to ask you. Why did you say I'd got to chuck Victor? Not that I cared about him, the poor fish, but I just wondered, especially after you'd told me to string him along."

"Because," replied Major Milligan, "the young what-not was trying to double-cross me."

"Good heavens, Tod—you ought to go on the talkies as Dog-faced Dick the Dope-King of the Underworld. Talk sense, darling."

"That's all very well, my girl, but your little Victor was getting to be a nuisance. Somebody had been talking to him—probably you."

"Me? that's good! There wasn't anything I could tell him. You never tell me anything, Tod."

"No—I've got some sense left."

"How rude you are, darling. Well, you see, I couldn't have split to Victor. Did you bump Victor off, Tod?"

"Who says he was bumped off?"

"A little bird told me."

"Is that your friend in the black and white checks?"

Dian hesitated. In an expansive and not very sober moment, she had told Tod about her adventure in the woods, and now rather wished she had not. Milligan took her silence for consent and went on:

"Who is that fellow, Dian?"

"Haven't the foggiest."

"What's he want?"

"He doesn't want me, at any rate," said Dian. "Isn't that humiliating, Tod?"

"It must be." Milligan grinned. "But what's the big idea?"

"I think he's on Victor's lay, whatever that was. He said he wouldn't be here if Victor hadn't popped off. Too thrilling, don't you think?"

"Um," said Milligan. "I think I'd like to meet this friend of yours. When's he likely to turn up?"

"Damned if I know. He just arrives. I don't think I'd have anything to do with him, Tod, if I were you. He's dangerous—queer, somehow. I've got a hunch about him."

"Your brain's going to mush, sweetest," said Milligan, "and he's trading on it, that's all."

"Oh, well," said Dian, "he amuses me, and you don't any more. You're getting to be a bit feeding, Tod." She yawned and trailed over to the looking-glass, where she inspected her face narrowly. "I think I'll give up dope, Tod. I'm getting puffy under the eyes. Do you think it would be amusing to go all good?"

"About as amusing as a Quaker meeting. Has your friend been trying to reform you? That's damn good."

"Reform me, nothing. But I'm looking horribly hag-like tonight. Oh hell; what's the odds, anyway? Let's do something."

"All right. Come on round to Slinker's. He's throwing a party."

"I'm sick of Slinker's parties. I say, Tod, let's go and gate-crash something really virtuous. Who's the stickiest old cat in London that's got anything on?"

"Dunno."

"Tell you what. We'll scoop up Slinker's party and go round and look for striped awnings, and crash the first thing we see."

"Right-ho! I'm on."

Half an hour later, a noisy gang, squashed into five cars and a taxi, were whooping through the quieter squares of the West End. Even today, a few strongholds of the grimly aristocratic are left in Mayfair, and Dian, leaning from the open window of the leading car, presently gave tongue before a tall, old-fashioned house, whose entrance was adorned with a striped awning, a crimson carpet and an array of hothouse plants in tubs upon the steps.

"Whoopee! Hit it up, boys! Here's something! Whose is it?"

"My God!" said Slinger Braithwaite. "We've hit the bull, all right. It's Denver's place."

"You won't get in there," said Milligan. "The Duchess of

Denver is heaven's prize frozen-face. Look at the chuckerou
in the doorway. Better try something easier."

"Easier be damned. We said the first we came to, and this
is the first. No ratting, darlings."

"Well, look here," said Milligan, "we'd better try the back
entrance. There's a gate into the garden round the other side,
opening on the car-park. We've more chance there."

From the other side, the assault turned out to be easy
enough. The cars were parked in a back street, and on
approaching the garden gate, they found it wide open, displaying a marquee, in which supper was being held. A bunch
of guests came out just as they arrived, while, almost on their
heels, two large cars drove up and disgorged a large party of
people.

"Blow being announced," said an immaculate person,
"we'll just barge right in and dodge the Ambassadors."

"Freddy, you can't."

"Can't I? You watch me." Freddy tucked his partner's arr
firmly under his own and marched with determination up to
the gate. "We're certain to barge into old Peter or somebody
in the garden."

Dian nipped Milligan's arm, and the pair of them fell in
behind the new arrivals. The gate was passed—but a footman
just inside presented an unexpected obstacle.

"Mr. and Mrs. Frederick Arbuthnot," said the immaculate
gentleman. "And party," he added, waving a vague hand
behind him.

"Well, *we're* in, anyhow," exulted Dian.

Helen, Duchess of Denver, looked round with satisfaction
upon her party. It was all going very nicely indeed. The
Ambassador and his wife had expressed delight at the quality
of the wine. The band was good, the refreshments more than
adequate. A tone of mellow decorum pervaded the atmosphere. Her own dress, she thought, became her, although
her mother-in-law, the Dowager Duchess, had said something
rather acid about her spine. But then, the Dowager was
always a little tiresome and incalculable. One must be fashionable, though one would not, of course, be vulgarly immodest. Helen considered that she was showing the exact
number of vertebrae that the occasion demanded. One less
would be incorrect; one more would be over-modern. She
thanked Providence that at forty-five she still kept her
figure—as indeed, she did, having been remarkably flat o
both aspects the whole of her life.

She was just raising a well-earned glass of champagne to

her lips when she paused, and set it down again. Something was wrong. She glanced hurriedly round for her husband. He was not there, but a few paces off an elegant black back and smooth, straw-coloured head of hair announced the presence of her brother-in-law, Wimsey. Hastily excusing herself to Lady Mendip, with whom she had been discussing the latest enormities of the Government, she edged her way through the crowd and caught Wimsey's arm.

"Peter! Look over there. Who are those people?"

Wimsey turned and stared in the direction pointed by the Duchess' fan.

"Good God, Helen! You've caught a pair of ripe ones this time! That's the de Momerie girl and her tame dope-merchant."

The Duchess shuddered.

"How horrible! Disgusting woman! How in the world did they get in? . . . Do you know them?"

"Not officially, no."

"Thank goodness! I was afraid you'd let them in. I never know what you're going to do next; you know so many impossible people."

"Not guilty this time, Helen."

"Ask Bracket how he came to let them in."

"I fly," said Wimsey, "to obey your behest."

He finished the drink he had in his hand, and set off in a leisurely manner in pursuit of the footman. Presently he returned.

"Bracket says they came with Freddy Arbuthnot."

"Find Freddy."

The Hon. Freddy Arbuthnot, when found, denied all knowledge of the intruders. "But there was a bit of a scrum at the gate, you know," he admitted, ingenuously, "and I daresay they barged in with the crowd. The de Momerie girl, eh, what? Where is she? I must have a look at her. Hot stuff and all that, what?"

"You will do nothing of the sort, Freddy. Where in the world is Gerald? Not here. He never is when he's wanted. You'll have to go and turn them out, Peter."

Wimsey, who had had time for a careful calculation, asked nothing better.

"I will turn them out," he announced, "like one John Smith. Where are they?"

The Duchess, who had kept a glassy eye upon them, waved a stern hand in the direction of the terrace. Wimsey ambled off amiably.

"Forgive me, dear Lady Mendip," said the Duchess, return-

160

ing to her guest. "I had a little commission to give to my brother-in-law."

Up the dimly-lit terrace steps went Wimsey. The shadow of a tall pillar-rose fell across his face and chequered his white shirt-front with dancing black; and as he went he whistled softly: "Tom, Tom, the piper's son."

Dian de Momerie clutched Milligan's arm as she turned.

Wimsey stopped whistling.

"Er—good evening," he said, "excuse me. Miss de Momerie, I think."

"Harlequin!" cried Dian.

"I beg your pardon?"

"Harlequin. So here you are. I've got you this time. And I'm going to see your face properly if I die for it."

"I'm afraid there is some mistake," said Wimsey.

Milligan thought it time to interfere.

"Ah!" said he, "the mysterious stranger. I think it's time you and I had a word, young man. May I ask why you have been tagging round after this lady in a mountebank get-up?"

"I fear," said Wimsey, more elaborately, "that you are labouring under a misapprehension, sir, whoever you are. I have been dispatched by the Duchess on a—forgive me—somewhat distasteful errand. She regrets that she has not the honour of this lady's acquaintance, nor, sir, of yours, and wishes me to ask you by whose invitation you are here."

Dian laughed, rather noisily.

"You do it marvellously, darling," she said. "We gate-crashed on the dear old bird—same as you did, I expect."

"So the Duchess inferred," replied Wimsey. "I am sorry. I'm afraid I must ask you to leave at once."

"That's pretty good," said Milligan, insolently. "I'm afraid it won't work. It may be a fact that we weren't invited here, but we aren't going to turn out for a nameless acrobat who's afraid to show his face."

"You must be mistaking me for a friend of yours," said Wimsey. "Allow me." He stepped across to the nearest pillar and pressed a switch, flooding that end of the terrace with light. "My name is Peter Wimsey; I am Denver's brother, and my face—such as it is, is entirely at your service."

He fixed his monocle in his eye and stared unpleasantly at Milligan.

"But aren't you my Harlequin?" protested Dian. "Don't be such an ass—I know you are. I know your voice perfectly well—and your mouth and chin. Besides, you were whistling that tune."

"This is very interesting," said Wimsey. "Is it possible—I

161

fear it is—I think you must have encountered my unfortunate cousin Bredon."

"That was the name—" began Dian, uncertainly, and stopped.

"I am glad to hear it," replied Wimsey. "Sometimes he gives mine, which makes it very awkward."

"See here, Dian," broke in Milligan, "you seem to have dropped a brick. You'd better apologize and then we'll clear. Sorry we crashed in, and all that—"

"One moment," said Wimsey. "I should like to hear more about this. Be good enough to come into the house for a moment. This way."

He ushered them courteously round the corner of the terrace, up a side path and by way of a French window into a small ante-room, laid out with tables and a cocktail bar.

"What will you drink? Whiskies? I might have known it. The abominable practice of putting whisky on top of mixed drinks late at night is responsible for more ruined complexions and reputations than any other single cause. There is many a woman now walking the streets of London through putting whisky on top of gin cocktails. Two stiff whiskies, Tomlin, and a liqueur brandy."

"Very good, my lord."

"You perceive," said Wimsey, returning with the drinks, "the true object of this hospitable gesture. I have established my identity, by the evidence of the reliable Tomlin. Let us now seek a spot less open to interruption. I suggest the library. This way. My brother, being an English gentleman, possesses a library in all his houses, though he never opens a book. This is called fidelity to ancient tradition. The chairs, however, are comfortable. Pray be seated. And now, tell me all about your encounter with my scandalous cousin."

"One moment," said Milligan, before Dian could speak. "I think I know the stud-book pretty well. I was not aware that you had a cousin Bredon."

"It is not every puppy that appears in the kennel-book," replied Wimsey carelessly, "and it is a wise man that knows all his own cousins. But what matter? Family is family, though indicated by the border compony (or gobony if you prefer that form of the word) or by the bend or baton sinister, called by most writers of fiction the bar sinister, for reasons which I am unable to determine. My regrettable cousin Bredon, having no particular right to one family name more than another, makes it his practice to employ them all in turn, thus displaying a happy absence of favouritism. Please help yourselves to smokes. You will find the cigars passable, Mr.—er—"

162

"Milligan."

"Ah the notor—the well-known Major Milligan? You have a residence on the river, I fancy. Charming, charming. Its fame has reached me from time to time through my good brother-in-law, Chief-Inspector Parker of Scotland Yard. A beautiful, retired spot, I believe?"

"Just so," said Milligan. "I had the pleasure of entertaining your cousin there one night."

"Did he gate-crash on you? That is exactly what he would do. And you have retorted upon my dear sister-in-law. Poetic justice, of course. I appreciate it—though possibly the Duchess will take a different view of the matter."

"No; he was brought by a lady of my acquaintance."

"He is improving. Major Milligan, painful though it may be to me, I feel that I ought to warn you against that cousin of mine. He is definitely not nice to know. If he has been thrusting his attentions upon Miss de Momerie, it is probably with some ulterior object. Not," added Wimsey, "that any man would need an ulterior object for such attentions. Miss de Momerie is an object in herself—"

His eye wandered over Dian, scantily clothed and slightly intoxicated, with a cold appraisement which rendered the words almost impertinent.

"But," he resumed, "I know my cousin Bredon—too well. Few people know him better. And I must confess that he is the last man to whom I should look for a disinterested attachment. I am unhappily obliged, in self-defence, to keep an eye on Cousin Bredon's movements, and I should be deeply grateful to be informed of the details of his latest escapade."

"All right, I'll tell you," said Dian. The whisky had strung her up to recklessness, and she became suddenly voluble, disregarding Milligan's scowls. She poured out the tale of her adventures. The incident of the fountain-dive seemed to cause Lord Peter Wimsey acute distress.

"Vulgar ostentation!" he said, shaking his head. "How many times have I implored Bredon to conduct himself in a quiet and reasonable manner."

"I thought he was too marvellous," said Dian, and proceeded to relate the encounter in the wood.

"He always plays 'Tom, Tom, the piper's son,' so of course, when you came along whistling it, I thought it was him."

Wimsey's face darkened in a most convincing manner.

"Disgusting," he said.

"Besides, you are so much alike—the same voice and the

163

same face as far as one can see it, you know. But of course he never took off his mask—"

"No wonder," said Wimsey, "no wonder." He heaved a deep sigh. "The police are interested in my cousin Bredon."

"How thrilling!"

"What for?" demanded Milligan.

"For impersonating me, among other things," said Wimsey, now happily launched and well away. "I cannot tell you in the brief time at our disposal, the distress and humiliation I have been put to on Bredon's account. Bailing him out at police stations—honouring cheques drawn in my name—rescuing him from haunts of infamy—I am telling you all these distressing details in confidence, of course."

"We won't split," said Dian.

"He trades upon our unfortunate resemblance," went on Wimsey. "He copies my habits, smokes my favourite brand of cigarettes, drives a car like mine, even whistles my favourite air—one, I may say, peculiarly well adapted for performance upon the penny whistle."

"He must be pretty well off," said Dian, "to drive a car like that."

"That," said Wimsey, "is the most melancholy thing of all. I suspect him—but perhaps I had better not say anything about that."

"Oh, do tell," urged Dian, her eyes dancing with excitement. "It sounds too terribly breath-taking."

"I suspect him," said Wimsey, in solemn and awful tones, "of having to do with—smug-druggling—I mean, dash it all—drug-smuggling."

"You don't say so," said Milligan.

"Well, I can't prove it. But I have received warnings from a certain quarter. You understand me." Wimsey selected a fresh cigarette and tapped it, with the air of one who has closed the coffin-lid upon a dead secret and is nailing it down securely. "I don't want to interfere in your affairs in any way at all, Major Milligan. I trust that I shall never be called upon to do so." Here he transfixed Milligan with another hard stare. "But you will perhaps allow me to give you, and this lady, a word of warning. Do not have too much to do with my cousin Bredon."

"I think you're talking rot," said Dian. "Why, you can't even get him to—"

"Cigarette, Dian?" interrupted Milligan, rather sharply.

"I do not say," resumed Wimsey, raking Dian slowly with his eyes, and then turning again to Milligan, "that my deplorable cousin is himself an addict to cocaine or heroin or

164

anything of that description. In some ways, it would be almost more respectable if he were. The man or woman who can batten on the weaknesses of his fellow-creatures without sharing them is, I admit, to me a singularly disgusting object. I may be old-fashioned, but there it is."

"Quite so," said Milligan.

"I do not know, and do not wish to know," went on Wimsey, "how you came to allow my cousin Bredon into your house, nor what, on his side, can have brought him there. I prefer not to suppose that he found there any other attraction than good drinks and good company. You may think, Major Milligan, that because I have interested myself in certain police cases, I am a consistent busybody. That is not the case. Unless I am forced to take an interest in another man's business, I greatly prefer to let him alone. But I think it only fair to tell you that I *am* forced to take an interest in my cousin Bredon and that he is a person whose acquaintance might prove—shall I say, embarrassing?—to any one who preferred to live a quiet life. I don't think I need say any more, need I?"

"Not at all," said Milligan. "I am much obliged to you for the warning, and so, I am sure, is Miss de Momerie."

"Of course, I'm frightfully glad to know all about it," said Dian. "Your cousin sounds a perfect lamb. I like 'em dangerous. Pompous people are too terribly moribund, aren't they?"

Wimsey bowed.

"My dear lady, your choice of friends is entirely at your own discretion."

"I'm glad to hear it. I got the impression that the Duchess wasn't too fearfully anxious to have both arms round my neck."

"Ah! the Duchess—no. There, I fear, all the discretion is on the other side, what? Which reminds me—"

"Quite right," said Milligan. "We have trespassed on your hospitality too long. We must really apologize and remove ourselves. By the way, there were some other members of our party—"

"I expect my sister-in-law will have dealt with them by now," said Wimsey with a grin. "If not, I will make a point of seeing them and telling them that you have gone on to—where shall I say?"

Dian gave her own address.

"You'd better come round and have a drink, too," she suggested.

"Alas!" said Wimsey, "duty and all that sort of thing, what? Can't leave my sister-in-law in the lurch, greatly as I

165

should enjoy the entertainment." He rang the bell. "You will excuse me now, I trust. I must see to our other guests. Porlock, show this lady and gentleman out."

He returned to the garden by way of the terrace, whistling a passage of Bach, as was his way when pleased.

"Nun gehn wir wo der Tudelsack, der Tudel, tudel, tudel, tudel, tudelsack . . ."

"I wonder, was the fly too big and gaudy? Will he rise to it? We shall see."

"My dear Peter," said the Duchess, fretfully, "what a terrible time you have been. Please go and fetch Mme. de Framboise-Douillet an ice. And tell your brother I want him."

CHAPTER XII

SURPRISING ACQUISITION OF A
JUNIOR REPORTER

VERY early one morning, a junior reporter on the *Morning Star*, of no importance to anybody except himself and his widowed mother, walked out of that great newspaper's palatial new offices and into the affairs of Chief-Inspector Parker. This nonentity's name was Hector Puncheon, and he was in Fleet Street at that time because a fire had broken out the previous night in a large City warehouse, destroying a great deal of valuable property and involving the spectacular escapes of three night watchmen and a cat from the roofs of the adjacent buildings. Hector Puncheon, summoned to the scene for the excellent reason that he had lodgings in the West Central district and could be transported to the scene of action in a comparatively brief time, had written a short stop-press notice of the disaster for the early country editions, a longer and more exciting account for the London edition, and then a still longer and more detailed report, complete with the night-watchmen's and eye-witnesses' stories and a personal interview with the cat, for the early editions of the *Evening Comet,* twin-organ to the *Morning Star* and housed in the same building.

After completing all this toil, he was wakeful and hungry. He sought an all-night restaurant in Fleet Street, accustomed to catering for the untimely needs of pressmen, and, having previously armed himself with a copy of the *Morning Star* as it poured out damp from the machines, sat down to a 3 a.m. breakfast of grilled sausages, coffee and rolls.

He ate with leisurely zest, pleased with himself and his good fortune, and persuaded that not even the most distinguished of the senior men could have turned in a column more full of snap, pep and human interest than his own. The interview with the cat had been particularly full of appeal. The animal was, it seemed, an illustrious rat-catcher, with many famous deeds to her credit. Not only that, but she had been the first to notice the smell of fire and had, by her anguished and intelligent mewings, attracted the attention of night-watchman number one, who had been in the act of brewing himself a cup of tea when the outbreak took place. Thirdly, the cat, an ugly black-and-white creature with a spotted face, was about to become a mother for the tenth time, and Hector Puncheon by a brilliant inspiration had secured the reversion of the expected family for the *Morning Star,* so that half a dozen or so fortunate readers might, by applying to their favourite paper and enclosing a small donation for the Animals' Hospital, become the happy owners of kittens with a prenatal reputation and a magnificent rat-catching pedigree. Hector Puncheon felt that he had done well. He had been alert and courageous, offering the night-watchman ten shillings on his own responsibility the very moment the big idea occurred to him, and the night-editor had okayed the stunt and even remarked that it would do quite well.

Filled with sausages and contentment, Hector Puncheon lingered over his paper, reading the Special Friday Feature with approval and appreciating the political cartoon. At length, he folded the sheet, stuffed it in his pocket, tipped the waiter extravagantly with sixpence and emerged into Fleet Street.

The morning was fine, though chilly, and he felt that after his night's labours, a little walk would do him good. He strolled happily along, past the Griffin at Temple Bar and the Law Courts and the churches of St. Clement Danes and St. Mary-le-Strand, and made his way up Kingsway. It was only when he got to the turning into Great Queen Street that he became aware of something lacking in an otherwise satisfactory universe. Great Queen Street led into Long Acre; off Long Acre lay Covent Garden; already the vans and lorries laden with fruit and flowers were rumbling in from all over the country and rumbling out again. Already the porters were unloading their stout sacks, huge crates, round baskets, frail punnets and long flat boxes filled with living scent and colour, sweating and grumbling over their labours as though their exquisite burdens were so much fish or pig-iron. And for the benefit of these men the pubs would be open, for Covent Garden interprets the London licensing regulations to suit its own topsy-turvy hours of labour. Hector Puncheon had had a successful night and had celebrated his success with sausages and coffee; but there are, dash it all! more suitable methods of celebration.

Hector Puncheon, swinging blithely along in his serviceable grey flannel bags and tweed jacket, covered by an old burberry, suddenly realized that he owned the world, including all the beer in Covent Garden Market. He turned into Great

Queen Street, traversed half the length of Long Acre, dodged under the nose of a van horse at the entrance to the Underground Station, and set his face towards the market, picking his way cheerfully between the boxes and baskets and carts and straw that littered the pavement. Humming a lively tune, he turned in through the swing doors of the White Swan.

Although it was only a quarter past four, the Swan was already doing a brisk trade. Hector Puncheon edged his way up to the bar between two enormous carters and waited modestly for the landlord to finish serving his habitual customers before calling attention to himself. A lively discussion was going on about the merits of a dog named Forked Lightning. Hector, always ready to pick up a hint about anything that was, or might conceivably be turned into news, pulled his early *Morning Star* from his pocket and pretended to read it, while keeping his ears open.

"And what I say is," said Carter the First, "—same again, Joe—what I say is, when a dawg that's fancied like that dawg is, stops dead 'arf way round the course like as if 'e'd a-bin shot, wot I say is, I likes to know wot's at the back of it."

"Ar," said Carter the Second.

"Mind you," went on Carter the First, "I ain't sayin' as animals is always to be relied on. They 'as their off-days, same as you an' me, but wot I says is—"

"That's a fact," put in a smaller man, from the other side of Carter the Second, "that's a fact, that is. An' wot's more, they 'as their fancies. I 'ad a dawg once as couldn't abide the sight of a goat. Or maybe it was the smell. I dunno. But show 'im a goat any time, and 'e got a fit of the trembles. Couldn't run all day. I remember one time when I was bringin' 'im up to run at the White City, there was a bloke in the street leadin' two goats on a string—"

"Wot did a bloke want with two goats?" demanded Carter the Second, suspiciously.

" 'Ow should I know wot 'e wanted with goats?" retorted the little man, indignantly. "They wasn't my goats, was they? Well, that there dawg—"

"That's different," said Carter the First. "Nerves is nerves, and a thing like a goat might 'appen to anybody, but wot I says is—"

"What's yours, sir?" inquired the landlord.

"Oh, I think I'll have a Guinness," said Hector. "Guinness is good for you—particularly on a chilly morning. Perhaps," he added, feeling pleased with himself and the world, "these gentlemen will join me."

169

The two carters and the little man expressed their gratification, and ordered beer.

"It's a queer thing, this business of nerves," said the little man. "Talking of Guinness, now, my old aunt had a parrot. Some bird it was, too. Learnt to speak from a sailor. Fortunately the old lady couldn't 'ear 'alf of wot it said, and didn't understand the other 'alf. Now, that there bird——"

"You seem to have had a wide experience with livestock," observed Hector Puncheon.

"I 'ave that," said the little man. "That there bird, as I was going to say, got fits of nerves as would surprise you. 'Unched 'isself up on 'is perch like, and shivered fit to shake 'isself to pieces. And wot was the reason of that, do you think?"

"Beggared if I know," said Carter the Second. "Your 'ealth, sir."

"Mice," said the little man, triumphantly. "Couldn't stand the sight of a mouse. And wot do you think we 'ad to give it to pull it round, like?"

"Brandy," suggested Carter the First. "Nothing like brandy for parrots. We got one at 'ome—one o' them green sort. My wife's brother brought it 'ome with 'im——"

"They ain't such good talkers as the grey ones," said Carter the Second. "There was a parrot at the old Rose & Crown dahn Seven Dials way——"

"Brandy?" scoffed the little man, "not 'im. 'E wouldn't look at brandy."

"Wouldn't 'e now?" said Carter the First. "Now, you show our old bird brandy, an' 'el'll 'op right out of 'is cage for it same as a Christian. Not too much, mind you, but give it 'im neat in a teaspoon——"

"Well, it wasn't brandy," persisted the little man. "Aunt's was a teetotal bird, 'e was. Now, I'll give you three guesses, an' if you gets it right, I'll stand drinks all round, and I can't say fairer 'an that."

"Aspirin?" suggested the landlord, anxious that the round of drinks should be stood by somebody.

The little man shook his head.

"Ginger," said Carter the Second. "Birds is sometimes wonderful fond o' ginger. Stimulates the innards. Though, mind you, some says it's too 'eatin', an' brings their fevvers aht."

"Nutrax for Nerves," suggested Hector Puncheon, a little wildly, his eye having been caught by that morning's half-double, which carried the intriguing headline: "WHY BLAME THE WOMAN?"

"Nutrax nothing," snorted the little man, "nor none o' yer

patent slops. No. Strong coffee wiv' cayenne pepper in it— that's wot that bird liked. Put 'im right in a jiff, it did. Well, seein' as the drinks ain't on me this time—"

He looked wistful, and Hector obliged again with the same all round. Carter the Second, jerking his beer off at one gulp and offering a general salute to the company, shouldered his way out, and the little man moved up closer to Hector Puncheon to make way for a florid person in evening dress, who had just shot his way in through the door and now stood swaying a little uncertainly against the bar.

"Scotch-and-soda," said this person, without preface, "double Scotch and not too bloody much soda."

The landlord looked at him keenly.

"Thass all right," said the newcomer, "I know what you're thinking, my boy, but I'm not drunk. Norra bittovit. Nerves a liddleoutavorder, 'tsall." He paused, evidently conscious that his speech was getting a little ahead of itself. "Been sittin' up with a sick friend," he explained, carefully. "Very trying to the system, sittin' up all night. Very hard on the conshi-conshishushion—excuse me—slight acshident to my dental plate, mush gettitsheento."

He leaned one elbow on the bar, pawed vaguely with his foot for the brass rail, pushed his silk hat well to the back of his head and beamed pleasantly upon the company.

The landlord of the Swan looked at him again with a practised eye, calculated that his customer could probably carry one more Scotch-and-soda without actual disaster, and fulfilled his order.

"Thanks verrimush, old feller," said the stranger. "Well, goo' luck, all. What are these gentlemen taking?"

Hector Puncheon excused himself politely, explaining that he had really had all he wanted and must now be going home.

"No, no," said the other, hurt. "Mustn't say that. Nottime to gome yet. Night yet young." He flung an affectionate arm round Hector's neck. "I like your face. You're the sortafeller I like. You must come along one day 'n see my little place. Roses roun' the porch an' all that. Give you my card." He hunted in his pockets and produced a note-case, which he flapped open on the bar-counter. A quantity of small pieces of paper flew out right and left.

"Dashitall," said the gentleman in dress clothes, "what I mean, dashit." Hector stooped to pick up some of the scattered oddments, but the little man was before him.

"Thanks, thanks," said the gentleman. "Wheresh card? Thatsh not card, thatsh my wife's shopping-list—you gorrawife?"

"Not yet," admitted Hector.

"Lucky devil," replied the stranger with emphasis. "No wife, no damned shopping-list." His vagrant attention was caught and held by the shopping-list, which he held up in one hand and tried, unsuccessfully, to focus with a slightly squinting gaze. "Alwaysh bringing home parcels like a blurry errand-boy. Where'd I put that parcel now?"

"You 'adn't no parcel when you come in 'ere, guv'nor," said Carter the First. The question of drinks seemed to have been shelved, and the worthy man no doubt felt it was time to remind the gentleman that there were others in the bar, besides the abstemious Mr. Puncheon. "Dry work," he added, "cartin' parcels round."

"Damn dry," said the married gentleman. "Mine's a Scotch-and-soda. Whaddid you say you'd have, ol' boy?" He again embraced Hector Puncheon, who gently disentangled himself.

"I really don't want—" he began; but, seeing that this reiterated refusal might give offence, he gave way and asked for a half-tankard of bitter.

"Talking about parrots," said a thin voice behind them. Hector started and, looking round, observed a dried-up old man seated at a small table in the corner of the bar, absorbing a gin-and-potash. He must have been there all the time, thought Hector.

The gentleman in dress clothes swung round upon him so sharply that he lost his balance and had to cling to the little man to save himself.

"I never mentioned parrots," he said, enunciating the words very distinctly. "I shouldn't think of talking about parrots."

"I once knowed a parson wot 'ad a parrot," continued the old man. "Joey, they called 'im."

"Wot, the parson?" asked the little man.

"No, the parrot," said the old fellow, mildly, "and that there parrot hadn't ever been out of the parson's family. Joined in family prayers, he did and said 'Amen' like a Christian. Well, one day this here parson—"

A rush of customers entering from the market drew the landlord's attention away and drowned the next sentence or so of the story. The carter hailed some acquaintances and joined them in a fresh round of beer. Hector, shaking off the intoxicated gentleman, who seemed now to be inviting him to join a cozy little fishing party in Scotland, turned to go, but found himself caught and held by the old man.

"—and old parson found the bishop sitting over the cage with a lump of sugar in his fingers, saying, 'Come on, Joey, say it! B ... b ... b ... !' And that, mind you," said the old man, "was a Church of England bishop. And what do you think the bishop did then?"

"I can't imagine," said Hector.

"Made the parson a canon," said the old man, triumphantly.

"Never!" said Hector.

"But that's nothing," pursued the old man. "There was a parrot I knew down in Somerset—"

Hector felt he really could not bear to hear about the parrot down in Somerset. He extricated himself politely and fled.

His next activity was to go home and have a bath, after which he coiled himself up on his bed and slept placidly till his normal breakfast-time at nine.

He breakfasted in his dressing-gown, and it was when he was transferring his various possessions from his grey flannels to his navy lounge suit that he came upon the little packet. It was neatly done up with sealing-wax in white paper, and bore the innocent label "Bicarbonate of Soda." He stared at it in surprise.

Hector Puncheon was a young man with a hearty and healthy digestion. He had heard, of course, of sodium bicarb, and its virtues, but only as a wealthy man hears of hire-purchase. For the moment he thought he must have accidentally picked the little package up in the bathroom and slipped it into his pocket unaware. Then he remembered that he had not taken his coat into the bathroom that morning, and that he had emptied out the pockets the previous night. He distinctly recollected that, when the summons to the fire had reached him, he had had to tumble hurriedly into them the few odds and ends he habitually carried about him—handkerchief, keys, loose cash, pencils and what-not, taken from his dressing-table. It was quite inconceivable that there should have been any bicarbonate on his dressing-table.

Hector Puncheon was puzzled. A glance at the clock, however, reminded him that he had no time for puzzlement just then. He had to get down to St. Margaret's, Westminster, by 10.30 to report the wedding of a fashionable beauty who was being married in the strictest secrecy at that unfashionable hour. He had then to hasten back to report a political meeting in Kingsway Hall, and thence he must gallop round the corner to attend a luncheon given to a distinguished airman in the Connaught Rooms. If the speeches were over by 3 o'clock, he could then make a dash for a train and get out to Esher, where a royalty was opening a new school and inaugurating it with a children's tea-party.

After which, if he were still alive, and had contrived to get his copy written up in the train, he could turn it in at the office and find time to think.

This strenuous programme was carried out without more than the usual number of exasperating hitches, and not until he had pushed the last sheet of copy over to the sub-editor, and was sitting, tired but conscious of work well done, in the Cock Tavern, tackling a beef-steak, did he give another thought to the mysterious packet of sodium bicarb. And now, the more he thought about it, the odder the incident became.

He ran over in his mind the various activities of the previous night. At the fire, he remembered now quite distinctly, he had put on his burberry and buttoned it up, by way of protecting his light grey flannels against showers of smuts and the spray of the firemen's hoses. The mysterious package could hardly have been placed in his jacket-pocket then. After that, there had been interviews with various people—including the cat—the writing of his copy in the *Morning Star* offices and his breakfast in the Fleet Street eating-house. To suppose that he had accidentally found and pocketed four ounces of bicarbonate on any of these occasions seemed to him fantastic. Unless, of course, one of his newspaper colleagues had put the thing there for a joke. But who? And why?

He went on to consider the walk home and the conversation in the White Swan. His exhilarated acquaintance in dress clothes was the kind of man, he thought, who might from time to time require the assistance of a mild digestive and carminative. Possibly in one of his more affectionate moments he might have slipped the packet into Hector's coat-pocket by mistake for his own. The two carters would not, Mr. Puncheon felt sure, be carrying drugs round with them. . . .

Drugs. As the word shaped itself in his mind—for Hector Puncheon usually thought articulately, and often, indeed, conversed quite sensibly aloud with his own soul—an enormous query shot up in his brain. Bicarbonate of soda, hell! He was ready to stake his journalistic reputation it was nothing of the sort. His fingers sought the packet, which he had thrust back into the pocket where he had found it, and he was on the point of opening it and investigating the contents when a better idea struck him. Leaving his rump-steak half finished, and muttering to the astonished waiter that he would be back in a minute, he ran out hatless to the establishment of the nearest chemist, one Mr. Tweedle, who knew him well.

174

Mr. Tweedle's shop was shut, but a light still burned within, and Hector hammered violently until the door was opened by an assistant. Was Mr. Tweedle in? Yes, he was in, but he was just going. On being assured that Mr. Puncheon wanted to see Mr. Tweedle personally, the assistant volunteered to see what could be done.

Mr. Tweedle, hatted and coated, appeared from the inner recesses of the shop with just enough delay to make Hector feel that he had acted with some precipitation and had probably started out upon a wild-goose chase. Once started, however, he had to go through with it.

"Look here, Tweedle," he said, "I'm sorry to bother you, and there's probably nothing in it, but I wish you'd have a look at this for me. It came into my hands in rather a curious way."

The chemist received the packet and held it balanced in his hand for a moment.

"What's wrong with it?"

"I don't know that anything's wrong with it. I want you to tell me."

"Bicarbonate of soda," said Mr. Tweedle, glancing at the label and at the sealed flaps of the package. "No chemist's name—the ordinary printed label. You don't seem to have opened it."

"No, I haven't, and I want you to bear witness to that, if necessary. It appears to be just as it came from the chemist, doesn't it?"

"It appears to be, certainly," rejoined Mr. Tweedle in some surprise. "The label seems to be the original label and the ends have apparently only been sealed once, if that is what you want to know."

"Yes, and I couldn't have sealed it up like that, could I? I mean, it looks professional."

"Quite."

"Well, now, if you're quite satisfied about that, open it."

Mr. Tweedle carefully inserted a penknife beneath one flap, broke the wax and opened up the paper. The packet was, as might have been expected, filled with a fine white powder.

"What next?" inquired Mr. Tweedle.

"Well, is it bicarbonate of soda?"

Mr. Tweedle shook some of the powder out into the palm of his hand, looked closely at it, smelt it, moistened his finger and took up a few grains, and then carried them to his tongue. Then his face changed. He took out his handkerchief, wiped his mouth, poured the powder from his palm carefully back into the paper and asked:

175

"How did you get hold of this?"

"I'll tell you in a moment," said Hector. "What is it?"

"Cocaine," said Mr. Tweedle.

"Are you sure?"

"Positive."

"My God!" cried Hector, jubilantly. "I'm on to something! What a day! Here, Tweedle, can you spare a moment? I want you to come round to our place and tell Hawkins about this."

"Where? What?" demanded Mr. Tweedle.

Hector Puncheon wasted no more words, but grabbed him by the arm. Thus, on Mr. Hawkins, news-editor of the *Morning Star*, there burst an agitated member of his own staff, with a breathless witness in tow, and an exhibit of cocaine.

Mr. Hawkins was a keen newspaper man and rejoiced in a stunt. He had, nevertheless, a certain conscience in such matters, so far as giving information to the police was concerned. For one thing, it does a newspaper no good to be on bad terms with the police, and, for another, there had only recently been trouble about another case in which information had been held up. Having, therefore, heard Hector Puncheon's story and scolded him soundly for having waited so long before examining the mysterious package, he telephoned to Scotland Yard.

Chief-Inspector Parker, with his arm in a sling and his nerves very much on edge, received the information in his own home, just as he thought his day's work was happily done with. He grumbled horribly; but there had been a good deal of fuss made lately at the Yard about dope-gangs, and things had been said which he resented. He irritably called a taxi and trundled down to the *Morning Star* offices, accompanied by a morose person called Sergeant Lumley, who disliked him, and whom he disliked, but who happened to be the only sergeant available.

By this time, Hector Puncheon's excitement had rather worn off. He was getting sleepy and stupid after a broken night and a hard day's work. He could not control his yawns, and the Chief-Inspector snapped at him. In answer to questions he managed, however, to give a fairly complete account of his movements during the night and early morning.

"Actually, then," said Parker, when the tale was finished, "you can't say with any certainty when you received this packet?"

"No, I can't," said Hector, resentfully. He could not help feeling that it was very clever of him to have received the packet at all, and that everybody ought, somehow, to be

176

grateful to him. Instead of which, they almost seemed to think he was to blame for something.

"You say you found it in your right hand coat-pocket. Did you at no time previously to that put your hand in that pocket for anything?"

"I should think I must have," said Hector. He yawned. "But I can't exactly remember." He yawned again, uncontrollably.

"What do you keep in that pocket?"

"Odds and ends," said Hector. He dipped into the pocket and drew out a mixed collection—a pencil, a box of matches, a pair of nail-scissors, some string, a thing for opening beer-bottles with patent caps, a corkscrew for opening ordinary beer-bottles, a very dirty handkerchief and some crumbs.

"If you could remember using any of those things during the night—" suggested Parker.

"I must have used the handkerchief," said Hector, gazing at it in some dismay. "I meant to take a clean one out this morning. I did, too. Where is it? Oh, in my trousers-pocket. Here it is. But of course," he added, helpfully, "this isn't the suit I wore last night. I had my old tweed jacket on then. I must have put the dirty handkerchief in this pocket with the other things instead of into the clothesbasket. I know it's the one I had at the fire. Look at the soot on it."

"Quite so," said Parker, "but can you remember *when* you used this handkerchief last night? Surely, if you had felt in your pocket at any time, you couldn't have failed to come on the packet if it was there."

"Oh, yes, I could," said Hector, brightly. "I shouldn't notice. I'm so accustomed to having a lot of junk in my pocket. I can't help you there, I'm afraid."

Another frightful yawn attacked him. He stifled it manfully, and it forced itself painfully out at his nose, nearly breaking his ear-drums on the way. Parker gazed crossly at his grimacing countenance.

"Do try to keep your mind on what I am asking you, Mr. Firkin," he said. "If only—"

"Puncheon," said Hector, annoyed.

"Puncheon," said Parker, "I beg your pardon. Did you at any time, Mr. Puncheon—?"

"I don't know," interrupted Hector. "I honestly don't know. It's no good asking. I can't tell you. I would if I could, but I simply can't."

Mr. Hawkins, looking from one to the other, discovered in himself a little elementary knowledge of human nature.

"I think," he said, "a small drink is indicated."

He fetched a bottle of Johnnie Walker and some glasses from a locker and set them on the desk, together with a siphon. Parker thanked him and, suddenly ashamed of himself and his bad temper, apologized.

"I'm sorry," he said. "I'm afraid I was a bit curt. I got my collar-bone broken a little time ago and it still aches a bit and makes me abominably peevish. Let's go about this business another way. Why do you suppose, Mr. Puncheon, that anybody should have picked you out to take charge of this hefty dose of dope?"

"I thought whoever it was must have mistaken me for some one else."

"So I should imagine. And you think that's more likely to have happened at the pub than anywhere else?"

"Yes; unless it was in the crowd at the fire. Because in the other places—I mean in this office and when I was interviewing people, everybody knew me, or at least they knew what I was there for."

"That seems sound," agreed Parker. "How about this restaurant where you had your sausages?"

"There's that, of course. But I can't recollect anybody coming near enough to me to shove things in my pocket. And it couldn't have been during the fire either, because I had my burberry on, buttoned up. But in the pub, I had my burberry open, and there were at least four people barging up against me—one of two carters who were there before me, and a little man who looked like a bookmaker's tout or something, and the drunken chap in dress clothes and the old boy sitting in the corner. I don't think it can have been the carter, though; he looked quite genuine."

"Had you ever been to the White Swan before?"

"Once, I think, ages ago. Certainly not often. And I think there's a new landlord since then."

"Well, then," said Parker, "what is there about you, Mr. Puncheon, that induces people to hand you out valuable cargoes of dope on sight and without payment?"

"Goodness knows," said Hector.

The desk telephone buzzed furiously, and Mr. Hawkins, snatching the receiver, plunged into a long conversation with some unknown person. The two policemen with their witness retired into a distant corner and carried on the inquiry in low tones.

"Either," said Parker, "you must be the dead spit of some habitual dope-peddler, or you must have led them in some way to imagine that you were the person they expected to see. What did you talk about?"

Hector Puncheon racked his brains.

"Greyhounds," he said at last, "and parrots. Chiefly parrots. Oh, yes—and goats."

"Greyhounds, parrots and goats?"

"We were swapping stories about parrots," said Hector Puncheon. "No, wait, we began about dogs. The little tout person said he'd had a dog that couldn't abide goats and that led on to parrots and mice (I'd forgotten the mice)—and doping parrots with coffee and cayenne."

"Doping?" said Parker, quickly. "Was that word used?"

"No, I don't know that it was. The parrot was frightened of mice, and they had to cure it of shock by giving it coffee."

"Whose parrot?"

"The little fellow's aunt's, I think. The old boy knew a parrot, too, but that belonged to a clergyman, and the bishop tried to teach it to swear and promoted the parson. I don't know whether it was blackmail, or just that he liked the parrot."

"But what did you contribute to the conversation?"

"Hardly anything. I just listened and paid for the drinks."

"And the man in dress clothes?"

"Oh, he talked about his wife's shopping-list and a parcel—yes, there was something about a parcel he ought to have brought with him."

"Was the parcel produced?"

"No, he never had a parcel."

"All right," said Parker, after a little more of this unsatisfactory conversation. "We'll go into the matter, Mr. Puncheon. We're very much obliged to you and Mr.—er—Hawkins for having called our attention to the matter. We will take charge of the packet, and if we want you again, we'll let you know."

He rose to his feet. Mr. Hawkins shot across from his desk.

"Got all you want? You don't want this story to go in, I suppose?" he added, wistfully.

"No; you mustn't say anything about it at present," said Parker, firmly. "But we're very much indebted to you, and if anything comes of it, you shall have the story first with all the details we can give you. I can't say fairer than that."

He left the office with Sergeant Lumley, mournful and silent, at his heels.

"It's a thousand pities, Lumley, that we didn't get this information earlier. We could have put a man in at that pub for the rest of the day. It's too late to do anything now."

"Yes, sir, it is," said Sergeant Lumley.

"The pub's the place, I fancy."

"Very likely, sir."

"The cargo of dope was a pretty large one. That means that it was meant for some one who distributes the stuff on a fairly extensive scale. And it didn't have to be paid for. That suggests to me that the man they expected to see was only a messenger for this distributor, who, no doubt, settles up direct with the top man by some other route."

"Very possibly, sir," said Sergeant Lumley, in an unbelieving tone.

"The thing is, what are we to do? We could raid the place, of course, but I don't think that would be advisable. We probably shouldn't find anything, and we should merely give the alarm to no purpose."

"That wouldn't be anything unusual," grunted the Sergeant, disagreeably.

"Too true. We haven't anything against the White Swan so far, have we?"

"Not that I know of, sir."

"We shall have to make certain about it first. The landlord may or may not be concerned in the business. Quite possibly he isn't, but we shall have to make sure. You had better arrange for at least two men to investigate the Swan. They mustn't make themselves conspicuous. They can drop in from time to time and talk about parrots and goats and see if anything peculiar happens to them. And they can try and get a line on those people—the little chap, and the old man, and the fellow in the boiled shirt. It ought not to be difficult. Put on two sensible, tactful men who are not teetotallers, and if they don't get anything in the course of a day or two, change them for two others. And see that they look like what they're supposed to be and don't wear regulation boots or anything foolish."

"Very well, sir."

"And for God's sake, Lumley, look a little more cheerful about it," said the Chief-Inspector. "I like to see duties undertaken in a pleasant spirit."

"I do my best," replied Sergeant Lumley, offended.

Chief-Inspector Parker went resolutely home to bed.

180

CHAPTER XIII

EMBARRASSING ENTANGLEMENTS
OF A GROUP-MANAGER

EXCUSE me, miss," said Tompkin, the reception-clerk, to Miss Rossiter, "but do you happen to have seen Mr. Wedderburn anywhere? He's not in his room."

"I think I saw him in with Mr. Ingleby."

"Thank you very much, miss."

Tompkin's cheerful face looked worried; and all the more so, when he reached Mr. Ingleby's room and found nobody there but Mr. Ingleby himself and Mr. Bredon.

He repeated his inquiry.

"He's just gone down to Bream's Buildings about an insertion in some magazine or other," said Ingleby.

"Oh!" Tompkin looked so non-plussed that Ingleby added, "Why, what's up?"

"Well, sir, as a matter of fact and strictly between you and I, a rather awkward thing has happened. I don't quite know what to do about it."

"In all social difficulties," said Bredon, "ask Uncle Ugly. Do you want to know how many buttons there should be on a dress waistcoat? how to eat an orange in public? how to introduce your first-wife-that-was to your third-wife-to-be? Uncle Ugly will put you right."

"Well, sir, if you will treat the matter in confidence, you and Mr. Ingleby—"

"Say on, Tompkin. We will be silent as a pre-talkie movie. Any sum from £5 to £5,000 advanced on your note of hand alone. No embarrassing investigations. No security required—or offered. What's your trouble?"

"Not mine, sir. As a matter of fact, sir, there's a young woman here, asking for Mr. Tallboy, and he's in conference with Mr. Armstrong and Mr. Toule, and I don't like to send a message."

"Well," said Ingleby, "tell her to wait."

"That's just it, sir, I did, and she said I was only saying that to put her off, while Mr. Tallboy got out of the building, and she took on terribly and said she was going to speak to

181

Mr. Pym. Well, sir, of course I don't know what the trouble is"—here Tompkin looked unnaturally blank and innocent—"but I don't think Mr. Tallboy would care for that, nor Mr. Pym neither. So I thought, seeing that Mr. Wedderburn is the gentleman who sees most of Mr. Tallboy, so to speak—"

"I see," said Ingleby. "Where is the young woman?"

"Well, I've put her in the Little Conference Room," said Tompkin, dubiously, with an accent on the "put," "but of course, if she was to come out again (and there's nothing to stop her) and was to go to Mr. Pym, or even to Miss Fearney— You see, sir, when parties like Miss Fearney are in an official position, they have to take notice of things, as you may say, whether they like to or not. It isn't the same as you or me, sir." Tompkins glanced from Ingleby to Bredon, dividing the "sir" impartially between them.

Bredon, who was drawing patterns on his blotter, looked up.

"What is she like?" he asked. "I mean"—as Tompkin hesitated—"do you think she is genuinely in distress or merely out to make trouble?"

"Well, sir," said Tompkin, "since you ask me, I should say she was a tough jane."

"I'll go and keep her quiet," said Bredon. "Be sure you tell Mr. Tallboy the moment he is free."

"Very good, sir."

"And try not to let it get round the office. It may be nothing at all."

"Quite so, sir. I'm not one to talk. But there's the boy on the desk, sir—"

"Oh! Well, tell him to hold his tongue."

"Yes, sir."

Bredon went out, looking as though he did not care for his self-imposed task. By the time he arrived at the door of the Little Conference Room, however, his face bore nothing but an expression of amiable helpfulness. He entered briskly, and in the first glance his practised eye took in every detail about the young woman who sprang up to face him, from her hard eyes and shrewish mouth to her blood-red, pointed finger-nails and over-elaborate shoes.

"Good afternoon," he said, brightly. "You want Mr. Tallboy, I think. He won't be long, but he's been called in to a conference with some clients and we can't rescue him, so they've sent me down to entertain you till he comes. Will you smoke, Miss—er—the clerk didn't mention your name?"

"It's Vavasour—Miss Ethel Vavasour. Who're you? Are you Mr. Pym?"

Bredon laughed.

"Good lord, no. I'm a very unimportant person—one of the junior copy-writers, that's all."

"Oh, I see. You a pal of Jim's?"

"Of Tallboy's? Not specially. I just happened to be there, so I came along, don't you know. They told me there was a very beautiful young lady asking for Tallboy, and I thought, What-ho! Why not buzz along and cheer her weary hours of waiting?"

"I'm sure it's frightfully good of you," said Miss Vavasour, laughing rather shrilly. "I expect what you mean is, that Jim's sent you along to see if you can talk me round. That's just like Jim. I suppose he's sneaked off the back way."

"I assure you, my dear young lady, that I haven't seen or spoken to Tallboy this afternoon. And I expect, when he hears that I've been along to have a chat with you, he'll be very fed-up with me. And no wonder. If you'd come to see me, I should loathe any other blighter who came and barged in."

"You can can that stuff," retorted Miss Vavasour. "I know your sort. You'd talk the hind leg off a donkey. But I can tell you this: if Jim Tallboy thinks he's going to get round me by sending his flash friends to shoot off a lot of hot air, he's mistaken."

"My dear Miss Vavasour, will nothing rid you of this misapprehension? In other words, you got me all wrong. I'm not here to forward Tallboy's interests in any way—except, perhaps, by offering the suggestion that this office is possibly not the most suitable spot for interviews of a personal and confidential kind. If I might presume to advise you, would not an appointment for some other place and time—?"

"Ah!" said Miss Vavasour. "I dare say. But if a fellow won't answer your letters or come and see you, and you don't even know where he lives, what is a girl to do? I'm sure I don't want to make trouble."

Here Miss Vavasour sniffed and applied a small handkerchief carefully to her made-up eye-lashes.

"Good heavens!" said Bredon. "How unkind and abominable!"

"You may well say so," said Miss Vavasour. "It's not what anybody would expect of a gentleman, is it? But there! When a fellow's telling the tale to a girl it's one thing, and when he's got her into trouble it's another. A girl doesn't hear so much about him marrying her then. Well, you tell him he's got to do it, see? Or I'll scream my way into old Pym's office and make him. A girl's got to look after herself these days. I'm sure I only wish I had somebody to do it for me, and now poor Auntie's dead, I haven't got a soul to stick up for me."

The handkerchief came into play again.

"But, my dear girl," said Bredon, "even Mr. Pym, great autocrat as he is, couldn't make Tallboy marry you. He's married already."

"Married?" Miss Vavasour took away the handkerchief revealing a pair of perfectly dry and very angry eyes, "the dirty beast! So *that's* why he never asked me to his home. Talking a lot of eye-wash about only one room and his landlady being very particular. I don't care, though. He's got to do it. His wife can divorce him. Goodness knows she's got cause. I've got his letters."

Her eyes turned, irresistibly, to her large and ornate handbag. It was a false move and she realized it instantly and gazed appealingly at Bredon, but he knew where he was now.

"So you've got them there with you. That was very—farsighted of you. See here, Miss Vavasour, what's the use of talking like this? You may just as well be frank with me. Your idea was to threaten to show those letters to Mr. Pym if Tallboy didn't pay up, wasn't it?"

"No, of course it wasn't."

"You're so devoted to Tallboy that you always carry his correspondence about with you?"

"Yes—no. I never said I'd got the letters with me."

"No? But you've admitted it now, you know. Now, you take the advice of a man double your age." (This was a generous estimate, for Miss Vavasour was an easy twenty-eight.) "If you make a disturbance here, nothing will happen, except that Tallboy will possibly lose his job and have no money at all for you or anybody. And if you try to sell him those letters—there's a name for that, and it's not a pretty one."

"That's all very well," said Miss Vavasour, sullenly, "but how about this trouble he's got me into? I'm a mannequin, see? And if a girl's got to chuck her job, and her figure ruined for life—"

"Are you sure you're not mistaken about that?"

" 'Course I'm sure. What do you take me for? An innocent?"

"Surely not," said Bredon. "No doubt Tallboy will be ready to come to a suitable arrangement. But—if I may presume to advise you—no threats and no disturbance. And—forgive me—there are other people in the world."

"Yes, there are," said Miss Vavasour, frankly, "but they're not so keen to take over a girl with encumbrances, if you know what I mean. You wouldn't yourself now, would you?"

"Oh, me? I'm not in the running," said Bredon, with perhaps more promptness and emphasis than was quite complimentary. "But, speaking generally, I'm sure you'll find it better not to make an explosion—not here, at any rate. I mean to say, you know, that's the point. Because this is one of those old-fashioned firms that don't like anything unpleasant or—er—undesirable to happen on their premises."

"You bet they don't," said Miss Vavasour, shrewdly, "that's why I'm here."

"Yes, but take it from me, you'll do no good by making a fuss. Really not. And—ah! here is the missing gentleman. I'll be pushing along. Hullo, Tallboy—I've just been entertaining the lady in your absence."

Tallboy, his eyes burning in a very white face and his lips twitching, looked at Bredon for a moment or two in silence. Then:

"Thanks very much," he said, in a stifled tone.

"No, don't thank me," said Bredon. "The gratification is entirely on my side."

He went out and shut the door upon the pair of them.

"Now, I wonder," said Mr. Bredon, reverting to his own detective personality as he went slowly upstairs to his room, "I wonder if it's possible that I'm all wrong about our friend Victor Dean. Can it be that he was merely a common or garden blackmailer, intent on turning his colleague's human weaknesses to his own advantage? Would that be worth cracking a fellow's skull for him and hurling him down a staircase, iron, one, murderers for the use of? The chap who could probably tell me is Willis, but somehow the good Willis is deaf as an adder to my well-known charm of speech. Is it any use sounding him again? If only I could be sure that he was not the gentleman who sandbagged my poor brother-in-law Charles and that he was not still harbouring designs upon my unworthy carcase. Not that I mind having designs harboured on me, but I don't want to make a confidant of the fellow I'm after, like the fat-headed hero in one of those detective stories where the detective turns out to be the villain. If only I had ever seen Willis engaged in any game or sport, I should know better where I stood, but he seems to despise the open-air life—and that in itself, if you come to think of it, is sinister."

After a little more thought, he went along to Willis' room.

"Oh, I say, Willis," he said, "am I disturbing you?"

"No. Come in."

Willis looked up from a sheet of paper which bore the engaging headlines: "MAGNOLIA-WHITE, MAGNOLIA-SOFT— that's what they'll say of your hands." He looked depressed and ill.

"See here, Willis," said Bredon, "I want your advice. I know we don't seem to hit it off very well—"

"No—it's my fault," said Willis. He seemed to struggle with himself for a moment, and then brought his words out with a rush, as though they had been violently forced from him: "I fancy I owe you some sort of apology. I appear to have been mistaken."

"What exactly did you have against me? I never could make out what it was, to tell you the truth."

"I thought you belonged to Victor Dean's beastly doping and drinking crowd, and thought you were trying to get Pamela—Miss Dean—in among them again. She tells me that's not the case. But I saw you there with her, and now she tells me it's my fault that you—that you—oh, hell!"

"What *is* the matter?"

"I'll tell you what's the matter," said Willis, violently. "You went and forced yourself on Miss Dean—God knows what you told her, and she won't tell me. You made out you were a friend of her brother's, or something—was that true, to start with?"

"Not quite, as you put it. I made Miss Dean's acquaintance over a matter connected with her brother, but I had never met him, and she knows that."

"What had it got to do with him, then?"

"I'm afraid I can't tell you that."

"It sounds damned queer to me," said Willis, his face darkening with suspicion. Then he seemed to recollect that he was supposed to be making an apology, and went on:

"Well, anyway, you took her to that disgusting place down there by the river."

"That's not altogether true, either. I asked her to take me, because I couldn't very well have got in without an introduction."

"That's a lie; I got in all right."

"Miss Dean told them to let you in."

"Oh!" Willis was disconcerted for a moment. "Well, in any case, you had no business to ask a decent girl to do anything of the kind. That was exactly what Dean and I had trouble about. A house like that is no fit place for her, and you know it."

"I do; and I regretted the necessity which compelled me to

186

ask her to go there. You may have noticed that I took care nothing should happen to her."

"I don't know that," grumbled Willis.

"You aren't a very good detective," said Bredon with a smile. "You must take my word for it that she was quite safe."

"I won't take your word, but I'd take hers. She says so, and I suppose I've got to believe it. But if you're not an out-and-out rotter yourself, why did you want to be taken there?"

"That's another thing I can't tell you. But I can offer you one or two reasonable explanations that might fit the case. I might be a journalist, commissioned to write an inside story about the newest kind of night-club. Or I might be a detective, engaged in tracking down dope-smugglers. Or I might be a zealot with a new brand of religion, trying to save the souls of post-war society sinners. Or I might be in love with somebody—say, if you like, the notorious Dian de Momerie—and threatening to commit suicide unless I got an introduction to her. I present you with those four solutions on the spur of the moment, and I dare say I could think of others, if I was put to it."

"You might be a dope-merchant yourself," said Willis.

"I hadn't thought of that. But if I were, I doubt if I should need Miss Dean's introduction to that particular crowd."

Willis muttered something unintelligible.

"But I gather," said Bredon, "that Miss Dean has more or less absolved me of being anything hoeplessly corrupt. So what's the trouble?"

"The trouble is," groaned Willis, "that you've—my God! you swine—you've thrown her over and she says it's my fault."

"You oughtn't to say a thing like that, old son," said Bredon, really distressed. "It's not done."

"No—I dare say I'm not quite a gentleman. I've never been—"

"If you tell me you've never been to a public school," said Bredon, "I shall scream. What with Copley and Smayle, and all the other pathetic idiots who go about fostering inferiority complexes, and weighing up the rival merits of this place and that place, when it doesn't matter a damn anyway, I'm fed up. Pull yourself together. Anybody, wherever he's been educated, ought to know better than to say a thing like that about any girl. Particularly when there isn't the slightest foundation for it."

"Ah, but there is," said Willis. "You don't realize it, but I do. I know a man's a man for a' that and all the rest of it, but people like you have a sort of glamour about them and women fall for it, every time. I know I'm as good a man as you are, but I don't look it, and that's where it is."

"I can only assure you, Willis—"

"I know, I know. You've never made love to Miss Dean—that's what you're going to say—never by word, look or deed and so forth and so on, given her the slightest ground—bah! I know it. She admits it. It makes it all the worse."

"I am afraid," said Mr. Bredon, "that you are a very foolish pair of people. And I really think you must be quite mistaken in Miss Dean's feelings."

"That's damned likely."

"I think so. In any case, you oughtn't to have said anything to me about it. And in any case, there's nothing I can do."

"She asked me," said Willis, miserably, "to apologize to you and bring you—and ask you—and put the matter right."

"There's nothing to put right. Miss Dean knows quite well that my interviews with her were merely a matter of business. And all I can say is, Willis, if you accepted any such commission, she must think you as soft as a pancake. Why on earth didn't you tell her you'd see me at the devil first? That's probably what she expected you to do."

"Do you think so?"

"Sure of it," said Bredon, who was not sure at all, but thought it best to appear so. "You mustn't go about creating intolerable situations, you know. It's very awkward for me, and I'm sure Miss Dean would be horribly upset if she knew what you'd been saying about her. All she meant was, I expect, that you'd taken quite a wrong view of a perfectly ordinary business acquaintanceship and been unnecessarily antagonistic and so on, and that she wanted you to put the thing straight, so that, if I needed her help again, there wouldn't be any awkwardness about it. Isn't that, in other words, what she said to you?"

"Yes," said Willis. It was a lie, and he knew that Bredon knew that it was a lie, but he lied manfully. "Of course that was what she actually said. But I'm afraid I put another interpretation on it."

"All right," said Bredon, "that's settled. Tell Miss Dean that my business is progressing very well, and that when I need her kind help again I shall have no hesitation in calling her to my assistance. Now, is that all?"

"Yes, that's all."

"You're sure—while you are about it—that there's nothing else you want to get off your chest?"

"N-no."

"You don't sound very sure about it. You've been trying to say all this to me for some time, I dare say."

"No, not very long. A few days."

"Since the day of the monthly tea-party, shall we say?"

Willis started violently. Bredon, with a wary eye on him, followed up his advantage.

"Was that what you came round to Great Ormond Street that night to tell me?"

"How do you know about that?"

"I didn't know, I guessed. As I have said before, you would not make a good detective. You lost a pencil on that occasion, I believe?"

He drew the pencil from his pocket and held it out.

"A pencil? Not that I know of. Where did you find that?"

"In Great Ormond Street."

"I don't think it's mine. I don't know. I think I've still got mine."

"Well, never mind. You came round that night intending to apologize?"

"No—I didn't. I came round to have an explanation with you. I wanted to bash your face in, if you must know. I went round there just before ten—"

"Did you ring the bell of my flat?"

"No, I didn't. I'll tell you why. I looked in your letterbox, and I saw a letter there from Miss Dean, and I—I didn't dare go upstairs. I was afraid I might let myself go. I felt like murdering you. So I went off and wandered about till I was too done-up to think."

"I see. You didn't make any attempt to get hold of me at all?"

"No."

"Oh, well, that's that." Bredon dismissed the matter with a wave of the hand. "It's quite all right. It doesn't matter. I was only a little bit puzzled about the pencil."

"The pencil?"

"Yes. I found it on the top landing, you see, just outside my door. I couldn't quite understand how it got there, that's all."

"It wasn't me. I didn't go upstairs."

"How long did you stay in the house?"

"Only a few minutes."

"In the front hall downstairs all the time?"

"Yes."

"Oh, well then, it can't have been your pencil. It's very odd, because those pencils aren't on the market, as you know."

189

"Perhaps you dropped it yourself."

"Well, perhaps I did. That seems the likeliest explanation, doesn't it? It's not of any importance."

There was a short and rather uncomfortable pause. Willis broke it by asking in a constrained tone:

"What did you want to ask my advice about?"

"About the old subject," said Bredon; "perhaps, now that we've had this little explanation, you may find it easier to tell me what I want to know. Circumstances have brought me up against the Dean family, and I feel a certain amount of curiosity about the late lamented Victor. From his sister I gather that he was a good, kind brother, but unfortunately a little wild in his morals—which means, I take it, that he became infatuated with Dian de Momerie. According to her, he took his sister to various places to meet the fair Dian; you interfered; Miss Dean then realized what the situation was, and withdrew from the association, while quite naturally and illogically resenting your interference; and finally Dian de Momerie shut down on Victor and sent him off home. That's true, as far as it goes, I imagine?"

"Yes," said Willis, "except that I don't believe Dean ever was really infatuated with the de Momerie woman. I think he was flattered, and I think he thought he could make something out of her. As a matter of fact, he was a mean little beast."

"Did she give him money?"

"Yes, she did; but he didn't get much out of that, because he found that crowd so expensive to run with. He wasn't naturally one of that sort. He didn't enjoy gambling, though he had to do it, to keep in with them; and he wasn't a drinker. In some ways, I'd have liked him better if he had been. He wouldn't dope, either. I expect that's why Miss de Momerie got tired of him. The worst of that crowd, you know, is that they can't rest till they've made everybody they have to do with as bad as themselves. If they'd only drug themselves into their graves and have done with it, the sooner they did it the better it would be for every one. I'd cheerfully hand the stuff over to them by the cartload. But they get hold of quite decent people and ruin them for life. That's why I got so worried about Pamela."

"But you say that Victor managed to remain undefiled."

"Yes, but Pamela's different. She's rather impulsive and easily—no, not easily led, but easily excited about things. She's high-spirited and likes to try everything once. If she once gets a sort of enthusiasm for a person, she wants to do the same as they do. She needs somebody—well, never mind that. I don't want to discuss Pamela. I only mean that Victor

190

was just the opposite. He was very careful of himself, and he had a very good eye for the main chance."

"Do you mean that he was the sort of man who makes what he can out of his friends?"

"He was the kind of man who never has his own cigarettes, and never happens to be there, if he can help it, when it's his turn to stand the drinks. And he'd pick your brains every time."

"He must have had a pretty good reason, then, for going round with Dian de Momerie's lot. As you say, they're expensive."

"Yes; he must have seen something remunerative in the distance. And when it came to sacrificing his sister—"

"Exactly. Well, that's all rather by the way. What I wanted to know from you was this: supposing he found out that somebody—say somebody in this office—as it might be yourself—had a skeleton in the closet, to use the pretty old metaphor, was Victor Dean the kind of fellow to—er—to dispose of that skeleton to an anatomist?"

"Blackmail, do you mean?" asked Willis, bluntly.

"That's a strong word. But call it that."

"I don't quite know," said Willis, after a few moments' consideration. "It's a devil of a thing to suggest about anybody, isn't it? But I can only say that the question gives me no shock. If you were to tell me that he had blackmailed somebody, it wouldn't surprise me very much. Only, as it's a pretty serious offence, it would have to be a very safe kind of blackmail, with the sort of victim who couldn't possibly afford to face a court of law. Mind you, I haven't the least reason to suppose he ever did anything of the kind. And he certainly never seemed to be particularly flush of cash. Not that that's much to go by, with a careful fellow like him. *He* wouldn't have let wads of bank-notes come tumbling out his desk."

"You think the tumbling about of notes affords a presumption of innocence?"

"Not a bit. Only of carelessness, and Dean certainly wasn't careless."

"Well, thanks for speaking so frankly."

"That's all right. Only, for goodness' sake, don't let Pamela know what I've been saying about Victor. I've had trouble enough about that."

Bredon assured him that he need not fear any such fantastic indiscretion, and took his leave, polite but still puzzled.

Mr. Tallboy was lying in wait for him at the end of the passage.

"Oh, Bredon, I'm very much obliged to you, of course. I'm

sure I can rely on you not to spread the thing any further than it's gone already. All quite absurd, of course. That fool Tompkin seems to have lost his head completely. I've ticked him off properly."

"Oh, yes, absolutely," replied Bredon. "Just so. Much ado about nothing. No real necessity for me to have butted in at all. But you never know. I mean to say, if you'd been detained and Miss Vavasour had got tired of waiting or—well, you know what I mean."

"Yes." Tallboy licked his dry lips. "It might have been very awkward. When girls get hysterical and so on, they sometimes say more than they mean. I've been a bit of a fool, as I dare say you've gathered. I'm cutting it all out now. I've settled everything all right. Worrying, of course, but nothing really desperate." He laughed uncomfortably.

"You're looking a bit over-done."

"I feel it. The fact is, I was up all night. My wife—well, the fact is, my wife had a baby last night. That was partly why—oh, hell, what's it matter, anyhow?"

"I quite understand," said Bredon. "Very wearing business. Why didn't you take the day off?"

"I didn't want to do that. It's my busy day. Much better to occupy one's mind. Besides, there wasn't any necessity. Everything went all right. I suppose you think I'm an awful swine."

"You're not the first, by any means," said Bredon.

"No—it's rather usual, I believe. It's not going to happen again, I can tell you."

"It must have put you in a hell of a hole—all this."

"Yes—at least—not so bad. As you say, I'm not the only man it's ever happened to. It doesn't do to let one's self be upset, does it? Well, as I said, thanks very much and—that's all, isn't it?"

"Absolutely. There's nothing whatever to thank me about. Well, sonnie, what do you want?"

"Any letters to go, sir?"

"No, thanks," said Bredon.

"Oh, stop a minute," said Tallboy. "Yes, I've got one." He searched in his breast-pocket and pulled out an envelope, all ready sealed. "Lend me a pen one moment, Bredon. Here, boy, take this penny-halfpenny and run along to Miss Rossiter and ask her for a stamp."

He took the pen Bredon held out, and bending over the desk addressed the envelope hurriedly to "T. Smith, Esq." Bredon, idly watching him, was caught by his eye in the act, and apologized.

"I beg your pardon; I was snooping. Beastly habit. One catches it in the typists' room."

"All right—it's only a note to a stockbroker."

"Lucky man to have anything to stockbroke."

Tallboy laughed, stamped the letter and tossed it to the waiting boy.

"And so ends an exhausting day," he observed.

"Toule very tiresome?"

"Not more so than usual. He turned down 'Like Niobe, all Tears.' Said he didn't know who Niobe was and he didn't suppose anybody else did either. But he passed this week's 'Tears, Idle Tears,' because when he was a boy his father used to read Tennyson aloud to the family circle."

"That's one saved from the wreck, anyhow."

"Oh, yes. He liked the general idea of the poetical quotations. Said he thought they gave his advertisements class. You'll have to think up some more. He likes the ones that illustrate well."

"All right. 'Like Summer Tempest came her Tears.' That's Tennyson, too. Picture of the nurse of ninety years setting his babe upon her knee. Babies always go well. (Sorry, we don't seem able to get off babies.) Start the copy, 'Tears are often a relief to overwrought nerves, but when they flow too often, too easily, it is a sign that you need Nutrax.' I'll do that one. Bassanio and Antonio: 'I know not Why I am so Sad.' Carry the quote on into the copy. 'Causeless depression, like Antonio's, wearies both the sufferer and his friends. Go to the root of the matter and tone up the overstrung Nerves with Nutrax." I can do that sort of thing by the hour."

Mr. Tallboy smiled wanly.

"It's a pity we can't cure ourselves with our own nostrums, isn't it?"

Mr. Bredon surveyed him critically.

"What *you* need," he said, "is a good dinner and a bottle of fizz."

CHAPTER XIV

HOPEFUL CONSPIRACY OF TWO
BLACK SHEEP

THE gentleman in the harlequin costume removed his mask with quiet deliberation, and laid it on the table.

"Since," he said, "my virtuous cousin Wimsey has let the cat out of the bag, I may as well take this off. I am afraid"—he turned to Dian—"my appearance will disappoint you. Except that I am handsomer and less rabbity-looking, the woman who has seen Wimsey has seen me. It is a heavy handicap to carry, but I can't help it. The resemblance, I am happy to say, is only skin-deep."

"It's almost incredible," said Major Milligan. He bent forward to examine the other's face more closely, but Mr. Bredon extended a languid arm and, without apparently using any force at all, pushed him back into his seat.

"You needn't come too close," he observed, insolently. "Even a face like Wimsey's is better than yours. Yours is spotty. You eat and drink too much."

Major Milligan, who had, indeed, been distressed that morning by the discovery of a few small pimples on his forehead, but had hoped they were not noticeable, grunted angrily. Dian laughed.

"I take it," pursued Mr. Bredon, "that you want to get something out of me. People of your sort always do. What is it?"

"I've no objection to being frank with you," replied Major Milligan.

"How nice it is to hear anybody say that. It always prepares one for a lie to follow. Fore-warned is fore-armed, isn't it?"

"If you choose to think so. But I think you'll find it to your advantage to listen."

"Financial advantage?"

"What other kind is there?"

"What indeed? I begin to like your face a trifle better."

"Oh, do you? Perhaps you may like it well enough to answer a few questions?"

194

"Possibly."

"How do you come to know Pamela Dean?"

"Pamela? A charming girl, isn't she? I obtained an introduction to her through what the great public—seduced by the unfortunate example of that incomparable *vulgari-sateur,* Charles Dickens—abominably calls a mutual friend. I admit that my object in obtaining the introduction was a purely business one; I can only say that I wish all business acquaintances were so agreeable."

"What was the business?"

"The business, my dear fellow, was concerned with another mutual friend of us all—with the late Victor Dean, who died, deeply regretted, upon a staircase. A remarkable young man, was he not?"

"In what way?" asked Milligan, quickly.

"Don't you know? I thought you did. Otherwise, why am I here?"

"You two idiots make me tired," broke in Dian. "Where's the sense of going round and round each other like this? Your pompous cousin told us all about you, Mr. Bredon—I suppose you've got a Christian name, by the way?"

"I have. It's spelt Death. Pronounce it any way you like. Most of the people who are plagued with it make it rhyme with teeth, but personally I think it sounds more picturesque when rhymed with breath. What did my amiable cousin say about me?"

"He said you were a dope-runner."

"Where my cousin Wimsey gets his information from, I am damned if I know. Sometimes he is correct."

"And you know perfectly well that one can get what one wants at Tod's place. So why not come to the point?"

"As you say, why not? Is that the particular facet of my brilliant personality that interests you, Milligan?"

"Is that the particular facet of Victor Dean's personality that interests *you?*"

"One point to me," said Mr. Bredon. "Till this moment, I was not sure that it was a facet of his personality. Now I do. Dear me! How interesting it all is, to be sure."

"If you can find out exactly how Victor Dean was involved in that show," said Mr. Milligan, "it might be worth something to you and to me."

"Say on."

Major Milligan reflected a little and seemed to make up his mind to lay his cards on the table.

"Did you learn from Pamela Dean what her brother's job was?"

"Yes, of course. He wrote advertising copy at a place called Pym's. There's no secret about that."

"That's just what there is. And if that infernal young fool hadn't gone and got killed, we might have found out what it was and done ourselves a lot of good. As it is—"

"But look here, Tod," said Dian. "I thought it was the other way round. I thought you were afraid of *his* finding out too much."

"That's true," said Milligan, scowling. "What would be the use of it if he found out first?"

"I don't follow all this," said Bredon. "Wasn't it his secret? Why not stop talking like a sensation novel and give us the dope straight?"

"Because I don't believe you know even as much as I do about the fellow."

"I don't. I never met him in my life. But I know a good deal about Pym's Publicity, Ltd."

"How?"

"I work there."

"What?"

"I work there."

"Since when?"

"Since Dean's death."

"Because of Dean's death, do you mean?"

"Yes."

"How did that happen?"

"I received information, as my dear cousin Wimsey's police pals would say, that Dean was on to something fishy about Pym's. So, since most fish have gold in their mouths like St. Peter's, I thought it wouldn't do any harm to try a cast or two over that particular pool."

"And what did you find?"

"My dear Milligan, you would make a cat laugh. I don't give away information. I dispose of it—advantageously."

"So do I."

"As you like. You invited me here tonight. I wasn't looking for you. But there's one thing I don't mind telling you, because I've already told Miss de Momerie, and that is, that Victor Dean was bumped off deliberately to prevent him from talking. So far, the only person I can discover who wanted him out of the way was yourself. The police might be interested to know that fact."

"The police?"

"Oh! I quite agree. I don't like the police. They pay very badly and ask a hell of a lot of questions. But it might be useful, for once, to get on the right side of them."

"That's all punk," said Milligan. "You're barking up the

196

wrong tree. I didn't kill the fellow. I didn't want him killed."

"Prove that," said the other, coolly.

He watched Milligan's impassive face, and Milligan watched his.

"Give it up," suggested Bredon, after a few minutes of this mutual scrutiny. "I can play poker just as well as you. But this time I fancy I hold a straight flush."

"Well, what do you want to know?"

"I want to know what you think Dean was in a position to find out."

"I can tell you that. He was trying to find out—"

"Had found out."

"How do you know?"

"If you want instruction in detective methods, you must pay extra. I say he had found out."

"Well, then, he had found out who was running the show from Pym's end."

"The dope-show?"

"Yes. And he may have found out, too, the way it's worked."

"*Is* worked?"

"Yes."

"It's still being worked the same way, then?"

"So far as I know."

"So far as you know? You don't seem to know much."

"Well, how much do you know about the way your own gang run the show?"

"Nothing whatever. Instructions are issued—"

"By the way, how did you get into it?"

"Sorry. Can't tell you that. Not even if you pay extra."

"How do I know I can trust you, then?"

Bredon laughed.

"Perhaps you'd like me to supply you," he said. "If you're not satisfied with your distribution, you can inscribe yourself upon the roll of my customers. Deliveries Sunday and Thursday. Meanwhile—and as a sample—you may be interested in the collar of my cloak. It is handsome, is it not? A rich velvet. A little ostentatious, perhaps you think—a little overmuch buckram? Possibly you are right. But very well made. The opening is almost invisible. We delicately insert the forefinger and thumb, pull the tab gently, and produce this dainty bag of oiled silk—fine as an onion-skin, but remarkably tough. Within it, you will discover sufficient inspiration for quite a number of enthusiasts. A magician's cloak. Such stuff as dreams are made on."

Milligan examined the contents of the little bag in silence.

They were, in fact, a portion of the famous packet obtained by Mr. Hector Puncheon at the White Swan.

"All right, so far. Where do you get it from?"

"I got it in Covent Garden."

"Not at Pym's?"

"No."

Milligan looked disappointed.

"What day did you get it?"

"Friday morning. Like yourself, I get it on a Friday."

"Look here," said Milligan, "you and I have got to be together on this. Dian, my child, run away and play. I'm going to talk business with your friend."

"That's a nice way to treat me in my own house," grumbled Miss de Momerie, but, seeing that Milligan meant what he said, she gathered up herself and her wraps and retreated into the bedroom. Milligan leaned forwards over the table.

"I'm going to tell you what I know," he said. "If you double-cross me, it's at your own risk. I don't want any funny business with that damned cousin of yours."

Mr. Bredon expressed his opinion of Lord Peter Wimsey in a few well-chosen words.

"All right," said Milligan. "You have been warned. Now, see here. If we can find out who works this thing and how it's worked, we can get in at the top. It pays fairly well as it is, in one way, but it's a devil of a risk and a lot of trouble, and it's expensive. Look at that place I have to keep up. It's the man in the centre of the ring that makes the big profits. I know, and you know, what we pay for the stuff, and then there's the bore of handing it out to all these fools and collecting the cash. Now, here's what I know. The whole stunt is worked from that advertising place of yours—Pym's. I found that out from a man who's dead now. I won't tell you how I fell in with him—it's a long story. But I'll tell you what he told me. I was dining with him one night at the Carlton, and he was a bit lit-up. A chap came in with a party, and this man said to me: 'Know who that is?'—'Not from Adam,' I said. He said: 'Well, it's old Pym, the publicity agent.' And then he laughed and said: "If he only knew what his precious agency was doing, he'd have a fit.' 'How's that?' I said. 'Why,' said he, 'didn't you know? All this dope-traffic is worked from there.' Naturally, I started to ask him how he knew and all about it, but he suddenly got an attack of caution and started to be mysterious, and I couldn't get another word out of him."

"I know that brand of drunkenness," said Bredon. "Do you think he really knew what he was talking about?"

"Yes, I think so. I saw him again next day, but he was

198

sober then, and got the shock of his life when I told him what he'd said. But he admitted it was true, and implored me to keep quiet about it. That was all I could get out of him, and the same evening he was run over by a lorry."

"Was he? How remarkably well-timed."

"I thought so myself," said Milligan. "It made me rather nervous."

"But how does Victor Dean come into it?"

"There," admitted Milligan, "I dropped a bad brick. Dian brought him along one evening—"

"Just a minute. When did this conversation with your indiscreet friend take place?"

"Nearly a year ago. Naturally, I'd been trying to follow the matter up, and when Dian introduced Dean and said he worked at Pym's, I thought he must be the man. Apparently he wasn't. But I'm afraid he got an idea about the thing from me. After a bit, I found out he was trying to horn in on my show, and I told Dian to shut down on him."

"In fact," said Mr. Bredon, "you tried to pump him, just as you are trying to pump me, and you found out that he was pumping you instead."

"Something like that," confessed Milligan.

"And shortly after that he fell down a staircase."

"Yes; but I didn't push him down it. You needn't think that. I didn't want him snuffed out. I only wanted him kept out of the way. Dian's too much of a chatterer, especially when she's ginned up. The trouble is, you're never safe with these people. You'd think common sense would tell them to keep quiet in their own interests, but they've got no more sense than a cageful of monkeys."

"Well," said Bredon, "if we fill them up with stuff that notoriously saps their self-control, I suppose we can't grumble at the consequences."

"I suppose not, but it's a damned nuisance sometimes. They're as cunning as weasels in one way, and sheer idiots in another. Spiteful, too."

"Yes. Dean never became an addict, did he?"

"No, if he had, we'd have had more control over him; but unfortunately, his head was screwed on the right way. All the same, he knew pretty well that he'd have been well paid for any information."

"Very likely. The trouble is that he was taking money from the other side as well—at least, I think he was."

"Don't you try that game," said Milligan.

"I've no wish to fall down staircases. What you want, I take it, is the way the trick's worked and the name of the man who works it. I dare say I can find that out for you. How about terms?"

"My idea is, that we use the information to get into the inside ring ourselves, and each strike our own bargain."

"Just so. Alternatively, I suppose, we put the screw on the gentleman at Pym's, when we've got him, and divide the spoil. In which case, as I'm doing most of the work and taking the biggest risk, I suggest I take 75 per cent."

"Not on your life. Fifty-fifty. I shall conduct the negotiations."

"Will you? That's pretty good. Why should I bring you into it at all? You can't negotiate till I tell you whom to negotiate with. You don't think I was born yesterday."

"No. But knowing what I do, I could get you shifted from Pym's tomorrow, couldn't I? If Pym knew who you were, do you suppose he'd keep you on his virtuous premises for another day?"

"Well, look here. We conduct the negotiations together, and I take 60 per cent."

Milligan shrugged his shoulders.

"Well, leave it at that for the moment. I'm hoping it won't pan out that way. What we want to aim at is getting the reins into our own hands."

"As you say. When we've done that, it will be time enough to decide which of us is going to crack the whip."

When he had gone, Tod Milligan went into the bedroom, and found Dian kneeling on the window-seat, staring down into the street.

"Have you fixed things up with him?"

"Yes. He's a twister, but I'll be able to make him see that it'll pay him to be straight with me."

"You had much better leave him alone."

"You're talking rubbish," said Milligan, using a coarser term.

Dian turned round and faced him.

"I've warned you," she said. "Not that I care a damn what happens to you. You're getting on my nerves, Tod. It's going to be great fun to see you come to smash. But you'd better keep off that man."

"Thinking of selling me, are you?"

"I shan't need to."

"You'd better not. Lost your head over this theatrical gentleman in tights, haven't you?"

"Why do you have to be so vulgar?" she asked, contemptuously.

"What's the matter with you, then?"

"I'm frightened, that's all. Unlike me, isn't it?"

"Frightened of that advertising crook?"

"Really, Tod, you're a fool sometimes. You can't see a thing when it's under your nose. It's written too big for you to see, I suppose."

"You're drunk," said Milligan. "Just because you haven't quite managed to get off with this joker of yours—"

"Shut up," said Dian. "Get off with him? I'd as soon get off with the public hangman."

"I dare say you would. Any new sensation would do for you. What do you want? A row? Because, if so, I'm afraid I can't be bothered to oblige you."

There is a dreary convention which decrees that the final collapse of a sordid liaison shall be preceded by a series of no less sordid squabbles. But on this occasion, Miss de Momerie seemed ready to dispense with convention.

"No. I'm through with you, that's all. I'm cold. I'm going to bed. . . . Tod, *did* you kill Victor Dean?"

"I did not."

Major Milligan dreamed that night that Death Bredon, in his harlequin dress, was hanging him for the murder of Lord Peter Wimsey.

CHAPTER XV

SUDDEN DECEASE OF A MAN IN
DRESS CLOTHES

CHIEF-INSPECTOR PARKER continued to be disturbed in his mind. There had been another fiasco in Essex. A private motor-boat, suspected of being concerned in the drug-traffic, had been seized and searched without result—except, of course, the undesired result of giving the alarm to the parties concerned, if they were concerned. Further, a fast car, which had attracted attention by its frequent midnight excursions from the coast to the capital, had been laboriously tracked to its destination, and proved to belong to a distinguished member of the diplomatic corps, engaged on extremely incognito visits to a lady established in a popular seaside resort. Mr. Parker, still incapacitated from personal attendance upon midnight expeditions, was left with the gloomy satisfaction of saying that everything always went wrong when he wasn't there himself. He was also unreasonably annoyed with Wimsey, as the original cause of his incapacity.

Nor had the investigation at the White Swan so far borne very much fruit. For a week in succession, tactful and experienced policemen had draped themselves over its bar, chatting to all and sundry about greyhounds, goats, parrots and other dumb friends of man, without receiving any return in the shape of mysterious packets.

The old man with the parrot-story had been traced easily enough. He was an habitué. He sat there every morning and every afternoon, and had a fund of such stories. The patient police made a collection of them. The proprietor—against whose character nothing could be proved—knew this customer well. He was a superannuated Covent Garden porter, who lived on an old-age pension, and every corner of his inoffensive life was open to the day. This excellent old gentleman, when questioned, recalled the conversation with Mr. Hector Puncheon, but was positive that he had never seen any of the party before, except the two carters, whom he knew well enough. These men also agreed that the gentleman in dress clothes and the little man who had talked about greyhounds were equally unknown to them. It was not, however, unusual for gentlemen in dress clothes to drop in at the Swan by way of a good finish to a lively night—or for gentlemen without dress clothes, either. Nothing threw any light on the mystery of the packet of cocaine.

Parker was, however, roused to some enthusiasm by Wimsey's report of his conversations with Milligan.

"What incredible luck you do have, Peter. People who, in the ordinary way, would avoid you like the plague, gate-crash into your parties at the psychological moment and offer you their noses to lead them by."

"Not so much luck, old man," said Wimsey. "Good guidance, that's all. I sent the fair Dian an anonymous letter, solemnly warning her against myself and informing her that if she wanted to know the worst about me, she had only to inquire at my brother's address. It's a curious thing, but people *cannot* resist anonymous letters. It's like free sample offers. They appeal to all one's lower instincts."

"You are a devil," said Parker. "One of these days you'll get into trouble. Suppose Milligan had recognized you."

"I prepared his mind to accept a striking resemblance."

"I wonder he didn't see through it. Family resemblances don't usually extend to details of teeth and so on."

"I never let him get close enough to study details."

"That ought to have made him suspicious."

"No, because I was rude to him about it. He believed me all the time, simply because I was rude. Everybody suspects an eager desire to curry favour, but rudeness, for some reason, is always accepted as a guarantee of good faith. The only man who ever managed to see through rudeness was St. Augustine, and I don't suppose Milligan reads the *Confessions*. Besides, he wanted to believe in me. He's greedy."

"Well, no doubt you know your own business. But about this Victor Dean affair. Do you really believe that the head of this particular dope-gang is on Pym's staff? It sounds quite incredible."

"That's an excellent reason for believing it. I don't mean in a *credo quia impossible* sense, but merely because the staff of a respectable advertising agency would be such an excellent hiding-place for a big crook. The particular crookedness of advertising is so very far removed from the crookedness of dope-trafficking."

"Why? As far as I can make out, all advertisers are dope-merchants."

"So they are. Yes, now I come to think of it, there is a subtle symmetry about the thing which is extremely artistic. All the same, Charles, I must admit that I find it difficult to

203

go the whole way with Milligan. I have carefully reviewed the staff of Pym's, and I have so far failed to find any one who looks in the least like a Napoleon of crime."

"But you seem convinced that the murder of Victor Dean was an inside job. Or do you now think that some stranger was hiding on the roof and did away with Dean because he was on the point of splitting on the gang? I suppose an outsider could get access to Pym's roof?"

"Oh, easily. But that wouldn't explain the catapult in Mrs. Johnson's desk."

"Nor the attack on me."

"Not if the same person that killed Dean attacked you too."

"Meaning that it might have been Willis? I take it that Willis is not the Napoleon of crime, anyhow."

"Willis isn't a Napoleon of anything. Nor, I fancy, is the chap with the catapult. If he had been, he'd have had the common sense to use his own catapult and burn it afterwards. As I see him, he is a person of considerable ingenuity but limited foresight; a person who snatches at the first thing that is offered him and does his best with it, but lacks just that little extra bit of consideration that would make the thing a real success. He lies from hand to mouth, as you may say. I dare say I could spot him without much difficulty—but that's not what you want, is it? You'd rather have the Napoleon of the dope-traffic, wouldn't you? If he exists, that is."

"Certainly I should," said Parker, emphatically.

"That's what I thought. What, if you come to think of it, is a trifle like an odd murder or assault, compared with a method of dope-running that baffles Scotland Yard? Nothing at all."

"It isn't, really," replied Parker, seriously. "Dope-runners are murderers, fifty times over. They slay hundreds of people, soul and body, besides indirectly causing all sorts of crimes among the victims. Compared with that, slugging one inconsiderable pip-squeak over the head is almost meritorious."

"Really, Charles! for a man of your religious upbringing, your outlook is positively enlightened."

"Not so irreligious, either. Fear not him that killeth, but him that hath power to cast into hell. How about it?"

"How indeed? Hang the one and give the other a few weeks in jail—or, if of good social position, bind him over or put him on remand for six months under promise of good behaviour."

Parker made a wry mouth.

204

"I know, old man, I know. But where would be the good of hanging the wretched victims or the smaller fry? There would always be others. We want the top people. Take even this man, Milligan, who's a pest of the first water—with no excuse for it, because he isn't an addict himself—but suppose we punish him here and now. They'd only start again, with a new distributor and a new house for him to run his show in, and what would anybody gain by that?"

"Exactly," said Wimsey. "And how much better off will you be, even if you catch the man above Milligan? The same thing will apply."

Parker made a hopeless gesture.

"I don't know, Peter. It's no good worrying about it. My job is to catch the heads of the gangs if I can, and, after that, as many as possible of the little people. I can't overthrow cities and burn the population."

"'Tis the Last Judgment's fire must cure this place," said Wimsey, "calcine its clods and set its prisoners free. There are times, Charles, when even the unimaginative decency of my brother and the malignant virtue of his wife appear to me admirable. I could hardly say more."

"You have a certain decency of your own, Peter," replied Parker, "which I like better, because it is not negative." Having given voice to this atrocious outburst of sentiment, he became extremely red in the face, and hastened to cover up his lapse from good taste. "But at the present moment I must say you are not being very helpful. You have been investigating a crime—if it is a crime—for some weeks now, and the only tangible result is a broken collar-bone for me. If you could confine yourself to breaking your own collar-bone—"

"It has been broken before now," said Wimsey, "and in no less good a cause. You shouldn't shove your beastly collar-bone into my affairs."

At this moment, the telephone-bell rang.

It was half-past eight in the morning, and Wimsey had been consuming an early breakfast with his brother-in-law, prior to their departure each to his own place of business. Lady Mary, who had been supplying their bodily necessities and leaving them to their argument, took up the receiver.

"It's from the Yard, darling. Something about that man Puncheon."

Parker took the instrument and plunged into an animated discussion, which ended with his saying:

"Send Lumley and Eagles along at once, and tell Puncheon to keep in touch with you. I'm coming."

"What's up?" inquired Wimsey.

"Our little friend Puncheon has seen his bloke in dress

205

clothes again," said Parker, cursing as he tried to get his coat over his damaged shoulder. "Saw him hanging about the *Morning Star* offices this morning, buying an early paper or something. Been chasing him ever since, apparently. Landed out at Finchley, of all places. Says he couldn't get on to the 'phone before. I must push off. See you later. Cheerio, Mary dear. Bung-ho, Peter."

He bounced out in a hurry.

"Well, well," said Wimsey. He pushed back his chair and sat staring vacantly at the wall opposite, on which hung a calendar. Then, emptying the sugar-bowl on the table-cloth with a jerk, he began, frowning hideously, to built a lofty tower with its contents. Mary recognized the signs of inspiration and stole quietly away to her household duties.

Forty-five minutes afterwards she returned. Her brother had gone, and the banging of the flat-door after him had flung his column of sugar-lumps in disorder across the table, but she could see that it had been a tall one. Mary sighed.

"Being Peter's sister is rather like being related to the public hangman," she thought, echoing the words of a lady with whom she had otherwise little in common. "And being married to a policeman is almost worse. I suppose the hangman's relatives are delighted when business is looking up. Still," she thought, being not without humour, "one might be connected with an undertaker, and rejoice over the deaths of the righteous, which would be infinitely worse."

Sergeant Lumley and P.C. Eagles found no Hector Puncheon at the small eating-house in Finchley from which he had telephoned. They did, however, find a message.

"He has had breakfast and is off again," said the note, written hurriedly on a page torn from the reporter's note-book. "I will telephone to you here as soon as I can. I'm afraid he knows I am following him."

"There," said Sergeant Lumley, gloomily. "That's an amachoor all over. 'Course 'e lets the bloke know 'e's bein' followed. If one of these newspaper fellows was a bluebottle and 'ad to follow an elephant, 'e'd get buzzin' in the elephant's ear, same as 'e'd know what 'e was up to."

P.C. Eagles was struck with admiration at this flight of fancy, and laughed heartily.

"Ten to one 'e'll lose 'im for keeps, now," pursued Sergeant Lumley. "Gettin' us pushed off 'ere without our breakfusses."

"There ain't no reason why we shouldn't have our breakfusses, seein' as we are here," said his subordinate, who was

206

of that happy disposition that makes the best of things. ".'Ow about a nice pair o' kippers?"

"I don't mind if I do," said the sergeant, "if only we're allowed to eat 'em in peace. But you mark my words, 'e'll start ringin' up again afore we 'as time to swallow a bite. Which reminds me. I better ring up the Yard and stop me lord Parker from traipsin' up 'ere. 'E mustn't be put about. Oh, no!"

P.C. Eagles ordered the kippers and a pot of tea. He used his jaws more readily for eating than for talking. The sergeant got his call, and returned, just as the eatables were placed on the table.

"Says, if 'e rings up from anywhere else, we better take a taxi," he announced. "Save time, 'e says. 'Ow's 'e think we're goin' to pick up a taxi 'ere. Nothing but blinkin' trams."

"Order the taxi now," suggested Mr. Eagles, with his mouth full, "so's to be in readiness, like."

"And 'ave it tickin' up the thruppences for nothing? Think they'll call that legitimate expenses? Not 'arf. 'You pay that out of your own pocket, my man,' that's what they'll say, the lousy skin-flints."

"Well, 'ave yer grub," suggested Mr. Eagles, pacifically.

Sergeant Lumley inspected his kipper narrowly.

" 'Ope it's a good one, that's all," he muttered. "Looks oily, it do. 'Ope it's cooked. Eat a kipper what ain't properly cooked through and you gets kipper on your breath for the rest of the day." He forked a large portion into his mouth without pausing to remove the bones, and was obliged to expend a painful minute rescuing them with his fingers. "Tcha! it beats me why Godamighty wanted to put such a lot of bones into them things."

P.C. Eagles was shocked.

"You didn't oughter question the ways of Godamighty," he said, reprovingly.

"You keep a civil tongue in your 'ed, my lad," retorted Sergeant Lumley, unfairly intruding his official superiority into this theological discussion, "and don't go forgettin' what's due to my position."

"There ain't no position in the eyes of Godamighty," said P.C. Eagles, stoutly. His father and his sister happened to be noted lights in the Salvation Army, and he felt himself to be on his own ground here. "If it pleases 'Im to make you a sergeant, that's one thing, but it won't do you no good when you comes before 'Im to answer to the charge of questionin' 'Is ways with kippers. Come to think of it, in 'Is sight you an' me is just the same as worms, with no bones at all."

"Not so much about worms," said Sergeant Lumley. "You

oughter know better than to talk about worms when a man's eating his breakfuss. It's enough to take any one's appetite away. And let me tell you, Eagles, worm or no worm, if I have any more lip from you— Drat that telephone! What did I tell you?"

He pounded heavily across to the insanitary little cupboard that held the instrument, and emerged in a minute or two, dismally triumphant.

"That's 'im. Kensington, this time. You 'op out an' get that taxi, while I settle up 'ere."

"Wouldn't the Underground be quicker?"

"They said taxi, so you damn well make it taxi," said Sergeant Lumley. While Eagles fetched the taxi, the sergeant took the opportunity to finish his kipper, thus avenging his defeat in religious controversy. This cheered him so much that he consented to take the Underground at the nearest suitable point, and they journeyed in comparative amity as far as South Kensington Station, and thence to the point indicated by Hector Puncheon, which was, in fact, the entrance to the Natural History Museum.

There was nobody in the entrance-hall who resembled Hector Puncheon in the least.

"Suppose 'e's gone on already?" suggested P. C. Eagles.

"Suppose 'e 'as," retorted the sergeant. "I can't 'elp that. I told 'im to telephone 'ere if 'e did or to let them know at the Yard. I can't do no more, can I? I better take a walk round, and you sit 'ere to see as they don't come out. If they do, you be ready to take up this other bird's trail and tell Puncheon to set 'ere till I come. An' don't let your bird see you talking to Puncheon, neether. And if they comes out and you see me a-follerin' of them, then you foller on be'ind an' keep yourself outer sight, see?"

Mr. Eagles saw clearly—as indeed he well might, for he knew quite as much about his duties as Sergeant Lumley. But the worm still rankled in the sergeant's breast. Mr. Eagles strolled over to a case of humming-birds and gazed at it with absorbed interest, while Mr. Lumley went heavily up the steps, looking as much as possible like a country cousin bent on seeing the sights.

He had been in the entrance-hall about ten minutes, and had almost exhausted the humming-birds, when he saw something reflected in the glass case which made him sidle softly round so as to command a view of the staircase. A portly person in an overcoat and a top-hat was coming slowly down, one hand thrust deep into his overcoat pocket, the other swinging carelessly at his side. P.C. Eagles looked past him up the stair; there was no sign, either of Hector Puncheon or of Sergeant Lumley, and for a moment the constable hesitated. Then something caught his eye. In the gentleman's left-hand overcoat pocket was a folded copy of the *Morning Star*.

There is nothing unusual about seeing a gentleman with a copy of the *Morning Star*. The readers of that great organ periodically write to the editor, giving statistics of the number of passengers on the 8.15 who read the *Morning Star* in preference to any other paper, and their letters are printed for all to read. Nevertheless, P. C. Eagles determined to take the risk. He scribbled a hasty note on the back of an envelope and walked across to the doorkeeper.

"If you see my friend that came in with me," he said, "you might give him that and tell him I can't wait any longer. I got to get along to my work."

Out of the corner of his eye, he saw the gentleman in the overcoat pass out through the swing-door. Unobtrusively, he followed him.

Upstairs, at the top of a dark staircase barred by a trestle bearing the words "No Entrance," Sergeant Lumley was bending anxiously over the inanimate form of Hector Puncheon. The reporter was breathing heavily in a way the sergeant did not like, and there was a nasty contused wound on his temple.

"Trust your amachoors to make a mess of it," reflected Sergeant Lumley, bitterly. "I only 'ope as that Eagles 'as got 'is 'ead screwed on the right way. But there you are. I can't be in two places at once."

The man in the overcoat walked quietly down the street towards the Underground Station. He did not look back. A few yards behind him, P.C. Eagles sauntered casually along in his wake. His eyes were on his quarry. Neither of them saw a third man, who emerged from nowhere in particular and followed a few yards behind P. C. Eagles. No passer-by gave so much as a second glance to the little procession as it crossed Cromwell Road and debouched upon the station.

The man in the overcoat glanced at the taxi-rank; then he seemed to change his mind. For the first time, he looked back. All he saw was P. C. Eagles purchasing a newspaper, and in this sight there was nothing alarming. The other follower he could not have seen, because, like the Spanish Fleet, he was not yet in sight, though P. C. Eagles might have seen him, had he been looking in his direction. The

209

gentleman appeared to reject the notion of a taxi and turned into the station entrance. Mr. Eagles, his eyes apparently intent upon a headline about Food-Taxes, wandered in after him, and was in time to follow his example in taking a ticket for Charing Cross. Pursued and pursuer entered the lift together, the gentleman walking across to the farther gate, Eagles remaining modestly on the hither side. There were already about half a dozen people, mostly women, in the lift, and just as the gate was shutting, another man came in hurriedly. He passed Eagles and took up a central position among the group of women. At the bottom of the shaft, they all emerged in a bunch, the strange man pressing rather hastily past the man in the overcoat, and leading the way towards the platform, where an eastward-bound train was just running in.

What exactly happened then, P. C. Eagles was not quite clear about at the time, though, in the light of after events he saw plainly one or two things that were not obvious to him then. He saw the third man standing close to the edge of the platform, carrying a thin walking-stick. He saw the man in the overcoat walk past him and then suddenly stop and stagger in his walk. He saw the man with the stick fling out his hand and grasp the other by the arm, saw the two waver together on the edge and heard a shriek from a woman. Then both toppled together under the advancing train.

Through the uproar, Eagles shouldered his way.

" 'Ere," he said, "I'm an officer of the law. Stand aside, please."

They stood aside, with the exception of a porter and another man, who were hauling out something between the train and the platform. An arm came up, and then a head— then the battered body of the third man, the one who had had the walking-stick. They laid him down on the platform bruised and bloody.

"Where's the other?"

"Gone, poor chap."

"Is that one dead?"

"Yes."

"No, he ain't."

"Oh, Betty, I'm going to faint."

"He's all right—see! He's opening his eyes."

"Yes, but how about the other?"

"Do stop shoving."

"Look out, that's a policeman."

"That's the live rail down there."

"Where's a doctor? Send for a doctor."

"Stand back, please. Stand right back."

"Why don't they shut off the electricity?"

"They have. That feller ran off to do it."

"How'll they get 'im out without moving the train?"

"Expect he's all in little bits, pore chap."

"That one tried to save 'im."

"Looked as if he was took ill, or drunk-like."

"Drunk, this time in the morning?"

"They ought to give 'im brandy."

"Clear all this lot out," said Eagles. "This one'll do all right. The other's done for, I suppose."

"Smashed all to blazes. 'Orrible."

"Then you can't do him any good. Clear the station and get an ambulance and another police officer."

"Right you are."

"This one's coming round," put in the man who had helped to haul the victim up. "How are you feeling now, sir?"

"Bloody," said the rescued man, faintly. Then, seeming to realize where he was, he added:

"What happened?"

"Why, sir, a poor gentleman fell off the platform and took you over with him."

"Yes, of course. Is he all right?"

"Afraid he's badly knocked about, sir. Ah!" as somebody ran up with a flask. "Take a pull at this, sir. Gently, you. Lift his head up. Don't jerk him. Now then."

"Ah!" said the man. "That's better. All right. Don't fuss. My spine's all right and I don't think anything's broken to speak of." He moved his arms and legs experimentally.

"Doctor'll be here in a minute, sir."

"Doctor be damned. I'm a doctor myself. Limbs all correct. Head apparently sound, though it aches like hell. Ribs— not so sure about those. Something gone there, I'm afraid. Pelvis intact, thank goodness."

"Very glad to hear that," said Eagles.

"It's the footboard of the train that got me, I fancy. I remember being rolled round and round like a pat of butter between two whatsinames," said the stranger, whose damaged ribs did not seem to impede his breathing altogether. "And I saw the wheels of the train get slower and stop, and I said to myself: 'This is it, You're for it, my lad. Time's stopped and this is Eternity.' But I see I was mistaken."

"Happily so, sir," said Eagles.

"Wish I'd been able to stop that other poor devil, though."

"I'm sure you did your best, sir." Eagles produced his notebook. "Excuse me, sir, but I'm a police-officer, and if you could manage to tell me just how it occurred—"

211

"Damned if I know myself," replied the other. "All I know is, I was standing just about here when the fellow passed me." He paused, catching his breath a little. "I noticed he was looking rather queer. Heart subject, I should think. He suddenly stopped and staggered and then came towards me. I caught hold of his arm and then he lurched over with all his weight and dragged me over with him. And then I can't remember anything but the noise of the train and the tremendous size of its wheels and the feeling of having the breath squeezed out of me. I must have dropped him, I suppose."

"And no wonder," said Eagles, sympathetically.

"My name's Garfield," went on the rescuer. "Dr. Herbert Garfield." He gave an address in Kensington and another in Harley Street. "I think I see one of my professional brethren arriving, and he'll probably say I'm not to talk." He grinned faintly. "Anyhow, I shall be filed for reference for the next few weeks, if you want more information."

P. C. Eagles thanked Dr. Garfield, and then turned to the body of the man in the overcoat, which had by now been disentangled from between the wheels of the train and laid upon the platform. It was an unpleasant sight. Even Eagles, accustomed as he was to casualties, felt a violent distaste for the necessary job of searching the dead man's pockets for evidence of identity. Curiously enough, he found none in the shape of visiting cards or papers. There was a note-case with a few pound-notes, a silver ˌcigarette-case filled with a popular brand of Turks, a little loose change, an unmarked handkerchief, and an H.T. & V. latch-key. Moreover—and this pleased him very much—in the overcoat pocket was a little rubber cosh, such as is sold for use against motor-bandits. He was in the act of hunting over the suit for the tailor's tab, when he was hailed by a local inspector of police, who had arrived with the ambulance.

Eagles was relieved to have the support of a colleague. He knew that he ought to get in touch with Sergeant Lumley and with Scotland Yard. An hour's energetic action on the part of all resulted in a happy reunion at the nearest police-station, where, in fact, Lumley had already arrived, after depositing the unconscious Mr. Puncheon in hospital. Chief-Inspector Parker came hot-foot to Kensington, heard the statements of Lumley and Eagles, reviewed the scene of the disaster and the remains of the mysterious man in dress clothes, and was annoyed. When a man whom you have been elaborately chasing all over London has the impudence to be killed just as you are on the point of catching him, and turns out to have no tailor's name on his clothes and nothing to identify him by; when, moreover, he has thoughtlessly permitted his face to be smashed into pulp by an electric train, so that you cannot usefully circulate his photograph for recognition, your satisfaction in feeling that there is something wrong about him is cancelled by the thought of the weary work that his identification is going to involve.

"There's nothing for it," said Chief-Inspector Parker, "but his laundry-mark, I suppose. And, of course, his dentistry, if any."

Irritatingly enough, the deceased turned out to have an excellent set of teeth and at least three laundry-marks. Nor were his shoes helpful, being ready-made, though by an excellent and much-advertised firm. In fact, the wretched man had gone to meet his Maker in Farley's Footwear, thus upholding to the last the brave assertion that, however distinguished the occasion, Farley's Footwear will carry you through.

In this extremity, Mr. Parker—perhaps stimulated by the thought of Messrs. Farley's advertising—rang up Pym's Publicity and desired to speak with Mr. Bredon.

That gentleman was closeted with Mr. Armstrong when the call came through. Whifflets were causing trouble. The sales of Whifflets had been considerably affected by the publicity methods of a rival brand, Puffin Cigarettes. The manufacturers of Puffins had had a brain-wave. They were giving away aeroplanes. In every packet of Puffins they enclosed a coupon, bearing the name of a component part of a popular little touring 'plane, suitable for amateur use. When you had collected your complete set of parts (numbering one hundred) you sent up your coupons, together with a brief essay on the importance of air-mindedness for British boys. The writer of the best essay each day became the recipient of a private 'plane, and a course of free instruction enabling him or her to take out an air-pilot's certificate. This happy scheme was supported by heavy advertising of a modern and sitmulating kind: "The Future is with the Air-Minded"—"The Highest Flight in Modern Cigarette Manufacture"—"Puff Puffins, and Reach the Height of your Ambition"—and so forth. If you were incapacitated, by reason of age or infirmity, from enjoying the ownership of an aeroplane, you received instead a number of shares in the new issue of the Aeroplane Company involved. The scheme had the support of several notable airmen, whose faces, adorned with flying helmets, stared and grinned from every page of the press in conjunction with their considered opinions that

Puffins were doing a valuable work in helping to establish British Supremacy in the Air.

Whifflets were upset. They demanded, with some annoyance, why Pym's had not had this brilliant idea first. They clamoured for an aeroplane scheme of their own, with a larger plane and a hangar to keep it in. Mr. Armstrong pointed out to them that the sole result of this would be to confuse the public mind between Whifflets and Puffins, which were already quite sufficiently similar in quality and appearance to confuse anybody.

"They're all alike," he said to Bredon, not meaning the cigarettes, but the manufacturers. "They follow each other like sheep. If Whifflets use large heads of film-stars, Puffin's want to come out with still larger heads of still more important stars. If Gasperettes give away timepieces, Puffins follow on with grandfather clocks and Whifflets with chronometers. If Whifflets announce that they don't damage the lungs, Puffins claim that they strengthen the pulmonary system and Gasperettes quote doctors who recommend them in cases of tuberculosis. They will try to snatch each other's thunder—and what happens? The public smoke them all in turn, just as they did before."

"Isn't that a good thing for trade?" asked Mr. Bredon, innocently. "If one of them got all the sales, the others would go bankrupt."

"Oh, no, they wouldn't," said Mr. Armstrong. "They'd merely amalgamate. But it would be bad for us, because then they'd all use the same agency."

"Well, what about it, then?" queried Bredon.

"We've got to cope. We must head them off aeroplanes. For one thing, the boom won't last. The country isn't ready to be cluttered up with aeroplanes, and fathers of families are beginning to complain about it. Even today, few fathers care about having private aeroplanes delivered to their daughters in quiet suburban areas. What we want is a new scheme, on similar lines but with more family appeal. But it must boost Britain. We've got to have the patriotic note."

It was in that moment, and while Chief-Inspector Parker was arguing over the line with the office telephonist, that Mr. Death Bredon conceived that magnificent idea that everybody remembers and talks about today—the scheme that achieved renown as "Whiffling Round Britain"—the scheme that sent up the sales of Whifflets by five hundred per cent in three months and brought so much prosperity to British Hotel-keepers and Road and Rail Transport. It is not necessary to go into details. You have probably Whiffled yourself. You recollect how it was done. You collected coupons for

214

everything—railway fares, charabancs, hotel-bills, theatre-tickets—every imaginable item in a holiday programme. When you had collected enough to cover the period of time you wished to spend in travelling, you took your coupons with you (no sending up to Whifflets, nothing to post or fill in) and started on your tour. At the railway station you presented coupons entitling you to so many miles of first-class travel and received your ticket to the selected town. You sought your hotel (practically all the hotels in Britain fell eagerly in with the scheme) and there presented coupons entitling you to so many nights' board and lodging on special Whifflet terms. For your charabanc outings, your sea-bathing, your amusements, you paid in Whifflet coupons. It was all exceedingly simple and trouble-free. And it made for that happy gregariousness which is the joy of the travelling middle-class. When you asked for your packet of Whifflets in the bar, your next-door neighbour was almost sure to ask, "Are you Whiffling too?" Whiffling parties arranged to Whiffle together, and exchanged Whifflet coupons on the spot. The great Whifflers' Club practically founded itself, and Whifflers who had formed attachments while Whiffling in company, secured special Whifflet coupons entitling them to a Whifflet wedding with a Whifflet cake and their photographs in the papers. When this had happened several times, arrangements were made by which Whiffler couples could collect for a Whifflet house, whose Whifflet furniture included a handsome presentation smoking cabinet, free from advertising matter and crammed with unnecessary gadgets. After this, it was only a step to a Whifflet Baby. In fact, the Whifflet Campaign is and remains the outstanding example of Thinking Big in Advertising. The only thing that you cannot get by Whiffling is a coffin; it is not admitted that any Whiffler could ever require such an article.

It is not to be supposed that the great Whiffle-Way, in all its comprehensive perfection, sprang fully armed from Mr. Bredon's brain when Mr. Armstrong uttered the words, Family Appeal. All that then happened was a mental association with the phrase Family Hotel, coupled with a faint consciousness of inner illumination. He replied, humbly, "Yes, I see; I'll try to work out something," gathered up some sheets of paper on which Mr. Armstrong had scribbled a few illegible notes and a thing that looked like a hedgehog, and made his way out. He had taken six steps down the passage when the idiotic slogan: "If that's what you want, you can Whiffle for it," took possession of his brain; two steps further on, this repellent sentence had recast itself as: "All you Want by Whiffling," and on the threshold of his own room, the first practical possibility of Whiffledom struck him like a sledge-hammer. Fired with excitement, he hurled himself at his desk snatched a scribbling-block, and had written the word "WHIFFLE" in capitals an inch high, when Miss Rossiter arrived with the message that Mr. Parker urgently requested Mr. Bredon to ring him up on the Whitehall number. Lord Peter Wimsey was so intimately in the skin of Mr. Death Bredon that he said: "Damn!" loudly and heartily.

Nevertheless, he obeyed the call, presented himself with leave of absence on urgent private business, and went down to Scotland Yard, where he surveyed the clothes and effects of the man in the dress suit.

"No doubt we shall end by having to circularize the laundries," said Parker. "Perhaps a photograph in some of the London and provincial papers would be as well. I loathe newspapers, but they do advertise one's requirements, and some of these laundry-marks may come from outside London. . . ."

Wimsey looked at him.

"Advertisement, my dear Charles, may be desirable in the case of laundries, but for people like ourselves it does not exist. A gentleman whose clothes are so well cut, and who yet deprives his tailor of the credit for them is, like ourselves, not of the advertising sort. This, I see, is his top-hat, mysteriously uninjured."

"It had rolled beyond the train, on to the farther line."

"Quite. Here again the maker's golden imprint has been removed. How absurd, Charles! One does not—at least, you and I and this gentleman do not—consider the brand to be the guarantee of quality. For us, the quality guarantees the brand. There are two hatters in London who could have made this hat, and you have doubtless already observed that the crown is markedly dolichocephalic, while the curve of the brim is also characteristic. It is a thought behind the present fashion; yet the article is undoubtedly of recent manufacture. Send one of your sleuths to each of these two establishments and ask for the customer with the elongated head who has a fancy for this type of brim. Do not waste your time on laundry-marks, which are, at best, tedious and, at worst, deceptive."

"Thanks," said Parker. "I thought you might be able to put your finger either on the hatter or the tailor."

The first hatter they visited proved to be the right man. He directed their researches to the flat of a Mr. Horace

Mountjoy, who lived in Kensington. They armed themselves with a search-warrant and visited the flat.

Mr. Mountjoy, they ascertained from the commissionaire, was a bachelor of quiet habits, except that he was frequently out rather late at night. He lived alone, and was waited upon and valeted by the staff belonging to the block of flats.

The commissionaire came on duty at 9 o'clock. There was no night porter. Between 11 p.m. and 9 a.m. the outer door was locked and could be opened by the tenants with their own keys, without disturbing him in his basement flat. He had seen Mr. Mountjoy go out the previous evening at about 7.45, in evening dress. He had not seen him return. Withers, the valet, would probably be able to say whether Mr. Mountjoy had been in that night.

Withers was able to say positively that he had not. Nobody had entered Mr. Mountjoy's flat but himself, and the chambermaid who did the rooms. The bed had not been slept in. That was nothing unusual with Mr. Mountjoy. He was frequently out all night, though he generally returned to breakfast at 9.30.

Parker displayed his official card, and they went upstairs to a flat on the third floor. Withers was about to open the door with his pass-key, which, as he explained, he was accustomed to use in the mornings, to avoid disturbing the tenants, but Parker stopped him and produced the two keys which had been taken from the corpse. One of them fitted the lock and established, without much doubt, that they had come to the right place.

Everything in the flat was in perfect order. There was a desk in the sitting-room, containing a few bills and some notepaper, but its drawers were all unlocked and it appeared to hold no secrets. Nor was there anything remarkable about the bedroom or the small dining-room. In the bathroom was a little cupboard containing the usual toilet articles and household medicines. Parker made a rapid inventory of these, pausing for a few minutes over a packet labelled "Bicarbonate of Soda," but touch and taste soon assured him that this contained exactly what it purported to contain. The only thing that could be considered in the slightest degree out of the ordinary in the whole establishment was the presence (also in the bathroom cupboard) of several packets of cigarette papers.

"Did Mr. Mountjoy roll his own cigarettes?"

"I never saw him do so," replied Withers. "He smoked Turkish Abdullas as a rule."

Parker nodded and impounded the cigarette-papers. A further search disclosed no loose tobacco. A number of boxes

217

of cigars and cigarettes were retrieved from the dining-room sideboard. They looked innocent and a few, which Parker promptly slit open, proved to contain excellent tobacco and nothing else. Parker shook his head.

"You'll have to go through everything very carefully, Lumley."

"Yes, sir."

"Any letters by the first post?"

There were none.

"Any visitors today?"

"No, sir. Not unless you count the man from the post-office."

"Oh? What did *he* want?"

"Nothing," replied Withers, "except to bring the new telephone directory." He indicated the two clean volumes which lay upon the sitting-room desk.

"Oh!" said Parker. This did not sound promising. "Did he come into the room?"

"No, sir. He knocked at the door when Mrs. Trabbs and I were both here. Mrs. Trabbs was sweeping, sir, and I was brushing Mr. Mountjoy's lounge suit. I took the books in, sir, and handed him out the old ones."

"I see. All right. And beyond sweeping and brushing and so on, you disturbed nothing?"

"No, sir."

"Anything in the waste-paper basket?"

"I could not say, sir. Mrs. Trabbs would know."

Mrs. Trabbs, produced, said there had been nothing in the waste-paper basket except a wine-merchant's circular. Mr. Mountjoy wrote very little and did not receive many letters.

Satisfied that there had been no interference with the flat since the occupant had left the night before, Parker turned his attention to the wardrobe and chest of drawers, where he found various garments, all properly marked with the names of the tailor or shirt-maker responsible for them. He noticed that all were by first-class artists in their own line. Another silk hat, similar to the one now resting at Scotland Yard, but with sweat-band and crown undisfigured, was found in a hat-box; there were also several felt hats and a bowler, all by first-class makers.

"Mr. Mountjoy was a rich man?"

"He appeared to be in very easy circumstances, sir. He did himself well; the best of everything. Especially during the last year or so."

"What was his profession?"

"I think he was a gentleman of independent means. I never heard of him being engaged in any business."

"Did you know that he had a silk hat from which the maker's name had been removed?"

"Yes, sir. He was very angry about it. Said that some friend of his had damaged the hat for a rag. I offered several times to get it put right, sir, but when he had cooled down he said it didn't matter. It wasn't a hat he very often used, sir. And besides, he said, why should he be a walking advertisement for his hatter?"

"Did you know that his dress suit had also lost the tailor's tab?"

"Had it indeed, sir? No, I can't say I noticed it."

"What sort of man was Mr. Mountjoy?"

"A very pleasant gentleman, sir. I'm very sorry to hear he has met with such a sad accident."

"How long has he lived here?"

"Six or seven years, I believe, sir. I've been here four years myself."

"When was the practical joke played on his silk hat?"

"About eighteen months ago, sir, if I remember rightly."

"As long ago as that? I fancied the hat looked newer."

"Well, sir, as I say, he didn't wear it above once or twice a week, sir. And Mr. Mountjoy didn't trouble about the fashion of his hats. There was one particular shape he fancied, and he had all his hats specially made to that pattern."

Parker nodded. He knew this already from the hatter and from Wimsey, but it was well to check matters up. He reflected that he had never yet caught Wimsey tripping in any fact pertaining to dress.

"Well," he said, "as you may have guessed, Withers, there will have to be an inquiry about Mr. Mountjoy's death. You had better say as little as possible to any outside person. You will give me all the keys of the flat, and I shall be leaving the police in charge here for a day or two."

"Very good, sir."

Parker waited to ascertain the name and address of the proprietor of the flats, and left Lumley to his investigations. From the proprietor he gained very little information. Mr. Mountjoy, of no profession, had taken the flat six years previously. He had paid his rent regularly. There had been no complaints. Nothing was known of Mr. Mountjoy's friends or relations. It was regrettable that so good a tenant should have come to so sudden and sad an end. It was much to be hoped that nothing would transpire of a scandalous nature, as those flats had always been extremely respectable.

Parker's next visit was to Mr. Mountjoy's bank. Here he

encountered the usual obstructive attitude, but eventually succeeded in getting access to the books. There was a regular income of about a thousand a year derived from sound investments. No irregularities. No mysterious fluctuations. Parker came away with an uneasy impression that Mr. Hector Puncheon had discovered a mare's nest.

CHAPTER XVI

ECCENTRIC BEHAVIOUR OF A
POST-OFFICE DEPARTMENT

THE Chief-Inspector voiced this opinion to Wimsey the same evening. His lordship, whose mind was still divided between detection and the new Whifflet campaign, which had taken clear shape during the afternoon, was curt with him:

"Mare's nest? Then what knocked Puncheon out? A kick from the mare's heel?"

"Perhaps Mountjoy merely got fed up with him. You'd get fed up yourself if you were pursued all over London by a Puncheon."

"Possibly. But I shouldn't knock him out and leave him to his fate. I should give him in charge. How is Puncheon?"

"Still unconscious. Concussion. He seems to have got a violent blow on the temple and a nasty crack on the back of the head."

"Um. Knocked up against the wall, probably, when Mountjoy got him with the cosh."

"No doubt you're right."

"I am always right. I hope you are keeping an eye on the man Garfield."

"He won't move for a bit. Why?"

"Well—it's odd that Mountjoy should have been snuffed out so inconveniently for you."

"You don't suppose that Garfield had anything to do with it? Why, the man was nearly killed himself. Besides, we've looked into him. He's a well-known Harley Street man, with a large West-end practice."

"Among the dope-maniacs, perhaps?"

"He specializes in nervous complaints."

"Exactly."

Parker whistled.

"That's what you think, is it?"

"See here," said Wimsey, "your grey matter isn't functioning as it ought. Are you tired at the end of the day? Do you suffer from torpor and lethargy after meals? Try Sparkletone, the invigorating vegetable saline that stimulates while it cleanses. Some accidents are too accidental to be true. When a gentleman removes his tailor's tab and takes the trouble to slice his hatter's imprint away with a razor, and goes skipping, for no reason at all, from Finchley to South Kensington Museum in his dress suit at unearthly hours in the morning, it's because he has something to hide. If he tops up his odd behaviour by falling under a train without the smallest apparent provocation, it's because somebody else is interested in getting the things hidden, too. And the more risks somebody else takes in the process, the more certain it is that the thing is worth hiding."

Parker looked at him and grinned quietly.

"You're a great guesser, Peter. Would you be surprised to hear that you're not the only one?"

"No, I shouldn't. You're holding something out on me. What is it? A witness to the assault, what? Somebody who was on the platform? Somebody you weren't inclined to pay much attention to? You old leg-puller, I can see it in your face. Out with it now—who was it? A Woman. A hysterical woman. A middle-aged, hysterical spinster. Am I right?"

"Curse you, yes."

"Go on, then. Tell me all about it."

"Well, when Eagles took the depositions of the witnesses at the station, they all agreed that Mountjoy had walked several paces past Garfield and then suddenly staggered; that Garfield had caught him by the arm and that both had fallen together. But this female, Miss Eliza Tebbutt by name, 52, unmarried, housekeeper, living in Kensington, says that she was standing a little way beyond them both and that she distinctly heard what she describes as a 'dreadful voice' say, 'Punch away, you're *for* it!' That Mountjoy immediately stopped as though he had been shot, and that Garfield 'with a terrible face,' took him by the arm and tipped him up. It may increase your confidence in this good lady when you hear that she is subject to nervous disorders, has once been confined in a mental home and is persuaded that Garfield is a prominent member of a gang whose object is to murder all persons of British birth and establish the supremacy of the Jews in England."

"Jews in England be damned. Because a person has a monomania she need not be wrong about her facts. She might have imagined or invented a good deal, but she couldn't possibly imagine or invent anything so fantastic as 'Punch away,' which is obviously her mishearing of the name 'Mountjoy.' Garfield's your man—though I admit that you're going to have some difficulty in fixing anything on

222

him. But if I were you, I'd have his premises searched—if it isn't too late by now."

"I'm afraid it probably is too late. We didn't get any sense out of Miss Tebbutt for an hour or so; by which time the heroic Dr. Garfield had, naturally, telephoned both to his home and to his consulting room to explain what had happened to him. Still, we'll keep an eye on him. The immediate matter of importance is Mountjoy. Who was he? What was he up to? Why did he have to be suppressed?"

"It's pretty clear what he was up to. He was engaged in the dope traffic and he was suppressed because he had been fool enough to let Puncheon recognize and follow him. Somebody must have been on the watch; this gang apparently keeps tabs on all its members. Or the wretched Mountjoy may have asked for help and been helped out of the world as the speediest method of disposing of the difficulty. It's a pity Puncheon can't talk—he could tell us whether Mountjoy had telephoned or spoken to anybody during his dash round town. Anyhow, he made a mistake, and people who make mistakes are not permitted to survive. The odd thing, to my mind, is that you heard nothing of any visit to the flat. You'd rather expect the gang to have made some sort of investigation there, just to make sure. I suppose those servants are to be trusted?"

"I think so. We've made inquiries. They've all got good histories. The commissionaire has an army pension and an excellent record. The valet and chambermaid are highly respectable—nothing whatever against them."

"H'm. And you've found nothing but a packet of cigarette-papers. Handy, of course, for wrapping up a grain or so of cocaine but, in themselves, no proof of anything."

"I thought you'd see the significance of the cigarette-papers."

"I am not yet blind or mentally deficient."

"But where is the dope?"

"The dope? Really, Charles! He was going to fetch the dope when friend Puncheon butted in. Haven't you yet grasped that this is part of the Milligan crowd and that Friday is their day for distributing dope? The Milligans get it on Friday and give house-parties on Friday night and Saturday, when it goes into the hands of the actual addicts. Dian de Momerie told me so."

"I wonder," said Parker, "why they stick to one day? It must add to the risk."

"It's obviously an integral part of the system. The stuff comes into the country—say on Thursdays. That's your part of the story. You don't seem to have done much about that,

223

by the way. It is taken to—somewhere or the other—that night. Next day it is called for by the Mountjoys and sent on to the Milligans, none of whom probably knows any of the others by sight. And by Saturday the whole lot is pushed out and everybody has a happy week-end."

"That sounds plausible. It certainly explains why we found no trace of anything either in the flat or on Mountjoy's body. Except cigarette-papers. By the way, is that right? If Mountjoy has the cigarette-papers, he ought to be the one who distributes to the addicts."

"Not necessarily. He gets it himself in bulk—done up as Bicarbonate of Soda or what not. He divides it into small packets and parcels them out—so many to Milligan, so many to the next retailer and so forth; when, or how, I don't know. Nor do I know how the payments are worked."

"Glad to hear there's something you don't know."

"I said I didn't know; not that I couldn't guess. But I won't bother you with guesses. All the same, it's rather surprising that Garfield & Co. left that flat alone."

"Perhaps Garfield meant to go there afterwards, if he hadn't got knocked out."

"No; he'd not leave it so late. Tell me again about the flat."

Parker patiently repeated the account of his visit and the interviews with the servants. Before he was half-way through, Wimsey had sat up in his chair and was listening with fascinated attention.

"Charles! What imbeciles we are! Of course, that's it!"

"What's what?"

"The Telephone Directory, of course. The man who brought the new volumes and took the old away. Since when has the Post Office taken to getting *both* new volumes out at once?"

"By Jove!" exclaimed Parker.

"I should think it was, by Jove. Ring up now and find out whether two new volumes were sent round to Mountjoy's address today."

"It'll be a job to get hold of O.C. Directories at this time of night."

"So it will. Wait a moment. Ring up the flats and ask if anybody else received any Directories this morning. My experience is that even Government departments do these things in batches, and don't make a special journey to every subscriber."

Parker acted on this suggestion. After a little trouble, he succeeded in getting into touch with three other occupants in the same block as Mountjoy's flat. All three gave the same answer. They had received a new L-Z volume about a fort-night previously. The new A-K volume was not yet due to be issued. One man went further. His name was Barrington, and he had only recently moved in. He had inquired when the new A-K volume would be out with his new 'phone number, and had been told that it would probably be issued in October.

"That settles it," said Wimsey. "Our friend Mountjoy kept his secrets in the telephone directory. That great work contains advertisements, post-office regulations and names and addresses, but particularly names and addresses. May we conclude that the secret nestled among the names and addresses? I think we may."

"It seems reasonable."

"Very reasonable. Now, how do we set about discovering those names and addresses?"

"Bit of a job. We can probably get a description of the man who called for the books this morning—"

"And comb London's teeming millions for him? Had we but world enough and time. Where do good telephone directories go when they die?"

"The pulping-mills, probably."

"And the last exchange of the L-Z volume was made a fortnight ago. There's a chance that it hasn't been pulped yet. Get on to it, Charles. There's more than a chance that it, too, was marked, and that the markings were transferred at each exchange from the old book to the new one."

"Why? Mountjoy might easily have kept the old marked set by him."

"I fancy not, or we should have either found it or heard about it from the manservant. The stranger came; the two current volumes were handed to him and he went away satisfied. As I see the plan, the whole idea would be to use the current volume, so as to rouse no suspicion, have nothing to conceal and provide a convenient mechanism for getting rid of the evidence at short notice."

"You may be right. It's a chance, as you say. I'll get on to the telephone people first thing in the morning."

The tide of luck seemed to have turned. A morning's strenuous work revealed that the old directories had already been dispatched by the sackful ot the pulping-mills, but had not, so far, been pulped. Six workers, toiling over the week-end among L-Z volumes collected from the Kesnington District, brought to light the pleasing fact that nine people out of ten marked their directories in some way or another. Reports came pouring in. Wimsey sat with Parker in the latter's office at Scotland Yard and considered these reports.

Late on Sunday night, Wimsey raised his head from a sheaf of papers.

"I think this is it, Charles."

"What is it?" Parker was weary and his eyes blood-shot with strain, but a note of hope was in his voice.

"This one. A whole list of public-houses in Central London have been ticked off—three in the middle of the L's, two near the end of the M's, one in the N's, one in the O's, and so forth and so on, including two in the middle of the W's. The two in the W's are the White Stag in Wapping and the White Stoat off Oxford Street. The next W after that is the White Swan in Covent Garden. I would bet any money that in the new volume that was carried away, the White Swan was duly ticked off in its turn."

"I'm not quite sure what you're driving at."

"I'm making rather a long cast, but I suggest this. When the stuff comes up to London of a Thursday, I think it is taken to which ever pub. stands next on the list in the directory. One week it will be a pub. with a name in A—say the Anchor. Next week it will be a B—the Bull & Dog, or the Brickmaker's Arms. The week after that, it will be a C, and so on to W,X,Y,Z—if there are any. The people who have to call for their dope wander into the pub. indicated, where it is slipped to them by the head distributor and his agents, probably quite without the knowledge of the proprietor. And since it never comes twice to the same place, your pretty policemen can go and talk parrots and goats in the White Swan till they are blue in the face. They ought to have been at the Yellow Peril or the York & Lancaster."

"That's an idea, Peter. Let's look at that list again."

Wimsey handed it over.

"If you're right, then this week was W week, and next week will be X week. That's unlikely. Say Y week. The next Y after the last one ticked is the Yelverton Arms in Soho. Wait a minute, though. If they have been taking them in alphabetical order, why have they got right down to the end of the M's in one case and only to WH in the other?

"They must have been through the W's once, and be starting again."

"Yes—I suppose there are quite a lot of M's. But then there are hundreds of W's. Still, we'll try it, Peter, any way. What is it, Lumley?"

"Report from the hospital, sir. Puncheon has come round."

Parker glanced through the report.

"Much what we expected," he said, handing the paper to Wimsey. "Mountjoy evidently knew he was being followed.

226

He put through a telephone call at Piccadilly Tube Station, and started off on a wild scamper across London."

"That was how the gang came to be ready for him."

"Yes. Finding he couldn't shake Puncheon off, he lured him into the Museum, got him into a quiet corner and laid him out. Puncheon thinks he was slugged with a weapon of some kind. So he was. He did not speak to Mountjoy. In fact, this report tells us nothing we didn't know, except that, when Puncheon first saw him, Mountjoy was buying an early copy of the *Morning Star* from a man outside the office."

"Was he? That's interesting. Well, keep your eye on the Yelverton Arms."

"And you keep your eye on Pym's. Do remember that what we want is the man at the top."

"So does Major Milligan. The man at the top is very much sought after. Well, cheerio! If I can't do anything more for you, I think I'll tootle off to bed. I've got my Whifflets scheme to get out tomorrow."

"I like this scheme, Mr. Bredon," said Mr. Pym, tapping his finger on the drafts submitted to him. "It has Breadth. It has Vision. More than anything else, Advertising needs Vision and Breadth. That is what determines Appeal. In my opinion, this scheme of yours has Appeal. It is going to be expensive, of course, and needs some working out. For instance, if all these vouchers were cashed in at once, it would send up the cost per packet issued to a figure that the profits could not possibly cover. But I think that can be got over."

"They won't all be cashed in at once," said Mr. Armstrong. "Not if we mix them up sufficiently. People will want time to collect and exchange. That will give us a start. They've got to look on the cost of the thing as so much advertising expenditure. We shall want a big press splash to start it, and after that, it will run itself quite happily in small spaces."

"That's all very well, Armstrong, but we've got to think of ourselves."

"That's all right. We make all the arrangements with the hotels and railways and so forth and charge our fee or commission on the work. All we've got to do is to average the thing out so that the claims won't amount to more than their estimated appropriation for the month. If the thing goes big they'll be willing enough to increase the appropriation. The other thing we've got to do is to see that each coupon bears more or less the same actual cash value, so as not to get into trouble with the Lottery Act. The whole thing comes down to this. How much of the profit on each shilling packet are they prepared to spend in advertising? Remembering that this scheme, if properly put through, is going to sweep every other fag off the market for the time being. Then we make our coupons up to that value minus an appropriation for the opening press campaign. At present their appropriation is sixty thousand and their sales ... have we got that report on sales?"

The two directors plunged into a maze of facts and figures. Mr. Bredon's attention wandered.

"Printing costs ... see that they have a sufficient distribution ... bonus to the tobacconists ... free displays ... tackle the hotels first ... news-value ... get the *Morning Star* to give it a show ... no, I know, but there's the Boost Britain side of it ... I can wangle Jenks ... reduce overheads by ... call it £200 a day ... Puffin's aeroplanes must be costing them that ... front-page splash and five free coupons ... well, that's a matter of detail. ..."

"In any case, we've got to do *something*." Mr. Armstrong emerged from the argument with a slightly flushed face. "It's no use telling people that the cost of the advertising has to come out of the quality of the goods. They don't care. All they want is something for nothing. Pay? Yes, of course they pay in the end, but somebody's got to pay. You can't fight free gifts with solemn assertions about Value. Besides, if Whifflets lose their market they'll soon lose their quality too—or what are we here for?"

"You needn't tell me that, Armstrong," said Mr. Pym. "Whether people like it or not, the fact remains that unless you continually increase sales you must either lose money or cut down quality. I hope we've learnt that by this time."

"What happens," asked Mr. Bredon, "when you've increased sales to saturation point?"

"You mustn't ask those questions, Bredon," said Mr. Armstrong, amused.

"No, but really. Suppose you push up the smoking of every man and woman in the Empire till they must either stop or die of nicotine poisioning?"

"We're a long way off that," replied Mr. Pym, seriously. "And that reminds me. This scheme should carry a strong appeal to women. 'Give your children that seaside holiday by smoking Whifflets.' That sort of thing. We want to get women down to serious smoking. Too many of them play about with it. Take them off scented stuff and put them on to the straightforward Virginia cigarette—"

"The gasper, in fact."

"Whifflets," said Mr. Pym. "You can smoke a lot more of

them in the day without killing yourself. And they're cheaper. If we increase women's smokes by 500 per cent—there's plenty of room for it—"

Mr. Bredon's attention wandered again.

"—all right, date the coupons. Let them run for three months only. That will give us plenty of duds to play with. And they'll have to see that their stockists are kept up to date with fresh goods. By the way, that makes a selling point—"

Mr. Bredon fell into a dream.

"—but you must have a good press campaign as well. Posters are good and cheap, but if you really want to tell people something, you've got to have a press campaign. Not a big one, necessarily, after the first big bang. But a good, short, snappy reminder week by week—"

"Very well, Mr. Bredon." The creator of the Whifflet scheme came out of his doze with a start. "We'll put this up to Whifflets. Will you see if you can get out some copy? And you'd better put a few other people on to it as well, Armstrong. Ingleby—it's rather his line. And Miss Meteyard. We want to get something out by the end of the week. Tell Mr. Barrow to put everything else aside and rough out some really striking displays." Mr. Pym gave the signal of dismissal, and then, as a thought struck him, called Bredon back.

"I want a word with you, Bredon. I'd almost forgotten what you were really here for. Has any progress been made in that matter?"

"Yes." The Whifflets campaign receded from Lord Peter Wimsey, dying along the distance of his mind. "In fact, the investigation is turning out to be of so much importance that I don't quiet know how I can take even you into my confidence."

"That's nonsense," said Mr. Pym. "I am enploying you—"

"No. There's no question of employment. I'm afraid it's a police job."

The shadows of disquiet gathered and deepened in Mr. Pym's eyes.

"Do you mean that those earlier suspicions you mentioned to me were actually justified?"

"Oh, yes. But it's a bigger thing than that."

"I don't want any scandal."

"Possibly not. But I don't quite see how it's to be avoided, if the thing comes to trial."

"Look here, Bredon," said Mr. Pym, "I don't like your behaviour. I put you in here as my private inquiry agent. I admit that you have made yourself very useful in other capacities, but you are not indispensable. If you insist on going beyond your authority—"

"You can sack me. Of course. But would that be wise?"

Mr. Pym mopped his forehead.

"Can you tell me this," he inquired anxiously, after a silence in which he seemed to be digesting the meaning of his employee's question. "Do your suspicions point to any particular person? Is it possible to remove that person promptly from our staff? You see my point. If, before this scandal breaks—whatever it is—and I really think I ought to be told—but so long as we can say that the person is no longer on the staff, it makes a difference. The firm's name might even be kept out of it—mightn't it? The good name of Pym's means a great deal to me, Mr. Bredon—"

"I can't tell you," said Wimsey; "a few days ago, I thought I knew, but just lately, other facts have come to my knowledge which suggest that the man I originally suspected may not be the right one. And until I know definitely, I can't do or say anything. At the moment it might be anybody. It might even be yourself."

"This is outrageous," cried Mr. Pym. "You can take your money and go."

Wimsey shook his head.

"If you get rid of me, the police will probably want to put somebody in my place."

"If I had the police here," retorted Mr. Pym, "I should at least know where I was. I know nothing about you, except that Mrs. Arbuthnot recommended you. I never cared for the idea of a private detective, though I certainly thought at first that you were of a somewhat superior type to the usual inquiry agent. But insolence I cannot and will not put up with. I shall communicate at once with Scotland Yard, and they will, I imagine, require you to state plainly what you imagine yourself to have discovered."

"They know it."

"Do they? You do not seem to be a model of discretion, Mr. Bredon." He pressed his buzzer. "Miss Hartley, will you please get Scotland Yard on the 'phone, and ask them to send up a reliable detective."

"Very well, Mr. Pym."

Miss Hartley danced away. This was meat and drink. She had always said there was something funny about Mr. Bredon, and now he had been caught. Pinching the cash, perhaps. She dialled the switch-board and asked for Whitehall 1212.

"Just one moment," said Wimsey, when the door had closed upon her. "If you really want Scotland Yard tell her to ask for Chief-Inspector Parker and say that Lord Peter

Wimsey would like to speak to him. Then he'll know what it's about."

"You are—? Why didn't you tell me?"

"I thought it might raise difficulties about the salary and prove embarrassing. I took the job on because I thought advertising might be rather good fun. So it is," added Wimsey, pleasantly, "so it is."

Mr. Pym put his head into Miss Hartley's room.

"I'll take that call in here," he said, briefly.

They sat mute till the call came through. Mr. Pym asked for Chief-Inspector Parker.

"There is a man here on my staff, calling himself—"

The conversation was a brief one. Mr. Pym handed the receiver to Wimsey.

"They want to speak to you."

"Hullo, Charles! That you? Have you established my credit? All right. . . . No, no trouble, only Mr. Pym feels he ought to know what it's all about. . . . Shall I tell him? . . . Not wise? . . . Honestly, Charles, I don't think he's our man. . . . Well, that's a different question. . . . The Chief-Inspector wants to know whether you can hold your tongue, Mr. Pym."

"I only wish to God everybody could hold his tongue," groaned Mr. Pym.

Wimsey passed on the reply. "I think I'll risk it, Charles. If anybody is going to be slugged in the dark after this, it won't be you, and I can look after myself."

He rang off and turned to Mr. Pym.

"Here's the brutal fact," he said. "Somebody's running an enormous dope-traffic from this office. Who is there that has far more money than he ought to have, Mr. Pym? We're looking for a very rich man. Can you help us?"

But Mr. Pym was past helping anybody. He was chalk-white.

"Dope? From this office? What on earth will our clients say? How shall I face the Board? The publicity . . ."

"Pym's Publicity," said Lord Wimsey, and laughed.

CHAPTER XVII

LACHRYMOSE OUTBURST OF A
NOBLEMAN'S NEPHEW

THAT week passed quietly. On Tuesday, Mr. Jollop passed, quite amiably, another of the new "Quotations" series for Nutrax "—And Kissed Again with Tears" ("But Tears, and Fallings-Out, however poetical, are nearly always a sign of Nerve-Strain"); on Wednesday, Green Pastures Margarine was Reduced in Price though Improved in Quality ("It might seem impossible to improve on Perfection but we have done it!"); Sopo adopted a new advertising figure ("Let Susan Sopo do the Dirty Work"); Tomboy Toffee finished up its Cricket Campaign with a huge display containing the portraits of a complete Eleven of Famous Cricketers all eating Tomboy; five people went on holiday; Mr. Prout created a sensation by coming to the office in a black shirt; Miss Rossiter lost a handbag containing her bonus money and recovered it from the Lost Property Office, and a flea was found in the ladies' cloak-room, causing dire upheaval, some ill-founded accusations and much heart-burning. In the typists' room, the subject of the flea almost ousted for the moment the juicier and more speculative topic of Mr. Tallboy's visitor. For, whether by the indiscretion of Tompkin or of the boy at the desk, or of some other person (though not of Mr. Ingleby or Mr. Bredon, who surely knew better) the tale had somehow seeped through.

"And how he does it on his salary I don't know," observed Miss Parton. "I do think it's a shame. His wife's a nice little woman. You remember, we met her last year at the Garden Party."

"Men are all alike," said Miss Rossiter, scornfully. "Even your Mr. Tallboy. I told you, Parton, that I didn't think old Copley was so much to blame as you thought in that other business, and now perhaps, you'll believe me. What I say is, if a man does one ungentlemanly thing, he'll do another. And as for doing it on his salary, how about that fifty pounds in an envelope? It's pretty obvious where *that* went to."

"It's always obvious where money goes to," said Miss

232

Meteyard, sardonically. "The point is, where does it come from?"

"That's what Mr. Dean used to say," said Miss Rossiter. "You remember how he used to chip Mr. Tallboy about his stockbrokers?"

"The famous firm of Smith," said Mr. Garrett. "Smith, Smith, Smith, Smith, Smith & Smith Unlimited."

"Money-lenders, if you ask me"' said Miss Rossiter. "Are you going to the cricket-match, Miss Meteyard? In *my* opinion, Mr. Tallboy ought to resign and leave somebody else to captain it. You can't wonder that people aren't keen to play under him, with all these stories going about. Don't you feel the same, Mr. Bredon?"

"Not a bit of it," said Mr. Bredon. "Provided the man can captain, I don't care a bit if he has as many wives as Solomon, and is a forger and swindler into the bargain. What's it matter?"

"It would matter to me," said Miss Rossiter.

"How feminine she is," said Mr. Bredon, plaintively, to the world at large. "She *will* let the personal element come into business."

"I dare say," said Miss Rossiter, "but you bet, if Hankie or Pymmy knew, there'd soon be an end of Mr. Tallboy."

"Directors are the last people to hear anything about the staff. Otherwise," said Miss Meteyard, "they wouldn't be able to stand on their hind legs at the Saff Dinner and shoot off the speeches about co-operation, and all being one happy family."

"Family quarrels, family quarrels." Mr. Ingleby waved his hand. "Little children, love one another and don't be such little nosey-parkers. What's Hecuba's bank-balance to you, or yours to Hecuba?"

"Bank-balance? Oh, you mean Mr. Tallboy's. Well, *I* don't know anything, except what little Dean used to say."

"And how did Dean know so much about it?"

"He was in Mr. Tallboy's office for a few weeks. Learning the work of other departments, they call it. I expect you'll be pushed round the office before long, Mr. Bredon. You'll have to mind your P's and Q's in the Printing. Mr. Thrale's a perfect tartar. Won't even allow you to slip out for coffee."

"I shall have to come to you for it."

"They won't let Mr. Bredon out of this department for a bit," said Miss Meteyard. "They're all up in the air about his Whifflets stunt. Everybody always hoped Dean would do better somewhere else. He was like a favourite book—you liked him so well that you were always yearning to lend him to somebody else."

"What a savage woman you are," observed Ingleby, coolly amused. "It's that kind of remark that gets the university woman a bad name." He glanced at Willis, who said:

"It isn't the savagery. It's the fact that there's no animosity behind it. You are all like that."

"You agree with Shaw—whenever you beat your child, be sure that you do it in anger."

"Shaw's Irish," said Bredon. "Willis has put his finger on the real offensiveness of the educated Englishman—that he will not even trouble to be angry."

"That's right," said Willis. "It's that awful, bleak, blank—" he waved his hands helplessly—"the façade."

"Meaning Bredon's face?" suggested Ingleby, mischievously.

"Icily regular, splendidly null," said Bredon, squinting into Miss Rossiter's mirror. "Strange, to think that a whole Whifflets campaign seethes and burgeons behind this solid ivory brow."

"Mixed metaphor," said Miss Meteyard. "Pots seethe, plants burgeon."

"Of course; it is a flower of rhetoric culled from the kitchen-garden."

"It's no use, Miss Meteyard," said Ingleby, "you might as well argue with an eel."

"Talking of eels," said Miss Meteyard, abandoning the position, "what's the matter with Miss Hartley?"

"The hipless wonder? Why?"

"She came up the other day to inform the world that the police were coming to arrest somebody."

"What?" said Willis.

"You mean, whom?"

"Whom, then?"

"Bredon."

"Mr. Bredon?" said Miss Parton. "What next, I wonder."

"You mean, what for? Why don't you people say what you do mean?"

Miss Rossiter turned on her chair and gazed at Mr. Bredon's gently twitching mouth.

"That's funny," she said. "Do you know, Mr. Bredon, we never told you, but Parton and I thought we saw you actually being arrested one evening, in Piccadilly Circus."

"Did you?"

"It wasn't you, of course."

"Well, as a matter of fact, it wasn't. Still, cheer up— it may happen yet. Only I suppose Pymmy doesn't keep his millions in the office safe."

"Nor yet in registered envelopes," said Miss Meteyard, casually.

"Don't say they're after our Mr. Copley!"

"I hope not. Bread-and-skilly wouldn't suit him at all."

"But what was Bredon being arrested for?"

"Loitering, perhaps," said a mild voice in the doorway. Mr. Hankin poked his head round the corner and smiled sarcastically. "I am sorry to interrupt you, but if Mr. Bredon could favour me with his attention for a moment on the subject of Twentyman's Teas——"

"I beg your pardon, sir," said Mr. Bredon, springing to attention and allowing himself to be marched off.

Miss Rossiter shook her head.

"You mark my words, there's a mystery about Mr. Bredon."

"He's a darling," objected Miss Parton, warmly.

"Oh, Bredon's all right," said Ingleby.

Miss Meteyard said nothing. She went downstairs to the Executive and borrowed the current volume of *Who's Who*. She ran her finger through the W's, till she came to the entry beginning: "WIMSEY, Peter Death Bredon (Lord), D.S.O., born 1890; second *s.* of Mortimer Gerald Bredon Wimsey, 15th Duke of Denver, and Honoria Lucasta, *d.* of Francis Delagardie of Bellingham Manor, Bucks. *Educ.* Eton College and Balliol." She read it through.

"So that's it," said Miss Meteyard to herself. "I thought so. And now what? Does one do anything? I think not. Better leave it alone. But there's no harm in putting out feelers for another job. One's got to look after one's self."

Mr. Bredon, unaware that his disguise had been penetrated, gave but a superficial consideration to the interests of Twentyman's Teas. He meekly accepted the instruction to prepare a window-bill with two streamers on the subject of a richer infusion with fewer spoonfuls, and a gentle rebuke in the matter of wasting time in the typists' room. His mind was in Old Broad Street.

"You are playing for us on Saturday, I see," said Mr. Hankin, at the conclusion of the interview.

"Yes, sir."

"I hope the weather will hold. You have played in first-class cricket, I believe?"

"A long time ago."

"You will be able to show them a bit of style" said Mr. Hankin, happily. "Style—one sees so little of it nowadays. I am afraid you will find us a scratch lot, and for some reason, several of our best players seem unable to attend this match.

A pity. But you will find Mr. Tallboy very good. An excellent all-round man, and quite remarkable in the field."

Mr. Bredon said that it was all too rare to find proper attention given to fielding. Mr. Hankin agreed with him.

"Mr. Tallboy is excellent at all games; it's a pity he can't give more time to them. Personally, I should like to see more organization of the athletic side of our social functions here. But Mr. Pym thinks it would perhaps be too absorbing, and I dare say he is right. Still, I can't help feeling that the cultivation of the team-spirit would do this office good. I don't know whether you, as a newcomer, have noticed a certain tension from time to time—"

Bredon admitted that he had noticed something of the sort.

"You know, Mr. Bredon," said Mr. Hankin, a little wistfully, "it is sometimes difficult for the directors to get the atmosphere of situations in the office. You people keep us rather in cotton-wool, don't you? It can't be helped, naturally, but I sometimes fancy that there are currents beneath the surface. . . ."

Evidently, thought Bredon, Mr. Hankin had realized that something was on the point of breaking. He felt suddenly sorry for him. His eyes strayed to a strip poster, printed in violent colours and secured by drawing-pins to Mr. Hankin's notice-board:

EVERY ONE EVERYWHERE ALWAYS AGREES
ON THE FLAVOUR AND VALUE OF TWENTYMAN'S TEAS

No doubt it was because agreement on any point was so rare in a quarrelsome world, that the fantastical announcements of advertisers asserted it so strongly and so absurdly. Actually, there was no agreement, either on trivialities like tea or on greater issues. In this place, where from morning till night a staff of over a hundred people hymned the praises of thrift, virtue, harmony, eupepsia and domestic contentment, the spiritual atmosphere was clamorous with financial storm, intrigue, dissension, indigestion and marital infidelity. And, with worse things—with murder wholesale and retail, of soul and body, murder by weapon and by poison. These things did not advertise, or, if they did, they called themselves by other names.

He made some vague answer to Mr. Hankin.

At one o'clock he left the office and took a taxi citywards.

He was suddenly filled with a curiosity to visit Mr. Tallboy's stockbroker.

At twenty minutes past one, he was standing on the pavement in Old Broad Street, and his blood was leaping with the excitement wich always accompanies discovery.

Mr. Tallboy's stockbroker inhabited a small tobacconist's shop, the name over which was not Smith but Cummings.

"An accommodation address," observed Lord Peter Wimsey. "Most unusual for a stockbroker. Let us probe this matter further."

He entered the shop, which was narrow, confined and exceedingly dark. An elderly man stepped forward to serve him. Wimsey went immediately to the point.

"Can I see Mr. Smith?"

"Mr. Smith doesn't live here."

"Then perhaps you would kindly let me leave a note for him."

The elderly man slapped his hand on the counter.

"If I've said it once, I've said it five hundred times," he snapped irritably. "There's no Mr. Smith here, and never was, to my knowledge. And if you're the gentleman that addresses his letters here, I'd be glad if you'd take that for an answer. I'm sick and tired of handing his letters back to the postman."

"You surprise me. I don't know Mr. Smith myself, but I was asked by a friend to leave a message for him."

"Then tell your friend what I say. It's no good sending letters here. None whatever. Never has been. People seem to think I've got nothing better to do than hand out letters to postmen. If I wasn't a conscientious man, I'd burn the lot of them. That's what I'd do. Burn 'em. And I will, if it goes on any longer. You can tell your friend that from me."

"I'm very sorry," said Wimsey. "There seems to be some mistake."

"Mistake?" said Mr. Cummings, angrily. "I don't believe it's a mistake at all. It's a stupid practical joke, that's what it is. And I'm fed up with it, I can tell you."

"If it is," said Wimsey, "I'm the victim of it. I've been sent right out of my way to deliver a message to somebody who doesn't exist. I shall speak to my friend about it."

"I should, if I were you," said Mr. Cummings. "A silly, tom-fool trick. You tell your friend to come here himself, that's all. I'll know what to say to him."

"That's a good idea," said Wimsey. "And you tell him off."

"You can lay your last penny I shall, sir." Mr. Cummings,

having blown off his indignation, seemed a little appeased. "If your friend should turn up, what name will he give, sir?"

Wimsey, on the point of leaving the shop, pulled up short. Mr. Cummings, he noticed, had a pair of very sharp eyes behind his glasses. A thought struck him.

"Look here," he said, leaning confidentially over the counter. "My friend's name is Milligan. That mean anything to you? He told me to come to you for a spot of the doings. See what I mean?"

That got home; a red glint in Mr. Cummings' eye told Wimsey as much.

"I don't know what you are talking about," was what Mr. Cummings actually said. "I never heard of a Mr. Milligan, and I don't want to. And I don't want any of your sauce, neither."

"Sorry, old thing, sorry," said Wimsey.

"And what's more," said Mr. Cummings, "I don't want you. See?"

"I see," said Wimsey. "I see perfectly. Good-morning."

"That's torn it," he thought. "I'll have to work quickly now. St. Martin's-le-Grand comest next, I fancy."

A little pressure at head-quarters produced what was required. The postmen who carried letters to Old Broad Street were found and interrogated. It was quite true that they frequently delivered letters for a Mr. Smith to Mr. Cummings' shop, and that these letters invariably were returned, and marked "Not known." Where did they go then? To the Returned Letter Office. Wimsey rang up Pym's, explained that he was unavoidably detained, and sought the Returned Letter Office. After a little delay, he found the official who knew all about it.

The letters for Mr. Smith came regularly every week. They were never returned to the sender in the ordinary course. Why? Because they bore no sender's name. In fact, they never contained anything but a sheet of blank paper.

"Had they last Tuesday's letter there?" No; it had already been opened and destroyed. Would they keep the next one that arrived and send it on to him? Seeing that Lord Peter Wimsey had Scotland Yard behind him, they would. Wimsey thanked the official, and went his way, pondering.

On leaving the office at 5.30, he walked down Southampton Row to Theobald's Road. There was a newsvendor at the corner. Wimsey purchased an *Evening Comet* and glanced carelessly through the news. A brief paragraph in the Stop Press caught his eye.

CLUBMAN KILLED IN PICCADILLY

At 3 o'clock this afternoon a heavy lorry skidded and mounted the pavement in Piccadilly, fatally injuring Major "Tod" Milligan, the well-known clubman, who was standing on the kerb.

"They work quickly," he thought with a shudder. "Why, in God's name, am I still at large?" He cursed his own recklessness. He had betrayed himself to Cummings; he had gone into the shop undisguised; by now they knew who he was. Worse, they must have followed him to the General Post Office and to Pym's. Probably they were following him now. From behind the newspaper he cast a swift glance about the crowded streets. Any one of these loitering men might be *the* man. Absurd and romantic plans flitted through his mind. He would lure his assassins into some secluded spot, such as the Blackfriars subway or the steps beneath Cleopatra's Needle, and face them there and kill them with his hands. He would ring up Scotland Yard and get a guard of detectives. He would go straight home to his own flat in a taxi ("not the first nor the second that presents itself," he thought, with a fleeting recollection of Professor Moriarty), barricade himself in and wait—for what? For air-guns? ... In this perplexity he suddenly caught sight of a familiar figure—Chief-Inspector Parker himself, apparently taking his early way home, and carrying a fish-monger's bag in one hand and an attaché case in the other.

He lowered the paper and said, "Hullo!"

Parker stopped. "Hullo!" he replied, tentatively. He was obviously not quite certain whether he was being hailed by Lord Peter Wimsey or by Mr. Death Bredon. Wimsey strode forward and relieved him of the fish-bag.

"Well met. You come most carefully upon your cue, to prevent me from being murdered. What's this, lobster?"

"No, turbot" said Parker, placidly.

"I'm coming to eat it with you. They will hardly attack both of us. I've made a fool of myself and given the game away, so we may as well be open and cheerful about it."

"Good. I'd like to feel cheerful."

"What's wrong? Why so early home?"

"Fed-up. The Yelverton Arms is a wash-out, I'm afraid."

"Did you raid it?"

"Not yet. Nothing happened during the morning, but during the lunch-hour crush, Lumley saw something being smuggled into a fellow's hands by a chap who looked like a tout. They stopped the fellow and searched him. All they found was some betting-slips. It's quite possible that nothing is

239

timed to happen before this evening. If nothing turns up, I'll have the place searched. Just before closing-time will be best. I'm going down there myself. Thought I'd step home for an early supper."

"Right. I've got something to tell you."

They walked to Great Ormond Street in silence.

"Cummings?" said Parker, when Wimsey had told his tale. "Don't know anything about him. But you say he knew Milligan's name?"

"He certainly did. Besides, here's the proof of it."

He showed Parker the stop-press item.

"But this fellow, Tallboy—is he the bird you're after?"

"Frankly, Charles, I don't understand it. I can't see him as the Big Bug in all this business. If he were, he'd be too well-off to get into difficulties with a cheap mistress. And his money wouldn't be coming to him in fifty-pound instalments. But there's a connection. There must be."

"Possibly he's only a small item in the account"

"Possibly. But I can't get over Milligan. According to his information, the whole show was run from Pyms."

"Perhaps it is. Tallboy may be merely the cat's paw for one of the others. Pym himself—he's rich enough, isn't he?"

"I don't think it's Pym. Armstrong, possibly, or even quiet little Hankie. Of course, Pym's calling me in may have been a pure blind, but I don't somehow think he has quite that kind of brain. It was so unnecessary. Unless he wanted to find out, through me, how much Victor Dean really knew. In which case, he's succeeded," added Wimsey, ruefully. "But I can't believe that any man would be such a fool as to put himself in the power of one of his own staff. Look at the opportunities for blackmail! Twelve years' penal servitude is a jolly threat to hold over a man. Still—blackmail. Somebody was being blackmailed, that's almost a certainty. But Pym can't have slugged Dean; he was in conference at the time. No, I think we must acquit Pym."

"What I don't quite see" said Lady Mary, "is why Pym's is brought into it at all. Somebody at Pym's is one thing, but if you say that the show is 'run from Pym's,' it suggests something quite different—to me, anyhow. It sounds to me as though they were using Pym's organization for something—doesn't it to you?"

"Well, it does," agreed her husband. "But how? And why? What has advertising got to do with it? Crime doesn't want to advertise, far from it."

240

"I don't know," said Wimsey, suddenly and softly. "I don't know." His nose twitched, rabbit-fashion. "Pymmy was saying only this morning that to reach the largest number of people all over the country in the shortest possible time, there was nothing like a press campaign. Wait a second, Polly—I'm not sure that you haven't said something useful and important."

"Everything I say is useful and important. Think it over while I go and tell Mrs. Gunner how to cook turbot."

"And the funny thing is," said Parker, "she seems to like telling Mrs. Gunner how to cook turbot. We could perfectly well afford more servants—"

"My dear old boy," said Wimsey. "Servants are the devil. I don't count my man Bunter, because he's exceptional, but it's a treat to Polly to kick the whole boiling out of the house at night. Don't you worry. When she wants servants, she'll ask for them."

"I admit," said Parker, "I was glad myself when the kids were old enough to dispense with a resident nurse. But look here, Peter, it seems to me you'll be wanting a resident nurse yourself, if you want to avoid nasty accidents."

"That's just it. Here I am. Why? What are they keeping me for? Something unusually nasty?"

Parker moved quietly across to the window and peered out from a little gap in the short net blind.

"He's there, I think. A repellent-looking young man in a check cap, playing with a Yo-Yo on the opposite pavement. Playing darned well, too, with a circle of admiring kids round him. What a grand excuse for loitering. There he goes. Three-leaf clover, over the falls, non-stop lift, round the world. Quite masterly. I must tell Mary to have a look at him, and take a lesson. You'd better sleep here tonight, old man."

"Thanks. I think I will."

"And stop away from the office tomorrow."

"I should, in any case. I've got to play in a cricket match at Brotherhood's. Their place is down at Romford."

"Cricket-match be damned. I don't know, though. It's nice and public. Provided the fast bowler doesn't knock you out with a swift ball, it may be as safe as anywhere else. How are you going?"

"Office charabanc."

"Good. I'll see you round to the starting-point."

Wimsey nodded. Nothing further was said about dope or danger until supper was over and Parker had departed for the Yelverton Arms. Then Wimsey gathered up a calendar, the telephone directory, a copy of the official report on the volume retrieved from Mountjoy's flat, a scribbling-block and a pencil, and curled himself up on the couch with a pipe.

"You don't mind, do you, Polly? I want to brood."

Lady Mary dropped a kiss on the top of his head.

"Brood on, old thing. I won't disturb you. I'm going up to the nursery. And if the telephone rings, take care it isn't the mysterious summons to the lonely warehouse by the river, or the bogus call to Scotland Yard."

"All right. And if the door-bell rings, beware of the disguised gas-inspector and the plain-clothes cop without a warrant-card. I need scarcely warn you against the golden-haired girl in distress, the slit-eyed Chink or the distinguished grey-haired man wearing the ribbon of some foreign order."

He brooded.

He took from his pocket-book the paper he had removed, weeks earlier, from Victor Dean's desk, and compared the dates with the calendar. They were all Tuesdays. After a little further cogitation, he added the date of the previous Tuesday week, the day when Miss Vavasour had called at the office and Tallboy had borrowed his pen to address a letter to Old Broad Street. To this date he appended the initial "T." Then, his mind working slowly backwards, he remembered that he had come to Pym's on a Tuesday, and that Tallboy had come into the typists' room for a stamp. Miss Rossiter had read out the name of his addressee—what had the initial been? "K," of course. He wrote this down also. Then with rather more hesitation, he looked up the date of the Tuesday preceding Mr. Puncheon's historic adventure at the White Swan, and wrote "W?"

So far, so good. But from "K" to "T" there were nine letters—there had not been nine weeks. Nor should "W" have come between "K" and "T." What was the rule governing the letter-sequence? He drew thoughtfully at his pipe and sank into a reverie that was almost a pipe-dream, till he was aroused by a very distinct sound of yells and conflict from the floor above. Presently the door opened and his sister appeared, rather flushed.

"I'm sorry, Peter. Did you hear the row? Your young namesake was being naughty. He heard Uncle Peter's voice and refused to stay in bed. He wants to come down and see you."

"Very flattering," said Wimsey.

"But very exhausting," said Mary. "I do hate disciplining people. Why shouldn't he see his uncle? Why should uncle be busy with dull detective business when his nephew is so much more interesting?"

"Quite so," said Wimsey. "I have often asked myself the same question. I gather that you hardened your heart."

"I compromised. I said that if he was a good boy and went back to bed, Uncle Peter might come up to say good night to him."

"And has he been a good boy?"

"Yes. In the end. That is to say, he is in bed. At least, he was when I came down."

"Very well," said Wimsey, putting down his paraphernalia. "Then I will be a good uncle."

He mounted the stairs obediently and found Peterkin, aged three, technically in bed. That is to say, he was sitting bolt upright with the blankets cast off, roaring lustily.

"Hullo!" said Wimsey, shocked.

The roaring ceased.

"What is all this?" Wimsey traced the course of a fat, down-rolling drop with a reproachful finger. "Tears, idle tears? Great Scott!"

"Uncle Peter! I got a naeroplane." Peterkin tugged violently at the sleeve of a suddenly unresponsive uncle. "Look at my naeroplane, Uncle! Naeroplane, naeroplane!"

"I beg your pardon, old chap," said Wimsey, recollecting himself. "I wasn't thinking. It's a beautiful aeroplane. Does it fly? ... Hi! you needn't get up and show me now. I'll take your word for it."

"Mummie make it fly."

It flew very competently, effecting a neat landing on the chest of drawers. Wimsey watched it with vague eyes.

"Uncle Peter!"

"Yes, son, it's splendid. Listen, would you like a speed-boat?"

"What's peed-boat?"

"A boat that will run in the water—chuff, chuff—like that."

"Will it float in my barf?"

"Yes, of course. It'll sail right across the Round Pond."

Peterkin considered.

"Could I have it in my barf wiv' me?"

"Certainly, if Mummie says so."

"I'd like a boat in my barf."

"You shall have one, old man."

"When, now?"

"Tomorrow."

"Weally tomowwow?"

"Yes, promise."

"Say thank-you, Uncle Peter."

"Fank-you, Uncle Peter. Will it be tomowwow soon?"

"Yes, if you lie down now and go to sleep."

Peterkin, who was a practically-minded child, shut his eyes instantly, wriggled under the bed-clothes, and was promptly tucked in by a firm hand.

"Really, Peter, you shouldn't bribe him to go to sleep. How about my discipline?"

"Discipline be blowed," said Peter, at the door.

"Uncle!"

"Good night!"

"Is it tomowwow yet?"

"Not yet. Go to sleep. You can't have tomorrow till you've been to sleep."

"Why not?"

"It's one of the rules."

"Oh! I'm asleep now, Uncle Peter."

"Good. Stick to it." Wimsey pulled his sister out after him and shut the nursery door.

"Polly, I'll never say kids are a nuisance again."

"What's up? I can see you're simply bursting with something."

"I've got it! Tears, idle Tears. That kid deserves fifty speed-boats as a reward for howling."

"Oh, dear!"

"I couldn't tell him that, though, could I? Come downstairs, and I'll show you something."

He dragged Mary at full speed into the sitting-room, took up his list of dates and jabbed at it with a jubilant pencil.

"See that date? That's the Tuesday before the Friday on which coke was being served out at the White Swan. On that Tuesday, the Nutrax headline was finally passed for the following Friday. And what," asked Wimsey, rhetorically, "was that headline?"

"I haven't the faintest idea. I never read advertisements."

"You should have been smothered at birth. The headline was, 'Why Blame the Woman?' You will note that it begins with a 'W.' White Swan also begins with a 'W.' Got that?"

"I think so. It seems fairly simple."

"Just so. Now on this date, the Nutrax headline was 'Tears, idle Tears'—a quotation from the poets."

"I follow you so far."

"This is the date on which the headline was passed for press, you understand."

"Yes."

"Also a Tuesday."

"I have grasped that."

"On that same Tuesday, Mr. Tallboy, who is Group-manager for Nutrax, wrote a letter addressed to 'T. Smith, Esq.' You get that?"

"Yes."

"Very good. That advertisement appeared on a Friday."

"Are you trying to explain that these advertisements are all passed for press on a Tuesday and all appear on a Friday?"

"Exactly."

"Then why not say so, instead of continually repeating yourself?"

"All right. But now perpend. Mr. Tallboy has a habit of sending letters on a Tuesday, addressed to a Mr. Smith—who, by the way, doesn't exist."

"I know. You told us all about that. Mr. T. Smith is Mr. Cummings; only Mr. Cummings denies it."

"He denies it, said the King. Leave out that part. The point is that Mr. Smith isn't always Mr. T. Smith. Sometimes he's other kinds of Mr. Smith. But on the day that the Nutrax headline began with a 'T,' Mr. Smith was Mr. T. Smith."

"And what sort of Mr. Smith was he on the day that the Nutrax headline began with a 'W'?"

"Unfortunately I don't know. But I can guess that he was Mr. W. Smith. In any case, on this date here, which was the day I came to Pym's, the Nutrax headline was 'Kittle Cattle.' On that day, Mr. Smith—"

"Stop! I can guess this one. He was Mr. K. Smith."

"He was. Kenneth, perhaps, or Kirkpatrick, or Killarney. Killarney Smith would be a lovely name."

"And was coke distributed the next Friday from the King's Head?"

"I'm betting my boots it was. What do you think of that?"

"I think you want a little more evidence on that point. You don't seem to have any instance where you can point to the initial, the headline and the pub. all together."

"That's the weak point," confessed Wimsey. "But look here. This Tuesday which I now write down is the date on which the great Nutrax row occurred, and the headline was altered at the last moment on Thursday night. On the Friday of that week, something went wrong with the supply of dope to Major Milligan. It never turned up."

"Peter, I do believe you've got hold of something."

"Do you, Polly? Well, so do I. But I wasn't sure if it would sound plausible to anybody but me. And, look here! I remember another day." Wimsey began to laugh. "I forget which date it was, but the headline was simply a blank line

245

and an exclamation mark, and Tallboy was horribly peeved about it. I wonder what they did that week. I should think they took the initial of the sub-head. What a joke!"

"But how is it worked, Peter?"

"Well, I don't know the details, but I imagine it's done this way. On the Tuesday, as soon as the headline is decided, Tallboy sends an envelope to Cummings' shop addressed to A. Smith, Esq., or B. Smith, Esq., according to the initial of the headline. Cummings looks at it, snorts at it and hands it back to the postman. Then he informs the head distributing agent, or agents. I don't know how. Possibly he advertises too, because the great point of this scheme, as I see it, is to have as little contact as possible between the various agents. The stuff is run across on Thursday, and the agent meets it and packets it up as Bicarbonate of Soda, or something equally harmless. Then he gets the London Telephone Directory and looks up the next pub. on the list whose name begins with the letter of which Cummings has advised him. As soon as the pub. opens on Friday morning, he is there. The retail agents, if we may call them so, have meanwhile consulted the *Morning Star* and the Telephone Directory. They hasten to the pub. and the packets are passed to them. The late Mr. Mountjoy must have been one of these gentry."

"How does the wholesaler recognize the retailer?"

"There must be some code or other, and our battered friend Hector Puncheon must have given the code-word by accident. We must ask about that. He's a *Morning Star* man, and it may be something to do with the *Morning Star*. Mountjoy, by the way, evidently believed in being early on the job, because he seems to have made a practice of getting his copy of the paper the second it was off the machine, which accounts for his having been in full working order at 4.30 a.m. in Covent Garden, and hanging round Fleet Street again in the small hours of the following Friday. He must have given the code-signal, whatever it was; Puncheon may remember about it. After that, he would make his supply up into smaller packets (hence his supply of cigarette-papers) and proceed with the distribution according to his own taste and fancy. Of course, there are a lot of things we don't know yet. How the payments are made, for instance. Puncheon wasn't asked for money. Tallboy seems to have got his particular share in Currency Notes. But that's a detail. The ingenuity of the thing is that the stuff is never distributed twice from the same place. No wonder Charles had difficulties with it. By the way, I've sent him to the wrong place tonight, poor devil. How he must be cursing me!"

Mr. Parker cursed solidly enough on his return.

"It's entirely my fault," said Wimsey, blithely. "I sent you to the Yelverton Arms. You ought to have been at the Anchor or the Antelope. But we'll pull it off next week—if we live so long."

"If," said Parker, seriously, "we live so long."

CHAPTER XVIII

UNEXPECTED CONCLUSION OF A
CRICKET MATCH

THE party from Pym's filled a large charabanc; in addition, a number of people attended in their own Austins. It was a two-innings match, starting at 10 a.m., and Mr. Pym liked to see it well attended. A skeleton staff was left to hold the fort at the office during the Saturday morning, and it was expected that as many of them as possible would trundle down to Romford by the afternoon train. Mr. Death Bredon, escorted by Lady Mary and Chief-Inspector Parker, was one of the last to scramble into the charabanc.

The firm of Brotherhood believed in ideal conditions for their staff. It was their pet form of practical Christianity; in addition to which, it looked very well in their advertising literature and was a formidable weapon against the trade unions. Not, of course, that Brotherhood's had the slightest objection to trade unions as such. They had merely discovered that comfortable and well-fed people are constitutionally disinclined for united action of any sort—a fact which explains the asinine meekness of the income-tax payer.

In Brotherhood's régime of bread and circuses, organized games naturally played a large part. From the pavilion overlooking the spacious cricket-field floated superbly a crimson flag, embroidered with the Brotherhood trademark of two clasped hands. The same device adorned the crimson blazers and caps of Brotherhood's cricket eleven. By contrast, the eleven advertising cricketers were but a poor advertisement for themselves. Mr. Bredon was, indeed, a bright spot on the landscape, for his flannels were faultless, while his Balliol blazer, though ancient, carried with it an air of authenticity. Mr. Ingleby also was correct, though a trifle shabby. Mr. Hankin, beautifully laundered, had rather spoilt his general effect by a brown felt hat, while Mr. Tallboy, irreproachable in other respects, had an unfortunate tendency to come apart at the waist, for which his tailor and shirt-maker were, no doubt, jointly responsible. The dress of the remainder varied in combining white flannels with brown shoes, white shoes

248

with the wrong sort of shirt, tweed coats with white linen hats, down to the disgraceful exhibition of Mr. Miller, who, disdaining to put himself out for a mere game, affronted the sight in grey flannel trousers, a striped shirt and braces.

The day began badly with Mr. Tallboy's having lost his lucky half-crown and with Mr. Copley's observing, offensively, that perhaps Mr. Tallboy would prefer to toss with a pound-note. This flustered Mr. Tallboy. Brotherhood's won the toss and elected to go in first. Mr. Tallboy, still flustered, arranged his field, forgetting in his agitation Mr. Hankin's preference for mid-on and placing him at cover-point. By the time this error was remedied, it wad discovered that Mr. Haagedorn had omitted to bring his wicket-keeper's gloves, and a pair had to be borrowed from the pavilion. Mr. Tallboy then realized that he had put on his two fast bowlers together. He remedied this by recalling Mr. Wedderburn from the deep field to bowl his slow "spinners," and dismissing Mr. Barrow in favour of Mr. Beeseley. This offended Mr. Barrow, who retired in dudgeon to the remotest part of the field and appeared to go to sleep.

"What's all the delay about?" demanded Mr. Copley.

Mr. Willis said he thought Mr. Tallboy must have got a little confused about the bowling order.

"Lack of organization," said Mr. Copley. "He should make out a list and stick to it."

The first Brotherhood innings passed off rather uneventfully. Mr. Miller missed two easy catches and Mr. Barrow, to show his resentment at the placing of the field, let a really quite ordinary ball go to the boundary instead of running after it. The eldest Mr. Brotherhood, a spry old gentleman of seventy-five, came doddering cheerfully round from the pavilion and sat down to make himself agreeable to Mr. Armstrong. He did this by indulging in reminiscences of all the big cricket matches he had ever seen in a long life, and as he had been devoted to the game since his boyhood, and had never missed a game of any importance, this took him some time and was excessively wearisome to Mr. Armstrong, who thought cricket a bore and only attended the staff match out of compliment to Mr. Pym's prejudices. Mr. Pym, whose enthusiasm was only equalled by his ignorance of the game, applauded bad strokes and good strokes indifferently.

Eventually the Brotherhoods were dismissed for 155, and the Pym Eleven gathered themselves together from the four corners of the field; Messrs. Garrett and Barrow, both rather ill-tempered, to buckle on their pads, and the remainder of the team to mingle with the spectators. Mr. Bredon, languid in movement but cheerful, laid himself down at Miss Meteyard's feet, while Mr. Tallboy was collared by the aged Mr. Brotherhood, thus releasing Mr. Armstrong, who promptly accepted the invitation of a younger Brotherhood to inspect a new piece of machinery.

The innings opened briskly. Mr. Barrow, who was rather a showy bat, though temperamental, took the bowling at the factory end of the pitch and cheered the spirits of his side by producing a couple of twos in the first over. Mr. Garrett, canny and cautious, stonewalled perseveringly through five balls of the following over and then cut the leather through the slips for a useful three. A single off the next ball brought the bowling back to Mr. Barrow, who, having started favourably, exhibited a happy superiority complex and settled down to make runs. Mr. Tallboy breathed a sigh of relief. Mr. Barrow, confident and successful, could always be relied upon for some good work; Mr. Barrow, put off his stroke by a narrowly missed catch, or the sun in his eyes, or a figure crossing the screens, was apt to become defeatist and unreliable. The score mounted blithely to thirty. At this point, Brotherhood's captain, seeing that the batsmen had taken the measure of the bowling, took off the man at the factory end and substituted a short, pugnacious-looking person with a scowl, at sight of whom Mr. Tallboy quaked again.

"They're putting on Simmonds very early," he said. "I only hope nobody gets hurt."

"Is this their demon bowler?" inquired Bredon, seeing the wicket-keeper hurriedly retire to a respectful distance from the wicket.

Tallboy nodded. The ferocious Simmonds wetted his fingers greedily, pulled his cap fiercely over his eyes, set his teeth in a snarl of hatred, charged like a bull and released the ball with the velocity of a 9-inch shell in Mr. Barrow's direction.

Like most fast bowlers, Simmonds was a little erratic in the matter of length. His first missile pitched short, rocketed up like a pheasant, whizzed past Mr. Barrow's ear and was adroitly fielded by long-stop, a man with a phlegmatic countenance and hands of leather. The next two went wide. The fourth was pitched straight and with a good length. Mr. Barrow tackled it courageously. The impact affected him like an electric shock; he blinked and shook his fingers, as though not quite sure whether his bones were still intact. The fifth was more manageable; he smote it good and hard and ran.

"Again!" yelled Mr. Garrett, already half-way down the pitch for the second time. Mr. Barrow accordingly ran and once again stood ready for the onslaught. It came; it ran up his bat like a squirrel, caught him viciously on the knuckle and glanced off sharply, offering a chance to point, who, very fortunately, fumbled it. The field crossed over, and Mr. Barrow was able to stand aside and nurse his injuries.

Mr. Garrett, pursuing a policy of dogged-does-it, proceeded systematically to wear down the bowling by blocking the first four balls of the next over. The fifty produced two runs; the sixth, which was of much the same calibre, he contented himself with blocking again.

"I don't like this slow-motion cricket," complained the aged Mr. Brotherhood. "When I was a young man—"

Mr. Tallboy shook his head. He knew very well that Mr. Garrett suffered from a certain timidity when facing fast bowling. He knew, too, that Garrett had some justification, because he wore spectacles. But he knew equally well what Mr. Barrow would think about it.

Mr. Barrow, irritated, faced the redoubtable Simmonds with a sense of injury. The first ball was harmless and useless; the second was a stinger, but the third he could hit and did. He whacked it away lustily to the boundary for four, amid loud cheers. The next kept out of the wicket only by the grace of God, but the sixth he contrived to hook round to leg for a single. After which, he adopted Mr. Garrett's tactics, stonewalled through an entire over, and left Mr. Garrett to face the demon.

Mr. Garrett did his best. But the first ball rose perpendicularly under his chin and unnerved him. The second came to earth about half-way down the pitch and bumped perilously over his head. The third, pitched rather longer, seemed to shriek as it rushed for him. He stepped out, lost heart, flinched and was bowled as clean as a whistle.

"Dear, dear!" said Mr. Hankin. "It seems that it is up to me." He adjusted his pads and blinked a little. Mr. Garrett retired gloomily to the pavilion. Mr. Hankin, with exasperating slowness, minced his way to the crease. He had his own methods of dealing with demon bowlers and was not alarmed. He patted the turf lengthily, asked three times for middle and off, adjusted his hat, requested that a screen might be shifted, asked for middle and off again and faced Mr. Simmonds with an agreeable smile and a very straight bat, left elbow well forward and his feet correctly placed. The result was that Simmonds, made nervous, bowled an atrocious wide, which went to the boundary, and followed it up by two mild balls of poor length, which Mr. Hankin very properly punished. This behaviour cheered Mr. Barrow and steadied him. He hit out with confidence, and the score mounted to fifty. The applause had scarcely subsided when Mr. Hankin, stepping briskly across the wicket to a slow and inoffensive-looking ball pitched rather wide to the off, found it unaccountably twist from under his bat and strike him on the left thigh. The wicket-keeper flung up his hands in appeal.

"Out!" said the umpire.

Mr. Hankin withered him with a look and stalked very slowly and stiffly from the field, to be greeted by a chorus of: "Bad luck, indeed, sir!"

"It *was* bad luck," replied Mr. Hankin. "I am surprised at Mr. Grimbold." (Mr. Grimbold was the umpire, an elderly and impassive man from Pym's Outdoor Publicity Department.) "The ball was an atrocious wide. It could never have come anywhere near the wicket."

"It had a bit of a break on it," suggested Mr. Tallboy.

"It certainly had a break on it," admitted Mr. Hankin, "but it would have gone wide nevertheless. I don't think anybody can accuse me of being unsporting, and if I *had* been leg before, I should be the first to admit it. Did you see it, Mr. Brotherhood?"

"Oh, I saw it all right," said the old gentleman, with a chuckle.

"I put it to you," said Mr. Hankin, "whether I was l.b.w. or not."

"Of course not," said Mr. Brotherhood. "Nobody ever is. I have attended cricket matches now for sixty years, for sixty years, my dear sir, and that goes back to a time before you were born or thought of, and I've never yet known anybody to be really out l.b.w.—according to himself, that is." He chuckled again. "I remember in 1892 . . ."

"Well, sir," said Mr. Hankin, "I must defer to your experienced judgment. I think I will have a pipe." He wandered away and sat down by Mr. Pym.

"Poor old Brotherhood," he said, "is getting very old and doddery. Very doddery indeed. I doubt if we shall see him here another year. That was a very unfortunate decision of Grimbold's. Of course it is easy to be deceived in these matters, but you could see for yourself that I was no more l.b.w. than he was himself. Very vexing, when I had just settled down nicely."

"Shocking luck," agreed Mr. Pym, cheerfully. "There's Ingleby going in. I always like to watch him. He puts up a very good show, doesn't he, as a rule?"

"No style," said Mr. Hankin, morosely.

"Hasn't he?" said Mr. Pym, placidly. "You know best about that, Hankin. But he always hits out. I like to see a batsman hitting out, you know. There! Good shot! Good shot! Oh, dear!"

For Mr. Ingleby, hitting out a little too vigorously, was caught at cover-point and came galloping out rather faster than he had gone in.

"Quack, quack," said Mr. Bredon.

Mr. Ingleby threw his bat at Mr. Bredon, and Mr. Tallboy, hurriedly muttering, "Bad luck!" went to take his place.

"What a nuisance," said Miss Rossiter, soothingly. "I think it was very brave of you to hit it at all. It was a frightfully fast one."

"Um!" said Mr. Ingleby.

The dismissal of Mr. Ingleby had been the redoubtable Simmonds' swan-song. Having exhausted himself by his own ferocity, he lost his pace and became more erratic than usual, and was taken off, after an expensive over, in favour of a gentleman who bowled leg-breaks. To him, Mr. Barrow fell a victim, and retired covered with glory, with a score of twenty-seven. His place was taken by Mr. Pinchley, who departed, waving a jubilant hand and declaring his intention of whacking hell out of them.

Mr. Pinchley indulged in no antics of crease-patting or taking middle. He strode vigorously to his post, raised his bat shoulder-high and stood four-square to whatever it might please Heaven to send him. Four times did he loft the ball sky-high to the boundary. Then he fell into the hands of the Philistine with the leg-break and lofted the ball into the greedy hands of the wicket-keeper.

"Short and sweet," said Mr. Pinchley, returning with his ruddy face all grins.

"Four fours are very useful," said Mr. Bredon, kindly.

"Well, that's what I say," said Mr. Pinchley. "Make 'em quick and keep things going, that's my idea of cricket. I can't stand all this pottering and poking about."

This observation was directed at Mr. Miller, whose cricket was of the painstaking sort. A tedious period followed, during which the score slowly mounted to 83, when Mr. Tallboy, stepping back a little inconsiderately to a full-pitch, slipped on the dry turf and sat down on his wicket.

Within the next five minutes Mr. Miller, lumbering heavily down the pitch in gallant response to an impossible call by Mr. Beeseley, was run out, after compiling a laborious 12. Mr. Bredon, pacing serenely to the wicket, took counsel with himself. He reminded himself that he was still, in the eyes of Pym's and Brotherhood's at any rate, Mr. Death Bredon of Pym's. A quiet and unobtrusive mediocrity, he decided, must be his aim. Nothing that could recall the Peter Wimsey of twenty years back, making two centuries in successive innings for Oxford. No fancy cuts. Nothing remarkable. On the other hand, he had claimed to be a cricketer. He must not make a public exhibition of incompetence. He decided to make twenty runs, not more and, if possible, not less.

He might have made much his mind easy; the opportunity was not vouchsafed him. Before he had collected more than two threes and a couple of demure singles, Mr. Beeseley had paid the penalty of rashness and been caught at mid-on. Mr. Haagedorn, with no pretensions to being a batsman, survived one over and was then spread-eagled without remorse or question. Mr. Wedderburn, essaying to cut a twisty one which he would have done well to leave alone, tipped the ball into wicket-keeper's gloves and Pym's were disposed of for 99, Mr. Bredon having the satisfaction of carrying out his bat for 14.

"Well played all," said Mr. Pym. "One or two people had bad luck, but of course, that's all in the game. We must try and do better after lunch."

"There's one thing," observed Mr. Armstrong, confidently to Mr. Miller, "they always do one very well. Best part of the day, to my thinking."

Mr. Ingleby made much the same remark to Mr. Bredon. "By the way," he added, "Tallboy's looking pretty rotten."

"Yes, and he's got a flask with him," put in Mr. Garrett, who sat beside them.

"He's all right," said Ingleby. "I will say for Tallboy, he can carry his load. He's much better off with a flask than with this foul Sparkling Pomayne. All wind. For God's sake, you fellows, leave it alone."

"Something's making Tallboy bad-tempered, though," said Garrett. "I don't understand him; he seems to have gone all to pieces lately, ever since that imbecile row with Copley."

Mr. Bredon said nothing to all this. His mind was not easy. He felt as though thunder was piling up somewhere and was not quite sure whether he was fated to feel or to ride the storm. He turned to Simmonds the demon bowler, who was seated on his left, and plunged into cricket talk.

"What's the matter with our Miss Meteyard today?" inquired Mrs. Johnson, archly, across the visitors' table. "You're very silent."

"I've got a headache. It's very hot. I think it's going to thunder."

"Surely not," said Miss Parton. "It's a beautiful clear day."

"*I* believe," asserted Mrs. Johnson, following Miss Meteyard's gloomy gaze, "*I* believe she's more interested in the *other* table. Now, Miss Meteyard, confess, who is it? Mr. Ingleby? I hope it's not my favourite Mr. Bredon. I simply *can't* have anybody coming between us, you know."

The joke about Mr. Bredon's reputed passion for Mrs. Johnson had become a little stale, and Miss Meteyard received it coldly.

"She's offended," declared Mrs. Johnson. "I believe it *is* Mr. Bredon. She's blushing! When are we to offer our congratulations, Miss Meteyard?"

"Do you," demanded Miss Meteyard, in a suddenly harsh and resonant voice, "recollect the old lady's advice to the bright young man?"

"Why, I can't say that I do. What was it?"

"Some people can be funny without being vulgar, and some can be both funny and vulgar. I should recommend you to be either the one or the other."

"Oh, really?" said Mrs. Johnson, vaguely. After a moment's reflection she gathered the sense of the ancient gibe and said, "Oh, really!" again, with a heightened colour. "Dear me, how rude we can be when we try. I do hate a person who can't take a joke."

Brotherhood's second innings brought some balm to the feelings of the Pymmites. Whether it was the Sparkling Pomayne, or whether it was the heat ("I do believe you were right about the thunder," remarked Miss Parton), more than one of their batsmen found his eye a little out and his energy less than it had been. Only one man ever looked really dangerous, and this was a tall, dour-faced person with whipcord wrists and a Yorkshire accent, whom no bowling seemed to daunt, and who had a nasty knack of driving extremely hard through gaps in the field. This infuriating man settled down grimly and knocked up a score of fifty-eight, amid the frenzied applause of his side. It was not only his actual score that was formidable, but the extreme exhaustion induced in the field.

"I've had—too much—gas," panted Ingleby, returning past Garrett after a mad gallop to the boundary, "and this blighter looks like staying till Christmas."

"Look here, Tallboy," said Mr. Bredon, as they crossed at the next over. "Keep your eye on the little fat fellow at the other end. He's getting pumped. If this Yorkshire tyke works him like this, something will happen."

It did happen in the next over. The slogger smote a vigorous ball from the factory end, a little too high for a safe boundary, but an almost certain three. He galloped and the fat man galloped. The ball was racing over the grass, and Tallboy racing to intercept it, as they galloped back.

"Come on!" cried the Yorkshireman, already half way down the pitch for the third time. But Fatty was winded; a glance behind showed him Tallboy stooping to the ball. He gasped "No!" and abode, like Dan, in his breeches. The other saw what was happening and turned in his tracks. Tallboy, disregarding the frantic signals of Haagedorn and Garrett, became inspired. He threw from where he stood, not to Garrett, but point-blank at the open wicket. The ball sang through the air and spread-eagled the Yorkshireman's stumps while he was still a yard from the crease, while the batsman, making a frantic attempt to cover himself, flung his bat from his hand and fell prostrate.

"Oh, pretty!" exulted old Mr. Brotherhood. "Oh, well played, sir, well played!"

"He must have taken marvellous aim," said Miss Parton.

"What's the matter with you, Bredon?" asked Ingleby, as the team lolled thankfully on the pitch to await the next man in. "You're looking very white. Touch of the sun?"

"Too much light in my eyes," said Mr. Bredon.

"Well, take it easy," advised Mr. Ingleby. "We shan't have much trouble with them now. Tallboy's a hero. Good luck to him."

Mr. Bredon experienced a slight qualm of nausea.

The remainder of the Brotherhood combination achieved nothing very remarkable, and the side was eventually got out for 114. at 4 o'clock, on a fiery wicket, Mr. Tallboy again sent out his batsmen, faced with the formidable task of making 171 to win.

At 5.30, the thing still looked almost feasible, four wickets having fallen for 79. Then Mr. Tallboy, endeavouring to squeeze a run where there was no run to be got, was run out for 7, and immediately afterwards, the brawny Mr. Pinchley, disregarding his captain's frantic appeals for care, chopped his first ball neatly into the hands of point. The rot had set in. Mr. Miller, having conscientiously blocked through two overs, while Mr. Beeseley added a hard-won 6 to the score, lost his off stump to the gentleman with the leg-break. With the score at 92 by the addition of a couple of byes, and three men to bat, including the well-meaning but inadequate Mr. Haagerdorn, defeat appeared to be unavoidable.

"Well," said Mr. Copley morosely, "it's better than last

year. They beat us then by about seven wickets. Am I right, Mr. Tallboy?"

"No," said Mr. Tallboy.

"I beg your pardon, I'm sure," said Mr. Copley, "perhaps it was the year before. You should know, for I believe you were the captain on both occasions."

Mr. Tallboy vouchsafed no statistics, merely saying to Mr. Bredon:

"They draw stumps at 6.30; try and stick it out till then if you can."

Mr. Bredon nodded. The advice suited him excellently. A nice, quiet, defensive game was exactly the game least characteristic of Peter Wimsey. He sauntered tediously to the crease, expended some valuable moments in arranging himself, and faced the bowling with an expression of bland expectation.

All would probably have gone according to calculation, but for the circumstance that the bowler at the garden end of the field was a man with an idiosyncrasy. He started his run from a point in the dim, blue distance, accelerated furiously to within a yard of the wicket, stopped, hopped, and with an action suggestive of a Catherine-wheel, delivered a medium-length, medium-paced, sound straight ball of uninspired but irreproachable accuracy. In executing this manœuvre for the twenty-second time, his foot slipped round about the stop-and-hop period, he staggered, performed a sort of splits and rose, limping and massaging his leg. As a result, he was taken off, and in his place Simmonds, the fast bowler, was put on.

The pitch was by this time not only fast, but bumpy. Mr. Simmonds' third delivery rose wickedly from a patch of bare earth and smote Mr. Bredon violently upon the elbow.

Nothing makes a man see red like a sharp rap over the funny-bone, and it was at this moment that Mr. Death Bredon suddenly and regrettably forgot himself. He forgot his caution and his rôle, and Mr. Miller's braces, and saw only the green turf and the Oval on a sunny day and the squat majesty of the gas-works. The next ball was another of Simmonds' murderous short-pitched bumpers, and Lord Peter Wimsey, opening up wrathful shoulders, strode out of his crease like the spirit of vengeance and whacked it to the wide. The next he clouted to leg for three, nearly braining square-leg and so flummoxing deep-field that he flung it back wildly to the wrong end, giving the Pymmites a fourth for an overthrow. Mr. Simmonds' last ball he treated with the contempt it deserved, snicking it as it whizzed past half a yard wide to leg and running a single.

He was now faced by the merchant with the off-break. The first two balls he treated carefully, then drove the third over the boundary for six. The fourth rose awkwardly and he killed it dead, but the fifth and sixth followed number three. A shout went up, headed by a shrill shriek of admiration from Miss Parton. Lord Peter grinned amiably and settled down to hit the bowling all round the wicket.

As Mr. Haagedorn panted in full career down the pitch, his lips moved in prayer, "Oh, Lord, oh, Lord! don't let me make a fool of myself!" A four was signalled and the field crossed over. He planted his bat grimly, determined to defend his wicket if he died for it. The ball came, pitched, rose, and he hammered it down remorselessly. One. If only he could stick out the other five. He dealt with another the same way. A measure of confidence came to him. He pulled the third ball round to leg and, to his own surprise, found himself running. As the batsmen passed in mid-career, he heard his colleague call: "Good man! Leave 'em to me now."

Mr. Haagedorn asked nothing better. He would run till he burst, or stand still till he hardened into marble, if only he could keep this miracle from coming to an end. He was a poor bat, but a cricketer. Wimsey ended the over with a well-placed three, which left him still in possession of the bowling. He walked down the pitch and Haagedorn came to meet him.

"I'll take everything I can," said Wimsey, "but if anything comes to you, block it. Don't bother about runs. I'll see to them."

"Yes, sir," said Mr. Haagedorn, fervently. "I'll do anything you say. Keep it up, sir, only keep it up."

"All right," said Wimsey. "We'll beat the b——s yet. Don't be afraid of them. You're doing exactly right."

Six balls later, Mr. Simmonds, having been hit to the boundary four times running, was removed, as being too expensive a luxury. He was replaced by a gentleman who was known at Brotherhoods as "Spinner." Wimsey received him with enthusiasm, cutting him consistently and successfully to the off, till Brotherhood's captain moved up his fieldsmen and concentrated them about the off-side of the wicket. Wimsey looked at this grouping with an indulgent smile, and placed the next six balls consistently and successfully to leg. When, in despair, they drew a close net of fielders all round him, he drove everything that was drivable straight down the pitch. The score mounted to 150.

The aged Mr. Brotherhood was bouncing in his seat. He was in an ecstasy. "Oh, pretty, sir! Again! Oh, well played, indeed, sir!" His white whiskers fluttered like flags. "Why on earth, Mr. Tallboy," he asked, severely, "did you send this man in ninth? He's a cricketer. He's the only cricketer among the whole damned lot of you. Oh, well placed!" as the ball skimmed neatly between two agitated fielders who nearly knocked their heads together in the effort to retrieve it. "Look at that! I'm always telling these lads that placing is nine-tenths of the game. This man knows it. Who is he?"

"He's a new member of the staff," said Tallboy, "he's a public-school man and he said he'd done a good deal of country-house cricket, but I hadn't an idea he could play like that. Great Scott!" He paused to applaud a particularly elegant cut, "I never saw anything like it."

"Didn't you?" said the old gentleman with asperity. "Well, now, I've been watching cricket, man and boy, for sixty years, and I've seen something very like it. Let me see, now. Before the War, that would be. Dear, dear—I sometimes think my memory for names isn't what it was, but I fancy that in the 'varsity match of 1910, or it might be 1911—no, not 1910, that was the year in which—"

His tinkling voice was drowned in a yell as the 170 appeared on the score-board.

"One more to win!" gasped Miss Rossiter. "Oh!" For at that moment, Mr. Haagedorn, left for an unfortunate moment to face the bowling, succumbed to a really nasty and almost unplayable ball which curled round his feet like a playful kitten and skittled his leg-stump.

Mr. Haagedorn came back almost in tears, and Mr. Wedderburn, quivering with nervousness, strode forward into the breach. He had nothing to do but to survive four balls and then, except for a miracle, the game was won. The first ball rose temptingly, a little short; he stepped out, missed it, and scuttled back to his crease only just in time. "Oh, be careful! Be careful!" moaned Miss Rossiter, and old Mr. Brotherhood swore. The next ball, Mr. Wedderburn contrived to poke a little way down the pitch. He wiped hs forehead. The next was a spinner and, in trying to block it, he tipped it almost perpendicularly into the air. For a moment that seemed like hours the spectators saw the spinning ball—the outstretched hand—then the ball dropped, missed by a hair.

"I'm going to scream," announced Mrs. Johnson to nobody in particular. Mr. Wedderburn, now thoroughly unnerved, wiped his forehead again. Fortunately, the bowler was also unnerved. The ball slipped in his sweating fingers and went down short and rather wide.

"Leave it alone! Leave it alone!" shrieked Mr. Brotherhood, hammering with his stick. "Leave it alone, you numb-skull! You imbecile! You—"

Mr. Wedderburn, who had lost his head completely, stepped across to it, raised his bat, made a wild swipe, which missed its object altogether, heard the smack of the leather as the ball went into the wicket-keeper's gloves, and did the only possible thing. He hurled himself bodily back and sat down on the crease, and as he fell he heard the snick of the flying bails.

"How's that?"

"Not out."

"The nincompoop! The fat-headed, thick-witted booby!" yelled Mr. Brotherhood. He danced with fury, "Might have thrown the match away! Thrown it away! That man's a fool. I say he's a fool. He's a fool, I tell you."

"Well, it's all right, Mr. Brotherhood," said Mr. Hankin, soothingly. "At least, it's all wrong for your side, I'm afraid."

"Our side be damned," ejaculated Mr. Brotherhood. "I'm here to see cricket played, not tiddlywinks. I don't care who wins or who loses, sir, provided they play the game. Now, then!"

With five minutes to go, Wimsey watched the first ball of the over come skimming down towards him. It was a beauty. It was jam. He smote it as Saul smote the Philistines. It soared away in a splendid parabola, struck the pavilion roof with a noise like the crack of doom, rattled down the galvanized iron roofing, bounced into the enclosure where the scorers were sitting and broke a bottle of lemonade. The match was won.

Mr. Bredon, lolloping back to the pavilion at 6.30 with 83 runs to his credit, found himself caught and cornered by the ancient Mr. Brotherhood.

"Beautifully played, sir, beautifully played indeed," said the old gentleman. "Pardon me—the name has just come to my recollection. Aren't you Wimsey of Balliol?"

Wimsey saw Tallboy, who was just ahead of them, falter in his stride and look round, with a face like death. He shook his head.

"My name's Bredon," he said.

"Bredon?" Mr. Brotherhood was plainly puzzled. "Bredon? I don't remember ever hearing the name. But didn't I see you play for Oxford in 1911? You have a late cut which is exceedingly characteristic, and I could have taken my oath that the last time I saw you play it was at Lords in 1911, when you made 112. But I thought the name was Wimsey— Peter Wimsey of Balliol—Lord Peter Wimsey—and, now I come to think of it—"

At this very awkward moment an interruption occurred. Two men in police uniform were seen coming across the field, led by another man in mufti. They pushed their way through the crowd of cricketers and guests, and advanced upon the little group by the pavilion fence. One of the uniformed men touched Lord Peter on the arm.

"Are you Mr. Death Bredon?"

"I am," said Wimsey, in some astonishment.

"Then you'll have to come along of us. You're wanted on a charge of murder, and it is my duty to warn you that anything you say may be taken down and used in evidence."

"Murder?" ejaculated Wimsey. The policeman had spoken in unnecessarily loud and penetrating tones, and the whole crowd had frozen into fascinated attention. "Whose murder?"

"The murder of Miss Dian de Momerie."

"Good God!" said Wimsey. He looked round and saw that the man in mufti was Chief-Inspector Parker, who gave a nod of confirmation.

"All right," said Wimsey. "I'll come with you, but I don't know a thing about it. You'd better come with me while I change."

He walked away between the two officers. Mr. Brotherhood detained Parker as he was about to follow them.

"You say that man's called Bredon?"

"Yes, sir," replied Parker, with emphasis. "Bredon is his name. Mister Death Bredon."

"And you want him for murder?"

"For murder of a young woman, sir. Very brutal business."

"Well," said the old gentleman, "you surprise me. Are you sure you've got the right man?"

"Dead sure, sir. Well known to the police."

Mr. Brotherhood shook his head.

"Well," he said again, "his name may be Bredon. But he's innocent. Innocent as day, my good fellow. Did you see him play? He's a damned fine cricketer and he'd no more commit a murder than I would."

"That's as may be, sir," said Inspector Parker, stolidly.

"Just fancy that!" exclaimed Miss Rossiter. "I always *knew* there was *something*. Murder! Only think! We might all have had our throats cut! What do you think, Miss Meteyard? Were you surprised?"

"Yes, I was," said Miss Meteyard. "I was never so surprised in my life. Never!"

CHAPTER X IX

DUPLICATE APPEARANCES OF A
NOTORIOUS PERSONALITY

IT'S a fact, old man," said Parker, as the police-car sped Londonwards. "Dian de Momerie was found this morning with her throat cut in a wood near Maidenhead. Beside the body was a penny whistle and a few yards away there was a black mask caught on a bramble bush, as if some one had flung it away in a hurry. Inquiry among her friends elicited the fact that she had been going about at night with a masked harlequin, one Bredon by name. Strong suspicion was accordingly directed against the said Mr. Bredon, and Scotland Yard, acting with commendable promptitude, tracked the gentleman down to Romford and secured his person. Accused, when charged, replied—"

"I done it," said Wimsey, concluding the sentence for him. "And so, in a sense, I have, Charles. If that girl had never seen me, she'd be alive today."

"Well, she's no great loss," said the Chief-Inspector, callously. "I'm beginning to see their game. They've not yet tumbled to the fact that you're not Death Bredon, and their idea is to put you on ice quietly till they've had time to settle up their affairs. They know you can't get bail on a murder charge."

"I see. Well, they're not quite as smart as I took them to be, or they'd have identified me long since. What happens next?"

"My idea is, that we take immediate steps to establish that Mr. Death Bredon and Lord Peter Wimsey are not one person but two. Is that chap still following us, Lumley?"

"Yes, sir."

"Take care he doesn't lose us in the traffic through Stratford. We're taking you to be questioned at Scotland Yard, and this josser shall see you safely into the building. I've arranged for some pressmen to be there, and we'll prime them with full details of the arrest and a lot about your hideous past. You, as Mr. Bredon, will then telephone to yourself, as Lord Peter Wimsey, to come and see you, with a view to arranging your defence. You will be smuggled out by the back entrance—"

"Disguised as a policeman? Oh, Charles, do let me be a policeman! I should adore it."

"Well, you're a bit under the regulation height, but we might be able to manage it; the helmet is very disguising. Anyway, you go home, or else to your club—"

"Not my club; I couldn't go to the Marlborough dressed up as a cop. Stop a bit, though—the Egotists'—I could go there. I've got a room there, and the Egotists don't care what one does. I like this. Go on."

"All right. You change there, and come down to the Yard in a temper, grumbling loudly about the trouble Mr. Bredon puts you to. You can give an interview about it if you like. Then you go home. The Sunday papers have a long bit about you, with photographs of you both."

"Splendid!"

"And on Monday you go before the magistrate and reserve your defence. It's a pity you can't be in court to hear yourself, but I'm afraid that's rather beyond our powers. Still, you can be seen immediately afterwards doing something conspicuous. You might ride in the Row and fall off—"

"No," said Wimsey. "I absolutely refuse to fall off. There are limits. I don't mind being run away with, and only saving myself by consummate horsemanship."

"Very well; I'll leave that to you. The point is that you must be in the papers."

"I will. I will advertise myself in some way. Advertising is my long suit. By the way, though, that'll mean I can't be at the office on Monday."

"Naturally."

"But that won't do. I've got to get that Whifflets campaign finished. Armstrong wants it particularly; I can't let him down. And besides, I've got interested in the thing."

Parker gazed at him in astonishment.

"Is it possible, Peter, that you are developing a kind of business morality?"

"Dash it all, Charles! You don't understand. It's a really big scheme. It'll be the biggest advertising stunt since the Mustard Club. But if that doesn't stir you, here's another thing. If I'm not at the office, you won't know the Nutrax headline next Tuesday, and won't catch the supplies being delivered."

"We can find that out without you, old man. It won't help us in the least to have you murdered, will it?"

"I suppose not. What I can't understand is, why they haven't murdered Tallboy yet."

"No: I can't understand that, either."

"I'll tell you what I think. They haven't matured their new plans yet. They're leaving him till after next Tuesday, because they've got to deliver one more consignment by the old route. They think that if I'm out of the way they can take the risk."

"Perhaps that's it. We must hope so, any way. Well, here we are. Out you come, and try and look as much like a baffled villain as possible."

"Right-ho!" said Wimsey, distorting his face into a disagreeable sneer. The car turned into the entrance to New Scotland Yard and drew up. The sergeant got out; Wimsey followed, and, glancing round, observed three obvious newspaper men hanging about the courtyard. Just as Parker emerged in his turn from the car, Wimsey tapped the sergeant lightly but efficiently under the chin and sent him staggering, tripped Parker neatly as he jumped from the running-board, and made for the gate like a hare. Two policemen and a reporter dived to intercept him; he dodged the bobbies, tackled the pressman and left him sprawling, swerved through the gateway and led a beautiful ding-dong chase down Whitehall. As he sped, he heard shouts and the blowing of whistles. Foot-passengers joined in the pursuit; motorists accelerated to cut him off; people in buses crowded to the windows and stared. He slipped nimbly into the whirl of traffic, dodged three times round the Cenotaph, doubled back on the opposite side of the street and finally staged a magnificent and sensational capture in the middle of Trafalgar Square. Parker and Lumley came up panting.

" 'Ere 'e is, mister," said the man who had grabbed hold of him—a large and powerful navvy, with a bag of tools. " 'Ere 'e is. Wot's 'e done?"

"He's wanted for murder," announced Parker, briefly and loudly.

A murmur of admiration arose. Wimsey cast an offensively contemptuous glance at Sergeant Lumley.

"You ruddy bobbies are all too fat," he said. "You can't run."

"That's all right," said the sergeant, grimly. "Hold out your hands, my lad. We're taking no more chances."

"As you please, as you please. Are your hands clean? I don't want my cuffs dirtied."

"That's quite enough of it, my lad," said Parker, as the handcuffs snapped home, "we don't want any more trouble from you. Pass along there, please, pass along."

The little procession returned to Scotland Yard.

"Rather prettily done, I flatter myself," said Wimsey.

"Ar!' said Lumley, caressing his jaw. "You didn't need to have hit quite so hard, my lord."

"Verisimilitude," said Wimsey, "verisimilitude. You looked lovely as you went over."

"Ar!" said Sergeant Lumley.

A quarter of an hour later, a policeman whose uniform trousers were a little long for him and whose tunic was slightly too large in the waist, came out from Scotland Yard by a side-entrance, entered a car and was driven along Pall Mall to the discreet entrance of the Egotists' Club. Here he disappeared, and was never seen again, but presently an immaculately dressed gentleman, in evening dress and silk hat, tripped out and stood on the steps to await a taxi. An elderly gentleman of military appearance stood beside him.

"You will forgive me, Colonel? I shall not be many minutes. This fellow Bredon is an abominable nuisance, but what can one do? I mean to say, one has to do something."

"Quite, quite," said the Colonel.

"I only hope this is the last time. If he's done what they say he has, it *will* be the last."

"Oh, quite," said the Colonel, "my dear Wimsey, quite."

The taxi appeared.

"Scotland Yard," said Wimsey, in very audible tones.

The taxi span away.

Miss Meteyard, skimming the papers in bed on Sunday morning, found her attention held by enormous headlines:

DE MOMERIE MURDER CASE ARREST

FAMOUS DUCAL HOUSE INVOLVED

INTERVIEW WITH LORD PETER WIMSEY

and again:

PENNY WHISTLE MURDER

ARREST OF MASKED MUMMER

CHIEF-INSPECTOR PARKER INTERVIEWED

and once more:

There followed lengthy and picturesque descriptions of the arrest; pictures of the place where the body was found; articles on Lord Peter Wimsey, on the Wimsey family, on their historic seat in Norfolk; on night-life in London and on penny whistles. The Duke of Denver had been interviewed, but refused to say anything; Lord Peter Wimsey, on the other hand, had said a good deal. Finally—and this puzzled Miss Meteyard very much, there was a photograph of Lord Peter and of Death Bredon standing side by side.

"It would be useless," said Lord Peter Wimsey in an interview, "in view of the remarkable resemblance between us, to deny that there is a relationship between this man and myself. In fact, he has on various occasions given trouble by impersonating me. If you were to see us together, you would notice that he is the darker of the two; there are also, of course, slight differences of feature; but, when we are seen separately, it is easy to mistake one of us for the other."

The Death Bredon of the photograph had certainly very much darker hair than the Peter Wimsey; his mouth was set in an unpleasing sneer, and he had that indefinable air of raffish insolence which is the hall-mark of the *chevalier d'industrie*. The newspaper article wandered on to give various unverifiable details.

"Bredon never went to a university, though he sometimes claims Oxford as his Alma Mater. He was educated at a public school in France where English sports are cultivated. He is a very fine natural cricketer, and was actually playing in a cricket match when arrested through the prompt and intelligent action of Chief-Inspector Parker. Under various names he is well known in the night-clubs of London and Paris. He is said to have met the unfortunate girl, with whose murder he is charged, at the house of the late Major Milligan, who met his death two days ago by being run down by a lorry in Piccadilly. Following representations by the Wimsey family as to his mode of life, he had recently taken a post in a well-known commercial firm, and was supposed to have turned over a new leaf, but . . ."

And so on, and so forth.

Miss Meteyard sat for a long time with the papers strewn about her, smoking cigarettes, while her coffee got cold. Then she went and had a bath. She hoped it might clear her brain.

The excitement at Pym's on the Monday morning was indescribable. The Copy Department sat in the typists' room and did no work at all. Mr. Pym telephoned that he was unwell, and could not come to the office. Mr. Copley was so unnerved that he sat for three hours with a blank sheet of paper before him and then went out for a drink—a thing he had never done in his life. Mr. Willis seemed to be on the verge of nervous collapse. Mr. Ingleby laughed at his colleagues' agitation and said that it was a grand new experience for them all. Miss Parton burst into tears and Miss Rossiter proclaimed that she had always known it. Mr. Tallboy then enlivened the proceedings by fainting in Mr. Armstrong's room, thus giving Mrs. Johnson (who was hysterically inclined) useful occupation for half an hour. And Ginger Joe, of the red head and sunny temper, astonished his companions by having a fit of the sulks and then suddenly cuffing Bill's head for no reason whatever.

At 1 o'clock Miss Meteyard went out to lunch, and read in the *Evening Banner* that Mr. Death Bredon had appeared before the magistrates at 10 a.m. on the murder charge, and had reserved his defence. At 10.30, Lord Peter Wimsey (picturesquely described as "the second protagonist in this drama of dope and death") had, while riding in the Row, narrowly escaped injury, owing to his horse's having been startled by a back-fire from a racing car; the animal had bolted and only Lord Peter's consummate horsemanship had averted a nasty accident. There was a photograph of Mr. Bredon entering the court at Bow Street in a dark lounge suit and soft hat; there was also a photograph of Lord Peter Wimsey returning from his ride in neat breeches and boots and a bowler; there was, needless to say, no photograph of the metamorphosis of the one gentleman into another, behind the drawn blinds of a Daimler saloon while traversing the quiet squares north of Oxford Street.

On Monday night, Lord Peter Wimsey attended a performance of *Say When!* at the Frivolity, companioning a Royal personage.

On Tuesday morning, Mr. Willis arrived at the office late

and in a great state of excited importance. He beamed at everybody, presented the typists' room with a four-pound box of chocolates and an iced cake, and informed the sympathetic Miss Parton that he was engaged to be married. At coffee-time, the name of the lady was known to be Miss Pamela Dean. At 11.30, it was divulged that the ceremony would take place at the earliest possible moment, and at 11.45 Miss Rossiter was collecting subscriptions for a wedding-present. By 2 o'clock, the subscribers were already divided into two opinionated and bitterly hostile factions, the one advocating the purchase of a handsome dining-room clock with Westminster chimes, and the other voting with passion for a silver-plated electric chafing-dish. At 4 o'clock, Mr. Jollop had turned down successively, "Sigh no more, Ladies." "Oh, Dry those Tears" and "Weeping Late and Weeping Early," which Mr. Toule had previously passed, and rejected with derision the proposed substitution of "If you have Tears," "O Say, What are You Weeping For?" and "A Poor Soul Sat Sighing." Mr. Ingleby, stimulated by a frantic request for new headlines, had flown into a passion because the *Dictionary of Quotations* had mysteriously disappeared. At 4.30 Miss Rossiter, feverishly typing, had completed "I Weep, I know not Why" and "In Silence and in Tears," while the distracted Mr. Ingleby was seriously contemplating "In that Deep Midnight of the Mind" (for, as he observed, "they'll never know it's Byron unless we tell them"), when Mr. Armstrong sent up word to say that he had persuaded Mr. Jollop to accept the copy of "O Say, What are you Weeping For?" combined with the headline "Flat, Stale, and Unprofitable," and would Mr. Ingleby kindly verify at once whether it was "Flat, Stale" or "Stale, Flat," and get the thing re-typed and hand it to Mr. Tallboy immediately.

"Isn't Mr. Armstrong marvellous?" said Miss Rossiter. "He always finds a way out. Here you are, Mr. Ingleby—I've looked it up—it's 'Stale, Flat.' The first sentence will want altering, I suppose. You can't have this bit about 'Sometimes you are tempted to ask yourself, in the words of the old game,' can you you?"

"I suppose not," grunted Ingleby. "Better make it: 'Sometimes you may be tempted, like Hamlet, to exclaim'—then the whole quote—and go on, 'yet if anybody were to ask you why—' and join it up there. That'll do. Courses of the world, please, not curses."

"T'chk!" said Miss Rossiter.

"Here's Wedderburn, panting for his copy. How's Tallboy, Wedder?"

"Gone home," said Mr. Wedderburn. "He didn't want to

269

go, but he's fagged out. He oughtn't to have come to the office at all today, but he would do it. Is this the thing?"

"Yes. They'll want a new sketch, of course."

"Of course," said Mr. Wedderburn, gloomily. "How they ever expect things to look right when they chop and change like this— Oh, well! What is it? 'Picture of Hamlet.' Have the Studio got a reference for Hamlet?"

"Of course not; they never have anything. Who does these sketches? Pickering? You'd better take him my illustrated Shakespeare with my compliments, and request him not to cover it with Indian ink and rubber solution."

"All right."

"And to return it sometime before Christmas."

Wedderburn grinned and departed on his errand.

About ten minutes later, the telephone tinkled in the typists' room.

"Yes?" said Miss Rossiter, in mellifluous accents. "Who is it, please?"

"Tallboy speaking," said the telephone.

"Oh!" Miss Rossiter altered her voice from the tone reserved for clients and directors to a tarter one (for she was not too well pleased with Mr. Tallboy), modified by the sympathy due to ill-health:

"Oh, yes? Are you feeling better, Mr. Tallboy?"

"Yes, thanks. I've been trying to get Wedderburn, but he doesn't seem to be in his room."

"I expect he's in the Studio, making poor Mr. Pickering work overtime on a new Nutrax sketch."

"Oh! that's what I wanted to know. Did Jollop pass that copy?"

"No—he turned the whole lot down. It's a new one—at least, new headline with the 'What are you Weeping for?' copy."

"Oh, a new headline? What is it?"

"Stale, Flat and Unprofitable. Shakespeare, you know."

"Oh! Oh, good! Glad something managed to get through. It was worrying me."

"It's quite all right, Mr. Tallboy." Miss Rossiter rang off. "Touching devotion to business," she observed to Miss Parton. "As if the world would stop turning just because *he* wasn't here!"

"I expect he was afraid old Copley would be butting in again," said Miss Parton, with a snort.

"Oh, him!" said Miss Rossiter.

"Well, now, young man," said the policeman, "and what do *you* want?"

"I want to see Chief-Inspector Parker."

"Ho!" said the policeman. "Don't want much, do you? Sure you wouldn't rather see the Lord Mayor o' London? Or Mister Ramsay MacDonald?"

"I say, are you always as funny as that? Cor lumme, don't it 'urt yer sometimes? You better buy yourself a new pair o' boots or you'll be gettin' too big for wot yer wearin'. You tell Chief-Inspector Parker as Mr. Joe Potts wants ter see 'im about this 'ere 'Arlequin murder. And look snappy, 'cos I gotter git 'ome ter me supper."

"About the 'Arlequin murder, eh? And wot do you know about that?"

"Never you mind. Just tell 'im wot I say. Tell 'im it's Joe Potts as works at Pym's Publicity and you'll 'ave 'im steppin' aht ter meet me wiv' a crimson carpet and a bokay."

"Oh! you're from Pym's. Got something to say about this Bredon, is that it?"

"That's it. Now, you 'op it, and don't waste time."

"You'd better come in here, young Cocky—and be'ave yourself."

"Right-oh! it's all the same to me."

Mr. Joseph Potts wiped his boots neatly on the mat, took his seat upon a hard bench, drew out a Yo-Yo from his pocket, and began nonchalantly throwing a handsome series of loops, while the policeman retired defeated.

Presently he returned and, sternly commanding Mr. Joseph Potts to put his top away, conducted him through a series of passages to a door, upon which he knocked. A voice said "Come in," and Mr. Potts found himself in a good-sized room, furnished with two desks, a couple of comfortable arm-chairs and several other seats of penitential appearance. At the farther desk sat a man in mufti, writing, with his back to the door; at the nearer, facing the door, was another man in a grey suit, with a pile of documents before him.

"The boy, sir," announced the policeman, and retired.

"Sit down," said the man in grey, briefly, indicating one of the penitential chairs. "Now then, what's all this you've got to tell us, eh?"

"Excuse me, sir, are you Chief-Inspector Parker?"

"This is a very cautious witness," observed the man in grey to the world in general. "Why do you particularly want to see Chief-Inspector Parker?"

" 'Cos it's important and confidential, see?" said Mr. Joseph Potts, pertly. "Information, that's wot it is. I likes ter do business with the boss, especially if there's anythink ain't bein' 'andled as it should be."

"Oh!"

"I want to tell this Parker that this case ain't bein' 'andled right. See? Mr. Bredon ain't got nothink to do with it."

"Indeed. Well, I'm Chief-Inspector Parker. What do you know about Bredon?"

"This 'ere." Ginger Joe extended an inky forefinger. "You been 'ad. Mr. Bredon ain't no crook, 'e's a great detective, and I'm 'is assistant. We're 'ard on the track of a murderer, see? And this here is just a mashi—macki—I mean it's jest a bobby-trap set by the 'ideous gang as 'e's out ter track to its lair. You been boobies ter let yerselves be took in by it, see? 'E's a sport, is Mr. Bredon, and he ain't never murdered no young woman, let alone bein' such a fool as ter leave penny whistles be'ind 'im. If you wants a murderer, Mr. Bredon's got 'is eye on one now, and you're jest playin' into the 'ands of the Black Spider and 'is gang—meaning to say, 'oever done this. Wot I meantersay, the time 'as come fer me ter divulge wot I know, and I ain't agoin'—cor lumme!"

The man at the farther desk had turned round and was grinning at Ginger over the back of his chair.

"That'll do, Ginger," said this person. "We know all about that here. I am obliged to you for your testimonial. I hope you haven't been divulging anything in other directions."

"Me, sir? No, sir. I ain't said a word, Mr. Bredon, sir. But seein' as 'ow——"

"That's all right; I believe you. Now, Charles, I think this is just the lad we want. You can get that headline from him and save ringing up Pym's. Ginger, was the Nutrax headline passed this afternoon?"

"Yes, sir, 'Stale, Flat and Unprofitable,' that's what it was. And lor', wasn't there a to-do about it! Took 'em all afternoon, it did, and Mr. Ingleby wasn't 'arf wild."

"He would be," said Wimsey. "Now, you'd better cut along home, Ginger, and not a word, mind."

"No, sir."

"We're much obliged to you for coming," added Parker, "but you see, we aren't quite such boobies as you think. We know a good deal about Mr. Bredon here. And by the way, let me introduce you to Lord Peter Wimsey."

Ginger Joe's eyes nearly popped out of his head.

"Coo! Lord Peter—where's Mr. Bredon, then? This *is* Mr. Bredon. You're pulling my leg."

"I promise," said Wimsey, "to tell you all about it this time next week. Cut along now, there's a good chap. We're busy."

On Wednesday morning, Mr. Parker received a communication from St. Martin's-le-Grand. Inside the official envelope was another, addressed in Tallboy's hand to "S. Smith, Esq." at Cummings' address in Old Broad Street.

"That settles it," said Wimsey. He consulted the marked Telephone Directory. "Here you are. The Stag at Bay, Drury Lane. Make no mistake this time."

It was not until Thursday evening that Miss Meteyard made up her mind to speak to Mr. Tallboy.

CHAPTER XX

APPROPRIATE EXIT OF AN
UNSKILLED MURDERER

IS LORD PETER WIMSEY at home?"

The manservant raked his questioner with a swift glance, which took in everything from his hunted eyes to his respectable middle-class boots. Then he said, inclining a respectful head:

"If you will be good enough to take a seat, I will ascertain if his Lordship is at leisure. What name shall I say, sir?"

"Mr. Tallboy."

"Who, Bunter?" said Wimsey. "Mr. Tallboy? This is a little embarrassing. What does he look like?"

"He looks, my lord, if I may so poetically express myself, as though the Hound of Heaven had got him, so to say, cornered, my lord."

"You are probably right. I should not be surprised if a hound of hell or so were knocking about the neighbourhood as well. Take a squint out of the window, Bunter."

"Very good, my lord. . . . I can observe nobody, but I retain a distinct impression that, when I opened the door to Mr. Tallboy, I overheard a footstep on the floor below."

"Very likely. Well, it can't be helped. Show him in."

"Very good, my lord."

The young man came in and Wimsey rose to greet him.

"Good evening, Mr. Tallboy."

"I have come," began Tallboy, and then broke off. "Lord Peter—Bredon—for God's sake, which are you?"

"Both," said Wimsey, gravely. "Won't you sit down?"

"Thanks, I'd rather . . . I don't want . . . I came . . ."

"You're looking rather rotten. I really think you'd better sit down, and have a spot of something."

Tallboy's legs seemed to give way under him, and he sat down without further protest.

"And how," inquired Wimsey, pouring him out a stiff whisky, "is the Whifflets campaign getting on without me?"

"Whifflets?"

274

"It doesn't matter. I only asked to show you that I really was Bredon. Put that straight down. Is that better?"

"Yes. I'm sorry to have made a fool of myself. I came to you—"

"You came to find out how much I knew?"

"Yes—no. I came because I couldn't stick it out any longer. I came to tell you all about it."

"Wait a minute. There's something I must tell you first. It's all out of my hands now. You understand? As a matter of fact, I don't think there's very much you can tell me. The game's up, old man. I'm sorry—I'm really sorry, because I think you've been having a perfectly bloody time. But there it is."

Tallboy had gone very white. He accepted another drink without protest, and then said:

"Well, I'm rather glad in a way. If it wasn't for my wife and the kid—oh, God!" He hid his face in his hands, and Wimsey walked over to the window and glanced at the lights of Piccadilly, pale in the summer dusk. "I've been a bloody fool," said Tallboy.

"Most of us are," said Wimsey. "I'm damned sorry, old chap."

He came back and stood looking down at him.

"Look here," he said, "you need not tell me a thing, if you don't want to. But if you do, I want you to understand that it won't really make any difference. I mean, if you feel like getting it off your chest, I don't think it will prejudice matters for you at all."

"I'd like to tell you," said Tallboy. "I think you might understand. I realize that it's all up, anyhow." He paused. "I say, what put you on to this?"

"That letter of Victor Dean's. You remember it? The one he threatened to write to Pym. He showed it to you, I fancy."

"The little swine. Yes, he did. Didn't he destroy it?"

"No, he didn't."

"I see. Well, I'd better begin at the beginning. It all started about two years ago. I was rather hard up and I wanted to get married. I'd been losing money on horses, as well, and things were not too good. I met a man in a restaurant."

"What restaurant?"

Tallboy gave the name. "He was a middle-aged, ordinary sort of person. I've never seen him since. But we got talking about one thing and another, and how tight money was and so on, and I happened to mention where I was working. He seemed to be thinking a bit after that, and asked a good many questions about how advertisements were put together and sent to the papers, and so on, and whether I was in a position to know beforehand what the headlines were going to be. So I said, of course, that there were some accounts I knew all about, such as Nutrax, and others I didn't. So then he mentioned the *Morning Star* half-double, and asked when I knew about the headlines of that, and I said, on Tuesday afternoon. Then he suddenly asked me if I could do with an extra thousand a year, and I said, 'Couldn't I? Lead me to it.' So then he came out with his proposal. It sounded pretty innocent. At least, it was quite obviously a dirty trick, but it wasn't criminal, the way he put it. He said, if I would let him know, every Tuesday, the initial letter of the headline for the following Friday, I should be well paid for it. Of course, I made a fuss about breach of confidence and so on and he raised his terms to twelve hundred. It sounded damned tempting, and I couldn't see, for the life of me, how it was going to harm the firm in any way. So I said I'd do it, and we fixed up a code—"

"I know all about that," said Wimsey. "It was very ingenious and simple. I suppose he told you that the address was simply an accommodation address."

"Yes. Wasn't it? I went to see the place once; it was a tobacconist's."

Wimsey nodded. "I've been there. It's not exactly an accommodation address, in the sense you mean. Didn't this man give you any reason for this rather remarkable request?"

"Yes, he did, and of course I oughtn't to have had anything to do with him after that. He said he was fond of having a bit of a bet with some friends of his about one thing and another, and his idea was to bet on the initial letter of each week's headline—"

"Oh, I see. And he would be betting on a certainty as often as he liked. Plausible; not criminal, but just dirty enough to explain the insistence on secrecy. Was that it?"

"Yes. I fell for it. . . . I was damned hard up. . . . I can't excuse myself. And I suppose I ought to have guessed that there was more to it than that. But I didn't want to guess. Besides, at first I thought it was all a leg-pull, but I wasn't risking anything, so I buzzed off the first two code-letters, and at the end of the fortnight I got my fifty pounds. I was heavily in debt, and I used it. After that—well, I hadn't the courage to chuck it."

"No, it would be rather hard, I should think."

"Hard? You don't know, Bredon—Wimsey—you don't know what it means to be stuck for money. They don't pay any too well at Pym's, and there are heaps of fellows who

276

want to get out and find something better, but they daren't. Pym's is safe—they're kind and decent, and they don't sack you if they can help it—but you live up to your income and you simply daren't cut loose. The competition is so keen, and you marry and start paying for your house and furniture, and you must keep up the instalments, and you can't collect the capital to sit round for a month or two while you look for a new job. You've got to keep going, and it breaks your heart and takes all the stuffing out of you. So I went on. Of course, I kept hoping that I might be able to save money and get out of it, but my wife fell ill and one thing and another, and I was spending every penny of my salary and Smith's money on top of it. And then, somehow, that little devil Dean got hold of it; God knows how!"

"I can tell you that," said Wimsey, and told him.

"I see. Well, he started to put the screw on. First of all he wanted to go fifty-fifty, and then he demanded more. The devil of it was, that if he split on me, I should lose my job as well as Smith's money, and things were getting pretty awful. My wife was going to have a baby, and I was behind with the income-tax, and I think it was just because everything seemed too utterly hopeless that I got mixed up with the Vavasour girl. Naturally, that only made things worse in the long run. And then, one day I felt I couldn't stand it any longer and told Dean I was chucking the whole show and he could do as he damn well pleased. And it wasn't till then that he told me what it was all about, and pointed out that I might easily get twelve years' penal servitude for helping to run the dope-traffic."

"Dirty," said Wimsey, "very dirty. It never occurred to you, I suppose, to turn King's Evidence and expose the whole system."

"No; not at first. I was terrified and couldn't think properly. And even if I'd done that, there'd have been awful trouble. Still, I did think of it after a bit, and told Dean that that was what I would do. And then he informed me that he was going to get his shot in first, and showed me that letter he was sending to Pym. That finished me, and I begged him to hold off for a week or two, while I thought things over. What happened about that letter exactly?"

"His sister found it among his things and sent it on to Pym, and he engaged me, through a friend, to enquire into it. He didn't know who I was. I thought there probably wasn't much in it, but I took the job on for the experience."

Tallboy nodded.

"Well, you've had your experience. I hope you haven't paid as heavily for it as I have. I could see no way out of it—"

He stopped speaking, and glanced at Wimsey.

"Perhaps I'd better tell you the next bit," said the latter. "You thought it over, and decided that Victor Dean was a wart and a scab, and would be no great loss to the world. One day, Wedderburn came along to your room, chuckling because Mrs. Johnson had caught Ginger Joe with a catapult and had confiscated it and put it in her desk. You knew you were a wonderfully good shot with any sort of missile—the kind of man who could spread-eagle a wicket from the other end of a cricket-field—and you realized how easily a man could be plugged through the skylight as he went down the iron staircase. If the blow didn't kill him, then the fall might, and it was well worth trying."

"You really do know all about it, then?"

"Nearly. You pinched the catapult, opening the drawer with Mrs. Johnson's keys during the lunch-hour, and you did a few practice shots from day to day. You left a pebble there once, you know."

"I know. Somebody came along, before I could find it."

"Yes. Well, then, the day came for putting Dean away—a nice bright day, when all the skylights were open. You dodged about the building a good bit, so that nobody should know exactly where you were at any particular minute, and then you went up on the roof. How, by the way, did you ensure that Dean would go down the iron staircase at the right moment? Oh, yes, and the scarab? It was a very good idea to use the scarab, because if anybody found it, they would naturally think it had tumbled out of his pocket as he fell."

"I'd seen the scarab on Dean's desk after lunch; I knew he often kept it there. And I had *The Times Atlas* in my room. I sent Wedderburn down to the Vouchers for something or other, and then I rang up Dean on my telephone. I said I was speaking for Mr. Hankin from the Big Conference Room, and would Mr. Dean please come down about the Crunchlets copy and bring *The Times Atlas* with him from my room. While he went for it, I pinched the scarab and slipped up on to the roof. I knew it would take him a bit of time to find the atlas, because I'd buried it under a whole heap of files, and I was pretty sure he'd go by the iron staircase, because that was the nearest way from my room to the Conference Room. As a matter of fact, it might have gone wrong at that point because he didn't come that way at all. I think he must have gone back to his own room for something after getting the atlas, but of course, I don't know. Anyway, he came along all right and I shot at him through the skylight when he was about four steps down the staircase."

"How did you know so exactly where to hit him?"

"Curiously enough, I had a young brother who was accidentally killed by being hit in just that place with a golf-ball. But I went and looked it up in a book at the British Museum to make sure. Apparently he broke his neck as well; I hadn't expected that. I stayed up on the roof till the fuss was over, and then came down quietly by the stairs. I didn't meet a soul, of course, they were all holding post-mortems and hanging round the corpse. When I knew I'd succeeded, I didn't care. I was glad. And I tell you this, if I hadn't been found out, I shouldn't care now."

"I can sympathize with that," said Wimsey.

"They asked me for a shilling for the little beast's wreath." Tallboy laughed. "I'd gladly have given twenty shillings, or twenty pounds even. . . . And then you came along. . . . I didn't suspect anything . . . till you started to talk about catapults. . . . And then I got badly frightened, and I . . . and I . . ."

"We'll draw a veil over that," said Wimsey. "You must have got a bit of a shock when you found you'd slugged the wrong man. I suppose that was when you struck a light to look for Pamela Dean's letter."

"Yes. I knew her writing—I'd seen it in Dean's room—and I knew her writing-paper, too. I really came round to find out whether you knew anything or whether you were just drawing a bow at a venture—that's rather appropriate, isn't it? Drawing a catapult at a venture would be better. When I saw that letter I felt sure there must be something in it. And Willis, too—he'd told me that you and Pamela Dean were as thick as thieves. I thought the letter might be telling you all about Dean and me. I don't know quite what I thought, to tell you the truth. Then, when I'd found out my mistake, I got frightened and thought I'd better not try again."

"I was expecting you. When nothing came of it, I began to think it hadn't been you at all, but somebody else."

"Did you know by then that the other thing was me?"

"I didn't know it was you; you were one of several possibles. But after the Nutrax row and the £50 in notes—"

Tallboy looked up with a shy, fleeting smile.

"You know," he said, "I was horribly careless and incompetent all through. Those letters—I ought never to have sent them from the office."

"No; and the catapult. You should have taken the trouble to make your own. A catapult without fingerprints is something very unusual."

"So that was it. I'm afraid I've made an awful mess of everything. Couldn't even do a simple murder. Wimsey—how much of this will have to come out? Everything, I suppose? Even that Vavasour girl . . . ?"

"Ah!" said Wimsey, without replying to the question. "Don't talk about the Vavasour girl. I felt a cad about that. You know, I did tell you not to thank me."

"You did, and it frightened me badly, because you sounded as if you meant it. I knew then that it hadn't been an accident about the catapult. But I hadn't an idea who you were till that infernal cricket match."

"I was careless then. But that damned fellow Simmonds rapping me on the funny-bone got my goat. You didn't fall for my impressive arrest then?"

"Oh, yes, I did. I believed in it implicitly and put up the most heartfelt thanksgivings. I thought I'd got off."

"Then what brought you round here tonight?"

"Miss Meteyard. She got hold of me last night. She said she'd believed first of all that you and Bredon were the same person, but now she thought you couldn't be. But she said that Bredon would be dead sure to split on me by way of currying favour with the police, and I had better get out in time."

"She said that? Miss Meteyard? Do you mean to say she knew all about it?"

"Not about the Nutrax business. But she knew about Dean."

"Good God!" Wimsey's natural conceit received a shattering blow. "How in Heaven's name did *she* know?"

"Guessed. Said she'd once seen me look at Dean when I didn't know she was there—and apparently he had once let out something to her. Apparently she'd always thought there was something odd about his death. She said she'd made up her mind not to interfere either way, but after your arrest she decided you were the bigger crook of the two. She could stand Lord Peter Wimsey doing a proper investigation, but not Mr. Dirty Bredon squealing to save his skin. She's an odd woman."

"Very. I'd better forget about all this, hadn't I? She seems to have taken the whole thing very coolly."

"She did. You see, she knew Dean. He tried to blackmail her once, about some man or the other. You wouldn't think it to look at her, would you?" said Tallboy, naïvely. "There was nothing much in it, she said, but it was the kind of thing old Pym would have been down on like a sledgehammer."

"And what did she do?" asked Wimsey, fascinated.

"Told him to publish and be damned. And I wish to God

I'd done the same. Wimsey—how much longer is it going to hang on? I've been in torment—I've been trying to give myself up—I—my wife—why haven't I been arrested before this?"

"They've been waiting," said Wimsey, thoughtfully, for his mind was pursuing two trains of thought at the same time. "You see, you aren't really as important as this dope-gang. Once you were arrested, they would stop their little game, and we didn't want them to stop. I'm afraid you're being the tethered kid, left there to trap the tigers."

All this time, his ear was alert to catch the tinkle of the telephone, which would tell him that the raid on the Stag at Bay had succeeded. Once the arrests were made and the gang broken, the sinister watcher in the street would be harmless. He would fly for his life and Tallboy would be able to go home to whatever awaited him there. But if he were to go now—

"When?" Tallboy was saying urgently, "when?"

"Tonight."

"Wimsey—you've been frightfully decent to me—tell me—there's no way out? It isn't myself, exactly, but my wife and the kid. Pointed at all their lives. It's damnable. You couldn't give me twenty-four hours?"

"You would not pass the ports."

"If I were alone I'd give myself up. I would, honestly."

"There is an alternative."

"I know. I've thought about that. I suppose that's—" he stopped and laughed suddenly—"that's the public school way out of it. I—yes—all right. They'll hardly make a headline of it, though, will they? 'Suicide of Old Dumbletonian' wouldn't have much news-value. Never mind, damn it! We'll show 'em that Dumbleton can achieve the Eton touch. Why not?"

"Good man!" said Wimsey. "Have a drink. Here's luck!"

He emptied his glass and stood up.

"Listen!" he said. "I think there is one other way out. It won't help you, but it may make all the difference to your wife and your child."

"How?" said Tallboy, eagerly.

"They need never know anything about all this. Nothing. Nobody need ever know anything, if you do as I tell you."

"My God, Wimsey! What do you mean? Tell me quickly. I'll do anything."

"It won't save you."

"That doesn't matter. Tell me."

"Go home now," said Wimsey. "Go on foot, and not too fast. And don't look behind you."

Tallboy stared at him; the blood drained away from his face, leaving even his lips as white as paper.

"I think I understand. . . . Very well."

"Quickly, then," said Wimsey. He held out his hand.

"Good-night, and good luck."

"Thank you. Good-night."

From the window, Wimsey watched him come out into Piccadilly, and walk quickly away towards Hyde Park Corner. He saw the shadow slip from a neighbouring doorway and follow him.

"—and from thence to the place of execution . . . and may the Lord have mercy upon your soul."

Half an hour later, the telephone rang.

"Bagged the whole crew," said Parker's cheerful voice. "We let the stuff go up to town. What do you think it went as? Traveller's samples—one of those closed cars with blinds all round."

"That's where they made it into packets, then."

"Yes. We watched our man into the Stag; then we pulled in the motor-boat and the car. Then we kept our eye on the pub. and let the birds hop out into our arms, one after the other. It went off beautifully. No hitch at all. Oh, and by the way—their code-word. We ought to have thought of that. It was just anything to do with Nutrax. Some of them had the *Morning Star,* showing the ad., and some of them just mentioned Nutrax for Nerves. One chap had a bottle of the stuff in his pocket, another had it written on a shopping-list and so on. And one frightfully ingenious chap was bursting with information about some new tracks for greyhound racing. Simple as pie, wasn't it?"

"That explains Hector Puncheon."

"Hector—? Oh, the newspaper fellow. Yes. He must have had his copy of the *Morning Star* with him. We've got old Cummings, too, of course. He turns out to be the actual top-dog of the whole show, and as soon as we collared him he coughed up the whole story, the mangy little blighter. That doctor fellow who shoved Mountjoy under the train is in it—we've got definite information about him, and we've also got our hands on Mountjoy's loot. He's got a safe-deposit somewhere, and I think I know where to find the key. He kept a woman in Maida Vale, bless his heart. The whole thing is most satisfactory. Now we have only got to rake in your murderer chap, what's his name, and everything in the garden will be lovely."

282

"Lovely," said Wimsey, with a spice of bitterness in his tone, "simply lovely."

"What's the matter? You sound a bit peeved. Hang on a minute till I've cleared up here and we'll go round somewhere and celebrate."

"Not tonight," said Wimsey. "I don't feel quite like celebrating."

CHAPTER XXI

DEATH DEPARTS FROM PYM'S PUBLICITY

SO YOU see," said Wimsey to Mr. Pym, "the thing need never come into the papers at all, if we're careful. We've plenty of evidence against Cummings without that, and there's no need to take the public into our confidence about the details of their distributing system."

"Thank Heaven!" said Mr. Pym. "It would have been a terrible thing for Pym's Publicity. How I have lived through this last week, I really don't know. I suppose you will be leaving the advertising?"

"I'm afraid so."

"Pity. You have a natural flair for copy-writing. You will have the satisfaction of seeing your Whifflets scheme go through."

"Splendid! I shall begin to collect coupons at once."

"Just fancy!" said Miss Rossiter. "Charge withdrawn."

"I always *said* Mr. Bredon was a darling," triumphed Miss Parton. "Of course the *real* murderer was one of those horrible dope-trafficking beasts. That was far more likely. I said so at the time."

"I didn't hear you, dear," snapped Miss Rossiter. "I say, Miss Meteyard, you've seen the news? You've seen that our Mr. Bredon is discharged and never did any murder at all?"

"I've done better," replied Miss Meteyard. "I've seen Mr. Bredon."

"No, where?"

"Here."

"*No!*"

"And he isn't Mr. Bredon, he's Lord Peter Wimsey."

"What! ! !"

Lord Peter poked his long nose round the door.

"Did I hear my name?"

"You did. She says you're Lord Peter Wimsey"

"Quite right."

284

"Then what were you doing here?"

"I came here," said his lordship, unabashed, "for a bet. A friend of mine laid me ten to one I couldn't earn my own living for a month. I did it, though, didn't I? May I have a cup of coffee?"

They would gladly have given him anything.

"By the way," said Miss Rossiter, when the first tumult had subsided, "you heard about poor Mr. Tallboy?"

"Yes, poor chap."

"Knocked down and killed on his way home—wasn't it dreadful? And poor Mrs. Tallboy with a small baby—it does seem awful! Goodness knows what they'll have to live on, because—well, you know! And that reminds me, while you're here, could I have your shilling for a wreath? At least, I suppose you'll be leaving Pym's now, but I expect you'd like to contribute."

"Yes, rather. Here you are."

"Thanks awfully. Oh, and I say! There's Mr. Willis' wedding-present. You know he's getting married?"

"No, I didn't. Everything seems to happen while I'm away. Whom is he marrying?"

"Pamela Dean."

"Oh, good work. Yes, of course. How much for Willis?"

"Well, most people are giving about two bob, if you can spare it."

"I think I can manage two bob. What are we giving him, by the way?"

"Well," said Miss Rossiter, "there's been *rather* a fuss about that. The Department was awfully keen on a clock, but Mrs. Johnson and Mr. Barrow went off on their own and bought an electric chafing-dish—such a silly thing, because I'm sure they'll never use it. And in any case, Mr. Willis did belong to the Copy Department and we ought to have had a voice in it, don't you think? So there are going to be two presents—the staff as a whole is giving the chafing-dish and the Department is giving its own present. I'm afraid we shan't be able to manage a chiming clock, though, because you can't very well ask people for more than two bob or so, though Hankie and Armstrong have been very decent and stumped up half a quid each."

"I'd better made it half a quid too."

"Oh, no," said Miss Rossiter. "You're a lamb, but it isn't fair."

"It's quite fair," said Wimsey. "There are excellent reasons

285

why I should contribute largely to a wedding present for Mr.
Willis."

"Are there? I thought you and he didn't get on very well. I
expect I'm being tactless, as usual. If you're quite sure—oh, I
forgot, I *am* a fool. Of course, if you're Lord Peter Wimsey,
you're simply frightfully rich, aren't you?"

"Fair to middling," confessed Wimsey. "It might run to a
cake for tea."

He had a word with Miss Meteyard.

"I'm sorry, you know," he said.

She shrugged her angular shoulders.

"It's not your fault. Things have to happen. You're one of
the sort that pushes round and makes them happen. I prefer
to leave them alone. You've got to have both kinds."

"Perhaps your way is wiser and more charitable."

"It isn't. I shirk responsibility, that's all. I just let things rip.
I don't make it my business to interfere. But I don't blame
the people who do interfere. In a way, I rather admire them.
They do make something, even if it's only mischief. My sort
make nothing. We exploit other people's folly, take the cash
and sneer at the folly. It's not admirable. Never mind. You'd
better run along now. I've got to get out a new series for
Sopo. 'Sopo Day is Cinema Day.' 'Leave the Laundry to ruin
itself while you addle your brains at the Talkies.' Muck!
Dope! And they pay me £10 a week for that sort of thing.
And yet, if we didn't do it, what would happen to the trade
of this country? You've got to advertise."

Mr. Hankin tripped along the passage and encountered
them.

"So you're leaving us, Mr. Bredon? In fact, I understand
that we've been nursing a cuckoo in the nest."

"Not so bad as that, sir. I'm leaving a few of the original
nestlings behind me."

Miss Meteyard evaporated quietly, and Mr. Hankin continued:

"A very sad business. Mr. Pym is very grateful for the
discretion you have shown. I hope you will lunch with me
some day. Yes, Mr. Smayle?"

"Excuse me, sir—about this window-bill for Green Pastures?"

Wimsey made his way out, exchanging mechanical
handgrips and farewells. At the foot of the lift, in the lower
vestibule, he found Ginger, with his arms full of parcels.

"Well, Ginger," said Wimsey, "I'm off."

"Oh, sir!"

"By the way, I've still got your catapult."

"I'd like you to keep it, please, sir. You see, sir—" Ginger struggled with a variety of emotions—"if I was ter keep that there catapult, I might get telling some of the boys about it, not meaning to, like. Woe I meantersay, it's 'istorical, like, ain't it, sir?"

"So it is." Wimsey sympathized with the temptation. It is not every fellow whose catapult has been borrowed for the purpose of committing a murder. "Well, I'll keep it, and thank you very much for all your help. Look here, I'll tell you what. I'll give you something in exchange. Which would you rather have—a model aeroplane, or the pair of scissors with which the steward of the *Nancy Belle* stabbed the captain and the purser?"

"Ooh, sir! 'As the scissors got the marks on 'em, sir?"

"Yes, Ginger. Genuine, original bloodstains."

"Then, please, sir, I'd like the scissors."

"You shall have them."

"Thank you *very* much, sir."

"And you'll never say one word to anybody about you know what?"

"Not if you was to roast me alive, sir."

"Right you are; good-bye, Ginger."

"Good-bye, sir."

Wimsey stepped out into Southampton Row. Facing him was a long line of hoardings. Enormous in its midst stretched a kaleidoscopic poster:

NUTRAX FOR NERVES

In the adjoining space, a workman with a broom and a bucket of paste was unfolding a still more vast and emphatic display in blue and yellow:

ARE YOU A WHIFFLER?
IF NOT, WHY NOT?

A 'bus passed, bearing a long ribbon display upon its side:

WHIFFLE YOUR WAY ROUND BRITAIN!

The great campaign had begun. He contemplated his work with a kind of amazement. With a few idle words on a sheet of paper he had touched the lives of millions. Two men, passing, stopped to stare at the hoarding.

"What's this Whiffling business, Alf?"

"I dunno. Some advertising stunt or other. Cigarettes, ain't it?"

"Oh, Whifflets?"

"I suppose so."

"Wonderful how they think of it all. What's it about, anyway?"

"Gawd knows. Here, let's get a packet and see."

"All right. I don't mind."

They passed on.

Tell England. Tell the world. Eat more Oats. Take Care of your Complexion. No More War. Shine your Shoes with Shino. Ask your Grocer. Children Love Laxamalt. Prepare to meet thy God. Bung's Beer is Better. Try Dogsbody's Sausages. Whoosh the Dust Away. Give them Crunchlets. Snagsbury's Soups are Best for the Troops. *Morning Star*, best Paper by Far. Vote for Punkin and Protect your Profits. Stop that Sneeze with Snuffo. Flush your Kindeys with Fizzlets. Flush your Drains with Sanfect. Wear Wool-fleece next the Skin. Popp's Pills Pep you Up, Whiffle your Way to Fortune. . . .

Advertise, or go under.